Praise for

Evenings at the Argentine Club

"A big, beautiful novel of love, family, and the close-knit community they inhabit. By turns touching, funny, tragic, and triumphant, it's the story of an endearing group of people in search of their own American dream."

—Susan Wiggs, *New York Times* bestselling author

"Julia Amante has created an enchanting community to fall into, true-to-life characters to fall in love with, and a rich story that will fall directly onto readers' keeper shelves. Amante's tale is tantalizing tango for the imagination."

—Lynda Sandoval, award-winning author of *Unsettling* and *Who's Your Daddy?*

Evenings at the Argentine Club

Julia Amante

GRAND CENTRAL PUBLISHING

NEW YORK BOSTON

This book is a work of fiction. Names, characters, places, and incidents are the product of the author's imagination or are used fictitiously. Any resemblance to actual events, locales, or persons, living or dead, is coincidental.

Grand Central Publishing
Hachette Book Group
237 Park Avenue
New York, NY 10017

Visit our Web site at www.HachetteBookGroup.com.

Printed in the United States of America

First Edition: September 2009
10 9 8 7 6 5 4 3 2 1

Library of Congress Cataloging-in-Publication Data

Amante, Julia.
Evenings at the Argentine Club / Julia Amante.
p. cm.
Summary: "Two families struggle to achieve their own versions of the American Dream"—Provided by publisher.
ISBN 978-0-446-58162-2
1. Argentines—United States—Fiction. 2. Immigrants—United States—Fiction. 3. Immigrant families—United States—Fiction. 4. Argentine Americans—Fiction. 5. Domestic fiction. I. Title.
PS3618.I567E84 2009
813'.6—dc22
2008048333

I dedicate this book to both my parents.

My mother, who has always been the anchor of my life, encouraging me to dream while being "realistic." She has also been the one who has taught me to love my country—the United States of America. She chooses to never notice our country's faults, only the opportunities it offers us; and she stands firm that there has never been and never will be a nation as great as ours.

My father, who was the dreamer. The one who always risked everything for the chance to reach the stars. He taught me that there are worse things than failing, namely never trying. Although he never said the words, his actions shouted loud and clear that there was no point in living if you didn't go all out. He was also the man who taught me to love my roots passionately. To learn about my culture and to know that it will always be part of who I am.

Mom, Dad, I owe you both so much. Thank you.
This book is for you.

Acknowledgments

I usually have a laundry list of people whom I want to acknowledge and thank. My family is always up there. They know that I love them and am grateful for every minute of my life that they have to share with my characters.

So this time I want to focus my appreciation on two special people, because this book would not exist without them.

The first is my agent, Kevan, who came on in the middle of this project and went beyond her job requirements to see this book in print. Kevan, thank you! I hope this is only the beginning of the work we create together.

And second, my editor, Selina, whom I dreamed of working with from the first time I heard her speak on a panel years ago. Every author reaches a point in her career where she needs to grow and stretch. Selina has provided me with this challenge and opportunity, supporting me every step of the way. And the result of our joint effort is this book. Thank you for helping me make my work the best it could be. You're a fabulous editor.

Evenings at the Argentine Club

Chapter One

To every Argentine immigrant, July 9 is a day that brings back memories of family celebrations centered around food, wine, and heart-pounding renditions of the national anthem playing on every radio and TV across the nation. July 9 is Independence Day. A day of freedom and liberty and new beginnings. But to those Argentines living in America, it's also a day to admit with a fair amount of guilt that they chose to give up their old life for the intangible, unexplainable dream of... something better.

Victoria Torres couldn't say she understood what it felt like to leave behind everything one had ever known for something new. Leave parents, siblings, friends, an entire way of life, to live among strangers who spoke differently than you did and believed in values that were foreign compared to those you grew up with. To do something of that magnitude took a sort of internal strength that she lacked. When she thought of immigrants and their decisions to leave their homes, she figured either life had to be so bleak in their own countries or their dreams had to be so immense that they were willing to risk everything just for the hope of a little magic—a chance to change destiny.

Victoria admired that kind of courage. So much so that she tried to be sensitive to what her parents went through every Argentine Independence Day, even if the melodrama appeared to go over the top. She'd learned after twenty-eight years of living with them to accept their ritual of lament followed by an evening of celebration.

The lament period had occurred this morning, with phone calls home and personal stories both her father, Victor, and her mother, Jaqueline, felt compelled to share with her yet again over breakfast.

"July is cold, not like here," her mother had shared. "We wore our best sweaters, and after the family barbecues we went dancing until the early hours of the morning."

"Don't forget the marches down Avenida de Mayo," her father added. "Remember the freezing year that it snowed? The first time since 1918! What was it, 1974?"

" 'Seventy-three," Jaqueline said,

" 'Seventy-four," Victor repeated with certainty this time.

Victoria drank her earthy café con leche and listened, not because she hadn't heard the stories a million times but because it made them so happy to reminisce. Argentine immigrants, in her view, were fanatical, proud people who would be forever tied to a country they would never return to again. Her father had once described that the way he felt about his country was the same as what a man feels for a woman he once loved and never got over. Tragic.

But the morning trip down memory lane didn't last long. Mostly because although July 9 might be an important date in Argentina, here in America it was just another workday, at least for her family, who owned a popular restaurant in downtown Burbank. And Sunday was the busiest day of all at La Parrilla.

The family traditions were put on hold until the evening, when they would attend the celebrations at the Argentine Club.

The Argentine Club itself was a piece of Argentina transplanted to American soil. A nondescript building in Burbank, California, that was the center of her community and a part of Victoria's life since the day she was born. It occupied so much of her life, and that of her parents, that she considered it a second home.

And since much of the preparations for the July 9 celebration fell on her shoulders, she urged her father out of the house so they could get to work at the family restaurant early. The sooner she could get her job done at the restaurant, the earlier she could head to the Argentine Club before the other members arrived.

Once at work, Victor set aside all thoughts of Argentine Independence Day and focused on the restaurant. They had a quick meeting to start the day, reviewing reservations or any special event going on. Victoria placed all the food orders, except liquor. She handled the planning of private party events. And she took care of the physical appearance of La Parrilla. Things her mother used to do, which had eventually been passed on to her with the idea of training her to one day assume complete control of the business.

Victor studied the meat requirements for the weekend. "Mirá," he said, handing her a sheet of paper. "Call the supplier and tell him to deliver a shipment of short ribs, Italian sausage, flank steak, and sweet chard to the Argentine Club, as well as the usual shipment to the grill."

The grill served a staggering amount of well-seasoned beef every night. Every day Victoria put in a fresh order. She scribbled the extra amount he suggested on her notepad, "I've got it."

"Last year they delivered a double order to the restaurant. Nothing to the club."

"I remember." She lowered the pad and smiled at her father. "I've got everything under control." She placed a hand on her father's shoulder and dropped a kiss on his cheek. "Don't worry."

Victor nodded. Never one to show emotion, that was sufficient to tell her he'd lay off. "What time are you getting to the club?"

Victoria loaded her notepad in her bag already full with books, her PalmPilot, iPod, and an assortment of colored pens. "Early enough to help with the setup but late enough to avoid listening to the well-meaning nagging from every mom and grandma at the club about my weight and lack of love life." Painful as it was to admit, she was a good fifty pounds overweight, and it collected mainly in the midsection and hips of her five foot five frame. In order to minimize the obvious, she shopped in the plus-size section of Nordstrom, choosing elegant wide-leg jeans, solid dark colors, tops that all hung loosely past her hips. But the truth was, she wasn't fooling anyone. Least of all men. Hence, her lack of love life.

"Hmm," he said. "I don't know why you don't tell them all to mind their own business." As they were exiting the back office, a shipment of wine came in and the bartender interrupted to ask Victor to sign for it. "I'll be right there," he said without breaking his stride into the already bustling restaurant, where waiters worked rapidly, preparing for the lunch crowd.

The popularity of the restaurant had taken some time to grow into what it was today. Victoria's father had opened it when she was about ten years old. She still remembered the day Victor had come home with the idea and shared it with her mother. Excited, they drove to the building he wanted to purchase in downtown Burbank. They'd looked through the filmy windows of the closed-down diner as a light drizzle fell on their heads. But no one noticed the weather. She and her sister ran up and down the sidewalk, happy because their parents smiled and spoke a mile a minute in Spanish about the possibilities.

Today, the restaurant was so much a part of the community, she couldn't imagine driving down San Fernando Boulevard and not seeing it there. But the inside was dark and felt outdated to her. Victor had upgraded the sound system a few years back, and rather than playing a Spanish radio station from tiny corner speakers, Victoria had convinced him to invest in quality classical music, which now softly filled the room. But she knew it wasn't the music or the intimate lighting or even the location that made the restaurant a success. It was the food itself, and Victor.

"Those women have nothing better to do than to stick their noses into everyone's business," Victor continued. "Who are they to tell you what you should look like or when to get married?"

Her father was in many ways her ally. Not that he didn't have his own ideas of how she should lead her life. But at least he didn't nag. He flat out said, "I don't like that man, he's not Argentine, get rid of him," or, in her younger years, "Don't embarrass your family by dressing like that." Or Victoria's personal favorite, "I didn't sacrifice my goals in life to watch you [fill in the blank]." Anything he hadn't agreed with—risking her life at a rap concert, throwing money away on self-improvement gurus, becoming a Protestant—he had squelched before they'd had a chance to grow. And once her father said what needed to be said, that was the end of the discussion. No matter how old she got. Her mother once told her that her father was right even when he was wrong. Who could argue with that?

"They mean well," Victoria said. "Besides, they're probably right. I could stand to lose a few pounds, and I should make an effort to find the right man before I'm too old to enjoy him."

Victor frowned. "So join a gym, give men something to look at, then pick one of the guys at the club. Easy enough."

"Great, Dad," she said, trying not to be hurt that he hadn't said that she looked fine the way she was. "Love that plan. Now I'm going to the office to work or I'll never get done and to the club in time."

At the Argentine Club, Jaqueline checked her vintage Omega gold wristwatch, which Victor presented to her on their thirtieth anniversary. The weight of the thick band reminded her of the minutes ticking by. And the shimmering diamonds surrounding the face, which were supposed to represent each glorious year together, looked too ostentatious. Besides, the years hadn't been that glorious. She lowered her wrist and asked herself for the twentieth time, *Where is Victoria*? She hoped Victor hadn't kept her at the restaurant too long. He knew everyone counted on her to help out on special days like today. And July 9 was the most special of all. Even the air was charged with excitement as the setup crew arrived to prepare the tables in the large auditorium-size hall and her friends Lucia and Nelly hurried to the back kitchen to make the postres.

She returned to the table they had placed by the front door, where she had a list of who had called to say they would attend. Opening the book and taking a seat, she waited for guests to begin arriving.

The club phone rang and she quickly answered. It might be Victoria or a cancellation. But it was neither. The call was from Hugo Oviedo, a charming Mexican musician who had been trying to convince Jaqueline for months to let him perform at the club. He had two children, and Jaqueline had her suspicions that he was interested in Victoria. Thankfully, other than urging her mother to let him perform at the club, Victoria didn't return his interest. Victor wouldn't accept a man with children who didn't have a solid job and, on top of it all, wasn't Argentine.

"Be more flexible," Hugo coaxed. "Variety is good, Jaqueline."

"I'm sorry, Hugo," she said. The board wouldn't approve any event that didn't fit their strict objectives for the club, which centered around the mission of celebrating the Argentine culture.

"I'm not going to give up. You guys would love me if you gave me the chance."

"I've listened to you. I do love your music."

"Then put in a good word for me."

"I'm busy, Hugo," she told him, even though she wasn't at the moment. "And the answer is still no."

"Is your beautiful daughter around?"

"No. And I told you, you're too old for her." That was another thing. The man was forty-one.

"She's too young for me, and you're married. Life is unfair," he joked.

"Hugo, you're a silly man." But a nice one. Maybe she would listen to Victoria and recommend him. "I'll suggest to the board that they let you perform. But no promises, understand?"

"Gracias," he said. "You're wonderful."

"Stop with the flattery. I've already fallen for it."

He laughed. "I mean every word of it."

"Call me in a couple of weeks and I'll let you know what we decide."

"I will. And Jaqueline?"

"What?"

"Happy Independence Day. See, I remembered."

She smiled. "Good-bye."

She made a note to bring him up at the next board meeting. Why not embrace a little variety?

In the back office of the restaurant, Victoria was ready to call it a day. She turned off the radio and sat behind the desk to finish up. They had a wedding party scheduled in two weeks, one retirement party, and a large group that just wanted tables grouped together next Saturday night rather than reserve the private room. Easy enough. She completed the paperwork and made a few phone calls.

As she filed away the forms, she noticed a thick file stuffed in the back. She tried to adjust it, but the file tore. She groaned and pulled it out. Half the paperwork tumbled out onto the floor.

Victoria bent and started picking up the papers. She placed them on the desk and went in search of a new file, but found instead an empty box that was supposed to hold file folders.

Great. She threw out the box. That was another errand for her to run—the office supply store.

She sat back down and started to straighten the papers, which were now partially upside down and turned around. But seeing her home address on one of the forms caught her attention. She frowned and pulled it out of the pile. She wasn't exactly sure what type of form she was holding, but the more she studied it, the more it looked like a bank loan with the house and even the business listed as collateral.

Although she'd gone to college for a few years as a business major to please her father, she'd hated it and quickly dropped out. Still, even she could understand that this wasn't good. What was her father doing?

She shuffled the paperwork and continued to read. Much of the legal vocabulary confused her, though words like *restaurant expansion* and *franchise* were clear enough.

"Victoria, I just had a thought," Victor's voice carried down the hall and he entered the office. "When you get to the club, why don't you—"

"What's all this?" she interrupted.

Victor glanced at the desk, squinted, then his face seemed to lose its color and close down. No expression readable.

"It says you've applied for a loan." She shuffled more papers. "You've got a business plan for two... no, ten restaurants? Ten? What in the world is this?"

Victor drew a breath and stepped forward. He placed a hand on his face and slowly drew it down across his mouth and down his chin. Then he took a seat across from Victoria, the desk between them. "That," he said, "is my legacy. For you and your sister."

Victoria frowned, not comprehending at all. "Dad, this is going to cost millions of dollars."

"I know."

"Mom agreed to this?" Victoria couldn't imagine that she had. Jaqueline was the one who wanted both her and her sister to get nice government jobs with guaranteed income, medical insurance, and retirement benefits.

He maintained eye contact, then started to shake his head. "I didn't need her agreement. The house and the restaurant are in my name."

Victoria narrowed her gaze. Bad answer.

"You know how your mother is," he said in defense. "She doesn't understand business. And all she can see is the negative side of things."

No, she was conservative and careful. And she would flip when she learned about this.

"But"—he sat straighter and looked into Victoria's eyes—"I turned sixty this year, gorda. I don't know how it happened. One day I was a young man, full of dreams and plans, and the next I woke up an old man."

"Dad, you're not—"

"Listen," he said. "I didn't come to America to get married, raise kids, and barely get by."

"Papi, you've done more than get by."

"Yes, but that's not the point. I could have stayed in Argentina and done that. I came here to be someone. To make something of myself. And I decided that it was now or never."

Victoria stared at her father, seeing someone she wasn't sure she knew. Wasn't he the one who said, "Listen to your mother and don't dream too big. Take things slowly. Don't ever rush into anything"? She had vague memories of him talking about making it big someday, but that had been ages ago. When she was a teen. He hadn't spoken like that in years. It was always caution, caution, caution that she heard from both her mother and her father.

"This restaurant has done well. Has done spectacular," he continued. "I'm going to open ten more within the next five years. Then when they've all proven themselves, I'm going to sell franchises. By the time your kids are your age, La Parrilla will be as well known as Ruth's Chris or Morton's The Steakhouse. They'll know their grandfather came to this country a poor man and became great."

Victoria shivered slightly in her seat at the chills running down her spine. His excitement was something strong and palpable and contagious. These feelings of future glory, of wanting greatness, were things she'd desired herself when she was younger and dreaming of her future, but she had always been afraid to voice them. She'd felt it was selfish to want more than what her parents had already provided. So she'd learned to be content. Still living at home, because it had been easy to stay put while in college, and because her parents had wanted it that way. Working here at La Parrilla part-time and at a boutique part-time. Owning a simple Saturn that got her around town. Life was easy.

Her father's plans made her heart beat faster. If he was going for it, if he wasn't satisfied with a satisfactory life, maybe it wasn't so bad to dream after all. But she was also well aware that he was risking everything on this dream. Success was never easily achieved, and he was the one who told her that. "I don't know what to say."

He shrugged. "I wasn't going to share any of this yet. The plans are still premature. The loans have been approved, and I'm now contacting angel investors to get a good starting capital. In a couple of months, I plan to break ground on the first two restaurants. One in Santa Monica and one in Newport Beach. Then I start looking for property outside of California."

Even though all the paperwork was still in her hands, Victoria stared at him in disbelief. "This is . . . exciting," she said stupidly.

Grinning like a little boy, he stood. "I'm glad you finally know. I've been dying from keeping this to myself. I can't wait to see your mother's face when I take her to the openings of the new restaurants."

"You're going to wait until then to tell her?"

"Yes. So keep this to yourself. Understand?"

She understood. But she didn't agree.

"In fact, while I'm getting these other two restaurants off the ground, I'll expect you to put more time into this one. You're ready to take on more responsibility, Victoria." With a pat on the back, he winked and walked out of the office.

Victoria sat in the chair, dumbfounded. Was he going to expect her to run this restaurant? She didn't want to be responsible for the restaurant. Truth was, she wasn't interested in this type of business at all. And now he wanted to open ten more. Victoria dropped her head into her hands. In her mind, hearing another door slam shut. Burdened, as always, with her father's plans for her life.

Chapter Two

Just when Jaqueline was about to panic, Victoria flew into the club, arms full of things, her wavy, brown hair all over the place, her clothes wrinkled.

Jaqueline stood from behind the welcome table. "Por fin, llegaste."

"Yes, I made it, Mami. I'm not late. Don't tell me you're panicking."

"No," she said, faking innocence, "but you know no one does anything until you get here to tell them what to do." Victoria had an eye for color and patterns and item placement unlike anyone else's.

"If only I had that much power." She glanced around. "Okay, we need to get the light blue and white tablecloths on the round tables. And the flowers should have arrived. Have they?"

"I don't know."

"How about the band?"

"Not yet."

"Okay." She dropped her bag on the table, on top of the notebook in which Jaqueline was checking people off as they arrived. "Let's go find out."

Victoria spun around and charged full speed ahead, almost running right into Lucia and Nelly, who had approached behind her. "Oh, Mrs. Ortelli, Mrs. Apolonia, hello."

"Nena, llegaste," Lucia said in a tone that meant to scold.

"But you didn't get dressed," Nelly said.

Victoria looked down at her olive-colored stretch twill pants and simple black blouse that tied at her waist—and in Jaqueline's opinion outlined her breasts too much and her unflattering waist even more—and shrugged. "Didn't I?"

"Today's a special day, Victoria," Nelly said. "You should wear something nicer."

"You're right, Mrs. Apolonia, but if I did, I'd be a mess by the time the night was over." She patted Nelly on the arm. "I appreciate that you ladies are always looking out for me, though."

Quickly, she stepped away and immediately got to work.

Jaqueline raised an eyebrow at her friends. "Don't look at me. I've done everything I could with her. She dresses like every other American girl her age." To herself she added that just because she was a big girl didn't mean she couldn't dress fashionably. After all, she was still young.

"I never had these problems with my Susana," Nelly said. "And now she's married, with three kids. She has a nice house. And all because I was strict with her."

Jaqueline caught Lucia's gaze over Nelly's shoulder, and Lucia rolled her eyes. More than anyone, Lucia understood that children didn't always behave how parents wanted, no matter what they might do. Her Eric left home when he turned twenty-one, turned his back on his family, on his culture, on everything he should have valued. As her only child, he broke his mother's heart. And she didn't speak of his betrayal. Ever. If she ever mentioned her son it was to say how well he was doing, how wealthy and successful he had become.

Lucia looked down, then tapped Nelly's shoulder. "Vamos, we can't all be perfect parents. Let's go help Victoria."

Jaqueline and Victor may not have been perfect parents, but they were lucky with how their two beautiful daughters had turned out. Jaqueline had no complaints. Victoria was the older and the more difficult one to mold, but she was kind and loyal. A dreamer like Victor. A free spirit. And Jaqueline loved her despite all her unfocused and undisciplined traits. And Carmen, her baby, had gone away to college three years ago. Victor wanted her to study closer to home. But Victoria and Carmen together sent applications to the farthest colleges in the country, and Carmen ended up in a premed program in Pennsylvania. When Jaqueline blamed Victoria for encouraging her sister to go so far away, Victoria simply looked at her sadly and said, "Let her do what I can't."

And Jaqueline had let it go. Victoria was right. Let Carmen be the one who becomes a woman with an education, a woman who lives her own life. She never had, and poor Victoria, as the first, had been her father's child from day one. She would inherit La Parrilla. She would live the life Victor wanted whether she wanted to or not. Sometimes Jaqueline wished she'd had a son for Victor to share his dreams with, rather than dominating Victoria.

"Mami," she called. "The band's here. Can you show them where to set up?"

"Si, como no." Jaqueline went to help, tucking her thoughts away—something she was well practiced at after over thirty years as a mother and wife.

Victoria didn't say much when she left work, Victor thought. She'd stayed in the office for some time after learning about his plans. He imagined she was going over every detail of the paperwork from the banks and lawyers. She was probably worried about her future and his and Jaqueline's. But she shouldn't be. He'd studied this idea. Had a financial plan created by a professional. This would work.

He glanced around La Parrilla and, as always, it was packed.

Regulars like the TV personality who brought his group of friends in at least once a week. Or the CEO of a major radio broadcasting company who dined here with his family the first Friday of every month. He knew all these guys on a first-name basis, and they loved him and his restaurant.

And they should have. La Parrilla was something to be proud of. It wasn't a greasy hole in the wall like some of the other Hispanic restaurants that were open a year or two and then closed. On the contrary, he owned an upscale steak house, and the Americanos paid a lot of money for good beef. Argentines were known around the world for two things: tangos and beef. So he'd given up trying to become un Americano and just accepted that he'd always be an Argentine living in a foreign country. If that meant selling well-seasoned, expensive beef, so be it. Not what he'd imagined he'd be doing with his life, but it had been a job that Jaqueline had accepted would pay the bills.

And he'd decided that now this noose around his neck would make him rich. He'd finally be able to go back to Argentina and live his retirement years in style. Yes, that would be something. He strolled around the tastefully presented tables, and smiled at his guests. "Are you finding everything satisfactory?"

"This is the best beef I've ever had. What *is* your secret?" said a guy sitting with a pretty girl.

Victor smiled, reached for the wine bottle on the table, and poured more into each glass—the elegant sound of wine flowing into the fluted glass reminding both guests and Victor that it wasn't just food he served, but a dining experience. "Argentines know how to cook beef."

"You're not kidding." The man motioned to his lady friend. "Isn't this the best barbecue you've ever had?"

They'd ordered the house specialty—an Argentine parrilla. The little, sizzling grill sat at the center of the table, and everyone picked out what they wanted to eat.

"Delicious," the woman said.

Victor thanked them and continued to make his rounds to all the tables, feeling almost drunk with happiness. He had a gorgeous wife. One daughter in college, another who would one day be his partner in the restaurant business, and a future that for the first time in thirty years he could say he looked forward to living.

Jaqueline had noticed the second Victor arrived at the club, dressed in his work clothes—an elegant black suit, which he'd have to take off because he would be manning the smoky barbecues. In fact, the other men were already at the grill, preparing the coals. Most of the members were gathered in groups socializing and listening to music, waiting for dinner to begin. Victor took off his shirt, coat, and tie and hung them in the closet to change back into later. Jaqueline tried to ask him about his day, but he just nodded, gave her a quick peck on the cheek, and said that things had been the same as always.

"What does that mean?" Jaqueline asked.

He frowned, blocking the sight of his beautiful eyes. Charcoal-gray eyes that he'd passed on to Carmen. "It means, it was work. What do you want me to say?"

She wanted…what they'd once had. Jaqueline had been only seventeen years old when she fell in love with Victor, the most exciting boy in her barrio. Though at first she hadn't been entirely interested in him, because he'd seemed so full of himself. He'd learned to speak English at the fancy private school he attended and bragged about how one day he'd travel to Norte America and make his fortune. Then he would return home to Argentina and buy a mansion in Buenos Aires.

Somehow, at one of the neighborhood bailes, she'd caught his attention on the dance floor, and he'd become determined to get her to date him. Every night, he'd show up at her apartment and call her, beg for her to come to the balcony and talk to him. He'd read her poetry, sing tangos full of passion, and call out his undying love.

Jaqueline's father cursed at him and told him to go home. He threatened to go down stairs and bash Victor's head in. But Victor kept coming back, not intimidated or thwarted by parental disapproval. He had even shown up at her high school and begged her to have a cup of coffee with him, go for a walk in el centro, sit on a park bench and tell him her dreams.

His charm and boldness had swept her off her feet.

She soon learned that Victor was a man who got what he wanted. And that he had been serious about traveling to the United States.

"We'll get married and go together," he'd promised.

"Victor, I can't leave my family, my life, for that kind of adventure," Jaqueline had said. "Forget all that. We can have a great life here."

But Victor couldn't let it go. It was his dream, and soon it became her dream. They'd gotten married two years later and received a big send-off by all their friends, who wished them a great life in the faraway land so full of promise.

Everything was new and exciting. Starting with the plane ride. Jaqueline had never been on an airplane before. She marveled at everything—the silverware, the small pillows, the way the chair tipped back. "See how little the houses look," she had said excitedly, as she held Victor's hand.

He had smiled, caressing her with those sexy eyes of his, holding his excitement in check even if she could feel it in his touch. "We're really doing it," he'd said.

"Do you think it will be very different over there?"

"Maybe."

"I'm scared."

He'd put his arm around her and said, "Don't be, my love. I'll always take care of you. I promise."

And he had. But at some point, buried under the stresses of work and raising children, they'd drifted apart. He might have stopped loving her. Or maybe she'd stopped loving him.

Her children had become her entire world. But now, they no longer needed her. And Jaqueline had a vacant hole in her chest that she couldn't seem to fill.

"I've got to go get the meat ready," he said.

"Then I guess you'd better go."

He nodded and hurried outside.

By nine that night, everyone who was going to show up for the July 9 celebration had arrived. Victoria sat down to a glass of wine and breathed a sigh of exhaustion, surveying all her hard work and feeling satisfied with her efforts. She'd been able to put aside her concerns about her father's revelation and get to work. She had dressed the tables, made sure the place settings were perfectly arranged using the club's best china, and set up the gardenia center pieces. At each end of the stage she placed three-foot decorative vases, and she'd instructed the three-man band—consisting of a keyboardist, a violinist, and an accordianist—on the songs that had been requested by their members so they could incorporate those into their performance. She had the guys put up the banner over the stage, called the photographer, who was late, checked on the food, and passed the cooking on to the men, including her father, who would handle all the barbecuing. In the kitchen, the women had salads and desserts under control.

They didn't even pay her to work this hard. She must be insane. Well, to be fair, no one got paid. This was a labor of love. They purposely never had an event catered, preferring to do it themselves the way they would have in Argentina. So in a way, she looked at it as if she were serving 250 members of her extended family.

Her cell phone alerted her that her sister was calling. Victoria couldn't talk to Carmen and not tell her about her father's plans. And tonight was not the time. She answered hurriedly, "Carmen, let me call you later, we're going to start dinner." And that actually wasn't a lie. The women brought baskets overflowing with bread to the tables, and the aroma drifting inside from the grills indicated that the meat would follow shortly.

"No problem. Have a great time. I'll give you a call tomorrow."

"Good idea. I need to talk to you, but not tonight." She got up and purposely moved closer to the stage so the music from the band would get louder, making conversation more difficult.

"That's okay. I can barely hear you anyway. Hasta mañana," Carmen said. She made a kissy sound and hung up.

Victoria didn't want to burden Carmen with news of their father's plans, but she had to tell someone. Tomorrow they could talk privately.

At about nine thirty, with the summer sun finally having set in California, they began serving the food. As in Argentina, everyone ate late. By eleven the dishes had been cleared and loaded into the heavy-duty dishwashers in the kitchen by the older women. The younger ones took to the dance floor first. Victoria searched out her parents. They used to love to dance, but in the last few years her mother disappeared into the kitchen to help wash dishes, and her father stayed on the back patio beside the grills, smoking a cigarette and socializing with Mr. Ortelli and a couple of other men.

And she was too physically and mentally tired to dance. Hell, exhaustion was her middle name. Most days she felt like she was thirty-eight years old, not twenty-eight. She decided that instead of dancing, she'd get a cup of coffee before she made the drive home. As she filled her cup from one of the silver coffee urns in the back of the dance hall, she heard an unusual group gasp, and voices quieting as if someone had gradually turned down the volume. Only the music continued. Victoria looked over her shoulder. A tall man in a sophisticated suit, probably custom made to fit his great body, had walked in and stood just inside the entrance. He scanned the room as if he were looking for someone. Then Nelly Apolonia ran out of the large hall and into the kitchen. She came back out with Mrs. Ortelli, who called out in a high-pitched shock, "Eric!"

Eric? Ortelli? Victoria stood by the coffee urns, staring like everyone else at the guy who had inspired so much gossip through the years. There had been stories that he'd had a big fight with his parents, or that he'd gotten a girl pregnant in another state over spring break, or even that he'd killed someone and was hiding out. Speculation ran the gambit from wild to ridiculous. Eventually, all the gossip died down until, out of respect for Lucia Ortelli, no one mentioned Eric at all. So much time had passed since Eric had left home that Victoria had started to wonder if maybe he'd been a figment of their collective imagination and he'd never existed at all. A sort of tall tale that had taken on a legendary quality over the years. Yet here he was, looking very real, and very handsome, and like he'd done extremely well for himself.

Mrs. Ortelli ran to her son and pulled this broad-shouldered man into an embrace. Eric closed his eyes and held his mother close. He kissed the top of her head as she pulled back to look at him. Taking in the same image as the rest of the club—an amazingly put-together guy with dark, angular features and black, wavy hair that if left to grow longer would probably have curls. Different from the skinny, dimpled boy who left home.

After a brief private moment in a sea of observers where mother and son shared who knew what with their gazes, Mrs. Ortelli turned around with a huge smile and said, "Surprise. He made it home tonight after all."

Was she going to try to pull off the lie that she *expected* him to show up? She'd been just as surprised as everyone else. But like her mother always said, Lucia should have been an actress because she lived her life pretending. Pretending her life was perfect.

She pulled Eric into the crowd, talking to everyone around her, calling for someone to bring him a plate of food. He offered a gorgeous smile as he shook hands and accepted hugs or kisses. Lucia led him to their family table, and Mr. Ortelli, who had been fetched from the patio, joined them. As if Eric were a celebrity or a war veteran come home, people passed by their table to welcome him—though Victoria knew it was more out of curiosity and nosiness than anything else.

"Can you believe this?" Jaqueline whispered, having come to stand beside her.

"What's he doing here?"

"I don't know, but to show up just like that, without warning, to such a public place. He has no shame," Jaqueline said.

"Mrs. Ortelli said she knew," Victoria offered. Often the target of club criticism herself, she felt a small need to defend Eric.

"Well what else is she going to say? Pobre Lucia."

Saving face. Such an Argentine trait. Too proud to say, "My son's a jerk." All around them people were doing the same kind of whispering as Victoria and Jaqueline.

"Let's go say hello and welcome him home," her mother continued, grabbing Victoria by the elbow.

Victoria frowned. "No, give them some privacy."

"It would be rude not to say something. Vamos."

Jaqueline pulled Victoria's arm and led her to the Ortelli table. "Eric, querido, what an amazing surprise," Jaqueline said, and hugged him.

Eric stood for the hundredth time and opened his arms to Jaqueline, dropping a kiss on her cheek. Then without pausing he said hi and kissed Victoria. Then he took his seat again.

Victoria checked him out. He'd grown thicker, more muscular, more solid. Still just as handsome as he'd been in high school. He sipped his wine with a relaxed arrogance that didn't seem quite proper, considering the commotion he'd caused.

"How have you been, Victoria?" Again, the question was one that would make sense if he'd been away a few months, maybe a year. But for someone who'd disappeared seven years ago, his attitude seemed too casual.

"Where should I start?" she said.

He chuckled. "Wherever you'd like. Have a seat. Do you mind, Mami?"

Now he was asking if his mother minded what he did?

"No, but you eat. Your food is getting cold."

"I'm not hungry." He eased the plate away. "I didn't come to eat, anyway. I actually went home, and when no one was there I remembered it was Sunday and figured you'd be here."

"It's not only Sunday," Victoria said. "It's Independence Day."

He frowned. "Oh, in Argentina. That's right." He glanced around. "No wonder all this."

No one said anything in response. To forget July 9 was too big an insult to comment on.

"I was actually just leaving," Victoria said. "So enjoy your dinner."

Jaqueline gave her a scowl. "You can stay a little longer. Talk to Eric for a while."

"We shouldn't intrude," Victoria said.

Antonio Ortelli, who had walked in from the grills with a surprised look on his face, had hugged his son, then sat to let his wife handle all the questions. Now he stood. "We have time to catch up when we get home." He patted Eric on the shoulder. "Let's continue to enjoy the celebration."

"Of course," Lucia said, and though she didn't appear to want to let Eric out of her sight for a second, she also stood. "I'm going to go finish up in the kitchen and let you get reacquainted with your friends. Your father's right, we'll have you all to ourselves later. There's plenty of time."

Eric squeezed her fingers with his large, dark hands. The guy had a spectacular tan the color of dark, golden honey.

"All the time in the world," he said, before his mother and Jaqueline returned to the kitchen. Lucia looked back at him twice as if she were afraid he'd disappear.

Faced with making casual conversation with a man she didn't know anymore, Victoria took a seat across from him and tried to remember who he had been when they'd last spoken. Fun came to mind. Mama's boy. Cheerful. He didn't look like any of those things anymore. He looked harder.

He sipped from his glass of wine with lips that could possibly also be hard, but right now they looked shiny and sexy surrounded by the five o'clock shadow on his face. "This place never changes."

"Some things never do." Nor do some people. Namely, her. He, on the other hand, was almost unrecognizable.

His light brown eyes rested on her face after doing a very quick, barely noticeable scan of her body. "Remember when we used to sneak up to the offices on the second floor and pretend to look for clues that this was a secret organization involved in some kind of plot to take over the world?"

She wanted to smile at the memories of their childhood games. They'd had so much fun. She and Eric and Susana and a handful of other kids who were now all grown and married. Except for her. And maybe Eric. After high school they'd all stopped being friends. And he'd disappeared. Maybe that was why she wouldn't allow herself to enjoy reminiscing with him.

"I don't think we knew what we were looking for," he continued. "Or even why our parents would want to take over the world."

"Maybe we just wanted to have fun."

"Yeah, or maybe we wanted to believe they were more than just lonely immigrants longing for a piece of their homeland."

The way he said that, with such derision, irritated her. But a part of Victoria wondered if that was true. Kids always thought their parents were all-powerful and important. But had she ever wished they were more than what they were? No. "Is that why you finally came home? Longing for everything you walked away from?"

He took another sip of wine, but kept his gaze on her, probably wondering how she'd had the nerve to ask him directly what everyone was wondering. "Maybe."

"Well, it's about time. Do you know how much your mother has suffered? Because I do. I've been here the entire time to watch her cry on my mom's shoulder. And age way quicker than she should have."

He clenched his jaw and stared at her coldly. "That's the way the world works, Victoria. Children grow up, move out, go on with their lives. You apparently haven't learned that yet."

Anger made its way up her body from her stomach and warmed her face. "I value my family. I know the meaning of the word *loyalty,* and I respect my parents for everything they have sacrificed for me."

"How very Argentine of you," he said, obviously not meaning it as a compliment. Then he grinned, making those old dimples pop up. "And very admirable. With those honorable values and being damned cute to boot, I can't believe you're not married yet."

The personal nature of his comment was inappropriate, like everything else about him. "And what values do you hold dear? Let me guess: freedom and wealth?"

His grin dwindled. "Man, Victoria, I never thought you'd turn into one of them." He gestured to the others in the club. "How did you let that happen?" he asked with obvious disappointment. "You need to loosen up."

"Who are you to tell me how—?"

"Who are you to tell *me?*" He lifted an eyebrow.

"No one," she admitted.

"That's not entirely true. We were pretty good friends once."

"Not as good as I thought." They'd played together at the club and sometimes at each other's houses when their parents visited one another. And as teens they'd sat together and watched movies or listened to music. And they'd talked about so many things. But he never once mentioned leaving home. She had. She'd been the one with dreams. She wondered if he remembered that.

More curious people stopped by the table, interrupting them to welcome Eric home. But she didn't mind. It gave her a perfect excuse to leave. She stood and said good-bye. Eric stood as well, took her hand, and pulled her toward him for another kiss on the cheek. "It really is good to see you again."

She couldn't say what was really on her mind with others listening to them. "Welcome home, Eric," she said instead, and left feeling depressed.

She didn't know why the arrival of a family friend's son should have that kind of effect on her. Maybe it was a combination of that and finding out about her father's restaurant expansion plans that had her emotions so low. Maybe it was the realization that everyone seemed to be living the life they wanted except her. Maybe it was the realization that she didn't have the slightest idea what it was she wanted out of life anymore, and that the last time she'd thought about it had been in high school.

Chapter Three

Victoria woke up to her cell phone playing her sister's favorite tune—"Irreplaceable" by Beyoncé—and groaned, burrowing further under her soft, cozy blankets. Why couldn't Carmen ever remember that it was three hours earlier in California? The phone stopped, then the happy tune started again. She tossed the covers off her head, reached for the nightstand, and clicked her phone on. "What?"

"Sounds like someone partied a little too long last night."

"And now I'm trying to sleep." Victoria rolled onto her back and hung an arm over her forehead, shielding her eyes from the sunshine coming through the window shades.

"Sorry, but it was call now or not at all, because I'm meeting a friend in ten minutes. We're going to amuse ourselves walking seeing-eye dogs before class. Crazy, I know, but it's her idea, and I thought I'd go along with it. Gets me outside, in the fresh air, some exercise, you know. And the dogs are so cute, they—"

"Carmen," Victoria moaned. "You woke me and you're rambling about some stupid dogs. I don't really care."

"Sorry. Okay, tell me what you wanted to tell me last night. Fast."

If her eyelids weren't feeling like itty, bitty, flat weights preventing her from opening her eyes, she'd roll them. Last night, she had decided not to tell Carmen about Dad's new restaurants yet. And now wasn't the right time, either. She blinked at the clock and saw that it was nine thirty, so she pushed herself up in bed and rested her back on the headboard. "Well, you'll never guess who showed up at the club last night."

"Beyoncé?" She laughed.

Victoria ignored her way-too-peppy personality. "Eric Ortelli."

"Get out!"

"Yep, he just strolled right into the club and made himself at home. Could have given Lucia a heart attack, the jerk."

"What did she do?"

"Hugged him and told everyone she was expecting him."

"Wow. Well, what does he look like?"

Victoria shrugged. "Great, like always. Amazing, really."

"He always was a cutie. Okay, I gotta go. Give him a kiss for me, and call me soon. You've got to get me through this last year of college. I'm so not loving it."

"Just finish. You have to."

"I know. Love you, sis."

"Love you, too." Victoria turned her cell off and headed to the shower.

Eric took a seat at the breakfast table because his mother insisted he do so the instant he walked into the kitchen. Lucia bounded out of her seat and headed for the coffee carafe.

"Morning," Antonio said.

"Good morning." Eric glanced around the familiar kitchen. Unlike the changes to the interior of the rest of the house, the kitchen remained the same. Same cabinets, same paint job, even the same appliances that had been here when he was a kid.

His mother, already neatly dressed and as efficient as always, placed the steaming coffee cup in front of him. "Sugar?" She held the sugar bowl and a spoon above his cup.

"Oh, ah, no. Thanks, Mom."

"Cream?"

"Black is good." He smiled somewhat awkwardly as she hovered over him.

She ran her fingers through his hair. "I'll get you some bread."

And she did. She cut fresh French bread for him as if he were a child incapable of doing it himself. Then she offered him orange marmalade, or dulce de leche, and practically spread it on his bread.

He stared down at the plate, bread loaded with dulce de leche. His mouth watered. He hadn't had the sweet caramel spread in so long.

"Did you want something different? Maybe you're used to eating a full American breakfast instead."

"This is fine, Mami, really."

He'd lived alone for so long that the thick attention and the somersaults she was performing in an attempt to please him felt a little uncomfortable. Meanwhile, his father sat silently drinking his coffee, not saying much, like always. It had taken Antonio almost an entire year to talk to him again when he'd left home. Their fight over Eric's future had been bitter, with angry words shouted back and forth. Antonio had predicted he'd come home with his tail between his legs and beg to be taken back in. That had caused Eric to stubbornly stay away just to prove his father wrong. There had been times when Eric had considered swallowing his pride and going home. But he hadn't. Couldn't.

"Sit down, Mom, please. If I need anything else, I can get it myself."

"But I haven't had the pleasure of doing anything for you in so long. To give you a decent breakfast is the least I can do."

"You have. Now, please, if you want to do something for me, sit down. Talk to me."

"Well." Lucia considered that. "Okay."

"The house looks great," Eric said. "You've redecorated." Although he spoke to his mother on the phone often enough, now that he was face-to-face with her, he didn't know what to say.

"Victoria helped me. She said it looked too *Three's Company* before. I guess that meant our things were outdated."

Eric chuckled. "I guess so. Well, she has good taste. I like it."

Antonio grunted. "So are you going to tell us what you're doing home?"

"Viejo," Lucia scolded.

"What? He shows up out of the blue. Don't I have a right to ask?"

Eric took a bite of bread and chewed as he watched his father. The battle was still there. He sensed it as if it were something physical pushing between them. Nudging, poking, irritating like a burr on the inside of a sock. *Who had been right? Who was the better man?* He shrugged. Older and hopefully wiser, he was willing to allow his father the power he deserved. He no longer had anything to prove. "You're always asking me to come home, so I finished my last deal and decided it was time."

"Just like that?" Antonio asked, as if waiting for more. Waiting for Eric to get down on his knees and say he'd been wrong. And he *had* been wrong about some things. Not about his career choice, but in turning his back completely on his old life—on his parents.

"Everything I own is in the back of my pickup, so yeah, just like that."

"We're happy to see you, and glad you're home," Lucia quickly added. "What your father is trying to say is, why couldn't you have called us or let us know you were coming? To show up at the club like that without warning made us look like..."

"Fools," Antonio said.

If they were waiting for something earth-shattering, Eric didn't have it. He'd simply begun to feel like he was closing one deal after another, collecting money in a bank account that meant little to him, and feeling very little satisfaction from life. All the women, all the great dinners, all the alcohol in the world, didn't fill the void that had begun to grow in his heart the past year or two. It was simply time to come home. At least for a while. Since he lived in whatever property he was renovating, he didn't have a permanent home to worry about. No wife, no children. Nothing to prevent him from going wherever he pleased.

"I should have called," he said. "But I didn't really have a plan. I just started driving, and I before I knew it I was home."

Lucia reached across and caressed his face. "Doesn't matter. We're just glad you're here where you belong."

Antonio nodded, a question still in his gaze.

Victor always liked to get to the restaurant early. After his morning café and newspaper, he usually left home. Mostly because Jaqueline interrupted his morning routine at least a dozen times with questions or gossip of one sort or another. He tried to be patient and listen, like this morning when all she could talk about was the Ortelli boy coming home. Victor didn't understand what the big deal was. Eric had always been a wild little boy, spoiled by Lucia. Then everyone was surprised when the kid just up and left. Victor hadn't been surprised. In many ways, Eric was like his father, Antonio. Victor liked Antonio, but the man was always involved in some crazy scheme or another. And Eric had turned out the same. When he mentioned his thoughts to his wife, Jaqueline turned a horrified gape at him.

"They're our friends. How can you say that?"

"Because it's true."

"You know how much Lucia has suffered, losing Eric."

Her words brought back memories of what his sister had said to him whenever he would call Argentina, referring to their own mother. He frowned. "She didn't lose him. He's back." And maybe part of the reason the boy left *was* his mother. A man has to be allowed to grow up. He can't be coddled forever.

"Yes, but for how long will he stay?"

Victor stood and folded his newspaper, since she wasn't going to let him read it anyway. "I guess we'll see. I've got to go."

Jaqueline looked disappointed, but she never voiced her feelings. She would never dream of complaining, even though he'd guessed that she was unhappy. He didn't know how to please her anymore, and this bothered him. He worked hard—always had. He was putting Carmen through college. Always made sure Victoria and Jaqueline had whatever they wanted. He spent Sundays at the club with their friends. What else was a man to do?

Victoria strolled into the kitchen, yawning. "Morning," she said. "Carmen called and woke me up this morning. Says she loves you."

Jaqueline placed a cup of café con leche on the table, and a plate of French bread, then she slid the butter and dulce de leche across the table. "Did you tell her I'm still angry that she chose to spend most of her summer break in Philadelphia rather than come home?"

Victoria took a seat. "Just coffee this morning, Mami. And you tell her you're angry every time you talk to her. Maybe you should stop being angry and tell her how proud you are of her. She got a 4.0 last year again. Do you know how hard that is to do with the type of classes she takes?"

Surprised, Jaqueline placed a hand on her hip. "I tell her I'm proud all the time. But why can't she come home when she has a break?"

"She got a part-time job and wanted to stay close to school. Every summer she comes home. Maybe she wanted to enjoy the city this time."

Jaqueline shook her head, not accepting the absence of her

baby. Victor understood how she felt. He missed Carmen, too, but he kept his feelings to himself. He pushed in his chair as the conversation between Jaqueline and Victoria continued.

"Why don't you want some bread? Coffee is not enough to keep you going all morning."

"I need to lose some weight. You're always telling me I'm too fat."

"I don't say that."

"Your mother never called you fat," Victor said, taking his last sip of coffee while standing beside the table.

"You both call me *gordita* all the time. What are you talking about?"

"That's an endearment," Victor explained.

"If I were your pet pig that would be endearing."

Jaqueline lifted her hands up into the air. "Fine. Losing some weight would be good for you. Right, Victor?"

"If she wants." He pulled his car keys out of his pocket, gave Jaqueline a quick kiss, and turned to Victoria. "I have the Lewis wedding party next weekend. Are you coming in to make sure all last-minute things are taken care of?"

"I've got it under control."

"Don't say that. That tells me nothing. Are you coming in or not?"

"Sure, Dad. I'll come in."

"Okay. See you later." He hurried to work, where he felt the most comfortable these days.

Victoria worked part-time at a neighborhood boutique owned by her friend and ex-art history teacher, Douglas. Not only did it give her something to do, but it also allowed her to indulge her creativity, and she loved it. Between the work she did at the boutique and helping her father at La Parrilla, it kept her busy and provided some spending money. Sadly, she wondered if she'd have to give it up as her father piled more responsibilities onto her.

Most women her age probably wouldn't be content living at home, having jobs that led nowhere, not having a husband or even a boyfriend, but Victoria was content. Not thrilled with her life, true, and Eric's little digs about her still being at home bothered her more than she cared to admit. Because it wasn't only the fact that she lived at home. It was the entire package. He was obviously successful at whatever he did. He had gone out into the world and started living. She, on the other hand, had done nothing with her life. Ten years had passed since high school and she was in the exact same place.

She helped Douglas arrange a window display. Douglas had been a teacher for thirty-five years. His life had been going pretty well. Then his wife got cancer and died, and he decided to quit his job and open the boutique they'd always talked about. He was in his fifties now and seemed, like her, content.

Placing a mirror strategically to reflect the display of books and flowers on the antique table, Victoria caught sight of herself. She looked terrible.

"Augh, I need to lose weight before our high school reunion," she said. She was proud of herself for skipping breakfast.

Douglas glanced at her. "Must be hard with all that great food your family makes."

"Yeah," she said.

"You sound depressed."

"Do you think I'm a loser, Douglas?"

He frowned. "Loser? Why would you say that?"

"I don't know. I should be doing something with my life."

"What do you want to do?"

She picked up a gorgeous vintage phone from the 1920s, and placed it gently on the table. "I don't know."

"Maybe you are doing what you want to do."

She glanced at him. "Sort of." She looked in the mirror again and didn't see anything appealing. "I want to lose weight. I feel like shit most of the time."

He handed her a basket of dried flowers. "Then you should."

She nodded and smiled. "I think I will."

Now that he was home, Eric couldn't say he had a plan. He didn't. All he knew was that his life lacked a sense of purpose. He'd lived the last twenty-eight years of his life for no one but himself. And he'd had a great time, no doubt about it. But something was missing. He wasn't sure what. The crazy thing was that it felt like whatever was missing was something inside himself. Not things. Not experiences—he'd had plenty of those.

So he sat in the living room, wondering what the hell to do now that he was home. He opened his laptop on the coffee table and visited the home auction site he commonly used to find investment properties. That was the only thing he knew how to do, so why not do it? He punched in a few of the nearby zip codes. A list of houses popped up on the screen. He scanned through the information, then leaned back on the sofa and lazily turned over the information in his head to see if any of them could be a good deal. California real estate was tricky, and he'd avoided it for good reason. Prices had been overinflated for years, and though people were able to make a profit, you had to be lucky to find the right house in the right neighborhood. However, the market had dropped in the past year. A good thing for an investor who wanted to buy cheap, unless the home continued to drop before you could unload it. Eric debated whether it was a risk he wanted to take.

"Hey," Antonio placed a hand on his shoulder. "What are you doing?"

Eric angled his head back. "A little work. Nothing important."

Antonio sat beside him. "I didn't know you'd be working while in town."

He shrugged. "I'm always looking for the next great deal."

Antonio stared at the computer screen. "Foreclosures?"

"Yep. It's the way to go these days."

"These are in our area?"

"I was curious what the market was like around here."

Antonio sat back and studied him the way he had when Eric was a boy. "Why?"

"That way I can stick around for a while if I find something good."

"You thinking of staying for more than a while? Working closer to home?"

Eric wasn't ready to commit to something like that. "California hasn't been an easy real estate market. We'll see if things are changing." He pointed to the screen. "These are going to be auctioned next week."

Antonio's interest was sparked. "Oh yeah? So what do you do? How do you choose one?"

"I do a quick inspection of the properties. If I like what I see, if I think I can do a quick fix on one and put it back on the market in a fair amount of time, I go to the auction and bid on it."

"That's it, huh?" Antonio laughed and rubbed his chin. "Now why didn't I find a moneymaker like this when I was younger?"

Eric couldn't help feeling a tinge of irritation at Antonio's downplaying the skill and work involved to actually be able to make money. "It's not as easy as I'm making it sound."

"You've done well. Haven't you?"

The question asked more than what it seemed. Had he made the right career choice? Had he been correct to follow his passion and not his father's plans of advanced degrees that led to a plush legal office in which to hang and show off those degrees? "I have, but it hasn't been easy," he said honestly.

Antonio lifted his chin and almost seemed happy that Eric's road to independence hadn't been effortless. Eric felt the *I told you so* phrase hovering between them. Not spoken, but thought. "Easy or not, you've got the life, *Pibe.* Gamble on property here and there. Do a little traveling, a little work, and cash in big-time when you're done."

Even though his father hadn't wanted this kind of life for Eric, *he* had always been interested in any and all ventures that involved speculation. Except that for Eric, there was no speculation. He didn't make the kind of money he made by taking stupid risks. Where Antonio had been impulsive and gullible, Eric had always carefully weighed each business deal. Where Antonio had been easy prey for crazy get-rich schemes, being a foreigner who believed in the impossible American dream, Eric was fully aware that the world was full of scams and trusted only his own intuition and solid, legitimate real-estate ventures.

Yes, sadly, his father believed every guy with a promise of gold at the end of the rainbow. Eric blamed his ignorance on the fact that he wasn't raised in this country. He was an easy target to suck in and fool. But Antonio was wrong about Eric—he was no gambler. And he was eager to show his father that even though he might not have become a well-dressed lawyer, he was every bit as successful doing what he loved.

Maybe if Antonio saw Eric running his business, he would understand. "Want to go with me to the auction?"

Antonio put a hand on Eric's shoulder. "I'd love to," he said.

Those three words meant more to Eric than Antonio could ever guess. Acceptance. In a minor way, maybe, but for a father who once told him that he had become the biggest disappointment of his life, this was huge. With a lump in his throat, Eric said, "Then I'd better go check out these houses and see what they look like."

All homes prior to auction were open to inspection, and Eric never bought a house he hadn't thoroughly checked out. That was also the way he lived his life. Looking at things from every angle. He hoped that for the first time he wasn't thinking with his emotions rather than his intellect. California real estate could be his downfall. As could being home again. But he had to give it a try. Living the life of a wanderer, with no roots, no connection to anyone, was slowly eating at his soul. And he feared that if he didn't attempt to make a change now, there would be nothing left of him soon.

Chapter Four

Friday afternoon, Eric parked his pickup in front of the fifth and last house he planned to inspect this week. Immediately he liked what he saw. The house looked like someone had used it as a dumping ground. Old couches, broken glass, tires, pieces of discarded toys littered the front yard. An overgrown pepper tree blocked much of the view of the front door and porch. An attached garage had practically caved in on itself. It would need an entirely new roof. Most potential home owners saw this kind of mess and kept right on driving to the next house on their list, not wanting to clean up someone else's trash. But cleanup was the easiest fix in the world.

He walked across the yard, stepping carefully around all the garbage. The front door had seen better days and would definitely have to be replaced. Stepping inside the house, left unlocked during open-house hours, he scanned the living room, trying to see where the immediate focal point of the room should be. He decided it had to be the brick fireplace. Looking down at the stained and torn carpet, he knew it had to come out. Walls looked good and sturdy, even if some of the paint around the fireplace looked to be chipping. Kitchen was large and at one time had been okay, but since the house had sat empty vandals had come in and taken everything of value. The sink, faucet, oven, and microwave were gone. And it looked like they'd tried to pull the cabinets out but failed. The house had three bedrooms, two bathrooms, a large living room, and a small den. The starting bid for this house was ridiculously low. Eric nodded to himself. This was it. He'd hire an inspector to check for structural soundness, roof leaks, termites, and mold. If all that checked out, he was in business. He swatted some kind of bug, probably a spider coming down from the ceiling, and made his way out through the front door.

Lucia kept dinner warm on the stove. She was washing a pot when Antonio came in and wrapped his arms around her plump middle.

"I'm starving," he said, and nuzzled her neck.

Lucia smiled, drying her hands on a kitchen towel. "I'm waiting for Eric to get home so we can eat together." She turned around in Antonio's arms. "Why don't you call him to see where he is?"

"Because I'm not going to hound and annoy him, and you shouldn't, either."

"I haven't seen my son in seven years. Do you think I'm going to pretend to be indifferent about spending time with him?"

"No, amorcito. But let him figure things out on his own. He's home. And he's home because he wants to be home. Just wait and see what happens."

Lucia placed her hands on Antonio's face and kissed his familiar and comforting lips. "I want my son back. For good."

Antonio sighed and nodded; he got the same look of regret that he always got when they spoke about Eric being gone. "If I could turn back time, he never would have left. But the past is the past, and I can't do anything about it."

"Of course you couldn't. He was young and needed the adventures that young men seem to need. After all, you were his age about the time you decided to move to this country. But he's older now, and maybe you can convince him that it's time to settle down. Have a man-to-man talk with him."

Antonio stepped back. He smiled. "I'm starving. Let's eat, huh?"

"Bueno. I guess I'll feed him when he gets home. I hope it's soon, though. I want to get to sleep. I've got to be to work early tomorrow. It's inventory time."

"Mmm," he said.

Antonio hated that she had to work when so many of her friends didn't. Take Jaqueline, for example. Sure, she helped out at the restaurant before Victoria took over, but she never *had* to work. Unlike other couples their age from the club, Lucia and Antonio struggled to make ends meet. Eric sent them money each month. She told him not to, but Antonio told her it would hurt his ego if they rejected his help. Still, she would rather have him living nearby than receive a check from him once a month. They deposited his checks in an account and never touched the money.

But also, Lucia liked working. She'd gotten a job at a department store as soon as Eric finished high school, figuring she'd have more time to work, plus she could use the money to help him get through college. Sadly, he dropped out and they didn't have college tuition payments for long, but she continued to work part-time. It got her out of the house. And even some great discounts at the store. She enjoyed it. And she didn't care if Antonio approved.

She placed a plate of ravioli with sauce and chicken in front of him and kissed the top of his head. Then she fixed her own plate.

"They make you work too hard during inventory, and you're always tired when you get home."

Lucia shrugged. "You can rub my feet and my legs and I'll be fine," she said.

He frowned as he ate his food, so she reached across and tugged at his chin. "And if I'm still tired, we can go to bed early."

His eyes met hers, and he smiled. "Okay."

They ate, and as they were finishing their meal, Eric walked in. Lucia shot right up. "Let me fix you a plate, querido. Sit down."

"That's okay. I ate already. "

Antonio shot him a disapproving look when Lucia stopped in her tracks and gazed at her son with surprise and hurt she couldn't keep hidden.

"Ah, I mean. It was a while ago." Eric placed his hand over his stomach. "In fact, now that I think about it, I *am* kind of hungry." He took a seat at the table.

Lucia turned around toward the stove and smiled. This was one of the reasons she loved Antonio so much. He'd taught Eric to respect and want to please her. She took pity on him and served him a small amount of food. "We don't have much left, Eric. I'm sorry."

"Oh, that's fine, Mom." When he had the plate in front of him, he took the fork and stabbed one of the ravioli and put it in his mouth. "Mmm. This is excellent. Mmm," he said again, and nodded his head for emphasis.

She watched him eat and couldn't help remembering when he was younger. How she'd loved to watch him drink from his bottle and eat baby food. The look of pure joy on his face. He had the same look now.

He glanced up and she realized that she was staring. "You need something to drink?" she asked.

"Sure. Water is fine."

She got him a glass of water. "What did you do today?"

He wiped sauce off his lips. "Just drove around town, getting reacquainted with the neighborhood. Downtown looks great. That town center they created is awesome."

"They did that about four years ago. Brings lots of business to the mall. And in fact, I'm going to turn in, because I have to be there early tomorrow." She kissed Eric and placed a hand on Antonio's shoulder. "I'll see you up there."

"I'll be right up, Amor."

"Good night, Mami." He watched her walk down the hall, then turned his gaze to his father and pushed his plate back.

"Thanks for eating that."

"It's good. I should have waited, knowing she'd cook for me."

"I had to beg her to feed me. She wanted to wait for you to get home."

Eric smiled. "Sorry."

"So, did you check out the houses?"

"Yep. And I think I've got a winner," he grinned. "So get your rest this weekend, Viejo. Monday morning we go to the auction."

Eric actually slept in on Sunday. And then spent a couple of hours in front of the TV set dressed in an old T-shirt and comfortable shorts, his feet on the immaculate cherrywood coffee table. Lucia kept his coffee cup full and placed a plate of bread and pastries on his lap. The combination of coffee and yeasty aromas with the satisfaction of not having to do anything but enjoy being at home made him settle in comfortably. He didn't care if he moved all day.

About noon however, his peaceful morning came to a halt. Lucia turned the TV off, took the empty plate, and pulled his coffee cup out of his hands.

"Time to get ready to go to the club."

"The club?" he asked, feeling like a bloated, spoiled cat.

"The Argentine Club. It's Sunday."

"Oh." He'd forgotten that his mother spent all morning in church and all afternoon and evening at the Argentine Club on Sundays. This morning she'd skipped church. Antonio never went with her to church, but he was the first one out the door to get to the club on time. The men played poker and took turns watching the barbecue. The women played canasta and gossiped. The kids used to have to take a Spanish class before they were allowed to run wild around the club. He'd hated it. Not sure what they did now. "I should go with you guys?"

"Of course."

Eric took his feet off the coffee table and lowered them to the floor. "What would I . . . do there?"

"Visit. Play cards with the men. Whatever you want."

He never could understand the draw of hanging out with people just because they happened to share the same cultural background as you.

His mother repeatedly reminded him in the past that it was up to the youth to keep the club going. If they didn't, then when the older generation died off the club would disappear, and so would any trace of their culture.

"Today, everyone is 'Latino,' as if South Americans, Central Americans, Mexicans, Cubans were all the same," she'd say with a sad expression. "And of course anyone who speaks Spanish in California is assumed to be Mexican. We get lost in the crowd, Eric. You have to work to keep the Argentine culture alive inside you."

Eric would nod, but inside he felt he wasn't actually Argentine. He was American. And he had very little interest in maintaining an active club. But he did love his parents. And for them, he'd endured the club. So that they'd have the slight connection to their birth country.

And today, he'd do so again. He stood. "Well…I'll go shower." As he walked away, he told himself he *should* go. It would make his mother happy. And he could pretend to like anything for a few hours. But he wasn't sure he believed his own encouraging thoughts.

During the day, the Argentine Club didn't look as appealing as it had last Sunday night when it had been all decked out. No fancy tables in the large meeting room. No flowers. No music. Just a couple of round gaming tables and a few long picnic tables for lunch, which wouldn't be served until about three in the afternoon when he'd be starving. They had the air-conditioning turned off because the back doors were open to allow the men to go in and out to check on the barbecue. So the place felt a bit warm and stuffy. Smelled of cigarette smoke and charcoal.

He shook about twenty-five men's hands and kissed about as many women's cheeks. And although everyone was polite, he sensed strong disapproval. The same as he'd felt from Victoria when he dropped in on their Independence Day celebration. He didn't get it. What the hell had he done to these people?

A big-screen TV took up a wall on the opposite end of the room behind the stage. A curtain had been drawn to reveal it. He recognized the younger group that had congregated there and strolled over.

Alex, who used to pee his pants in Spanish class, and who went through a goth period in high school, was there looking like a normal guy. Eric sort of laughed at himself. What had he expected? Time changed all people. Eric recognized Christian, who was sort of cool and on the quiet side; Adrian, another quiet dude he used to share music interests with; Eduardo, a sports buff, and Esteban, who went by Steve and had always been a sort of jerk. They all stood around staring at the big screen.

Eric didn't care much for soccer. He was a football fan all the way. "Hey," he said.

Eduardo glanced over his shoulder for just a second, then his attention went back to the screen. "Hey, Eric, welcome home, man."

"Thanks."

No one else said a word. He shoved his hands into his pockets, and looked around. "Where are the women?"

"Cooking or doing crafts with the kids," Adrian said. "Enjoy the peace and quiet while you can."

Again, no one looked at him. "I'm going to get a beer." If he had to put up with hours of this, he'd better start drinking now.

They had a self-serve honor-system bar. Eric found a beer and put five bucks in the box under the counter, figuring this would cover him for a second one later. Then he climbed the wooden stairs with the same red runner they'd had since he was a kid. He was curious to see if they still had a library up there. They did. He looked through the volumes of Argentine history, literature, and art. He pulled out a book by Julio Cortázar and sat to read the first few chapters. After about an hour, he closed the book and put his empty beer bottle in a waste can.

He was bored stiff, not because of the book—in fact, he planned to ask if he could borrow it—but because he wasn't the type of guy that could happily sit inside for long. He climbed back down. The guys were still watching the soccer game. The older men were playing cards. With a smile, he thought it was actually sort of cool that they all enjoyed the routine of hanging out together every Sunday. The day was warm and comfortable. The only problem was that after so many years away, he felt sorely out of place.

He walked to the back, where the kids had a playroom, and caught sight of Susana, Victoria, Luisa, Anna, and a few other women he remembered. One little boy asked Victoria why the gaucho had to have such stupid-looking pants. She told him the pants weren't stupid, and that they were called bombachas, which got a laugh out of all the kids, because in modern times, bombachas were women's underwear.

"Jeans on cowboys look better," the boy told Victoria.

She shrugged. "When you're right, you're right."

Eric smiled.

"Okay, I'm done," said a little girl. "And I'm hungry. Can we be done now?"

"Yes, I'm starving, too," Victoria said.

"We should check first to make sure the food is ready," Susana said.

"Fine. I'll check." Victoria turned around and stopped walking when she saw him peeking into the room.

"Hi," he said with a smile, and stepped back to let her through.

She walked out of the schoolroom. "Didn't know you'd be here today."

"Neither did I. Not my idea of how to have a good time on Sunday afternoon, but I guess the old folks are creatures of habit."

"Yes, we're all seriously flawed and terribly boring. You're right." She walked past him.

"Hey," he said, and grabbed hold of her arm.

Steve turned the corner and walked into the hallway. "What's going on?" he asked with a frown.

"Eric was just sharing how quaint he finds us all." She faced him. "Please, let go of my arm."

He released her arm. "I wasn't trying to put you down, Victoria."

"Yeah, right," Steve said, coming to Victoria's side like he was planning to protect her from Satan. "You come back here acting too good to watch soccer with us, too American to have a glass of wine, and pushing yourself on the women. I think you'd better step back and leave Victoria alone."

"He wasn't—," Victoria started to say.

"I'll take care of this, Victoria." Steve stepped between them.

"You're a jerk, Steve. See what I mean, things never do change around here." Eric smiled, refusing to get into an argument about how he lacked Argentine sensibilities. He didn't. He didn't always see the point in creating a minicommunity within their American world, true. At least not for himself. But he understood that for his parents it was a connection to their past, and he was okay with this.

Steve frowned and pushed on Eric's shoulder enough to give a small shove and make his point. "Head on back to the main hall."

Was this guy for real? "Who the fuck are you?" Eric laughed. "Security?" He stepped around Steve, hoping he would go back to the big screen and mind his own business.

"I'm not kidding, man," Steve said, shoving Eric again and standing between him and Victoria.

"Steve," Victoria said. "Cut it out."

This time Eric didn't smile or laugh. If this guy had a screw loose, Eric was willing to tighten it for him. He shoved Steve right back. Without warning, Steve pulled his arm back and popped Eric right in the face, knocking him onto his back. Victoria's jaw dropped as she gasped. He himself lay stunned on the floor, and Steve shook his hand and cursed. The women ran out of the classroom, gasping and talking all at once. Susana hurried the children back to their seats and closed the door.

Eric stumbled to his feet and glared at Steve. "Are you crazy?" he shouted. He wanted to pound Steve into the ground but restrained himself for the sake of the women watching.

The older women from the kitchen ran into the hallway. Lucia brought a hand to her chest. "Oh, my, what happened?"

"This idiot hit me." Eric found it unbelievable. The last time he'd been in a fight, he was probably eighteen. He was no wimp, but he wasn't into acting like a macho idiot to prove he was a man. He scowled at Steve. What the hell was wrong with this guy?

"What? *Why?*" Lucia asked.

"He was harassing Victoria," Steve defended.

The older women looked at Victoria, and she turned twenty shades of red. She glanced at him, and his jaw tightened when she didn't speak up right away. He wasn't harassing her and she knew it.

"You need ice," Lucia said, cutting past the tense silence.

"I'll get it," Victoria said, and left the room.

"You men should be ashamed of yourself. Fighting in front of the kids," Mrs. Apolonia said. "We won't have this here. You both understand?"

Steve placed a hand on her shoulder. "Si, Doña. I'm sorry. I lost my temper. It won't happen again."

Lucia patted Eric's face. "You want to apologize too, don't you, Eric?"

He *wanted to apologize*? *Was she kidding?* But from the look on her worried face, he could see she wasn't kidding. She wanted him to make nice. "Yes, I'm sorry, too, Mrs. Apolonia." He didn't look at Steve.

Victoria came back with the ice. "Here," she said.

"I'm leaving." He stepped back. "I don't need that."

"No, you're not leaving," Lucia said firmly. "Not with your eye like that. Go eat," she ordered everyone else and waved her arms. "Victoria, bring the ice." She made him sit down in a small office to the side of the schoolroom. "Now get that ice on his eye before it swells shut," she told Victoria. "I'm going to find a small bandage. He's bleeding from that cut by his eyebrow."

Victoria came to his side. "Tilt your head back."

"Just give it to me."

"Shut up and tilt your head back."

He drew a breath and did as she asked. She gently put the plastic bag, covered by a towel, on his eye. He flinched. Damn it. It hurt.

"Sorry," she said, softly easing hair off his forehead with her spare hand.

"You should be. I wasn't bothering you."

"*I* didn't hit you."

"You might as well have."

She stared down at him and held the ice to his eye. A pink flush made her cheekbones more prominent and her creamy skin glow. Here was a girl that needed very little makeup. Huge, dark, almost black eyes. Absolutely luscious red lips.

Hmm, very pretty face, he decided. "Are you dating him or something?" Eric asked.

"God, no. You're right, he's a jerk."

"Don't let him hear you say that, or you might be the next one he punches out." Eric began to feel his temper subside. No point in letting one loser ruin the rest of his day.

"I'll take my chances. You okay?"

"I'll live."

"Okay, I'm going to go, then. Hold the ice to your eye."

He reached up and held the ice bag in place. "Thanks. And Victoria, I wasn't trying to insult you or the club. Seriously."

"Fine."

He closed his eyes, letting the ice fall to the side of his face. "Tell you the truth, I don't know what the hell I'm doing here."

She placed her hand over his, shifting the clumps of ice directly over his eye.

He opened the good eye and gazed at her, finding the feel of her hand over his oddly comforting. And the heat of her body beside his again—it was nice enough for him to allow her to take care of him. “Life sometimes gets complicated. What you think you know, you don’t,” he said.

She watched him with an adorable, perplexed frown. “What did you think you knew?”

He pulled the ice bag away from his frozen eyeball. “What I wanted, what I didn’t want. I thought I knew all the answers. But I’m finding I don’t know much of anything.” He sighed. “I’m not making any sense. Forget it.”

“Probably realizing that you don’t know everything is a good thing.”

He gazed at her, feeling like Quasimodo. “Yeah? I subscribe to the idea that what you don’t know can hurt you. And it did.” He tried to smile, but it didn’t work too well.

“Okay, here we go,” Lucia said, hurrying back into the room.

Victoria turned to face Lucia. He let the gaze of his good eye travel down to her jean-covered butt. He probably shouldn’t be looking. But he couldn’t help himself. Interest in the female shape was written into men’s DNA, wasn’t it? And hers was nice and curvy.

“Sorry about this, Mrs. Ortelli. What happened was Steve’s and my fault. Eric didn’t do anything wrong.”

She nodded. “Esteban is a troublemaker. Stay away from him, Victoria.”

“I do. We never even talk. He just wanted to find a reason to show Eric who’s boss. You know how he is. The other guys humor him, because they know he’s a pitiful loser with no balls. Excuse me,” she said.

Lucia smiled. “What? You think the truth offends me?”

Victoria blushed again. “I’ll see you later,” she said, then she glanced his way one more time. “Sorry, Eric,” she said, and left.

Eric sat up as Victoria walked out.

Lucia noticed that her son seemed particularly interested in watching Victoria disappear down the hall. “Why did he hit you?”

As if distracted, he forced his attention back to the two of them. "Hell if I know. They all hate me here, as if they take it personally that I left or something. Steve said I think I'm too good for them. Why would he think that?"

"Probably because I always told them how good you were doing. How you were traveling and didn't miss home at all. That you were happy to leave behind this ordinary life." She shrugged, full of guilt. "That's what I always told myself."

He gazed at her with sadness and an eye that was red and puffy. "Truth is, I *was* happy not to have to hang out here every Sunday once I left. But, I was just out of my teens. Not exactly the place a young man wants to spend his free time. But that was years ago. They have a problem with that?"

"They'll come around. Give them a chance. And Victoria's right. Esteban acts like he's very tough. Brags to all the men about the women he...entertains, gets into fights with neighbors, and is always involved in one legal dispute or another. He has no friends except the men from this club, and they only put up with him because he's Argentine."

"Bull. It's because his dad donates thousands every year to this club. Always has."

"That, too." Lucia smiled. "Anyway, relax and just be yourself. Like any dysfunctional family we're a strange mix, but this is the only family we have, Eric."

"Yeah. I know."

She reached across and caressed his hair like she used to when he was a little boy. "Maybe next week we'll have a barbecue at home."

Eric smiled. "Thanks, Mom."

Eric and Antonio got to the auction early. The convention center buzzed with excitement. Eric wrote a check for the deposit that every bidder was obligated to pay in order to bid, and got his paddle. Antonio waited in the hall while Eric took care of the pre-auction business. Once he finished, he got a cup of coffee for himself and one for Antonio. Eric found him chatting with a guy in a tan sport coat and blue pants and passed him the hot Styrofoam cup.

"Hey, this is my son," Antonio said as Eric stood beside him.

The man shook his hand. "I'm Jim. Your father tells me you're a pro at this."

"I'm okay."

Antonio smiled. "Jim does tax lien certificates as well as real estate."

"Yeah?" Eric said. "Great. Nice to meet you, Jim. We should get in there, Dad."

"Oh, okay." He gave Jim a business card from the auto dealership where he worked. "Give me a call, Jim, and we'll talk."

"You bet."

Eric frowned. "Talk about what?"

"The tax lien certificates. What a good deal. Do you know he made—?"

"I know about those." An investor would pay a property owner's back taxes and make a hefty hunk of change when the home owner got current, or end up owning the home if the taxes were not paid and the government seized the property. "But each state and each county has different rules, Dad. It's a pain in the ass. Plus you have to tie up your money for too long. Not a good deal."

"But he's gotten thousands of dollars and two properties by buying those certificates and waiting. And he didn't have to remodel any houses."

They found a seat. "Like I said, it takes a lot of homework. And you don't get a return on your investment for months, sometimes years."

Antonio shrugged. "Aren't you being a little close-minded?"

"I do what I do best. And I do it again and again and again. And I don't do anything else." Unlike his father, who was always trying something new.

"But you could be missing out on some great opportunities."

"Dad." Eric put an arm around his father. "I make my own great opportunities."

And by the end of the day, Eric owned a new house. At least for the couple of months it would take him to flip it.

Antonio watched Eric work, bidding, getting outbid, and bidding again. The fast-talking auctioneer and the general excitement of the speedy process held a definite appeal, and he could see how a young man would enjoy the game and final win. There was no denying that Eric was a serious investor, and Antonio's heart filled with pride. He regretted that he'd wasted so many years being angry with him. So the boy didn't finish college. So he didn't follow the plan Antonio had for him from the day he was born. So what? He was a good man. And in the end each man had to decide his own future and create his own destiny.

As they left the bidding hall to fill out the paperwork for the property in another room, Antonio patted Eric on the back. "Let's go celebrate."

Eric grinned. "What did you have in mind?"

He looked so much like an all-American boy that it made Antonio's heart ache. He'd so wanted the Argentine son that would share soccer scores and speak perfect Castilian, but it was time to begin accepting who Eric truly was, not who he had wished him to be. "How about we head out to Angel Stadium? They're playing at home tonight, and I bet we can get tickets. How many hot dogs can you eat?"

"More than you," he said, obviously pleased with the idea. "Let me finish up here and you've got a deal."

Antonio headed to the lobby and pulled out his cell to call Lucia.

"Lucia, habla Antonio, mi amor."

"Hi, how did the auction go, querido? Is it over?"

"It's over. He bought a house."

"Oh, I'm *so* happy," she said, because no doubt she viewed this as another step Eric was taking to return home.

"He's going to fix this place up and sell it, Lucia. Remember that."

"Well, it takes time to fix and sell a home, doesn't it? That's time he's going to spend close to us. And I'm thrilled."

He chuckled. "Listen, we're going to celebrate his successful bid. Go to a ball game. So we won't be home for dinner. I'm sorry, but—"

"Don't be sorry. I love that you and Eric are spending time together. Don't worry about me. I'm too tired to cook tonight, anyway."

"All right, amorcito. We'll see you tonight." He ended the call.

She was a good woman. A great woman. By being a pigheaded idiot and alienating Eric, he'd hurt his wife unintentionally. And for that he'd never forgive himself. But from the second Eric had walked into that club and stepped back into their lives, he decided he'd do whatever he had to in order to make it up to both of them.

Chapter Five

Victoria set her alarm clock to ring early. She'd decided to take up running in order to get in shape and feel healthier. This would be her first day out on the track, and she was sort of looking forward to it. She put on a pair of shorts and tied her new running shoes loosely on her feet. Fully geared and ready to get started on her goal to a slimmer self, she drove to the high school a quarter mile from her house. Parking by the football field, she walked to the track. The middle of July meant that the temperature was already in the eighties. Today would be a miserably hot day. A plane flew overhead, drowning out the sounds of the early morning birds.

To warm up she continued to walk a couple of laps, then began an easy jog. But after covering half a lap, she found she couldn't suck in enough air to even partially fill her lungs. As she took each new step, her thighs felt as if they were being shredded and pulled apart, and the arch of her left foot was practically numb with pain. She stopped jogging and continued to walk the rest of that lap, and even struggled to finish one more. Four laps equaled one mile. She remembered that from high school. And it had probably been that long since she'd run.

Like a wounded dog, she limped back to the car. Sweat covered her forehead and her neck. Yuck. She didn't like to sweat. Maybe tomorrow, she'd simply walk. There were no rules that said you had to run to exercise. The running could come later, after she'd lost some weight.

When she got home, Jaqueline and Victor were at the breakfast table, each drinking a cup of coffee and reading a part of the newspaper. Coexisting in the same room but each barely noticing the other. The smell of coffee in the house made her stomach growl and her mouth water.

"Victoria," Jaqueline said, surprised. "I didn't know you were up. Where have you been?"

"I went for a jog." She sat at the table, her legs sore and achy.

"Oh." Again a look of surprise. "Well, go take a shower and get dressed. The Ortellis invited us over for a Sunday barbecue today."

Wonderful. A week had passed since Eric got punched by that idiot, Steve, and she hadn't stopped feeling guilty. Not that it was her fault that Steve decided to defend her, though she was sure that was simply an excuse to take a shot at Eric. The guilt came from how coldly she'd treated him. She tried to be kind and tolerant of everyone, even those she didn't like, even Steve. But for some reason, having Eric return home flaunting his success irritated her and brought out a rude part of her personality that she wasn't proud of. "Tell Lucia that I appreciate the invite, but that I won't be able to make it."

"Why not?"

"I have plans to meet some friends at the mall for lunch." A nice, cool mall.

"But... it won't be the same without you there."

"What about the Argentine Club? Aren't you supposed to be there today?"

"Lucia thinks it's best if she takes a break from the club after that incident with Eric last week. So we're not going this week, either. But don't change the subject."

"Mom, I have other plans. I'm sorry."

"But Lucia wants to celebrate having Eric home again. Remember how much you liked him when you were young?" Jaqueline asked.

"Mom, yes, we were friends, but that was a long time ago. I'm happy for Mrs. Ortelli, but I made other plans today." If she kept repeating it, would it make an impression on her mother?

"Maybe you can stop by later in the day," Victor suggested finally, lowering his newspaper. Not that he cared if she showed up or not, she was sure, but he knew this would appease her mother.

"Maybe," Victoria conceded, but made no promises. She forced herself to stand and headed to her bathroom. She showered and dressed. Then she left for the mall to meet her friends. They had decided to have lunch at the Cheesecake Factory of all places, where she could suffer the full effect of dieting. They'd made the lunch date before she'd decided to start the diet, so she simply closed her eyes when she walked past the display of desserts. Figuring a mile didn't entitle her to indulge in much of a lunch, she ordered the herb-crusted salmon salad and enjoyed spending time away from her family. Being among non-Argentine friends was a treat. She sometimes forgot that women her age didn't spend all their time catering to their parents. They had their own lives, complete with husbands and children, or at least boyfriends. They visited their parents for Thanksgiving and called them once a month. Victoria didn't exactly want that, but some space would be nice.

On her way home, she considered blowing off the idea of stopping by the Ortellis', but decided it would be easier to make an appearance than to answer her mother's questions about why she hadn't. So, resigned, she got on the freeway and headed to Mr. and Mrs. Ortelli's house.

* * *

Eric watched Lucia in amazement as she ran around trying to make everything just right for the Torres family. "Mom," he said. "Let me help you with something."

"Oh, no," she said, as she pulled the vacuum out to touch up the carpet she'd vacuumed the night before. "Just relax. Go watch TV with your father so you don't walk on the carpet."

He eased the vacuum out of her hands. "I'll do this. You go finish in the kitchen."

She fought him, trying to grab hold of the handle again, but he insisted. He squeezed her tight and kissed her, and pointed her in the direction of the kitchen.

She laughed. "No fair. You've gotten bigger and stronger than me."

"Yep. So you might as well stop fighting me."

"Okay, but when you finish with that, put it back in the closet and go change."

"Change?" He wore comfortable shorts and a clean shirt.

"We're having this lunch in your honor. You have to look... you know."

He didn't know, but he had a suspicion and he wasn't happy about it. "You want me to wear church clothes."

She laughed. "I remember when you used to call it that." She shook her head and walked away with a silly grin on her face.

He smiled as he turned on the vacuum and it screamed to life. Quickly, he ran it across the carpet. It made little lines on the well-cared-for fibers. Back and forth. Up and down. Then he shut it off and put it away just the way she liked. And he went to change his clothes. It didn't take much to make her happy. If he had to be uncomfortable for a couple of hours, he'd deal with it.

By the time he got back into the living room, Mr. and Mrs.

Torres had arrived. Mrs. Torres kissed him on both cheeks. "Nene, you've gotten so handsome. I know we've told you already, but we're so glad you're home."

He smiled and kissed her back. "Thank you." He shook Mr. Torres's hand and offered them a seat on the couch.

Mrs. Torres beamed. "I feel like my own son has come home. Lucia's joy is my joy."

What did he say to that? "My mom's lucky to have such a good friend."

"So," Mr. Torres said, as if he were tired of all the bullshit. "What have you been up to all these years?"

Eric shrugged. "Not much."

Antonio patted Eric on the shoulder. "He's been busy becoming a wealthy man."

"Doing what?" Mr. Torres asked.

"Real estate," Eric said, and upon further questioning he explained what he did. Mr. Torres, who insisted Eric call him Victor, seemed particularly interested in the details of house flipping.

"So, how do you find properties cheap?"

"Victor, leave the poor boy alone." Mrs. Torres patted her husband's leg.

"Actually, let's eat," Lucia said. "Or should we wait for Victoria?"

"She had a prior obligation," Mrs. Torres explained. "She's going to try to stop by a little later, because she really is as excited as we are that you're back, Eric." She smiled at him. "So we can eat without her."

Victoria excited he was back? Right. Or course, he didn't blame her for skipping this little celebration. Hell, he'd skip it if he could.

After lunch, Victor invited Eric to join him for a cigarette while the ladies cleaned up. Antonio found the Argentine soccer game he'd recorded last week off one of the premium sports channels. They walked out to the front porch, where the heaviness of the afternoon heat was more pronounced, making him wish he hadn't eaten so much.

"Do you mind if I ask you a little more about finding the right property at the right price?"

"Not at all." He shoved his hands into his pockets, and stretched his tight shoulders that were suffering from lack of work. "You thinking of buying some investment properties?"

"Well, not exactly." Victor lit his cigarette and Eric's.

Eric enjoyed a cigar every once in a while. Didn't care much for cigarettes, but he joined Victor just the same.

"I'm not announcing this to anyone yet, but I'm going to be opening up a chain of restaurants like the one I currently own."

Eric raised an eyebrow. "Hmm, sounds big."

"It's going to be huge," Victor confided. "The only thing I'm not informed enough on is how to find the right locations. I know the cities I'd like to open up in. But specific locations, I don't know."

"It's just a matter of spending some time in the city you're interested in. Doing a little research. Looking at what properties or lots are available and comparing them to what you want to spend. Maybe checking out what areas are in need of your type of restaurant. What communities have the population that will spend money on a quality dinner."

"Sounds easy for someone like you who knows how to find properties."

Eric smiled. No way was he getting sucked into being a scout for someone else. Even a friend of his parents. "I buy homes that need a little repair and resell them. I'm not an expert in commercial property. You can do the same thing I can. Spend a little time on the Internet doing research. Once you find a retail center that interests you, contact the company leasing the space and they'll have demographic snapshots, info from the city on future development, and pretty much everything you need to decide if this is a good spot for you."

Mr. Torres didn't look enthusiastic about this aspect of expanding his business. Maybe he expected Eric to jump in and volunteer to do it all for him. "Why don't you use Victoria to scout out the right places?" Eric asked.

"Victoria?"

"Sure. She works with you, doesn't she?"

"Yes," Victor frowned, and blew smoke out the side of his mouth. "But... Victoria is my daughter and I love her, but she's not like you and me. We see the future. We've got an entrepreneurial spirit."

"She doesn't have to have great vision or even be a super businessperson to do this."

"She'd have to be able to spot the right place for the restaurant to be a success. That would be asking a lot from a girl who's never had to do more than organize a dinner or two."

"Maybe you're underestimating her. If I remember right, she always did way better than I did with research projects at school." Eric laughed.

"Victoria is my precious daughter," Victor said with obvious affection in his voice. "But she's sort of like... a butterfly. She flies from here to there. Tries a little of this and a little of that. So beautiful to watch. She makes people happy wherever she lands. That's her gift. But what I need requires expertise she doesn't have. I can't afford to fail. Besides, I'm not sure I want to lease a spot from a developer. I may want a pad to build on."

"Well, then you may want to hire a professional real-estate broker. It'll cost you more than if you do it yourself, but sounds like you might need that." Eric wasn't sure if what Victor said about Victoria was true or not. He never remembered her being stupid. The way Victor described her seemed pretty damned insulting. He squatted down and put the cigarette he hadn't smoked out in the dirt. Then he looked at the decorative stone wall that had been a part of the house facade since they moved in years ago. It needed a good cleaning.

He stood. "I'm sure my father's got the game ready. I'm going to stay out here and do some work on the outside of the house."

"Yes," he said, obviously still considering Eric's suggestion. "I better get inside."

They both went into the house. Eric changed back into his shorts and got the power sprayer out of the garage. He'd unloaded his truck with all his tools when he got here, and now they were taking up parking space. Time to put some of it to good use.

When Victoria pulled up in front of the Ortelli house, Eric was in the front yard painting the shutters. Looked like he'd pressure-washed the decorative stone wall facade earlier. The equipment lay on the grass, and the front of the house looked new and fresh. She was glad he was actually making himself useful.

She opened the car door and forced her sore legs to carry her out and across the yard. Her arches were killing her. The heels she had decided to wear didn't help. Low heels, but they were excruciatingly painful just the same.

Eric smiled when he noticed her making her way toward the front door. He didn't look angry with her anymore. "Hey. I was wondering if you'd succumb to your parents' demands and come see me today."

Victoria offered him a smile and tried not to notice the yellowish fading bruise around his left eye. "And how do you know I wasn't dying to be subjected to your charming company again?"

He crouched down to dip his brush in the paint can. He smiled up at her, letting his eyes, the color of warm golden oak, first travel up her legs. "You're a little overdressed today. Trying to impress me?"

"I went out to lunch with some friends." He wore a pair of worn shorts and a sleeveless T-shirt that made him look more gorgeous than he had at the Independence Day party, where he'd been properly dressed.

He rose to his feet. "Well, I am flattered that you cut your lunch short to see me. You must be feeling guilty about something." He turned away so she didn't catch his expression.

"I have nothing to feel guilty about," she said, though she felt guilty as hell.

He brushed the shutter and grinned, offering a small wink. "You're right. So don't worry about my eye. I've been punched before. Wasn't your fault. I was just pissed when I implied it was—sorry."

She nodded. He seemed sincere. "Since you're the star of this celebration, shouldn't you be inside with the old folks?"

"I've been fawned over enough for one day. So I left our dads in front of the TV in the living room and our moms in the kitchen cleaning up from lunch. I snuck out to spend some time in the sunshine."

Again, she noticed his great tan. He must spend a lot of time out in the sunshine. It looked good on him. "Getting tired of all the attention already?"

"My mom is driving me crazy. And your mom has pointed out how much stronger I look, how nice I trim my hair, how wonderful I dress—before I changed into this—and how deep my voice has gotten." He shook his head. "I feel like a specimen in a science lab."

Victoria laughed.

"And your dad hasn't stopped asking me questions about my work since the second I told him I deal in real estate." He dipped the brush in paint again.

Victoria felt her back tighten at the mention of her father and business. "Real estate? What do you do?"

"Not you, too?"

"Sorry. I should leave you alone to finish painting."

"No, have a seat." He pointed to a bench on the porch. "I'll be done soon."

"I should let my mom know I'm here."

"Later. Unless you're hungry and want to go in for a bite."

"No." Well, yes, she *was* hungry, but she had to work on that willpower, and no way would she admit to him that she wanted to eat again after telling him she'd come from eating lunch.

"Good, then stay with me a bit." He brushed across the slats of the shutters quickly and expertly.

"Okay." She sat on the bench like he suggested, because being on her feet in her current shoes was akin to torture. "What should we talk about if you don't want to tell me what you do in the real-estate world?"

"You."

She blushed. "Nothing much to tell. Besides, you seemed to know a lot about what I've been doing the other night when you made your grand reappearance."

"Why do you say that?" He worked his way down the shutter.

"You knew I still lived with my parents. And that I wasn't married."

"Oh, that." His expression gave nothing away. "My mom keeps me up-to-date on things when I call her every week. Usually she uses you as an example of what good Argentine kids do. Stay home. Take care of their parents." He smiled. "I had to take the first opportunity I got to tell you you're making the rest of us look bad."

Victoria crossed her tired legs, then uncrossed them again when her thigh muscles stretched and reminded her of how angry they were at her. "You're the only bad boy, Eric. The rest of us are doing what's expected. Susana is married with children. Adrian is a practicing psychologist. Eduardo runs his father's body shop. Ana teaches elementary school."

"And you, sweet Victoria? Continue to fill in at the grill and run errands for your father like you always have?"

"Actually, I'll be taking over the restaurant soon." Admitting that she was doing pretty much the same thing she'd done the last time he'd seen her was beyond humiliating.

Eric raised an eyebrow. "He's retiring?"

"No." She wasn't free to discuss any of it yet, so she tried to change the subject. "Now back to you. What do you do?"

"Never mind. Tell me about taking over the restaurant. I didn't think you had any interest in that."

"I don't. But it's a job."

"There are lots of jobs. Didn't you want to be an interior designer once?"

So he remembered her grand plans. One rainy weekend in particular came to mind, when their parents had gotten together. Carmen sat on the phone talking to her friends for hours, then actually did homework. She and Eric settled in his room, their shoes off, radio on. He playing video games and she drawing new interiors for his room. "How about this?" she'd say, interrupting his game. "I'm not changing my room," he'd said over and over again to each of her new designs. He barely looked at what she'd done, keeping his eyes on the TV screen. They'd been, what? Fifteen.

She watched him now give a final stroke of the brush to his mother's shutters and wondered what he thought of the way she'd redecorated his old room. "I do that for fun," she said. "I helped your mom decorate her place."

"She told me. You did a great job."

"Thanks." Neither one of them mentioned his room. She'd

found all her old designs packed away in his closet and left them where she'd found them. Instead of using any of those teen sketches, she painted his room in a nice, neutral taupe, exchanged his twin bed for a mature double with dark, masculine bedspreads instead of the sports quilt. Only one wall highlighted his childhood and provided evidence that this had been his personal space. A display case held his trophies, rock collections, model cars, airplanes, and houses. And a collection of pictures of Eric from baby to young man were framed in various sizes and hung on the wall beside the display case. Lucia had cried and told her again and again that she loved it, even though she'd been hesitant to let her touch his room at the beginning.

He watched her as he took his paintbrush over to the hose and ran water through it, droplets spraying in all directions. "I know your dad's not retiring. He told me about his business plans."

Victoria found that hard to believe. Why would he tell Eric of all people about something he was being so secretive about?

"He asked me if I'd be interested in finding good, cheap commercial property for him. Scouting out good locations for his expansions."

Victoria listened and frowned. "Why you?"

"Well I asked myself that, too, especially because I have a feeling he thinks I'm a major fuckup. But I guess my dad convinced him that I do know what I'm doing."

"Which is?"

"I'm a real-estate investor. I buy houses, fix them up, and resell them at a profit. Apparently your dad figured I would know where to find what he's looking for."

Victoria nodded. "Would you?"

"Possibly. But I turned him down."

"Why?"

He shrugged. "I work for myself."

That was a typical, self-centered Eric response. "I see."

"I suggested he use you, but he wasn't thrilled with that idea. Didn't think it would be something you could do."

"He's right. I don't know where he should open new restaurants," she said, though it stung to hear that her father had told Eric that he lacked confidence in her abilities. "In fact, all this is very new to me. I just learned of his plans recently, and I'm not sure how I feel about it."

He dried his hands on a towel he'd hung on the porch rail and walked around the porch. "You weren't in on the planning stage?"

Seen through his eyes, she realized how it must look. She didn't know what was going on in the family business. He must think she was either an idiot or self-absorbed to the point that she didn't care what went on, or what was closer to the truth—her father didn't think enough of her to let her in on the daily running of the business until now. "I found his paperwork in the back office, and he explained what he was doing when I questioned him. I'm sort of worried about this huge venture, to tell you the truth."

"Why?"

"Well." She wondered how much to say. But Eric was a businessman so maybe he could put her worries to rest. "He's emptied his entire savings, borrowed money against his restaurant, our house... It's a little... scary."

"It's risky." He took a seat beside her, using the towel to wipe perspiration from his face. "Something I would expect from my dad, but not yours."

Wonderful. Just what she wanted to hear. "I want to believe he knows what he's doing." Then, feeling unfaithful, she amended. "I'm sure he does."

Eric didn't comment.

"He's always wanted to make millions and go back to Argentina a success." Victoria smiled at how many times she'd heard her father's dream. And Jaqueline always remind him that they had to be practical. "He's always talked about it, but I never expected him to actually do it, I guess."

"Victoria, every Argentine guy I've ever known has wild ideas of making millions and returning to Argentina a big shot. My dad was the same."

"Yeah. I guess I just thought he'd gotten over all that."

"Where does all this leave you?"

"Putting in more time at the restaurant, I suppose."

"Don't trust that your parents are always going to take care of you, Victoria. Especially if your father has gotten a wild hair up his ass about striking it rich."

"I don't." And she resented that he assumed she was nothing but a mooch living off her parents. They *wanted* her to live at home. Her father expected her to help out with the family business. It wasn't like she had a choice.

"What if the restaurant you think you're going to run ends up having to close down? Then what will you do?"

Be free, she thought, then chased the thought away. "My father is not going to fail."

Eric leaned back and shook his head. "That's what he tells me."

Victoria stared out at the trees swaying in the warm afternoon breeze. She could hear traffic driving down neighboring streets, but this block was quiet. A perfect summer weekend, but her life didn't feel so perfect. She'd expected Eric to tell her that she was being silly for worrying, that her father was a genius, that his plan was brilliant, and instead he was giving her more to worry about. And now she was defending her father, when a moment ago she was telling Eric she had doubts. *He must think I'm a psycho*, she thought. She glanced back at him; he was watching her with a gentle look of concern.

But he quickly hid it as he stretched his arms up in the air and stood. "I better get this mess cleaned up." He wrapped the cord around the pressure washer, clamped it under his arm, and picked up the can of paint. "Be right back." He disappeared into the garage.

Victoria stood, then bent and picked up the brush he'd been using. She walked around the porch to the garage on the side of the house. She peeked inside. "Here's your brush."

He smiled and took it. "Thanks." He pointed to the crooked shelves that held household cleaners, rolls of paper towels, and bags of rags. "I organized all this for my parents when I was a kid. I remember putting those up. My mom used to let me keep my model-building tools up there. And the various bugs and lizards I'd caught in jars." He chuckled. "I thought she was so cool to let me take charge of the garage. She probably did it so I wouldn't bring all my junk into the house. Boys collect a lot of junk."

Victoria leaned on a cool, white washing machine and smiled as she listened to him reminisce. Something warm touched her heart, and she could almost picture him the way he used to look. She thought of all the times she'd heard people say how cold and uncaring Eric had been to leave his family behind so easily. But something told her that maybe it hadn't been so easy after all.

He shrugged and offered a crooked smile. "Strange how some places can take you back in time."

"Strange and sort of wonderful," she said softly.

He nodded. Then he leaned on the washer next to her and crossed his arms. "I'm sorry if I was out of line out there. I tend to look at all the negatives and see the pitfalls of a project way more than most people, I guess. I know the kind of trouble you can get into by rushing into a deal."

"My father hasn't rushed into this." But was he prepared to operate a business that would grow as rapidly as he planned?

And would other restaurants that he didn't personally run do as well as the original?

"Got it," he said, then he unfolded his arms and held out a hand. "Friends?"

She took his warm, slightly callused hand. "Only if you promise to say good-bye the next time you leave town."

Eric ran his thumb across her knuckles before he let her hand slip out of his. "I promise."

Chapter Six

Lucia peeked out of the kitchen window. "I don't see them out there anymore." She let the curtain fall. "You know men will do anything for love. And Victoria would be perfect for him."

Jaqueline wasn't so sure that Eric was perfect for Victoria. Of course, her daughter was getting older, and though she was pretty enough, she was overweight—and men usually didn't like that. Plus, she was too unpredictable for most men. One day she cooed over babies at the Argentine Club, and the next she was lost in her own world listening to that iPod with who knew what kind of crazy music. Then again, maybe Eric *could* be the man for her. If anyone should understand unpredictability, it should be him.

"You don't mind if I encourage him a bit, do you?" Lucia sat across from her. "We'd finally be related by marriage."

"No, I don't mind," Jaqueline sighed. "I suppose she has to get married someday."

"Of course," Lucia looked at her as if she had said something ridiculous. "I thought you *wanted* her to get married. You're always telling me you're worried no man will ever be interested in her because of the way she dresses and how little she cares about her appearance in general." She placed a hand over Jaqueline's. "But I know what she's really like inside, and I love her. Eric can, too."

"No, it's not that I don't want her to get married. It's

just...didn't you think being married would be different than...what it is?"

"What do you mean?"

She felt ridiculous voicing her thoughts. "I mean you start out so in love, and you think there's nothing you can't do together, and little by little you realize...how wrong you've been."

Lucia frowned. "Marriage isn't perfect, Jaqueline, but what's the alternative?"

Jaqueline had had plenty of alternatives at one point in her life. She'd been young and beautiful. She'd had tons of friends and a loving family. But she'd left all that behind in Argentina to follow Victor and his crazy dreams. Dreams she'd been foolish enough to believe in. Dreams that had all fallen apart, one by one. Women should never believe in men. She wouldn't encourage Victoria to take an interest in someone like Eric, who was just as wild as Victor and Antonio. But she could understand why Lucia thought it was a good idea. Maybe a permanent relationship *would* calm the boy down. "I know," she said. "I don't want Victoria to be alone forever. I'd love for her to have children."

Lucia beamed. "Grandkids! Can you imagine what gorgeous kids Eric and Victoria would have?"

Eric led Victoria into the house to let her parents know she'd arrived. After getting a very strange look from both moms, he left Victoria in the kitchen while he took his father and Victor outside to show off his clean-up job.

"Your mother is going to be ecstatic," Antonio said. "She's been after me for years to do something about those old stones."

"Well, she's right," Eric said. "You should actually replace them with stucco, but at least now they're clean."

"We've lived with it like this for twenty-five years, and we can continue to live with it as it is. I can't afford to waste money on cosmetic changes."

Eric disagreed. He'd gotten used to having his homes look exactly as he wanted them to.

Victor seemed quiet, sort of preoccupied. Maybe he was upset that Eric had decided he couldn't help him with his real-estate problem. Although he appreciated that Victor thought enough of him to ask for his help, commercial properties were not Eric's thing.

The women came out to the porch with pastries and mate, a strong green tea.

"Oh, Eric, it looks brand-new," Lucia said. She kissed his cheek. "Gracias. I love it."

He smiled. Then they all sat on the porch to enjoy the treats. Eric reached for a round pastry with dulce de leche in the middle. Heaven.

"Having you back is like coming back to life after being in a coma for years," Lucia said. "I feel so alive." She spooned some sugar into the gourd that held the mate leaves, then added hot water.

Eric hadn't had a mate in years. When he'd first moved away, he'd taken his own mate and bombilla and searched for Latin markets that sold the yerba tea. But since he traveled so much, eventually he gave up and packed away his mate gourd for good. He took the drink when his mother offered him the first sip. "Thanks, Mami. I'm glad to be home, too."

"Cariño," Antonio said. "Eric is here for a visit, okay? Don't go laying a guilt trip on him."

"I'm not."

"It's okay, viejo," Eric said. "I'm glad she's happy." He looked across to Victoria, wanting to change the subject. "So you know my mom kept me updated on your marital status." He angled his head. "But she didn't say anything about a boyfriend."

"You mean do I have a boyfriend?" Victoria asked.

"You know that's what I mean."

"Eric!" Lucia said, though it appeared to him that she looked pleased.

Victor frowned.

Jaqueline and Antonio didn't say a word.

"What?" he shrugged. "I'm just curious."

Victoria looked amused. "No, no boyfriends. My dad chases away any man who shows any interest. And my mom scares them by talking about weddings and babies on our first date."

Eric laughed.

Now it was Jaqueline's turn to look horrified. "I don't scare away your boyfriends. What a thing to say."

Eric noticed that Victor didn't deny his part in making Victoria's love life difficult.

"I just wanted to ask Victoria if she was interested in getting together some of our old high school friends. Maybe we can all go out while I'm in town. And I didn't want some jealous boyfriend trying to kill me. One black eye is enough."

"I don't hang out with anyone from high school anymore, Eric. In fact, the only ones I still see are the ones that go to the Argentine Club."

Eric passed the mate back to his mother, who refilled the gourd with sugar and water and offered it to Victoria.

She took it. "But we can look them up if you're interested."

"Would be fun, wouldn't it?" He wasn't sure how long he was going to stick around. Part of it depended on how the flip went. It also depended on whether he could live this close to his family again after all this time. He watched Victoria sip from the bombilla, which was a special metal straw that filtered out the tea leaves as you drank, and thought, not for the first time since seeing her again, that she'd grown amazingly beautiful.

"No problem," she said. "Let's get together next week and go through the last numbers I had on everyone." She gave the mate back to Lucia.

"What a great idea! You can plan a reunion without waiting for the school to do it," his mother said, reminding him for the millionth time that his ten-year high school reunion was this fall. Every time he called, she asked if he was planning to attend. And now he was sure she'd insist he hang around at least until then. She'd latch onto anything that gave him a reason to stay close by. He leaned over and placed a kiss on her cheek. He might just let her convince him.

Victoria spent the entire following week preparing for the Saturday wedding party that had reserved the back of the restaurant for their reception. Although she rarely worked the floor serving customers—the waiters in black and white suits with bow ties did that—this day, she helped to set all the tables, to prepare the plates for the waiters to serve, to cut the wedding cake, and to clean up after the last of them went home. Victor had been in during the morning and lunch rushes, then had gone to an investment meeting he was holding at the Argentine Club. He'd joined a venture capital association and contacted a few angel investors who appeared interested. He'd drawn up a business profile and had meetings during the week, and he said he also wanted to present it to friends from the club.

He came back to the restaurant late at night to help close up. La Parrilla had been closed for an hour. Tables had been cleaned, floors swept and mopped, and the kitchen prepped for the following day. Now it was quiet. Even the music had been turned off.

"How did it go?" Victoria asked, her feet up on a chair.

"Good. Great. How did it go here?"

"Busy." She drank a glass of cranberry juice with lemon soda, while Victor poured a cup of coffee. She filled him in on the details of the evening. Victor would lock up the cash and receipts in the safe tonight and go to the bank in the morning.

Victoria planned to sleep in tomorrow. She was exhausted, but she couldn't seem to push herself off the stool.

"On Monday, I'm interviewing a manager to run this restaurant while I'm away getting the other two started."

This caught Victoria's attention and helped to stir her quickly dwindling energy. "I thought you wanted *me* to run this restaurant."

"No," he said quickly. "Not everything. I want you to put more time in. Keep an eye on how things are going. But you can't do it all. Not yet. Little by little."

Agreed. Nor did she want to do it all. But the way he said it gave her the impression that he didn't think she was capable of running it on her own, and that irritated her. "I'd like to sit in on the interview."

"Why?"

"I'll have to work with the person, so I'd like to have some say on if you hire her or not."

"Him," he corrected.

Victoria already knew he'd hire a man to be the manager. After all these years, his sexist attitude against women being in charge didn't surprise her. She was more amused by his macho ideas than offended, and she enjoyed giving him little nudges every once in a while to remind him that his ideas were from another era.

"I'll make sure you can work with him. But I'm not going to have this man thinking he has to answer to my daughter."

"Why not? He should know that he *does* have to answer to me."

"Look Victoria. All I want you to do is keep your eyes open. Make sure things continue to run well. If anything doesn't look right, call me, tell me."

Victoria didn't want more responsibility, but she was either going to assume more control or she wasn't. She didn't appreciate being used as a spy. She sighed. "Dad, if you're really going to go through with all this, then you need to include me more. According to you, I'm supposed to inherit a chain of restaurants one day that I know nothing about. That I've had no part in building."

"But I don't want you to have any part in it."

"What's that supposed to mean?"

He rubbed his temples. It had been a long day and she didn't want to give him a hard time, but she had to know where she stood.

"Victoria, I've given my life to this restaurant. It's been hell. I don't get vacations. No real days off. Even when we're closed, my mind is here. I'm constantly asking myself, 'Have we put in all the orders for the next week? Have I set the alarm properly? Will we pass the next city inspection?' I've been a slave to this business for eighteen years. Do you think I want that for you?"

"I thought you did. If not, then why the expansion?"

"I plan to oversee it all. Eventually hire a board to run the franchises. I want you to sit back and collect the checks."

Victoria smiled. "That's nice, but not practical. I should be informed. Know about the business."

"Victoria." He looked uncomfortable. "You couldn't even grasp the college classes in business. Just... let me handle everything. Haven't I always taken care of you?"

She wasn't sure what emotion she felt more prominently: anger, offense, humiliation, or what. She dropped her legs off the stool and stood.

"Victoria," he said.

"It's late. I'm leaving."

"You're going to run the restaurant. But not alone. And I can't be here much in the next few months to get you ready. Try to understand that I'm doing what I think is best."

"Even if that means treating me like a second-rate employee."

"I treat you that way because that's the way you act. You come and go as you please." He raised his voice. "You show more interest in painting your toenails than you do in business. Start taking this job seriously and I'll start treating you like a serious partner."

Except that wasn't entirely true. He kept her at arm's length and doled out her responsibilities like he was feeding baby food to a three-month-old. Not that she'd cared in the past. She didn't want to spend more time here; he was right. She had no passion for this work and *would* rather paint her toenails than waste hours ordering beef. "You're right. Hire a manager and leave me out of the whole thing. I have better things to do with my life."

"Victoria!" he shouted.

She whirled and glared at him. "I hope you make your billions, Papi, but I don't intend to be Paris Hilton, holding a dog and smiling because that's the only thing people think I can do. I'm twenty-eight years old and you're still treating me like I'm eighteen."

"What the hell do you want from me?"

"I want you to see that I can stand on my own two feet. That I'm capable of doing more than blowing up balloons." Her voice cracked and tears sprung to her eyes, but she couldn't stop. "That I can choose my own men. That damn it, I have my own dreams in life, and they have nothing to do with running this restaurant."

His face grew red, and he eased himself off his stool.

Her voice grew soft. "But if I'm going to spend my life here, I want to be treated like your partner, not like your incompetent daughter. *Now*, not in ten years."

He took a few steps her way, and she thought he was going to say something, but instead his gaze dismissed her as he brushed past her out of the restaurant. The door closed and he was gone.

Victoria wanted to cry and scream. *Why* was it so hard for him to see her? He said he loved her, she did every damn thing he wanted her to do, and yet he didn't really know her. All he ever did was dismiss her interests and opinions. Damn him. She wandered to the back office, picked up her purse, set the security system, walked out, and locked the door—her hand shaking at the sound of the *click*. She knew tonight would be the last time she ever performed those tasks. And she drew a breath, thick with both relief and anxiety about the uncertainty of what would happen next.

Chapter Seven

Jaqueline poured coffee for both Victor and Victoria Sunday morning. They sat on opposite sides of the table, he behind his newspaper, Victoria reading a book. Jaqueline might as well have been a servant for all the attention they paid her.

"How did the wedding reception go?" she asked.

"Fine," Victoria said, glancing up from her book. "Thanks, Mami." She began adding sugar to her coffee. "I should skip this, but I can't drink Argentine coffee black." She added a little milk.

"A little sugar won't hurt you." Jaqueline sat beside Victoria. "That Mexican musician, Hugo, called again wanting to perform at the club. I wonder how we can fit him in."

Victoria raised an eyebrow. "Coming around, are you?"

Jaqueline liked the man. She wanted to help him out. But she shrugged. "Our events calendar is so full, I don't know how we'd work it out."

"Just choose one of those boring Sunday get-togethers and turn it into a Mexican Day celebration. We could invite three or four different acts. Would be fun."

"Maybe," she said. She glanced at Victor who was still to say more than "morning." "You want some toast, Viejo?"

"No." He put the paper down and stood. "I've got to go open the restaurant. I'll see you at the club later."

Jaqueline knew something was wrong but wasn't sure what.

He was even more distant than he normally was. She placed a hand on his arm. "Is everything okay?"

"Fine." He offered her a peck that was so different from the kisses they'd once shared. She wasn't even sure why she noticed those things lately. It had probably been years since they'd been truly affectionate with each other.

The phone rang and Jaqueline answered it. "Hello, Eric. Yes, she's here, but she's going to work with her father now."

Victoria glanced up. "No, I'm not. Is it for me?"

Jaqueline held her hand over the mouthpiece. "It's Eric."

Victoria stood. "I'll take it." She reached for the phone. "Eric, hi. Yes, I'd love to. Where? I'll be there in half an hour. Okay. See you." She took another drink of her coffee, then took the cup to the sink and washed it out. "I'm going to breakfast with Eric. See you later, Mami." She walked past Victor without saying good-bye to him or discussing if she was going to stop by the restaurant.

Victor turned away and left.

With a sigh, Jaqueline cleaned up the spotless kitchen table. She glanced at the white board on the refrigerator where she kept the schedule for the day. Not so long ago, it would have been packed with obligations. PTA meetings, laundry, bank runs for Victor, take Carmen to soccer practice, Victoria to art class, shop for groceries, cook, volunteer at the Argentine Club. There was never enough time to do it all. Now time seemed to stretch out in front of her in an endless emptiness.

After neatly organizing the receipts for July expenditures—now that the month was over—into a file for the Argentine Club, she had the rest of the day open. She went to the bathroom and opened the makeup drawer. She gazed in the mirror, wondering when her smooth, creamy face had begun looking so thin and creased with wrinkles. She applied some makeup to cover what lines she could. On her tired, lifeless brown eyes, she dabbed firming cream to refresh tired lids. A little shadow, and some lipstick. Then she brushed her hair and teased it into the same bell shape she'd worn for twenty-five years.

She gazed at the reflection, barely recognizing the woman she'd become. She wondered if Victor felt the same way when he looked at her. If he asked himself, *Who is this woman that I have to come home to every night?* She went into her bedroom and dressed for the day in a pair of brown slacks and an olive green blouse.

Finally ready, she went to sit at the computer where she'd begun to visit the blogs and Web sites that kept her company during the day.

Victoria drove to the shopping center down the street from Eric's house. He said he'd be sitting at the outside patio of a doughnut shop, and she spotted him right away, at a round table under a blue umbrella. She was grateful for an excuse to get away from her father. Did he plan to ignore her the rest of his life? He was impossible.

Eric noticed her before she got to the table and stood. He kissed her on the cheek, as was the Argentine custom. Then he resumed his place at the table. "I didn't get you a coffee yet because I didn't want it to get cold. But I bought plenty of doughnuts."

"That's fine. I brought my address book. We can divide up the names and start calling."

"That's what I like, a girl with a plan."

She realized she hadn't said hello properly or made any kind of chitchat at all. "I'm sorry. I'm . . . I decided to confront my father last night about taking more control over the restaurant, because everything you said had been bothering me. And we had a big fight. I barely slept, so I'm tired.

"I'm sorry," he said. "We could have done this another time."

"No," she shrugged. "Doesn't matter."

"I hate to ask, but what did I say to cause a fight?"

"Maybe it was more how I felt about doing exactly the same thing I've been doing since high school. Seeing you again made me remember that I once wanted my own life."

"Sorry," Eric said again. He reached across the table and placed a hand over hers. "Victoria, there's nothing wrong with staying close to your family and doing what they expect you to do. I didn't mean to criticize.... Part of me wishes *I* could have done that. You make me feel guilty as hell for my choices."

She smiled. "I'm so glad we bring out the best in each other."

"So what happened with your dad exactly?"

She told him the whole story. "I can't go back to that restaurant," she said. On a beautiful August morning like this, they should have been discussing the get-together with friends, enjoying their coffees and the heavenly smells coming out of the glass door every time a customer went in and out. Instead, she was unloading her irritations with her father on poor Eric.

He sipped his coffee, not looking at all bothered by her rantings. "Then don't," he said.

"What am I going to do? Even being at home is impossible."

He bit into his fourth or fifth doughnut and watched her as he chewed. He swallowed, and said, "I have a suggestion."

Victoria stared at the doughnuts, wanting one. "What?" she asked.

He pushed the bag of doughnuts across the table in front of her. "Help me with my flip."

"Help you with your flip? What does that mean?" She pushed the bag back.

"I've bought a house I'm going to fix up and sell while I'm in town. I'm usually my own project manager, but I hire subs to do a lot of the work. I need an interior designer. And I'll need help with staging when I'm ready to sell. The crew I usually use is in Austin. I'm putting together a crew here in LA. You can be my designer."

"You're offering me a job?"

"Not exactly. I'm suggesting you make me one of your new clients. Start your own interior design business."

"I can't start my own business."

"Mmm," he said, as he took another swig of coffee. "So your dad is right. You're too stupid to run a business. Then go back and be his errand girl for the next fifty years."

"Shut up," she said.

He grinned. "Want one of these?"

"Of course I do, but I'm on a diet. I need to lose weight."

"Help me with my flip and I'll keep you so busy you'll lose tons of weight. What do you say? And if you want, you can move into the house with me until we're ready to sell."

Now she laughed.

"What's so funny?"

"We haven't even been out on a proper date together and you want me to move in with you."

"I didn't mean it like that." He kept his smile. "But what do *you* mean? Do you want to go out on a date? Should I have asked you out? I didn't think you wanted me to."

"I don't. I mean, I wasn't hinting at anything. I'm just saying that... I'm not going to move in with you."

He shrugged easily. "I always live in the houses I flip. Mostly because I have nowhere else to live. But also because it makes me finish faster and I start to get a feel of what the house needs."

"I've lived with my parents for twenty-eight years and you

think I can move out just like that." Victoria snapped her fingers in the air.

"That's the way you do it. Swift and terrible. You'll feel like a new woman." He grabbed the bag of doughnuts, crumpled it up, and tossed it in the trash. "Good willpower," he said.

"That killed me. You can't eat those kinds of things in front of me again."

He nodded. "I'm all for getting healthy. But you know you look pretty damn cute the way you are, don't you?"

"I look fat. And I don't want to be cute. Carmen was always the smart one. I was always the cute one. I want guys to look at me and say, 'Man, she's hot.' "

He raised an eyebrow. "Hot?"

"Think I can pull it off?"

He stood and cleared his throat. "Sure." His eyes were bright with amusement. "Absolutely. Want to go see the house?"

Victoria figured she didn't have anything to lose. "Why not?"

Eric walked her though the front yard, which was littered with trash and overgrown weeds. "First thing I'm going to do as soon as we close escrow next week is get a Dumpster and start cleaning up. Then we can begin demo."

Victoria carefully made her way through the junk. Inside, he pointed out the changes he wanted to make, taking her room by room. "I'm going to completely gut the kitchen," he said.

The place smelled like cats and urine. Damn. He wondered if a family of cats might be spending their nights in the house. Victoria wrinkled her nose but didn't comment on the smell as she examined the kitchen. "You definitely need new cabinets and flooring. And I'd put in an extra window or maybe a skylight."

He nodded. "Exactly. That's where you come in. I'd like you

to choose the cabinets. The flooring. Come up with the color scheme. Suggestions on lighting. Then at the end, help me stage it so it looks good enough to sell."

She walked out of the kitchen and into the living room, looking around at all the work that had to be done. "And if I do this, I get paid when?"

"When we sell it."

"What if you don't sell it?"

"Of course I'll sell it. I should make about a hundred and fifty thousand if the market doesn't tank on me. I'll give you five percent."

She raised an eyebrow. "How about fifteen?"

He laughed. And here he thought she'd be impressed with five. "Ten."

She narrowed her eyes. "This seems very risky. How do you live like this? You might make way less than what you project."

"True. When I started, I had quite a few flips that ended up making me peanuts. But I've learned. I got this house at a good price. I know exactly what to put into it to turn it around at a good profit." He walked up beside her, and placed a hand on her shoulder. "What do you say? Are you in?"

She gazed at him, then tipped her head back and closed her eyes. Her pulse skipped like crazy. "Oh God, Eric, what am I doing? I should go back and apologize to my father. He needs me now that he's starting this major business expansion." She raised her head and looked him in the eye. "He's worked his whole life to pass his business on to me and my sister. Carmen doesn't want it."

"And you do?"

"No, but how can I walk away from him? And for what? To help you flip houses?—No offense."

"Vicki, this has nothing to do with me. I just happen to know you enjoy being creative, and you have a talent for decorating. And I need someone to be my interior designer." He lowered his arm and stepped in front of her. "I do understand your loyalty to your father, but in the end, you have to be able to step back and ask yourself what you really want."

Her dark eyes gazed deeply into his. "I envy that you were able to do that, Eric. Just leave everything behind, free to travel and do what you like. But I'm not sure I can do that."

"Don't envy me," he said. Sometimes when you blindly chased your independence, you got it. And he wasn't sure if he'd ended up losing much more than he'd gained. "Everyone thinks I'm an asshole."

"No," she argued, but she wasn't very convincing.

He smiled. "It's okay. I know what people have said. And I don't blame them. I was supposed to go to college. Go to law school in LA. And I abandoned everything and embarrassed my parents. That's what everyone sees. So of course they're judging me harshly." He stared into her big, understanding eyes. "And maybe they're all right, and I was wrong. I could have been a big-time lawyer and on my way to a great career. Instead, here I am hoping the whole real-estate market doesn't completely tank and leave me holding my . . . well, leave me in deep financial trouble."

"So why did you leave? Why take a chance?" She asked as if she really wanted to know—as if his answer mattered.

He sighed. "The short answer is I just wanted to get the hell out of here. I wanted to see something different. I wanted to make my own way in the world. And I had a passion for restoring houses, so I went for it." He angled his head. He'd never told this to a soul, and he hoped he wasn't making a mistake by telling her, but it felt good to talk about his past decisions to someone who knew him. "The extended answer is that even if I'd stayed, I wouldn't have been able to continue on to law school. My dad got into a bit of trouble financially and there was no money in my college fund by my third year at Claremont McKenna. My mom doesn't know any of this. She thought my dad had been saving for twenty years. But he'd never made enough for law school so he invested what he had, hoping it would magically grow into thousands, and things hadn't worked out like he'd hoped."

"Invested?"

"Aggressively."

"That's too bad, but you could have gotten a scholarship if—"

"If I really wanted to be a lawyer. But I didn't. So I used that as an excuse to quit. Pissed my dad off big-time and hurt my mom when their only son thumbed his nose at parental goals and traditions. So now..." He shrugged and walked across the room, then sat on a window ledge. "I'm stuck doing the only thing I know how to do. To those looking at me from the outside, I became a bargain hunter and a gambler." He watched her. "But I'm doing what I love."

"That's wonderful, Eric. It really is."

"Don't go back to your dad because you think you owe him something. You'll be miserable the rest of your life. I feel guilty, and I wish I had done things differently, but I'm not sorry I followed my passion. I would have made a lousy lawyer."

"And I'll make a lousy restaurant owner, I know. But it's the easiest road."

"So, you'll go back to doing something you don't like, because you're afraid go out on your own?"

"I am." Her voice was soft and sweet. "Pathetic, I know, but I'm scared to try something risky and fall flat on my face."

"Follow your heart and you won't." He smiled. "Hey, that's

what I did when I left home and when I decided to return. Something inside me said it was time. And everything has felt right ever since."

She smiled. "All right," she said. She stepped in front of him and offered her hand. "Fifteen percent?"

He never paid a designer that much money. But he pressed his palm to hers. This was the second time they shook hands. And the deals they made were getting progressively more interesting. "You got it." He held on to her hand.

"My heart is beating out of control. This is such a big step for me."

He felt the pulse on her wrist with his thumb. Gently, he rubbed it. "What, doing a little remodel job with me?"

"No. Moving on with my life."

He squeezed her hand, then released it. "And here I thought it was holding my hand that was sending you into overdrive."

She laughed. Nervously? "Let's go give some of our old friends a call now. Okay?" she said.

Eric watched her walk out the sliding glass door into the backyard. He'd spent the last seven years enjoying temporary women—not because he was a jerk, but because he never stayed in one town long enough to develop a long-term relationship. Being at home, with family, and old friends like Victoria made him think that maybe he was missing out on one of life's great gifts—real connections to other people.

They sat on the edge of the backyard pool, their legs dangling into an empty pit that was in need of serious cleaning and repair. The rest of the yard looked just as neglected, with weeds growing around wide patches of dirt. The wooden fence needed to be torn down, especially since many boards were already loose and half falling into the yard.

"So what are we proposing. Dinner? Drinks? Dancing?"

"How about all three? I'll book one of those dinner cruises off of Newport Beach, and buy out the boat for our party."

"Ah, that sounds nice, but—"

"Great. Let's do it."

"You're going to pay for that?"

"Sure."

"All right." She shrugged. "When?"

"Next weekend?"

"Too soon. People might have plans. How about next month? If we're going to be working on this house, you'll still be in town."

"Yep. Okay, next month it is."

Eric had a list of about five friends to call, Victoria about a dozen. She started with those she was still in contact with. Eduardo was first on her list, because he not only went to their high school but was a member of the Argentine Club. She called him at the auto shop and told him she and Eric wanted to get a group of friends together .

"Sounds great, Victoria," he said. "But you know Kelly plans all our events. And we have the kids to find sitters for. I'm not sure we'll be able to make it."

"Why don't you talk to her and call me back?"

"Yeah, I'll do that. Talk to you soon, nena."

Victoria moved on to Susana, even though she wasn't her favorite person, and regretted doing so almost immediately. Susana started in about what a disgrace it was that Eric showed up at the club after all these years and didn't even warn his parents first. Then had the nerve to make a scene by fighting with Steve.

"Really," she said, "I'm surprised you're even talking to him, much less helping him find friends."

She wasn't helping him find friends. She was helping him

reconnect with friends, and Susana obviously wasn't one of them. "Our parents are close friends, Susana. How can I not talk to him?" she asked quietly, standing and moving away from Eric, even though he was on his own phone and probably wasn't paying attention to her conversation.

"Well, of course we have to be polite, but you don't have to become his best buddy. Though, you and he *were* kind of close, weren't you? Did you actually, you know, have a relationship?"

Victoria rolled her eyes. "Susana, he's going to book a dinner cruise for us all. I think it'll be nice."

"Sure, now that he has money, he wants to buy us back."

Although Victoria had had more than one unpleasant thought about Eric through the years—and had once even agreed that he was dog shit for thinking he was better than they were and leaving—she would rather hang out with Eric a million times more than she would with Susana. Especially now that she knew that there was more to the story than what they had all believed.

"Susana, I think he came back because he's lonely. He missed his family. He missed us. Can't you let the past go and help welcome him back?"

"He was always an arrogant prick who shunned his Latino heritage. He wanted to go out there and pretend he was something he wasn't. Let him go back, Victoria. Don't get involved with him. Do yourself a favor."

"Yeah," she said, wondering if everyone, Susana and herself included, weren't all a little jealous of Eric. "But you might want to think of Lucia."

"I'll be polite to him at the club. But I'm not going out to dinner with him."

And that was that. After she ended the call, she decided to change tactics and not call anyone from the Argentine Club after all. She'd call their other high school friends instead.

An hour later, she'd gotten five yeses, and Eric had gotten two.

"Are you sure you want to book an entire dinner cruise for so few people?"

"It'll be almost twenty of us with spouses and girlfriends and boyfriends. It'll be fun," he said, excited.

Victoria smiled. She didn't care what Susana thought. Eric was okay, and she was glad he'd come home.

Chapter Eight

Mid-week Jaqueline met with the ladies at the Argentine Club, and they completed their plans to bring in an Argentine artist to talk about his work and display his paintings. But her mind was on Victoria and Victor. They weren't speaking to each other, and neither one would tell her why.

Lucia passed the paperwork across the table for Jaqueline to sign. Jaqueline stared down at it, then scrawled her name and passed it along.

"So, Jaqueline, you must be so excited about Victor's expansion plans," Nelly said.

Jaqueline took the stack of mini art prints and fixed them back into the binder. The artist was good, though she didn't know much about art. She glanced at Nelly. "Expansion?"

"For the restaurant."

What was this woman talking about? Nelly was a nice person, but... well, maybe she was getting tired of the politics at the Argentine Club. All the work it required, and for what? "Oh, the restaurant," she said, pretending she knew what Nelly was talking about. "Yes, it's going well."

"Hector invested quite a bit. I guess he must really believe in Victor's idea."

Invested? What, money? Jaqueline smiled. Though she wasn't pleased that her husband was asking their friends for money.

Was he crazy? Were they having money problems? "Really? He liked Victor's idea?"

"He won't stop talking about it. How about you? Are you nervous about it?"

She was nervous, all right. "A little," she admitted.

Lucia frowned. "What are you two talking about?"

"Victor's restaurant expansion," Nelly said.

"I didn't know he was doing that," Lucia said.

Neither did Jaqueline. But she planned on finding out what was going on immediately. "I'll have to tell you about it later. Oh, by the way, I'm proposing we have a Mexican fiesta day in celebration of our closest Latino neighbors," she said to the rest of the group. "Here's my proposal." She passed out a sheet of paper that she spent all last night preparing with Victoria's help. It included having a variety of performers, primarily Hugo's band, and indulging in a selection of Mexican food samples. She gave them an estimate of the cost.

She ignored all the frowns and mumbling about the unprecedented idea. "Read it over. We can discuss it next time. If it works out, we might want to consider highlighting a different Latino country every quarter."

Lucia made a "why not" face and then smiled. "I kind of like that idea. Just think of the variety of foods we can try and the diversity of entertainment we can enjoy."

"That's exactly what I was thinking," Jaqueline said, and stood. "I'll see you all next Sunday."

"Well, hold on, let's walk out to the parking lot together. I want to tell you something," Lucia said.

"Sure."

Lucia hooked her arm with Jaqueline's. "Good news, loca."

"Qué?"

"Eric said Victoria agreed to work with him to fix up a house."

"Fix up his house? I didn't even know he had a house."

"Not *his* house. *A* house. He buys and sells properties. I told you, remember?"

"Oh, yes." Was this what Victor was so upset about? She felt very misinformed about the things going on with her family. And she was going to get to the bottom of all of it.

"Well," Lucia smiled. "That's good news, no? They're going to be spending more time together."

Jaqueline nodded absently. "Maybe. Victor is angry at her, so it might not be so good."

Lucia made a growling sound in the back of her throat. "He needs to give that girl some space. She has to be allowed to spend some time with people her own age."

"Lucia, you're so transparent." She gave her a quick hug. "I've got to go."

"If this works between them, we will have major celebrating to do. My best friend will become my in-law."

Jaqueline laughed. "Let's keep our fingers crossed."

Victoria told Douglas about helping Eric with his flip. "Do you think we can keep my hours flexible? I'm not sure when he's going to need me."

"Of course." He rang up a customer's purchase. "Here you go, Mrs. Thorpe. If it doesn't look perfect in your living room, you bring it back, understand?"

Mrs. Thorpe took her purchase and held it close to her body. "It's not coming back, Douglas." She smiled. "Good-bye. 'Bye, Victoria."

Victoria hurried to open the door for her. "Take care, Mrs. Thorpe."

"I've got it, I've got it. I'm old, not feeble."

Victoria held her hands up, and stepped out of her way.

"Excuse me," Mrs. Thorpe said, practically running into someone on the sidewalk.

As Victoria turned back in, Douglas called her over. He held out a brochure. "I've been meaning to give you this. Now might be the perfect time."

Victoria looked at the pamphlet for a college. They were offering a special night class for store owners on designing displays. Looked interesting. "You want me to go to this?"

"No. I thought you might take a look at the college. They have an interior design program. Since you already have all of your lower division classes, you might be able to complete this fairly quickly."

Victoria flipped open the glossy pamphlet. She arched an eyebrow and looked at Douglas. "I'm too old to go back to school."

Douglas laughed. "Sweetheart, I wish I was as old as you." He walked out from behind the counter. "If you're seriously thinking of pursuing a career in decorating, it might be worth taking a look."

"Maybe." Even as she heard her voice say it, she hated her indecisiveness. Why was she always so damned wishy-washy? "So you think helping Eric with this flip is a good idea?"

"Yes, I think it's a good idea on many levels. I'm going to go unpack some boxes in the back. Watch the store?"

"Sure. Wait, Douglas."

He paused.

"I'm excited and scared and worried. I think I can really be a good interior designer, and I think I'd love it. But what if I'm wrong? What if I fall flat on my face?"

"So what if you do?" He turned around and gripped the counter with both hands, and his eyes that always looked sort of sad, twinkled. "Would that be worse than knowing for the rest of your life that you wanted something but were too chicken to go for it?"

"That's a good question."

"Thanks," he said. "I thought so, too." He winked and turned away.

He left her alone in the store with her thoughts. Taking on Eric's interior decorating job must be a good idea, because she was excited about life for the first time in so long.

Stunned, as if someone had hit him over the head with a side of beef, Victor walked back to his car. Away from Douglas's novelty shop, away from his daughter. He'd come to talk to her. To tell her that he'd hired a manager because it was the right thing to do, but that he saw her point also and was ready to include her in more of the restaurant's daily operations. He was ready to concede, at least in part, that Victoria was capable of handling more. An altruistic gesture on his part, he thought.

But after that old woman came bustling out of the shop in a cloud of perfume, he stood on the verge of entering and listened to Victoria and Douglas discuss her future. His heart sank. He had no *idea*. No idea that Victoria had dreams. He'd always looked at her decorating talent as something of a hobby that came in useful at the restaurant. He never knew that she loved doing it so much that she seriously considered it as a career. And listening to her voice her fears made him almost physically sick. Not only should she have been having that discussion with him instead of Douglas, but she should have done it years ago.

Reaching his Honda Civic, he leaned his arms on the car's roof and gazed back in the direction of the shop. How could he have become the kind of father that was blind to his children's dreams? He'd always sworn that no son of his would ever have to work even one hour at a job he disliked. He'd never have to sacrifice his dreams or curb his ambitions to please someone else. Because he'd never had a son, those promises to himself had been forgotten. Never in his wildest dreams had he imagined that women had the same desires of success as men. He felt like a stupid, thickheaded, outdated old fool. He thought he was being a good father by taking care of her. Involving her in the restaurant enough to give her something to do, but not saddling her with the headaches. Letting her be free enough to do nothing at all with her life.

Victor had turned away from that shop as fast as he could, before Victoria could notice him. Douglas had said all the right things. Things he himself should have said. He wanted to be the one his children confided in and looked to for wisdom. But Carmen always confided in either Jaqueline or Victoria. And Victoria, who he thought would turn to him, in the end found she couldn't.

He lowered his head and got in the car. A crazy empty feeling settled in the pit of his stomach. He wanted to run into that store and pull Victoria into his arms, hold her like when she was a little girl. He wanted to be her father again. The man she needed and who never let her down. But he realized he *had* let her down, and the best thing he could do for her now was leave her alone. Let her stand or fall. Let her make mistakes. As much as it killed him. As much as he ached inside to drive away from her, he knew it was way past time to admit that she had to be allowed to spread her wings.

Eric wasn't thrilled to see his father show up at the bank where he was finalizing the agreement for his house.

"I thought we might do this together," he said, slightly out of breath, excitement evident in his voice.

Trying not to show his surprise, and his horror, Eric simply frowned. "Do what together, Dad?"

"Sign the paperwork. Flip this house together. You know, it'll be our project. Together."

"Dad, I don't need a partner. I mean, it's a nice thought. And if you want to help—"

"No, I've got a little money saved up. We can buy it together."

Eric didn't know how to tell his father that there was no way in hell he was going to go into a financial project with him. "Down payment's been made already." He planted a hand on Antonio's shoulder. "But why don't we go to a soccer game while I'm in town?"

"Well what about the expense of the remodel itself? You're going to need help with that."

Holding his frustration in check, Eric said, "Yeah, and I've got that covered. Really, Dad, this is my job, I don't need any money." But maybe Antonio did. Maybe he was short and wanted to get in on the project to make some money. Eric hoped he hadn't gotten into trouble again. "Besides, you don't want to risk your cash at this point in your life. Right?"

"Sure, you gotta risk a little to make a little."

"I do. You don't. Your house is paid. You're happy. Mom's happy. Why risk what you have?"

"I just though it would be nice to work together. I'm proud of all you've accomplished, Eric."

"Thanks, Dad. Look, I'm going to hire a couple of subs. You can help out. I'll pay you like I would them. We can hang out together. But this is *my* deal. Okay?"

Antonio didn't seem to like that, but tough. That was the way it was going to be.

Victor hired a manager for La Parrilla. A UCLA graduate who had run a chain restaurant for three years. The boy was sharp, handsome, and enthusiastic. Even though it had caused Victoria to walk out on him, he couldn't have made a better move.

Victoria didn't have the heart to run a business like his. Besides, he never wanted her to have that kind of pressure. In the end it would work out, hopefully, for both of them.

He was relieved to leave the operation of this site to someone else at this point, since he barely had time to think lately. He was signing papers like crazy, working with contractors and architects to break ground next month for both restaurants simultaneously, getting home late, going to bed, and getting up and doing it all over again.

Once he got the two new California restaurants up and running, the others would be easier to establish. The architectural plans for the layout and design of all the La Parrillas would be identical. Later he'd get an interior designer to make sure each restaurant was decorated the same on the inside, as well. He'd followed Eric's advice and hired a market research firm, which he would be meeting with this week to find the best locations for the new restaurants. The speed at which this was moving was making his head spin.

But it seemed he had other problems on the home front. Jaqueline wanted to talk to him. Called him a few times and wanted to know about the expansion. Now that things were under way, he feared that news would reach her. Too many people were involved. But he hoped, probably unreasonably, that he could avoid a full discussion. He'd told her it was no big deal, and that he'd talk to her about it soon. When she insisted, he'd told her he had an emergency to deal with and hung up.

Cowardly of him, but he couldn't deal with sharing this with Jaqueline just yet. He had wanted to have all his financing in place and the new restaurants under construction, at least, before he shared his news, or gossip reached her. The truth was, he was afraid of her reaction and he would avoid the confrontation as long as possible.

So when she showed up at the restaurant, he was thrown off balance. "What are you doing here?"

"Nice way to greet your wife."

"Sorry." He pulled out a chair for her and kissed her cheek. "Un cafecito?"

"Bueno."

He waved at the guy behind the counter and signaled him to bring two coffees. "So what I meant was, what brings you by?"

"I wanted to talk."

"As long as you make it quick. I'm busy."

She looked around. At three in the afternoon, not many people crowded his tables. "I can see how busy you are."

He frowned. "I mean I need to plan for tonight."

The coffees arrived.

"I won't take much of your precious time. What I want to know is why are my friends telling me that you're asking them for money to expand the restaurant? What are you planning to expand? It's plenty big."

"I didn't ask our friends for money." He gazed at her. Maybe she didn't know the whole story after all. Did she think he was just planning to enlarge *this* building? Didn't she realize he always thought bigger than the obvious? "It's an investment opportunity for them. I just mentioned it and they wanted in. No big deal."

"Why would they want to give you money?"

"They're not giving me money. Look, vieja, that's the way business works. People invest money, and they get a share of the profits. Okay? Don't worry about it."

"Of course I worry. If we need money, I mean if we are struggling, I can come back and work here. You can let a couple of your guys go and I can come in and—"

"No, no, no. We don't need money. We're doing fine. Great, in fact. That's why I'm expanding."

She looked unsure. Victor couldn't take his eyes off her. She was still the most beautiful woman he'd ever seen. And she'd been a great wife. Loyal, helpful, forgiving, understanding, sexually amazing, and supportive. She'd also given him the best children a man could ask for. Both girls were intelligent and loving and strong. And soon, he'd be able to turn over an empire to his kids and give his wife anything she wanted.

He placed his hand over hers as she held her coffee cup. "I know I'm working a lot right now, but once I get my plans off the ground, we'll be able to take a little vacation together. Would you like that?"

"A vacation? Together?"

Why did she look so surprised? Just because they hadn't had time to do much traveling in the past didn't mean he wouldn't have enjoyed vacationing and sightseeing, or simply relaxing by a pool with his wife. And it wasn't too late now that the girls were grown. Might be nice. Get to know each other again. He pulled his hand back. "We'll talk about it when I get things straightened out here."

"There's always a 'when' for you Victor."

"What do you mean?"

"*When* we move to America we'll make millions and be happy. *When* we start the restaurant, we'll be secure enough to buy a house. *When* we have enough money saved, we can move back to Argentina. *When* the restaurant is self-sufficient, we can take our children on a cross-country vacation. *When* they graduate and leave home, we can spend more time together. When, when, when. Well, the kids are grown, and we never made the road trip. We never took them to Argentina, either, like we promised we'd do. And soon, we'll both be dead and there won't be anymore 'whens.'"

"That's life, Jaqueline. The years go by and . . . you do the best you can."

She shook her head. "I'm asking you to be my husband *now*, not when it's more convenient for you."

"I *am* your husband. What are you talking about?"

"I mean a husband who wants to share his life with me. One who notices I'm alive."

"You're talking crazy, Jaqui."

"No, I'm not. You're always here at the restaurant. You come home to sleep. That's it."

"I'm doing all this for us."

"No, Victor. I don't believe that anymore. You're doing it for you."

He drew a breath and ground his teeth. "Fine. I'm doing it for me. For once, I want to do something for myself."

"For once?" She shrieked. "It's always been about you and *your* dreams and *your* plans."

That made his blood boil. She was the one who wanted kids, and a house, and even the restaurant because it would bring in stable money. "I thought it was *our* plans."

Jaqueline scoffed. "I never wanted any of this. It was just a way to give you some of the success and independence you wanted."

Wonderful. Just what he needed to hear. She'd suggested he slave away at a restaurant all his life to make him feel *successful.* Was she kidding?

She spoke again, this time barely a whisper. "All *I* wanted was you."

A sharpness cut into his heart, but deep down he knew that she was right. She'd hung around and supported his dreams because she loved him. But, he had to be honest. "Men need more than just a wife and children."

She looked at him like he'd slapped her.

"I didn't mean—," he tried to correct himself.

"That's okay." She stood and took her purse, which had been hanging on the back of the chair. "See you at home whenever you feel like dropping by."

Long after she'd walked out the door, he sat in the same spot.

Finally, he slammed his fist on the table, making the coffee cups bounce and spilling the coffee that was left. He *was* going to follow his dream. Even if he had to do it alone. In the end, Jaqueline and Victoria both would understand what he'd sacrificed for all of them. They would see. And they would forgive him.

Chapter Nine

Almost two weeks after agreeing to work with Eric, Victoria returned to the remodel to begin with cleanup and demo and found that Eric and two other guys were already working. A box of doughnuts and empty coffee cups littered the counter, which would be coming out today. A large Dumpster now sat at the curb in front of the house. In the kitchen, Eric had boxes of gloves and face masks. After saying hello, he told her to put on both. "There's going to be a lot of dust."

"So where do we start?"

"Getting rid of all the trash."

"Fun."

He grinned. "Okay, follow me." He covered his mouth and nose with the mask and winked as he headed outside.

The three guys he hired started throwing trash into the Dumpster. Victoria joined in. She tossed in pieces of broken CDs, old lamps, chairs, and tons of clothes.

"Leave the heavy stuff to us," Eric said, as he walked by carrying a dirty, warped stroller.

A little later she had raked glass and small pieces of other trash into a pile.

"Victoria," Eric called. "Careful with that glass. There's a shovel in the—"

"Got it," she said, and held it up. "I can handle this part."

The front yard looked almost normal three hours later as they raked up the last of the debris. Eric pulled a trash bag out of a roll he'd set up on the porch and came over. "Hold the bag, I'll shovel."

"*You* hold the bag and *I'll* shovel," she said.

He wiped his sweaty forehead with his shirtsleeve and squinted from the bright sunlight. Then he flapped the bag open. "Yes, ma'am."

She poured the trash into the bag and watched him. She never thought she'd find a dirty, sweaty man appealing, but *God*, he was sexy. "You haven't become one of these macho guys who thinks girls can't do anything, have you?"

"Of course not." He frowned. "Why would you ask that?"

"You're doing a bit of micromanaging."

"Sorry, I like my crew to be safe. Men *and* women."

And he'd been guiding the other guys as well, if she were honest. "Did it look like I wasn't being safe?"

"No. I guess I have been keeping my eye on you a little more closely." He winked. "You're much more enjoyable to watch than those two guys."

She poured the last of the trash into the plastic bag. "Should we pour some of the crap you're dishing out in here, too?"

He laughed and tied the bag. "Time for the inside."

He tossed the full trash bag into the bin and headed into the house. The guys followed him. He gave some orders in pitiful Spanish.

"Eric, honey," she said, pulling him aside. "*Rompan* los cabinetes y *tirenlo* en la basura. Not romper los cabinetes y tirar a la basura." She was amused and a bit appalled at his poorly spoken Spanish.

He shrugged sheepishly. "They understand what I'm saying."

The guys began breaking cabinets apart. Pounding and kicking them to pieces. Victoria stepped out of the way as wood and tile crashed around her. Eric was right; they had understood his meaning. It took them less than twenty minutes to completely tear apart the kitchen. She couldn't believe it. Once the sounds of splintering wood and shattering ceramic stopped, and the dust cleared, Victoria carried away as many chunks of broken cabinets as she could. The guys put down their hammers and electric screwdrivers and helped.

As soon as they made enough space on the floor to continue working, they started hammering kitchen walls until the drywall broke to pieces. They ripped out carpet and pulled off linoleum.

"Eric, what about if we take out this half wall?" A half wall separated the entrance from the livingroom. It created a more defined entryway but at the same time blocked the traffic flow into and out of the house.

He wiped his forehead on his sleeve and glanced her way. "No, I like it."

"If we take it out, I think you'd like it better. The room will look larger."

"Yeah, but I like the separation. Makes the entrance stand out. Almost like it's its own room."

Even though she disagreed, this was his house, so she decided to let it go. "Okay."

"Don't you think the entrance should stand out?" Eric asked.

"Yes, but it already does. You don't need something obvious like a half wall to announce to visitors that this is the entrance. But if you like it this way, that's okay."

"Hmm," he said, and got back to work.

Victoria, too, moved on to other things. She took down all the old lighting fixtures, carried trash out, swept, and when her stomach grumbled she checked her watch and noticed it was almost two in the afternoon. So she dropped everything, washed her hands outside with a hose, and went for a late lunch run.

As if they hadn't eaten in a month, the guys devoured the

giant garbage burritos—appropriately named for containing everything but the kitchen sink—and slurped down the monster sodas. And Victoria herself practically inhaled her smaller bean and rice burrito. And she didn't even feel guilty eating the heavy meal. She'd had quite a workout already.

Eric sat beside her, sipping on his soda when he finished eating. "I appreciate you being here today. You didn't have to be involved in this part."

"*Now* you tell me," she said, then smiled. "I wanted to be here."

"Thanks for picking up lunch."

She ate the last bite and wiped her lips. "No problem."

He gazed sleepily at her.

"What?"

"I never thought I'd be sitting across from you, casually eating lunch again. It's weird."

"Weren't you ever planning to return home?"

He shook his head. "Nope." He stood and tossed his trash into a plastic bag. "I wasn't ever going to come back." He patted his stomach as if satisfied. "Back to work."

She got on her feet, too. "Hey, wait a minute. You can't leave me with just that. Why weren't you ever going to come back?"

"I didn't think there was anything for me here anymore. Come on." He jerked his head toward the house.

"What about your parents? Didn't you miss them?"

"Honest?"

"That would be nice."

He offered one nod. "I was young and angry when I left. I missed the easy home-cooked meals and the comforts of home. I didn't miss my parents the first couple of years. It was them I was trying to get away from."

"Where did you go?"

He narrowed his gaze and stared out at the yard. "All over.

I stayed in the States for a while. Paid my dad's debts off, then took off to Europe with some friends. Traveled all over until I ran out of money." He chuckled. "My friends magically disappeared then. So I came back to America and started seriously working in real-estate investment. The last two years I've been in Austin. Nice college town. Lots of culture, believe it or not."

"So why did you come home?"

He glanced at her. "I don't know."

But she thought he did know. He just didn't want to say that he'd gotten lonely. That he'd needed to reconnect with his past. That it was inevitable for people to return home. "That's okay. It's not always important to know every why."

Then he turned and placed a hand on her lower back. "Thanks."

She followed him inside. His helpers did, too.

"Here," Eric handed her the sledgehammer.

"What?" He didn't actually think she was going to swing that heavy, oversized hammer at anything, did he?

"I've decided you're right about that half wall."

She smiled, pleased that he had decided to trust her, and follow her first major recommendation. "Good. It's going to make a big difference in here."

He put the sledgehammer in her hands and walked her to the wall. "Go for it."

"I don't think—"

"Come on," he coaxed. "Give it a good swing. You wounded me with that comment of me being a macho construction worker, so come on."

She eyed him skeptically. She might be big, but that didn't mean she was strong. Still, he looked so excited about her tearing down that wall. So she lifted the heavy, menacing-looking tool and swung it at the stuccoed wall. It made a small dent.

Eric laughed. "I could have made a bigger hole if I kicked it. Slam the damn thing."

Victoria nodded, lifting the sledgehammer with more determination.

Eric stood beside her making an ugly face. "Hard. Think of putting it clear through to the other side."

The other two men came to watch.

Victoria pulled it back as far as she could and swung, hitting the dry wall and chipping a piece off. A small piece. She pulled back again and hit it again and again and again. The men all cheered and yelled things like "Slam it," "Think of your ex-boyfriend," "You got it."

Finally, the muscles in her arms started to burn, and she was laughing too much to continue. She stepped back, and all the guys lunged forward as if they were just waiting to take over. They kicked at the wood beams that were left until the entire wall lay in pieces on the floor. Then they cheered, congratulated each other, and patted her on the back. The entire episode reeked of too much testosterone, so she allowed Eric to dust her off and take the sledgehammer out of her hands. "Wasn't that fun?" he asked

"A blast," she said, breathing heavily.

He laughed. "That's how I'm going to feel when you start asking me what color carpet matches what color walls and what flooring works best with what cabinets."

"I wasn't going to ask you."

"Well, then." He stepped back. "I've hired the right woman for the job."

By nightfall, she understood why he said she wouldn't have to work out if she helped him. Not only had her arms gotten a workout, but with all the trips she'd made to the Dumpster she must have walked ten miles. Even her back was sore.

He sat on the front porch steps drinking his hundredth soda. She finished sweeping up the last of the broken glass and tile, then joined him. It was still warm outside, but a breeze was starting to cool things off. This was actually her favorite time of day. Birds flew from tree to tree trying to find just the right spot to settle in for the night. Some mowers could be heard in the background as people got home from work and tackled the chore. The air was scented with cooking smells coming from neighboring kitchens and outdoor grills. From the relaxed look on Eric's face, she guessed it was his favorite time of day, too. And from the look of the house right now, this was the best place to be.

"We didn't leave a thing intact in there," she said.

With a lazy grin, he turned to look at her. "Demo is always the most fun."

"Yes, I saw the look of satisfaction on your face when you took your sledgehammer to those bathroom cabinets earlier. A lot of hidden aggression, I think."

"You think correctly." He placed a hand on her knee. "Thanks for your help."

Every time he touched her—and he did so a lot—she became instantly aware of him as a man. Strong and confident and so different from the boy he used to be. She had to continuously remind herself that this flirtatious man *was* just Eric. "No problem. It was sort of fun, even if it looks like all we've done is mess up a perfectly good house."

"I've got about a six- to eight-week window to get this all done. If we finish by the end of September, I'll only have to make two house payments. I can put the house on the market in October. Tomorrow, I'd like you to pick out the kitchen cabinets and appliances, because they take the longest to come in. I'll give you my American Express and your limit."

"Ah, shopping. Now you're talking."

"Remember, we want nice, but we don't want to go overboard."

"You sure you want me doing this?"

He squeezed her knee and let go. "Positive."

"Okay. Then I'm off to take a shower and go to sleep. I'm exhausted." She stood.

"Victoria."

"Hmm?"

" 'Night," he said, though she was sure that wasn't at all what he wanted to say.

"Good night, Eric."

He watched her, making no move to get up and go anywhere. He wanted to sit outside by himself for a little while. After so many years on his own, he enjoyed the solitude. Although he could have sat on this porch talking to Victoria all night. Once they got this place cleaned up, he'd take possession of one of the rooms and move in. Life was looking up.

Victoria took a long, warm, heavily scented shower, absorbing the moisture into her pores and relaxing her tired muscles. Then she wrapped herself in a long bathrobe and brushed her teeth. Wiping the steam off the mirror with a towel, she gazed at herself. If someone had told her last month that she was going to be hammering walls with Eric Ortelli, considering going into business for herself, *and* maybe going back to college, she would have told them they were on drugs. All of that involved work. Not to mention a belief that she could be successful with any of it.

She let the bathrobe fall and turned to look in the full-length mirror on the bathroom door. Her belly bulged forward. Her hips flared way further than the natural bone and muscle structure forced them to. Rolls of fat padded her back and her legs.

Her breasts were large, but they actually looked firm and good. She had one thing going for her.

Mentally cringing, she pulled out the scale. The red digital numbers lit up and rewarded her with a number that said she was five pounds lighter than she was two weeks ago. Amazing. In the adjoining bedroom, her cell phone played Beyoncé. Victoria hurriedly slipped on the bathrobe and reached for her phone.

"Hey, Carmen."

"You sound out of breath," Carmen said. "What were you doing?"

"Nothing fun. I just got out of the shower."

"Well, I have something to confess."

Victoria sat on her bed. When someone confessed something, it usually wasn't good. "Yeah?"

"I enrolled in business classes this year instead of the planned genetics, metabolic biochemistry, and molecular structure classes. I need to see if there's something I'm better at than all those science courses."

"Better? Carmen, you're an excellent student. You can't do much better than straight As."

"I struggle for those grades and the next aren't going to look so good. Labs didn't go well."

"I'm sorry."

"I'm trying something different. Hopefully, you and Dad won't freak."

"Why would *I* freak?"

"You might not agree with what I have in mind."

"Which is?"

"Let's see how I do in these business classes first, then we'll talk."

Business? Victoria wasn't following. "Carmen, you can always talk to me, you know?"

"I know."

"Okay. I've got something to confess, myself."

"You found a guy and he's not Argentine."

"Worse. I quit La Parrilla." She told Carmen the whole story, even the part about working with Eric.

"Oh, my God. I'm speechless, Victoria."

"Think I'm crazy?"

"No! I think it's all great. I love that Dad's planning to have more than one restaurant. And you being a professional designer? What can be more perfect?"

"Dad's really pissed at me. I hurt him, Carmen." The line was silent for a few seconds too long. "Carmen?"

"I'm here. I was just thinking that if he hadn't chosen our career paths for us, maybe he wouldn't be hurt."

"If he starts to struggle or it looks like he's going to lose what he's invested, I'm going to have to step back in."

"Vic, maybe instead of thinking you can go back and help him out of a financial bind doing something you hate and you're not good at—and I'm only repeating what you've told me; I'm not being critical—you should start building your own career."

"I know. I've been thinking that, too. I want to have the money to save their house if Dad's new restaurants don't do well and he can't pay the banks."

"I hate to say this, but I wasn't implying you do that to save Dad, but yourself."

Victoria was the one who was quiet this time. "Let's just see how it all works out."

"Love you, Vic."

"I love you, too."

Jaqueline couldn't dwell on the lack of connection with Victor forever. He made his feelings clear, and sadly, she couldn't say his words were a surprise. His mind had always been occupied with plans that rarely included her. So why let it bother her now? In the past, she'd focused on her daughters and the truth had been easy to bury. Today it wasn't as easy, but she tried. She called Hugo.

He answered his cell but seemed distracted. "Jaqueline, it's so good to hear from you."

"Bad time?" she asked. A child cried loudly in the background.

"No," he said. "Well, I have my children with me and I'm having one of those days," he admitted. "But it's still good to hear from you."

She smiled, remembering what "one of those days" felt like. "Are you driving?" Sounded like he was in a cave of sorts, and she heard the children.

"Yes, I'm in traffic—missed my son's soccer practice while they cleared an accident. He's pouting. And now my daughter is crying, because I won't take her to buy a dress for her piano recital tomorrow. She didn't tell me in time, and it's too late now. As it is, it's probably going to be McDonald's again tonight, because I don't have time to cook."

Whew, he really is overwhelmed right now, Jaqueline thought.

She didn't know why he was a single father, but she felt for him. "Hang in there, Hugo. I just wanted to let you know that I put in a good word for you at the club. We're going to try to work something out for your band."

"Ah, gracias, Jaqueline. I appreciate it."

"You're welcome."

He cursed. "Damn it, I missed my exit."

"I'd better let you go."

"I'm sorry," he said.

"Don't be. And Hugo?"

"What?"

"If you're close to a mall, pull over and buy your daughter that dress. Then take lots of pictures at the recital. You won't regret it."

He sighed, obviously distraught. "Okay. If you think I should."

"Trust me. Buy the dress. Eat at McDonald's. Let the world go by, and enjoy your kids."

"Okay, Jaqueline. Thanks."

She ended the call and smiled. "Goodness." She didn't envy him. Well, maybe she did, a little. And she asked herself—what would she do to have that again?

Chapter Ten

Taking the next step toward her new life, Victoria checked out the interior design degree offered at the institute Douglas recommended. She'd laid in bed a long time after she'd gotten off the phone with Carmen last night, thinking about what they'd talked about. She couldn't go into the designing idea halfheartedly. If she was going to do it, she had to be prepared to succeed. The institute had a campus right in Burbank, so she wouldn't have to fight LA traffic or move out of town to attend. That was a plus.

She asked to speak to a counselor, but the size of the university allowed them to be much less formal than a major university that specialized in everything from plant reproduction to granting medical degrees. Instead, she was introduced to a facilitator, who walked her through the curriculum that the university offered for Interior Architecture. Fancy name for a designer. They had courses like color, lighting, fabrics and textiles, presentation boards. She had to be honest with herself. It all sounded interesting and exciting.

"You'd be coming in as a transfer student," the woman told her.

"Yes. I've completed all my general division classes."

"Wonderful. Then you can jump right into the design courses." She stood. "Let me walk you around campus."

Victoria followed her as she pointed out the various modern buildings and showed off the green grounds. That was all nice, but Victoria had little interest in university life. "I don't want to spend years completing this degree. To be honest, I'm not sure I want to put in a bunch of time to do something that I already do without a degree."

"We have an accelerated program," she said, "created for working adults like yourself, and we even offer weekend classes. There are those, Victoria, who present themselves as designers when they have no training. But if you're thinking of making interior design a career—a profession—you owe it to yourself to invest in the proper education. Our graduates are competent design experts who have been hired by top firms and won prestigious awards. You couldn't do better for your future than to post a degree from our university on your office wall."

Victoria nodded, still not sure she wanted to invest the time. She completed her tour and left the university with a folder full of forms and brochures. As she drove down Glen Oaks Boulevard, she had to fight the desire to go straight to La Parrilla and give up all these insane ideas. Working in the back office of the restaurant, unnoticed and with minimal responsibility, held an appeal that was hard to explain to people like that facilitator, who probably spent most of her day talking to starry-eyed eighteen-year-olds. Or even Eric, who was never really handed anything and had to work to create his own destiny. Victoria could simply sit back and accept what her father was building and do nothing.

But that was where the problem rested. She had to do nothing, and in return she felt like nothing.

She made a few turns and headed to Eric's property.

She found him in the backyard, covered with sweat. He had a bandana—though it looked more like an old rag—tied around his head and wore long shorts and a sleeveless tee. Involved in a heated discussion with a couple of guys who were standing around the pool, he didn't notice her.

Victoria paused, thinking maybe she should have called his cell first before showing up. There really wasn't anything for her to do here yet. In fact, she was supposed to choose the flooring this week. Then again, she didn't know the measurements of each room, so that might be a good place to start.

He turned his head when the other men watched her walk out to the back porch. "Hey, Victoria," he said with no particular emotion, though his voice maintained its rough edge.

"I, I came to measure the rooms, but... I don't have a tape measure."

He immediately unhooked a tape measure from his belt, took eight long steps toward her and handed her his.

She took it. "Thanks."

"Sure." Then he went back to telling those guys that they either work their sorry, lazy asses off to complete the pool by the end of the week or not come back at all.

Jeesh, she thought, and went back into the house. Eric wanted to install the same flooring in the dining room, living room, and hall. When she'd mentioned hardwood, he'd gotten excited, so wood it was. In the kitchen, she'd install hardy eighteen-inch tile. The three bedrooms would be recarpeted.

Taking the tape measure in hand and dropping her purse in a corner, she got to work. She borrowed a notepad from a guy working on the electrical in the kitchen.

"It's Eric's," he said. "Sure, use it."

She had to get her act together if she was going to do this. The electrician helped her measure the kitchen. She was able to handle the living room and dining room on her own. Then she moved on to the bedrooms.

Eric strolled in while she worked. He crossed his arms and leaned on the wall. "Need help?"

"No, I got it." She took notes. "Bad day?"

"Nah," he said. "Just a tense last half hour."

She walked past him to the other bedroom. "Wanna share?"

"The pool guys I hired were sent home by my dad and replaced by these jerks, who tell me I'm not only going to have to repaint the pool but install a whole new pump."

"Hmm." She measured the room quickly, since it was almost identical to the previous room. "Don't you plan for unexpected things like that?"

He raised an eyebrow. "Yes, I do."

"So you're not upset about the paint and the pump, but about what your dad did."

"I found those guys sitting on their butts drinking beer, and it pissed me off, that's all. They said it was too hot to work, and they were waiting until the sun went down."

"You didn't believe them?"

He laughed. "I don't care. I want them to finish today, if possible. It they don't want to work in the heat, someone else will."

Victoria left and entered the master bedroom with a private bath. She still thought that what really bothered him was his father's interference, but if he didn't want to acknowledge that, she wasn't going to ask again.

He took the end of the tape measure and helped her hold it while she measured the room. They worked in silence. "Thanks," she said, then wrote down the last of her needed numbers. He let his end go, and it snapped back into the roll. "Okay, I'm done."

He smiled. "How was *your* day?"

She shrugged. "I checked out a university that offers interior design degrees. Felt completely incongruous walking around the campus full of young, skinny kids. I'll be the oldest and fattest student in the program, but I'm considering it."

"Now why would those be the only things you noticed about the university?"

"Good question," she said. "I'm insecure?"

He took the tape measure from her hand. "You're not too old to finish your college degree. And you look good. You really do."

"You're too kind."

"I'm not. I'm honest." He held the tape measure under her own nose. "Get your own supplies from now on, and get the floors ordered *mañana*. Okay?"

"And if I don't, I shouldn't come back. Right?"

"Oh no." He grinned. "*You* I want back."

For a second she wondered if there was a hidden meaning in there somewhere, but she ignored his words, wished him a good night, and took off.

Jaqueline turned on her computer. A Christmas gift from Victoria last year, which she'd thought at the time to be an absurdly expensive gift for an old woman. And here it was August and she couldn't imagine what she'd do all day without it.

She pulled up the Google page and stared at it. Then out of curiosity, she typed in *lonely mom*. Everything from lonely women looking for sex to mommies wanting to chat about their babies popped up on the screen. Then she saw a site on empty nesters and wondered if that was what she was. Her children were gone. Well, Victoria still lived at home, but she was never around. And her husband...well, she saw him in bed at night, where they slept side by side like strangers.

She clicked on the Web site. Read some interesting articles and took down notes on books they recommended. Books with titles like *The Next Fifty Years: A Guide for Women at Mid-Life and Beyond* and *Awakening at Midlife*. She ordered them and a couple of others.

Then she read some of the messages in one of the chat rooms and sighed. Speaking to a bunch of strangers struck her as bizarre. Why would she want to share her personal business with a bunch of people she didn't know? Enough people knew about her personal life at the Argentine Club. Besides, she had friends. It wasn't new friends she was looking for, it was . . . a life.

With another sigh, she was about to exit when she got an instant message, saying simply, *hi*.

"What in the world?" She pushed some hair out of her face. The question *male or female?* flashed on the screen. Hesitating, she looked around the living room that she knew to be empty, but she still felt self-conscious about spending time frivolously playing on the computer. She typed *female*.

Kids?

Yes, she wrote.

I mean how old?

They're both adults.

Married?

She blushed. Was this a man she was talking to? Silly as it was, she felt unfaithful. Regardless of the fact that Victor hadn't always been faithful to her, she'd respected him, her children, and herself enough to honor her marriage vows. *Yes,* she wrote.

Happily?

She fumbled with the mouse, ready to turn off the computer. She had no business in a chat room for lonely women. She might not be happy with her husband, but that was no one's business but her own.

I'll take your silence as a no. Me neither. My husband and I hate each other.

Jaqueline paused. Her husband? So this wasn't a man. A ripple of relief washed over her. And she settled further into her chair. *I don't hate my husband,* she started . . . .

Victor spent an entire week at the Santa Monica site going over details. He hired a firm that would be in charge of staffing both restaurants once they opened in about five months. So much to think about.

The woman they assigned to him from the firm took him out for drinks. She was only slightly older than Victoria. Made him feel old when these kids were running the world.

"You're staring," she said.

He shook himself mentally. Then reached for his drink. "Sorry. I was thinking about what I'd give to be young again."

She laughed, feminine and delicate. "You don't look old."

He looked okay for his age. Sort of like Sean Connery and Anthony Hopkins had, he'd aged well. "Too old to be noticing women half my age."

"Once you become a millionaire, women won't care how old you are."

Victor shook his head. That might be the case, but he wasn't interested in fucking a teenager. In his younger days, he'd done his share of fooling around. Jaqueline had even caught him once. She'd stayed with him because the kids were young and she was dependent on him. But she'd probably stopped loving him that day.

If he could take back what he'd done, he would. Prior to his affairs, Jaqueline used to look at him like he was the most intelligent, most amazing man in the world. She hung on his every word. Worshipped him in a way that made him feel unstoppable.

Until he'd blown it. After that, she'd simply tolerated him. As the years went by, she'd learned to like him again. Maybe even respect him for being a good father and provider, but love... it was gone.

Maybe he'd finally find a way to earn it back. "The only woman I really want is my wife back."

"Did she leave you?"

"No. She should have. But she didn't." He ordered another

drink and decided that was as much as he wanted to share about his personal life with this very beautiful young woman. "Now, let's talk about staffing my restaurants."

Standing beside a sparkling, brand-new backyard pool with his father in front of him, Eric ran his fingers through his hair for the tenth time. "All I'm saying is that if you're going to hire anyone to work on my house, you run it by me first."

"I hired professionals. You hired a couple of day laborers."

"No." Eric raised his voice. "I hired a couple of college kids that work at a pool service company. They were cheap and they knew what they were doing. Your guys cost me three times as much and I had to threaten them to get them to do their job."

Antonio shrugged. "They did a great job." He looked at the clear blue pool.

Eric wasn't getting through to him, and he didn't have any more time to discuss it. "Yes, they did. Now, just don't hire anyone else, okay? I've got everything covered."

"What about the wall in that back bedroom? Who's going to replace the drywall in there?"

"Why would I want to replace the drywall?"

"It's rotting or something."

"What?" Eric marched into the house. Like a torpedo, he zeroed in on the problem.

"Right there," Antonio pointed to a discoloration on the wall.

Eric balled his fist and hit the wall a few times. "Son of a bitch." He looked up. "It's moist." Hurrying outside, he propped a ladder against the house and climbed onto the roof. When he got to the top he didn't see a problem with the roof. There was no water getting through there. Besides, there wasn't enough rain in California at this time of year to cause the wall to have permanent moisture. That meant that pipes from the laundry room on the other side of the bedroom must be leaking. Fucking great.

Eric climbed down.

"See, you need to replace that drywall."

"Dad," Eric said. "I've got bigger problems than that." And he went inside to call his electrician. The guy said he had a plumber he worked with who was good and reasonable. Whatever that meant.

After he got that settled, he went back outside. Antonio rested in the sunshine beside the pool. The sight of his old man calmed him down and reminded him that job-related problems were unimportant. He'd get things fixed. Didn't matter. "Relaxing?"

"It's nice out here. So, you want to go out to dinner? Take something back to your mother?"

"No, actually, I need to go home and change. I'm going out with Victoria tonight."

"Oh?"

"With some of our friends from high school."

"Good for you. And Victoria is a nice girl. Your mother really likes her."

Eric grinned and took a seat beside Antonio. "She does, huh?"

"I'm just saying... if you've got interests aside from friendship, your mother would be all for it."

Nodding, he gazed at his old man. "Thanks for the tip."

"No problem."

"I dated this girl once. She was cute, had a kid. I bought a couple of properties in her neighborhood. I thought maybe things were going somewhere. I really liked her son. But... she didn't feel like home."

"When the right woman comes along, you know it. You don't have to force it," Antonio said. "I knew I wanted to marry your mother after only a minute of talking to her."

"You were trying to sell her a vacuum," Eric said, unable to hide his smirk and wondering why any woman would be interested in a corny guy forced to sell vacuums door to door.

"I was trying to sell *her mother* a vacuum, and the second they answered the door and I realized they were Argentine, I knew I had the sale." He stared at the pool and smiled. "Your mother listened to my bullshit sales pitch and references to Argentina and didn't buy any of it, but her mother did. When she went to write me a check, Lucia told me I had a gift and that if I used it well, I would probably be a powerful man one day."

"Was that her way of telling you you should become a politician?" Eric laughed. "Maybe you should have—you always have been better at selling yourself than products."

"I was about to leave thinking, *I don't care what her opinion of me is, I got the sale*. And then she invited me to the Argentine Club so I wouldn't have to feel so melancholic about missing my country, and I knew she had me. She knew I'd used our country as a gimmick to get her mother to feel an affinity to me, and now I was stuck. I had to pretend I was excited about spending time with other Argentines. After I'd practically cried about how much I missed my country, how could I not go?" He chuckled. "Her mother took my address, my phone number, and made sure I showed up at the club. But by then I wanted to go anyway to see that smart, pretty girl who trapped me in my own sales pitch."

"Well, you hit the jackpot with Mom."

"I did. And you will too one day, son."

Eric leaned back in the chair, wove his fingers together, and rested his head in his hand. He wanted to have the kind of marriage his parents had. In all the years growing up with them, he never once heard them raise their voices or fight. They disagreed about things, but they always worked things out.

"You know why I asked Victoria to help me with this house?"

he asked, then continued without waiting for an answer. "I really couldn't give a shit whether she had any skill at decorating or not. It was because when I walked into my old bedroom and saw what she'd done, I had to fight back tears. It was perfect."

"Sometimes I go in there and look at the pictures of you as a boy."

Eric stared at his father, a lump growing in his throat. "I wanted to go knock on her door, wrap my arms around her, and hold her tight. She captured my childhood on one wall. She captured me."

"She's a special girl."

"Yeah. I'm not saying she's it or anything, but I look at her, talk to her, and I feel... at home."

Chapter Eleven

After a hot shower and refreshing shave, Eric got dressed and packed the rest of his clothes into his three suitcases that held almost all his belongings. He looked in the mirror. *Ready as I'll ever be*, he thought. He carried the suitcases out to the living room.

His mother, who was sitting on the couch with a basket of red, green, and gold yarn, noticed immediately. She put her knitting needles down on her lap. "What in the world are you doing?"

"The house is ready enough for me to move into it."

"But... you're fixing it up to sell. Why would you want to live in it?"

Eric sat beside her. "I like to live in the houses I fix up. That way I'm working on it constantly. Taking notes on what works or doesn't work. Making changes."

Jaqueline frowned. "But, nene, it's been so nice having you home."

"I'm not going far, Mami. I'm a short phone call away."

Her gaze locked with his. "I know you're a man and need your privacy, but we've tried to stay out of your way."

Taking one of her hands, strong from work, he held it in his own much larger and much rougher hands. "You've been fantastic," he said. "But let's pretend I never went away. I'd still have my own place by now, right?"

"Maybe, but—"

"No maybes. I would. And since my return has turned into more than just a few days' visit, I don't want to bunk in my childhood room indefinitely. Okay?"

"Not really okay." She pouted with a smile. "But I'm happy that you're staying longer to work. Promise you'll come have dinner with us."

"Not every night, but often."

"Ahi, Eric. You don't make mothering easy."

He laughed.

"Going out with your friends tonight?"

"Yes."

"With Victoria?"

"Yes."

"You like her?"

"Always have."

"I like her."

"I've heard."

She laughed under her breath and leaned across to kiss him. "Maybe you do need your own place. Can't bring girls home to your parents' house, can you?"

"That's not why I need my own place. But in a weird way, I'm glad you understand. Can I leave my radio and computer equipment here for a while?"

"Of course," she said.

He stood. "Thanks for understanding, Mom."

"What are moms for?" she said, somewhat resigned.

He dropped one more kiss on her cheek and headed out. That hadn't been as difficult as he'd anticipated. Strange, but his mother seemed to be handling things better than his father.

Victoria took care to dress well for the dinner cruise Eric had booked. The weight she'd lost made her clothes fit better. A pretty summer chiffon dress she bought last summer, because it flared out over her hips without clinging to them, was now loose around her back and chest. She was looking forward to seeing some of her friends from high school as much as he was. Everyone had gone away to college or gotten jobs and were busy building careers. And though she'd gotten together with some of them the first few years after school was over, eventually she'd let those friendships dissolve.

Eric suggested picking her up at her house and driving to Newport Beach together. Her first reaction had been that she could drive herself. They weren't going as a couple, and she didn't want him or anyone else to get that idea. But when she told him she'd rather meet him there, he insisted that it was dumb to take two vehicles.

"I'll pick you up," he said.

He came to the door dressed in light tan Dockers and a tropical button-up shirt, looking carefree and happy. He chatted with her parents. Jaqueline was wonderful to him, as always. But her father, who was still not speaking to her, grunted and hid behind an Argentine newspaper.

Eric tried to engage him in conversation a couple of times, and finally Victor put the paper down on his lap. "You came to pick up my daughter. It looks like she's ready."

Eric glanced over his shoulder to where Victoria stood, taking items from her purse and placing them in her evening bag. Victoria wanted to apologize for her father's behavior, but instead she said, "Yes, I'm ready."

Jaqueline sat across from Victor. "You didn't have to be so rude."

"Is she dating him?"

"I'm not sure. She's working with him on that house he

bought, which seems crazy to me. Why don't you talk to her? Why isn't she helping out at the restaurant anymore?"

He shrugged. "She doesn't want to."

"What do you mean, she doesn't want to?"

"How is she helping Eric?" he asked.

"She said she's helping him design the inside. Then she's going to decorate it when he's finished so he can sell it. I can't believe you're going to stand by and let her do that."

Victor sighed. "She's a grown woman. What am I supposed to do?"

"What if...? Lucia wants them to get together."

Victor snorted. "That's her business, I guess."

Jaqueline didn't understand him. Usually he criticized every man Victoria dated. Questioned her. Drove her crazy until Victoria got tired and ended the relationship. "He's too unpredictable. He'll break her heart," she said to herself.

Victor watched her from behind his newspaper, even if he pretended not to. "Hmm," he said.

"Whatever she did, you have to forgive her, Victor."

"She didn't do anything. And I have forgiven her. That's why I'm staying out of her way. Let her do whatever she has to do." He lowered the newspaper. "Work where she wants. Date who she wants. Fall or stand on her own two feet. That's what she said she wanted."

Jaqueline knew that couldn't be easy for Victor. She drew a breath. "She said that?"

"Yes."

Took her long enough to stand up to her father, Jaqueline thought. "She's just like you, Victor." Dying to be set free. To challenge the world. Her love for Victor was the only thing that had kept her in check. Jaqueline wondered what she'd do now that he was no longer setting limits.

"Yeah, just like me," he grumbled. "That's what I'm afraid of."

* * *

"Is he pissed at me?" Eric asked, as they got on the road.

"I don't know. He's still mad at me. Probably has nothing to do with you."

"It's because I didn't help him out with the property location. Or maybe because he doesn't want me dating you."

"You're not."

He smiled. "I'm not?"

"This isn't a date."

"It can be. Our first."

He was supposed to be a family friend, that was all. Besides, she told herself, Eric wouldn't seriously be interested in her in a romantic way. "It's not nice to tease a homely fat girl."

He laughed a deep, very real laugh. "You're adorable and I have no problems with your body. Want me to prove it?"

"Well *I* have lots of problems with my body. And I'm kind of shy around men—so don't say things like that."

"Shy? Are you kidding?" He smiled and looked away from traffic a couple of times.

"Not really. I mean I date occasionally, of course. But I'm not what you'd call very confident about men looking at or touching my body. I can't even believe I'm admitting this to you."

He drove, a few shadows fell on his angular face, as the sun began to set. "Vicki, you've gotta accept yourself better. Your dreams, your body. It's who you are."

She considered that. Easy to say. "I'm trying. Now tell me how the house is doing."

He didn't push the body image issue. Instead, he told her that the pool had been refinished and the motor replaced, and it was now filled with water. The plumber had found corroded, leaking pipes leading from the laundry room out to the sewer, and that had been a huge expense Eric hadn't expected. She told him that she had ordered the flooring and the cabinets for the kitchen and the bathroom. Four weeks into the project and everything was going according to his schedule, but it was way over budget, he said.

"So, will you leave when it's finished and sold?"

He kept his eyes on the road. "Probably."

"Hmm." Not what she wanted to hear. "Have you told your mom?"

"We don't talk about that. But I'm moving into the flip as of tonight. She couldn't understand why I'd want to live in an empty house instead of 'at home'. I want her to understand that *her* home is not *my* home anymore."

"It'll always be your home, Eric." Victoria shifted in her seat and looked out the window. *You can't ever really escape your roots*, she thought. *They're there, a part of you forever.*

They got to the pier, and gradually everyone started to arrive. The sky had now grown a dark blue-gray with a hint of light on the horizon. The night promised to be warm, clear, and beautiful. As they sailed out into the harbor, Victoria spent the first couple of hours so engrossed in everyone's life and catching up that she barely noticed the time go by. The crew provided a buffet-style dinner with amazing seafood and vegetables. Everyone filled up their plates and walked around, chatting in small groups.

Her friends all seemed to have found great guys to marry and had pictures of children to share and great jobs to complain about. In her mind, everyone had a better life than she had. She decided she wasn't going to go to her ten-year reunion in the fall. It would be more of the same. *What do you do? I'm a dentist. I'm a teacher. I'm the manager of some great company. And what about you, Victoria? Well, I'm still trying to figure out what I'm going to do when I grow up*. Pathetic.

She went out on the small deck and enjoyed the spray of the salt air on her face.

Eric followed her out. Well, maybe not followed her, but he came out about ten minutes later. He placed an arm around her and leaned in close. "Hi."

"You're still acting like we're out on a date."

"You're still acting like we're not."

She chuckled and shook her head. "Come on, Eric. You're my friend. And soon you'll be gone again, so I don't want to start something."

He frowned and seemed to consider this. "What if I don't go?"

She raised an eyebrow. "You'd stay in LA?"

"If I can make money doing what I do. And if I can't, maybe you can come away with me. We'd make a pretty good team."

She laughed. "Sure."

He reached across and touched her hair. "I like watching you laugh. You're beautiful."

She arched an eyebrow.

"And I'm attracted to you." His fingers slipped into her hair and combed down. When she continued to stare, too surprised to respond, he chuckled. "To be completely honest," he added.

"Oh." *Stupid, stupid, say something else.* "I don't think I've ever met a guy as *honest* as you."

His deep, sexy chuckle continued. "Direct, you mean? Sorry. I'm curious what could happen if we got to know each other better, and I don't believe in wasting time playing games."

She angled her body and faced him, liking the feel of his fingers in her hair, the touch of his gaze on her face. "You know me pretty well." Was he *really* attracted to her? Not that she was ugly, and some guys liked bigger girls, so it wasn't the attraction that surprised her. It was that it was Eric saying this.

"I knew you as a kid. I'd like to get to know the woman."

That had so many meanings attached to it that she wasn't going to touch it. "I haven't changed all that much. That's the problem. I'm still the same, and I'm tired of being me."

"Don't be. I'm glad you haven't changed." His stare appeared to fall to her lips.

Eduardo from the Argentine Club and his wife, Kelly, decided they could make the cruise after all and chose that moment to come outside.

"Great night to be out on the water," Eduardo called, as they walked toward them. "Eric, you sure know how to do things right."

Eric maintained eye contact with Victoria, then finally looked away. He and Eduardo started chatting and Victoria listened to Kelly talk about how little Eddy, who was three, spelled five words with magnetic letters on her refrigerator.

On the drive home, Victoria and Eric didn't have much to say to each other. After discussing all the changes in their friends, they grew quiet. But it wasn't an uncomfortable silence. She sort of enjoyed driving through the freeway and city streets peacefully.

He pulled up in front of her house. Then he touched her shoulder and leaned closer.

"Eric," she said.

But he softly brushed his lips against hers before she could say more. He took his time, kissing little sections of her lips. Tingles of awareness spread quickly, warming her skin and making every cell feel alive. Then he slanted his head and deepened the kiss. The hand on her shoulder moved sensually up the front of her neck and slipped behind to cradle her head. Victoria had a delayed reaction, but the moment was so sweet that she began kissing him back, inhaling the intoxicating scent of salt air and masculine cologne on his skin. Marveling at the feel of his tongue in her mouth, even though she knew deep inside that this shouldn't be happening.

Though her blood was simmering and she didn't want the kiss to end, he eased back. "I was right. That was nice," he said.

Victoria stared at him, feeling the frown between her eyebrows. What was he doing? And why was he doing it? Why her? "I better get inside." She walked into the house with the unanswered questions still in her head while at the same time thinking, yes, that *was* nice.

The next evening at the Argentine Club they had a guest speaker—an artist who lived in some of the worst slums of Buenos Aires just so he could do what he loved—paint—until one day he was "discovered" and invited to show some of his work at a prestigious gallery on *Calle 9 de Julio*. Now he sold his paintings for thousands of dollars. One of the rooms in the club was set up to display his work—all along the walls and on large easels.

After the inspirational talk, Victoria strolled through the exhibit room, curious about the paintings.

"What do you think?"

Victoria glanced over her shoulder and found Eric staring at her. "When did you get here?"

"About halfway through his talk." He moved up and stood beside her.

Victoria stepped away, moving from painting to painting. "Wouldn't it be something to be this talented?"

Eric made a derisive sound. "Sure, I guess."

"You don't like his work?"

"I don't get art. What makes this better than something else?"

"The artist's style. The color he uses. The distinctive way he looks at the world."

Eric raised an eyebrow. "I didn't know you knew anything about art."

"I don't."

He stepped closer to her again. "Sounds like you do."

No, she simply appreciated people who were brave enough to believe in themselves and live their dreams. There was something to be said for people who didn't play it safe, who didn't wake up every day to a boring, predictable life. Like she had for so long. She gazed at Eric, grateful that he'd come home, grateful that her father had decided to do what he'd come to America to do so many years ago, grateful that she was finally asking herself what she wanted from life.

"I'm sorry for that kiss the other night. I—"

"Why *did* you kiss me?"

He held his arms out apologetically. "Why does any guy kiss a woman?"

"I'm not just any woman. Our parents have been friends forever. If something went wrong between us, we'd end up seeing each other for the rest of our lives, having to pretend that nothing happened."

He smiled. "What could go wrong?"

She gave him a look that made him nod and drop the smile. "I hear you." He took one of her hands. "And you're right, you're not just any woman. I know that. You're someone I have a history with. You know me. And I think I need that in my life right now."

Victoria closed her fingers around his. Their bond tight. "I'm willing to be in your life. We're friends."

"Vicki, I—"

But his words were cut off by Jaqueline, shouting in the next room.

Alarmed, Victoria spun around and ran out of the exhibit room. Eric was right behind her. She stopped short when she noticed her mother and father having a full-blown fight in the small room where they stored the card tables.

Victoria stared in stunned surprise. Jaqueline was a private person, and even in the club where everyone seemed to know everyone else's business, she tried extra hard to be reserved. So, to see her have a public fight with her father concerned her more than if they had been home.

Jaqueline noticed her. "And *you!*" She pointed a finger at her. "You knew what he was doing with the restaurant and you didn't tell me."

Victoria gazed at her father, understanding exactly what was going on and wishing he'd been up front with Jaqueline from day one.

"She just found out not too long ago herself," Victor said. "Leave her out of this."

Jaqueline glared at Victoria. "You're supposed to be my daughter. You're supposed to stand by me and protect me the way I always protected you!"

Victoria blinked, closing her eyes momentarily, and shook her head. Then she said, "Mom, I'm sorry."

"This one"—she pointed at her father—"risks our entire life savings on his crazy dream, and now you... you're just like him."

"Mom, calm down."

"Calm down! I've been calm for thirty-five years, and what has it gotten me? Not even the security of my home. I'm going to be in a worse place than when I came to this country. At least back then I had my youth."

"I'm not going to lose anything," Victor said. "I keep telling you."

"You are a lying, scheming, betraying bastard, and I want you gone."

"Mom!" Victoria said, starting to get a sick feeling in the pit of her stomach. "What are you saying?"

"Vieja," Victor begged.

"Out, Victor. I don't want to see you ever again."

Victoria touched her mother's shoulder. "Stop it, Mom. He's not going anywhere. Have you lost your mind?"

"Victoria," her father shouted. "Apologize to your mother this instant."

"But—"

"Apologize."

"Don't bother. I'm going home," Jaqueline said. She stormed past them and the group that had gathered at the door.

Victoria started to follow after her, but Eric grabbed her arm.

"Let me go," she said.

"Maybe you should let *her* go."

"I'm going home to be with her."

Victor stood rooted in place, looking down, his fists clenched.

"Let's go for a ride," Eric said, and tugged her gently toward the door.

Victoria pulled her arm loose. "I'm going home." And she turned to Victor. "I suggest you do the same." And she hurried out.

When Victoria got home, Jaqueline was curled up on the couch. She'd been crying but had wiped the tears away, and now she sat and somberly stared out the sliding glass door.

"I found out on July ninth, but he wanted to surprise you and asked me not to say anything. He thought you'd freak if you knew, and he was right."

"Shut up, Victoria. I don't want to talk to you right now."

Taking a step closer, she stared sadly at her mother. "I was just as surprised as you about all this. Just as angry. Just as worried. But... Mom, maybe we have to see that he needs to do this."

"What about what *I* need? Does anyone in this house ever think about what *I* need?"

Victoria swallowed her tears. She had thought about how her father's plans would affect her, yes. And she had been worried about what would happen if he failed. But her mother was asking about more than this one instance. "Probably not enough."

"You have no idea what it's like to be me. To love your husband and your children so much and watch everyone go on with their lives. To be nothing more than the next meal or a closet of clean laundry."

"Oh, Mom," she said, and took a seat beside her. "You know you're everything to us. And I don't want you to worry. I won't let you lose this house. I'll make sure you have the money to keep it."

"It's not just that. I can't be this pitiful person anymore, Victoria." She shook her head. "Living my life around the rest of you. Depending on you all to feel fulfilled."

Victoria gazed into her mother's bright eyes full of tears.

"Carmen called and told me she's not coming home this summer at all. Not even for a week or two."

"I didn't know," Victoria said immediately so she wouldn't be blamed for yet another thing.

Jaqueline almost smiled. "I know. She told me you had nothing to do with her decision, but that she wanted to spend more time researching her courses for next quarter." Jaqueline grew quiet for a moment. "She's doing wonderful. And you. You should go back and help your father with the business. It's going to be yours, Victoria, and you should do what you can to learn it and make it successful. Don't ever rely on a man. Understand me?"

Victoria nodded.

"I think I'm going to go to Argentina," Jaqueline said.

Victoria's heart skipped a beat.

"I need to see my family. I need to remember who I was before I gave up my life to be Victor's wife."

"For how long? I mean, you can't go alone. Mami, you—"

"It's my country. Of course I can go alone." She reached across and placed her hand on the side of Victoria's face. "I'm sorry I yelled at you."

"It's okay, Mami." She reached forward and drew her mother in for a hug. She held her close.

Victor walked in. They pulled back from each other and gazed at him. Without a word he walked to the bedroom.

Victor packed his suitcase in the quiet buzz of the bedroom. He couldn't believe he was leaving his home. She had no right to throw him out of his own place. He'd worked hard all his life to pay for this home. And now he was risking it all for them. To give Jaqueline something even better and grander and to make their lives what they'd always dreamed. He tossed a dozen or so pairs of underwear into his suitcase. Well, maybe what *he'd* always dreamed. Jaqueline claimed to never have wanted any of it. His heart clenched when he remembered her exact words. *All I wanted was you.*

His arms fell to his sides and his throat constricted. What the hell was he trying to prove to himself?

Victoria stepped into his bedroom and zeroed in on his suitcase. "Where are you going?" she asked.

"I don't know," he said, reaching for a pair of pants so she wouldn't see the pain in his eyes. "But I have to leave for a while."

"How is that going to help? Do you know that she says she's going to go to Argentina?"

He snapped his attention away from packing. "What?"

"You should have done this differently. You should have spoken to her."

"She wouldn't have agreed. It's a risk, and she doesn't deal well with risks. But it will pay off for all of us. We'll never have to worry about money again." He prayed he was right. That all this was for something.

"Dad, we don't worry about money now—"

"You don't, but I do."

"I could have helped out. You guys just never let me—"

"No!" Victor shouted. He loved his daughter, but how could she possibly understand that a man didn't want his children taking care of him? "This will all work out, and you will never have to work again in your life."

"But I *want* to work. That's what you don't seem to get. I want to be a productive member of this family. You treat me like I'm incapable of contributing anything."

Victor didn't want to listen to any of this now. He'd already decided his daughter was a grown woman and she could do what she wanted. Except think she was ever going to give him a dime. "We've already established that you're free to do what you like, haven't we? Now go do it."

His daughter's stubborn chin lifted, and he knew he was going to have another fight on his hands. She could be so much like her mother sometimes.

"That's right, Victoria. Go lead your own life. That's what you want, go do it."

"You think I can't, don't you? You're waiting for me to fail. To come crawling back so you can say I told you so."

That wasn't at all what he wanted. He might not understand

his wife much, but he understood the desire Victoria felt to have something of her own. So he decided to give her the extra push out the door. "You want to show me you're so goddamn independent? You think it's easy to go out there and make something of yourself on your own? Then maybe you should be packing your bags, too. When I left Argentina, sweetheart, I left. No one held my hand."

Tears filled Victoria's large expressive eyes, but she nodded. "Fine."

"Fine," he said, and turned back to his packing. Then, as an afterthought, he remembered Jaqueline. If he was leaving, and Victoria was leaving, who the hell was going to take care of Jaqueline? "Wait," he said, before Victoria could walk out of the bedroom. "Your mother. You can't leave yet."

"You're the one who's married to her and the one who needs to stay," she said in a voice that sounded tired and sad and that almost did him in.

"But she threw me out."

"Then sleep in the garage. It's your job to take care of this family, remember?" she said with a hint of sarcasm.

He thought about this for a second. "You're right. The garage. Good idea."

She wiped her tears and turned away.

"Victoria," he said, unable to let her go through with this. "Damn it, you can pursue your dreams without leaving home. I... didn't mean that."

"It's okay," she said softly. "I'll start looking for a place tomorrow."

His jaw tightened. This was never what he wanted. Hell, he wanted to make things better, and instead his life was falling apart.

Victoria left him alone in the room he'd shared with his wife since before she was born. How had things gone so wrong? How had he managed to mess up so badly? And he wasn't thinking of just what he'd decided to do with the restaurant. No, it was the first time Jaqueline had needed him and he'd been too busy. It was the first time he'd felt justified in finding comfort in the bed of another woman because his wife was too tired taking care of little girls to satisfy him. Truth was, even in Argentina, he knew he didn't deserve a girl like Jaqueline. Hell, she'd always been too good for him. And here they were years later, and he'd let her down over and over again.

He pulled his suitcase off the bed and headed to the garage.

Chapter Twelve

Victoria spent half of the next day choosing lighting for Eric's house. He gave her a budget that was pretty tight, and after flooring, cabinets, and appliances she had little left to splurge on fancy lights. But she drove to the city of Ontario, where she'd located a warehouse that sold most of their discontinued items direct to the public. She was able to purchase a ceiling fan and a great chandelier for the dining room, as well as couple of nice lamps. She would have to pay retail for the rest of the items, like the canned lighting and the bathroom lights, but she was sure she had enough to cover that now.

She took her finds to Eric's place and stored them in his garage, which now had a new roof and a new door. Then she went into the house to look for him. His car sat in the driveway, but she didn't see him in the house. In fact, no one was working, which was bizarre, since he kept everyone jumping and on target.

She called him and got no response. Frowning, she peeked out of the sliding glass door and made a mental note to ask him if he wanted to replace it with a French door. It would look much nicer. She noticed him swimming laps in the pool.

Stepping outside, she called, "Must be nice."

He lifted his head and swam to the edge of the pool. "Hey! Didn't know you were stopping by today." The water began to settle, winking at her here and there as the sun touched it. His dark hair was slicked back. He wiped away drops from his smiling face.

"I purchased most of our lighting and wanted to drop it off. Where is everyone?"

"Roofers finished work in the garage this morning. I didn't schedule anyone else today. Wanna join me?"

"In the pool? Ah, no."

"Come on," he coaxed with a huge, inviting grin.

"I didn't bring a swimsuit. I'm working."

He angled his head and offered a wicked sneer. "You don't need a swimsuit."

Victoria smiled and joked. "What kind of girl do you think I am?"

"I think you're a sexy woman, not a girl at all. But I wasn't suggesting what you think. You can borrow a pair of my shorts, and use your bra. Instant swimsuit."

"I hate to admit this, but I don't think I can fit into your shorts. Besides, I'm going to spend the rest of the afternoon going through the paper to look for a place to live. I'm moving out of my parents' place."

He pulled himself out of the pool with strong, tanned arms that were kept in shape by hard work, not by a gym. He took a seat on one of the fold-up aluminum chairs with plastic straps that he'd placed on the deck. "Sit down."

She did.

"What happened? How's your mom?"

"Pissed. I've never seen her this upset. She's serious about my dad moving out."

"I'm sorry."

Victoria's heart ticked a little louder. He was so easy to talk to. "My dad asked me to move out, too."

"What? Why?"

"He was angry; he didn't mean it. But I decided it's time. My only concern is leaving my mom alone."

He nodded. "What are you going to do?"

"My dad is going to move into the garage. And I'm going to check in on her every day for a while." She drew a breath. "God, Eric, I'm worried about them both."

He placed a hand on Victoria's shoulder. His skin was almost dry, it was so hot outside. But his hair was still wet, and he looked gorgeous. "Everything will work out."

"I hope you're right."

"Now, about that swim." He offered a smile.

She shook her head. "I told you, I've got to look for an apartment."

"You can do that tomorrow. Come on."

Victoria gazed into his eyes and thought, *Why the hell not?* She nodded and followed him inside, where he offered her a pair of his swimming trunks.

"I'll take a T-shirt, too. I'm not going in there with a bra."

"Why not?"

She raised an eyebrow. "Because I'm not."

He grumbled but offered her a sleeveless white T-shirt that he'd probably be able to see right through.

"You're kidding."

He chuckled and headed for the door. "I'll wait in the pool."

She put on the shorts and the T-shirt over her bra, then met him outside. She climbed into the cold water, shivering slightly at the temperature difference. He swam over and watched the water soak into the T-shirt.

"You kept your bra on."

"Of course. What did you expect?"

He smiled at her question. And she had to smile, too.

"Sure you don't want to pull the T-shirt off, then? It'll be easier to swim."

"I'm fine. Race you to the other side."

"Okay." He splashed her and performed a perfect backstroke. Effortlessly, he made it to the opposite end of the pool. They swam up and down the length of the pool about a dozen times. He paused, stood up, and leaned back against the edge of the pool. "So Victoria, I'd really like you to take one of the rooms in this house. Seems kind of foolish for you to go rent an apartment when I've got this big empty house available."

Victoria tried to control her breath as she stopped beside him. Would she ever get in shape? She hadn't had any sugar for over a month, and she'd cut all her portion sizes. For all her effort, she'd lost very little weight—maybe ten pounds. "Thanks, but I'll need to get an apartment eventually, anyway."

"So take your time looking for one, and in the meantime move in here. We're about a month away from completion. Then we've got to sell it, and that's when I'm really going to need your help with staging. You might as well move in."

She turned around in the pool and rested her arms on the edge. She lay the side of her face on her arms as she watched him. He was beyond sexy. "Why didn't you ever get married, Eric?"

A corner of his lips hitched up. "Never met the right girl."

"How many have you lived with?"

"Zero."

She continued to look at him, blinking away drops of water that fell on her lashes. They shared a special relationship. One that never got a chance to blossom past friendship. And she wondered if maybe life...fate...was giving them a new opportunity. "Come here," she said.

He leaned closer.

"Be honest. Are you asking me to *live* live with you? Or are you offering me a room?"

"I'm offering you a room, no strings attached. But...I'm totally and completely interested in you as a woman, Victoria."

She hadn't forgotten his words about being attracted to her. Or the kiss. Yes, she believed that he was interested. Without thinking, she leaned in closer. His breath seemed to catch and his gazed dropped to her mouth before he gently, hesitantly, touched his lips to hers. The kiss remained sweet and exploratory, ending much too quickly as he pulled back with a smile.

"We shouldn't do this, you know," she whispered.

He shrugged. "If you're taking about sharing the house, it's no big deal. If you mean the kiss, it feels right. Being home feels right." He ran a hand down her back to her waist. "You feel right."

"I'm not sure if it feels right to me. But I'm in the mood to do a few things that don't feel exactly right."

He chuckled. "It's settled, then. Move in." He eased back, swam away, got out of the pool, and disappeared. He returned with a couple of towels.

She followed him out, took a towel, and dried off.

He brushed her wet hair back with his fingers. "Offering you a room is just because you're a friend, Vicki, and it's business. Nothing more, I promise. "

"Got it. You're not doing it to have sex with me. You're just being nice."

His fingers froze, and his voice seemed lodged in his throat as he cleared it. "Ah, I'm not saying that, either."

She laughed, enjoying the fact that she felt comfortable enough with him to loosen up and be flirtatious.

He caressed the side of her face as he slowly pulled his hand back from her hair. "Victoria," he said.

"Eric."

"What you said at the club last night about our parents being friends, and all that. I want you to know... I understand what you meant." He touched her lips with his thumb. "But maybe their friendship shouldn't have anything to do with you and me."

She eased her head back from his touch, because it was distracting. "It's not just them. Lately, there's so much going on in my life. I feel like I'm just getting to know who I really am."

He dropped a kiss on her forehead. "You want me to back off?"

"Maybe not completely."

He smiled. "Okay. Good. I'll take your lead, then."

She gazed into his eyes and they were warm. With him she felt comfortable. He seemed to understand her like no one else. What a wonderful, unexpected thing to feel understood and accepted. She pulled his head down and kissed him with all her heart.

Victoria got up early the next morning and went for a two-mile walk. When she got back home, she took a shower and began packing.

Jaqueline walked in with a plate of fresh fruit and placed it on Victoria's two-person table, which she used as everything from desk to craft table to dinner table when she didn't want to intrude on her parents' alone time. Not that either of them ever cared to share a romantic dinner alone, but Victoria wanted to give them the opportunity if they wanted it.

"Thanks, Mami," Victoria said. "That looks wonderful."

Jaqueline sighed and took a seat at the table. "I don't understand why you have to live with Eric in that broken-up house. Victoria, we didn't raise you to live with a man. It's not right."

"Mami, we're working together. It's just easier if we're both there."

"It's just as easy if you drive there in the morning."

Victoria got up off the floor, where she was folding clothes and deciding which she wanted to put in her suitcase. She sat across from Jaqueline. "I'll get my own place soon."

"But why do you have to do that? *This* is your house. If your father doesn't manage to lose it, it will be yours and Carmen's."

Victoria placed a hand over her mother's. "Dad won't lose the house. I won't let that happen. That's why I plan to work with Eric and save money. If the bank takes this house, I plan to buy it right back. It's *your* house."

Jaqueline shook her head. "It doesn't feel like my home anymore with you girls grown. Especially if you move out. And with Victor gone."

"He's in the garage. You can ask him to move back in anytime." The detached garage sat at the end of the driveway.

"I'm not going to do that. In fact, I want him gone farther than the garage."

"No, you don't."

She stood. "If you're determined to leave, I guess I can't stop you. But you're making a mistake, Victoria."

She probably was, but she didn't care. She was excited and looking forward to the future. When had she ever felt that?

"You can leave whatever you want until you get your own place," Jaqueline said. "You don't have to take all your things now."

"Thanks." Victoria's stomach grew queasy, and not just because she was always hungry.

Jaqueline left, and Victoria felt alone in her big bedroom. This was home. This was safety. She knew it was normal to feel trepidation when facing an unknown future. Everyone who left home probably felt exactly the same way. But the knowledge that she wasn't the only one to ever go through this type of anxiety didn't make her feel any better. She pushed aside her fears and continued to pack her suitcase.

Beside her closet, she had a plastic trash bag for all the clothes she never wanted to wear again—sizes 18 and even 20. She'd worn them for a while one particularly horrible year when she couldn't seem to stop stuffing things into her mouth. That had been when she dropped out of college and had to tell her father she couldn't handle all those classes on statistics and business writing. She'd pick up venti mocha cappuccinos and extra large muffins on the way to class. Ate king-size Butterfingers between classes, then doughnuts and more coffee before heading to the restaurants in the evenings. Then her mother would offer her a huge steak before she started work, and she'd accept it and eat a baked potato loaded with butter and sour cream. Every night.

Ugh. She tossed the clothes in the plastic bag and vowed never to fit into those again. Even her current size 16 she planned to discard as soon as possible. She loved food, but life was too short to hate the way you looked every time you looked in the mirror. And lately, she didn't feel so much like stuffing herself with things that were bad for her. Especially when she was around Eric, who looked so healthy and vibrant. Because he knew what he wanted and went for it, she decided. That's what she wanted for herself.

A couple of hours later, she had two suitcases packed with clothes, shoes, belts, and other accessories. One bag full of makeup, brushes and combs, her blow-dryer, hair straightener, curler, lotions, creams, deodorants, toothbrushes, and birth control pills. She'd been taking those since she'd turned eighteen, and at times she asked herself why she bothered. Her face warmed now as she wondered if she would need them soon enough.

Eric made it pretty clear that he was offering her a room as he might offer a business partner a spare office. Was he interested in sleeping with her? She'd have to say yes. And she'd lie if she said she wasn't just as interested. Sex had always been a complex thing for her. The female part of her craved the touch of a man. But then came the overthinking. Not wanting to undress unless it was completely dark, not wanting a man to run his hands up and down her body and feel all the flab. When you were overweight and hated your body, that kind of intimacy held a painful amount of anxiety.

But with Eric, that wasn't the reason she might hesitate entering into a sexual relationship. She looked better today than she had in years. No, it was more that their families had been friends and would probably continue to be friends forever. Would sex mess things up if they didn't get emotionally involved? Probably, Victoria reluctantly admitted to herself.

She dragged her bags to the living room. Then she went in search of her mother and found her in her bedroom, surrounded by boxes and boxes of stuff. "What in the world are you doing?"

"I'm doing some packing and cleaning up, too. Maybe it's time for all of us to leave."

Victoria opened her mouth to respond, but didn't know what to say. Leave? This was where both her parents belonged. "What are you packing?"

"Things I plan to give away and things I'd like to keep."

She walked in. "Like?"

Jaqueline had piles of old clothes. Cardboard boxes full of pictures; other pictures sat in albums. Plastic bins full of crafts and trinkets she and Carmen had made through the years. Victoria picked up a picture frame she'd made out of popsicle sticks and soft drying clay back in third grade. A picture of herself smiling with overgrown front teeth stared back at her.

"Would you like some of those?" Jaqueline asked.

"No."

"Would it hurt your feelings if I chose just the most special to keep?"

"Of course not." Victoria found a spot on the bed to sit. She picked up old cameras. "I remember when you used to use these huge things."

Jaqueline nodded. "That's when it took skill to take a good picture. Not like now that everyone uses those digital things with automatic settings."

Victoria put the camera down and peeked into a box of pictures. "Wow, Mom, I never saw any of these." There were tons of pictures of Jaqueline with Victor when they were young. They wore heavy coats and hats, and the scenic backgrounds of mountains and ice made it look as if they were in Antarctica.

"Most of those we took when we went to Bariloche for our high school graduation trip. Back then, as soon as you started high school your parents started to make monthly payments to a travel agency. By the end of the fifth year, they had paid for a one-week trip to the Patagonia. Your father met me there, since he wasn't at the same school as I was. My parents never knew that he'd done that." Jaqueline blushed.

Victoria smiled. "You had a whole week alone in an exotic, isolated Patagonian town?" She raised an eyebrow. "What did you do?"

Jaqueline's fair skin turned even more red, and she looked away. "Nothing. Explored."

"Each other?"

Now Jaqueline looked directly at Victoria and frowned. "Victoria!"

"Sorry." She looked back at the pictures. "These look like postcards, Mom."

"Mmm," she said, and stacked old books in boxes.

"Did you take all these?"

"All the ones I'm not in, yes."

"They're great."

"Thanks." She got a faraway look in her eyes. "I loved to take pictures. I used to imagine that I would sell some to a magazine like *National Geographic.* We didn't have Internet back in the mid-seventies when I took those, and the magazine was available at the newsstands, but it was so expensive. I would buy one every few months and wonder how those photographers managed to get their pictures in there."

Victoria gazed at her mother. "Really?" she said gently. "Why didn't you pursue photography once you moved to America?"

Jaqueline shrugged and brushed aside the idea with a huff. "Who had time to do that? I had to take care of you girls and help your father at the restaurant. I didn't have time to play like when I was a teenager in Argentina."

"But you could have made money selling your photos."

"Victoria, don't be silly."

That was her answer to everything. It annoyed her. "Mom, dreams aren't silly."

"It wasn't my dream. It was just for fun."

Fine. She stood. "Save some of those pictures for me."

"Some day, when I have time, I'll have to organize them."

"Good idea." She bent down and kissed her mother. "I've gotta go. Love you."

Jaqueline looked at her like she was moving to another continent. "Good-bye."

"I'll see you soon. Okay?" Victoria ignored the guilt that she told herself she shouldn't feel. She was twenty-eight, for goodness sake. Most American kids left home the second they hit eighteen. She had to go. It was now or never.

Jaqueline watched Victoria leave and didn't move until she heard the front door close. Then she let out the gush of air she'd been holding in her lungs to keep from calling her back. Her last child was gone, and she felt the last bit of life drain from the house. How could she stay here alone? Tears clouded her vision. She reached for a pillow and let out a shaky sob that had been building for hours. She cried into the soft feathers covered by warm cotton. Hot tears flowed from her eyes, and grief and fear from her soul. Her whole life, everything she worked for and lived for, was gone. It all came down to this. Boxes full of pictures and an empty house. Once she released much of the pain she'd been holding in check, she felt better. Drained, but better. She straightened, setting the pillow aside. "Estupida," she scolded herself.

She wiped her eyes, glad she had nowhere to go today. No one to see. She reached across to the box of pictures Victoria took so much interest in. One day when she had time, she would organize them, she'd told her. An ironic laugh escaped her lips. Time was all she had these days. She decided to put the rest of these pictures into albums. Then she'd offer some to Victoria, some to Carmen, and some to Victor. The rest she'd keep for herself.

She stared at a picture she took of a group of penguins. She and Victor had enjoyed Bariloche so much that a couple of years later, she'd traveled back to the Patagonia to Peninsula Vales. She'd photographed penguins and glaciers and places most people would never see because of its remoteness. Gorgeous sceneries. Her country had magnificent sites that nature had sculpted and humans had not had a chance to destroy. And Victor had wanted to leave all that behind. Granted that even in Argentina, they had lived in a city where they weren't lucky enough to enjoy the stark beauty of the south very often. But they would have been so much closer. They would have been home.

Jaqueline let the photograph drop back into the box. This was getting her nowhere. Those days, those times, were over. And she had to face life as it was now. And maybe it wasn't too late to reclaim the girl and the woman who took those pictures.

Maybe the lie she'd told Victoria about not having dreams could be remedied. Why not? She wasn't dead yet.

Victoria carried one suitcase at a time into Eric's home. He wasn't there. She could tell men had been working in the kitchen today. The cabinets had arrived and been placed like a jigsaw puzzle where they would sit, but they hadn't been screwed together or attached to the wall.

In the bedroom that Eric had offered her, everything had been completed. The carpet was new, the walls and ceiling had been painted, the lighting she'd chosen had been installed. The awesome closet organizer made the previous plain closet with a wooden pole look like a hole in the wall. She unzipped her suitcases and began emptying her clothes, finding places in the closet to fill up.

But as she worked she became increasingly more depressed. Her clothes might fill the closet, but a coldness filled her spirit. She felt truly alone. So she sat in the center of the empty bedroom and wondered where her father was, what Carmen was up to, and if her mother was cooking for herself tonight. Jaqueline would.

"Hey, what are you doing?" Eric stood at her door.

Victoria hadn't even heard him walk in. "Moving in."

He took a seat on the middle of the floor next to her. "Is this like a meditation-moving-in thing?"

She smiled. "Maybe. I was trying to make this room feel like mine, which is kind of stupid. I'm only going to be here for a few weeks."

"You asked me a few weeks ago where I went when I left home. Remember?"

"Yes."

"The first place I stayed in was a dump. Well, the first place was my car, actually. But then I found this run-down shack. It had one bedroom, a tiny bathroom, and a kitchen covered in roaches."

"Ugh," Victoria said. "And you stayed there?"

"I started cleaning it up, then called an exterminator. We took out all the drywall and found roaches even inside the walls and in the insulation."

"Eric!" She shuddered, imagining crawling things running up and down her back. "You're creeping me out."

"It was gross." He smiled like a little boy. "I'd sit in my car at night, sometimes shivering and close to tears. I wondered what the hell I'd gotten myself into. I missed my mom's great meals, and my bed, and I started to think I should have stayed where I was and figured out how to finish school, and like it."

Victoria listened.

"But I stuck it out. Within a couple of weeks we had the entire house clean. I laid the flooring, got the drywall back up and painted, and finally moved into the place. I made a whole ten grand off the place in the end. It wasn't much, but it was like gold to me. I was so proud of the way it turned out. I'd taken a dump and made it a nice place to live."

She smiled.

"Being on your own is sort of scary. Even without the cockroaches."

"I'm not scared. Just sort of sad that my life as I knew it is over."

"Isn't that what you wanted?"

"Yes and no."

Eric leaned forward. "Let me help you finish unpacking. Then let's meditate over the roasted chicken and salad I brought. Hungry?"

"A little."

He got on his feet opened one of her suitcases, and began gathering shorts, T-shirts, socks, bras, and underwear.

Victoria pulled the items out of his hands. "I'll do it."

He shrugged. "Sure you don't want my help?"

"I'm sure. Actually, let's go eat. I'll do more of this later."

"Good." He put everything down and headed to the living room. On a card table was a bag from the grocery store. He pulled out the delicious-smelling chicken and prepared salad. Then he dug some paper plates out of another paper bag.

"Is this the way you're used to living?"

He nodded and pulled out a French bread.

She smiled. His mother apparently had some influence over him, Argentines ate bread with every meal. She loved it but would have to control herself and limit her portion to one slice.

"The kitchen will be finished this week, and we'll be able to cook then. But I'm used to making do without a kitchen or furniture. The second a house gets livable I sell it and start over." He tore a piece of bread off and handed it to her, then took a chunk for himself and bit into it.

"I tell you, Eric, I don't think I could get used to this." She took a napkin and placed her bread on it.

He cut the chicken and served a leg and breast on each plate, then spooned the salad beside the chicken. "It gets tiring. I'm ready for something more permanent, but the problem is that you have to work wherever you find a house."

"You found this one. Why can't you find more and establish a home base?"

He took his plastic fork and knife and began eating, but he watched her with sort of a crooked smile. "Has my mom hired you? She makes the same argument."

Victoria took a bite of chicken. It was tender and garlicky with a hint of rosemary. Delicious. "I'm sorry. It's none of my business."

"No problem. I would like to find a great house, fix it up, and actually keep it someday." He held up his fork. "Have real silverware and a real dining table."

"How about real mortgage payments? Those are the ones that worry me."

"I don't plan on having those. I'll pay cash for my house."

She lifted an eyebrow. "Really? I'm impressed."

He chuckled. "Not having anything allows me to save a lot." He finished his food and put his plate and utensils in a plastic bag he was using for trash. Victoria gave him her plate. She'd had enough.

He stood and took the bag outside, where they had a large can to toss construction debris. Then he returned. "Okay, now we can go back to your room and unpack your undies?"

She shook her head. "I wondered when you were going to mention those."

"I'll let you see mine, if you'd like."

She stood, still feeling completely inadequate with Eric. She looked...well, the way she did. And he looked like he had just walked out of a workingman's calendar. "I don't play that game," she joked.

"Ah." He looked amused. "Too bad for me." He turned away, then paused. "Although, you do play some games. You forget that I know some of the guys you dated in high school, which was why you surprised me with that comment about being shy. I know you weren't such an angel."

What did he mean by that? "I wasn't?" she asked with surprise.

"Evan Greene and Saul Anaya."

Victoria frowned and followed Eric into her bedroom. "What about them?"

"Spin the bottle?" Eric said, raising an eyebrow.

Victoria laughed. She and Evan had dated a couple of months

until her father had put his foot down. She could see him at school but no dating. At sixteen, she wasn't about to listen to that nonsense. So when she spent the night at her best friend's house, the guys came over and they played spin the bottle. "That was an innocent kid game."

Eric reached back into her suitcase, but instead of pulling out panties he took some of her tops and placed them in a drawer in the closet. "Not what Evan said."

She rolled her eyes. "He never got past... second base." She laughed.

He laughed too. "And Saul?"

"No comment." She dated him for a year and a half, until they graduated and he joined the navy. He was her first real boyfriend.

"Hmm," Eric said, and handed her a pile of shorts.

She put away her shorts. "My dad hated him."

Finally he pulled out her bras and panties, and handed them to her. "And if you and I started dating. Seriously. Would he hate me, too?"

"You're Argentine."

He stepped closer. "That makes a difference?"

"To him."

"And to you?"

"No difference at all."

Eric leaned closer, and he placed a hand on her waist. "Being with you makes me happy, Vicki. Do you think it's because you remind me of when I was a kid and still innocent?"

She couldn't answer that. "It's because I let you touch my underwear," she whispered.

He smiled. "That must be it." He kissed her cheek. "You going to be okay sleeping in here all by yourself?"

"I'll be fine."

"Too bad." He eased back. "Good night, then."

Victoria's heart was beating a little too fast. Whatever she was doing, it gave her a rush she found irresistible. Out of all the risks she was taking lately, spending time with Eric was probably the most dangerous, but also the most enjoyable.

Chapter Thirteen

Victoria officially enrolled in the Institute of Design the following week. She planned to attend twice a week during the fall quarter. That gave her plenty of time to complete work on Eric's property, put in some hours at the boutique, and look for more design work. Eric wouldn't be paying her until he sold the house—that was their agreement. And that was fine. She didn't need the money. Her expenses had been so minimal while living with her parents that she had enough money saved to last her a long time. So that didn't worry her, but she was excited to begin building her business.

As part of her registration process, she had a counseling session. Victoria spent a couple of hours discussing her goals and planning her courses.

The counselor tapped his notepad. "I pointed out your reference, Douglas Glen, to one of our instructors, Mrs. Hendrickson. They used to teach together at Burbank High."

Victoria smiled. "Douglas is the one who recommended I get my degree. He's my cheerleader and my friend. He's right about absolutely everything."

"Mrs. Hendrickson would like to speak with you when we finish here—and we *are* actually done. Unless you have any questions."

She had a plan for next year, and it all looked doable and exciting. So she didn't have any questions. She closed her notebook and slipped it into her canvas bag. "I'm all set."

He wrote on a sticky pad. "This is Mrs. Hendrickson's office number."

Victoria took it. "Thank you."

She stopped by the woman's office next. Mrs. Hendrickson was one of the few older people she'd met here—even the professors seemed young and stylish—although she looked amazing. She invited Victoria into her office.

"I don't remember you from Burbank High," Victoria said.

"I worked there ages ago. Douglas was suited for that environment. I'm afraid I didn't enjoy dealing with teen hormones half as much."

Victoria smiled. "I don't think I would, either."

"Victoria, I spoke with Douglas earlier and he thinks a lot of you."

Victoria loved Douglas.

"Would you be interested in being paired up with a design company this quarter and getting some work experience?"

Sounded like working for free. "Ah, I don't know."

"Occasionally we manage to put some of our students into prestigious firms. The experience you get working with these professionals is worth gold, I assure you. If you're interested, Victoria, I can recommend you as a possible candidate. We'll arrange everything. I'll talk to the counseling office, and you'll get credit as well as a paycheck while you learn."

Course credit *and* a paycheck? Now *that* sounded good. "I don't know how to thank you."

"Learn, and represent us well." She took a few notes. Then stood and held out a hand. "A pleasure, Victoria. I'll be in touch."

"Thank you." Taking her cue, she stood and left her office.

Beyond excited, she flew from the university to see Douglas. Even though a few customers were milling around the store, she went around the counter and wrapped her arms around him.

"Hey." He chuckled and held his arms up in the air. "What's this about?"

"I just love you. I registered at the university today, and I'm so excited I can barely stand it." She squeezed him tight one more time, then let him go.

He smiled down at her. "Wonderful."

"And I spoke with a colleague of yours who is going to help place me with a design firm."

"Andrea. Yes, she called me. It's a great opportunity for you, kiddo."

"I know. It's amazing. Thank you so much, Douglas."

He nodded and shrugged as if it were no big deal. "It's time for you to move on."

"Move on?"

"Sure." He sat on the stool he kept behind the counter for the few times when things got slow and he had a chance to sit. "I've watched you prepare for this for the last five years, Victoria. Some people know what they want right away. And they charge after it. Others, like you, sit with things a long time and then make their move. You're ready, and I'm excited for you."

"I feel like I am ready."

"So I accept your resignation. We should go out for celebratory drinks when I close tonight."

"Resignation?" Victoria's bubbling happiness fizzed away.

"Isn't that what you came to tell me? That you'll be busy studying and working on your ID career? And you quit?"

"Of course not."

"Sure you did. And don't feel bad. I support your decision one hundred percent."

"But, Douglas, that wasn't what—"

He stood and placed a hand on her shoulder. "Yes. It was."

"I love working here," she said softly. It was the one part of her day she'd always loved. She suffered through the hours at the restaurant. But working at the boutique was like playtime.

"You're going to be a fantastic interior designer," Douglas said.

Maybe she would be and maybe she wouldn't, but that was where her time needed to be spent. He knew it and she knew it. But like always, she couldn't seem to make the jump forward without a huge shove. She looked away with tears in her eyes, and nodded.

He patted her back and walked around her, leaving her behind the counter alone. She watched him approach a customer. Damn, he was a great teacher. She reached for the sticky notepad, wrote "Thank you" on it, and stuck it on the computer screen. Then she left the store before she broke into tears.

Jaqueline answered the door and thanked the UPS man for the box he delivered. Inside, she opened it and pulled out the books she ordered. She read the back covers with anticipation. Maybe these would provide some answers to questions she didn't even know she had about what to do with her life. If someone had told her when she was changing diapers and struggling to make meals and keep the house clean while still squeezing out hours to help Victor with the restaurant that one day she'd be sitting in this kitchen searching for something to do, she'd have laughed at them.

She poured herself a cup of tea and started reading one of the books.

Two hours later, Lucia rang her doorbell. Jaqueline was

expecting her. She placed her books in a drawer and called out, "It's unlocked. Come in."

"Che, cómo estás?" Lucia strolled inside and kissed her hello, placing a bag of pastries on the kitchen countertop.

"Bien. Té?"

"Oh, yes, iced tea, please."

Jaqueline wrinkled her nose. Didn't matter how hot it got, she couldn't drink tea cold. "I made some fresh mate cosido."

"Oh, well, in that case, I'll take that. How are you adjusting to Victoria being gone?" She took a seat at the table.

"I'm not. She's only been gone two days and I've called her both days to ask her to run an errand for me that I could have done on my own."

Lucia clicked her tongue. "You've got to stop that. It gets easier."

"No, it doesn't. How can you say it gets easier not to live with someone you spent the last twenty-eight years worrying about, sharing things with, protecting, loving—?"

"At least you know where she's at. I couldn't even see Eric when he chose to leave." She reached for a pastry that Jaqueline took out of the bag and placed on a plate at the center of the round table. "And I had to pretend I didn't know what was going on between him and Antonio."

"I don't know how you didn't kill your husband for losing your boy's college money. I would have left Victor if he had done that to the girls."

Lucia sipped her mate cosido and gently smiled. "How could I kill him when I loved him so much? He didn't intend to lose the money." She placed her cup down. "Jaqui, don't take this the wrong way, but... maybe Victor didn't share his plans about the restaurant with you because you're too harsh."

"How can you say that?"

"Because we're both married to good men. Not perfect men."

"Some are more perfect than others."

"You're always so ready to attack. Why don't you put some trust in him and accept that he's doing the best he can?"

Jaqueline stood and faced away from Lucia, putting more water in the teakettle. "Victor hasn't always deserved my trust, Lucia." She turned around again and leaned on the counter. "How many times has Antonio been unfaithful?"

"None," she said, as if shocked by the question. Then her expression darkened. "Victor?"

Jaqueline nodded. "It was a long time ago, but something died inside me when I found out. Though I forgave him—I *had* to forgive him—things were never the same. It's like he always tries too hard to please me by buying me things or working harder, and none of it means anything to me."

"Why didn't you ever tell me, loca?" Lucia said, full of compassion.

"I didn't want to think about it. It was over."

Lucia stood and hugged her. Jaqueline felt no emotion at all. She'd mourned the passionate, innocent, romantic part of her marriage long ago. That didn't hurt anymore. But now she missed the friendship part that they'd developed in later years.

Jaqueline eased back. "Listen, I think I'm going to go spend some time in Argentina."

Lucia's eyes opened wide. "How much time?"

"A few months. I don't know. I need to get away. I want to see if I can find the part of myself that I lost."

Lucia frowned and stared at her for a long time. "I have a better idea. I mean, you can still go to Argentina, but what if we take a little vacation together first?"

Jaqueline smiled. "What kind of vacation?"

"I don't know. A cruise?"

Jaqueline lifted an eyebrow. "A cruise?"

"Sure. It'll be fun. Just us girls. We can chat until three in the morning every night. Sing karaoke, sunbathe without having to worry about how we look because no one will know us."

Jaqueline laughed. "That sounds fun. But what will Antonio say?"

"He'll hate it. He won't want me to go, of course."

"I don't want to cause you any trouble. One of us contemplating divorce is enough."

Lucia went back to her chair. "You're not getting divorced and neither am I. But we are going to remind both those men how terrible life would be without us. "

Jaqueline doubted Victor cared one way or another if she was gone. "So where should we go?"

Eric opened the fridge and pulled out a carton of orange juice. He was about to take a couple of swigs from it when he remembered he wasn't living there alone. So he reached for a glass and poured. As he drank, he looked out the kitchen window to the backyard. His guys were carrying in two huge pine trees. "What the hell?" He put the glass down. "Victoria," he called.

She walked out of her bedroom.

"Did you order pine trees for the backyard?"

"No." She frowned, joined him at the window, and gazed at the same spot.

As they watched the men lower the trees into the ground beside the fence, Antonio followed them into the yard, directing them.

Eric cursed.

"He's only trying to help," Victoria said.

"For the last time," he said, and walked out the sliding glass door.

"Hóla, nene." Antonio smiled. "Good morning."

Eric sent the two workers home and turned to his father. "What are you doing here with these trees?"

"What do you think of them?"

"What do I think of pine trees? They look great in the mountains. What are they doing here?"

"You need landscaping by the pool."

"I know that. But what am I supposed to do with pine trees?" He tried to keep his frustration in check, but it wasn't working.

Antonio pulled off his button-up shirt and hung it on the fence. Underneath, he had on a white T-shirt. "If you put one on each corner of your backyard, laying in your pool will feel like you're in a lake in the mountains, and—"

"Wait a minute." Eric motioned for him to pause. "This doesn't have anything to do with trees. Just like firing my pool guys and hiring your own wasn't about the pool. Just like wanting to redo my walls didn't have anything to do with the damned walls. What's up?"

"I'm just trying to help."

"You're not."

"Well, I'm sorry." He frowned, like he didn't understand what the big deal was, and wiped beads of sweat off his forehead with the back of his hand.

"Why would you do anything without talking to me? I have a plan for this house. I have a budget. And I need to stick to both."

"Like I said, I'm trying to help."

"Fine, stop it. Don't help me anymore." Eric headed for the door.

"Eric, wait." Antonio pointed to the trees. "What should I do with these?"

The perfect suggestion was on the tip of his tongue. He turned and stared at his father. "Ah, fuck. Let's get the damn things in the ground." He grabbed two shovels and handed one to Antonio. Each corner of the yard had large four-by-five-inch planters with overgrown ornamental grasses and impatiens that needed too much water and made a mess on the patio. He'd planned to pull them out and put in crotons. The large green and yellow leaves would look decorative without dropping flowers near the pool. Along with some decorative stones, it would have been perfect. Now, he had pine trees for an area he was sure would be too small once the trees grew.

He began to dig out clumps of grasses, stabbing the shovel into the soil. "So, you gonna help me?" he asked Antonio, irritation in his tone.

"Yeah." Antonio went to the opposite planter. "I'm trying to, you know, get involved in your interests. You don't have to get so upset."

Eric suspected something like this, but found it hard to be sympathetic. "My interests?" He plunged the shovel into the ground. "This isn't like playing catch with me because I like baseball. This is my job."

"I know."

Bull. He didn't know crap. And he didn't understand that butting into his business was no way to spend time together. "This is my work; it isn't a hobby. You can't just jump in and fix things you think I'm doing wrong."

Antonio yanked out handfuls of grasses. "You never were one to let anyone help you."

Eric glared at him as he bent over to yank out the flowers on the edges of the planter. He tossed them over his shoulder.

"Even as a boy. Remember when you were building that bird feeder and I kept telling you you were doing it wrong? But did you listen? No. You built it the way you wanted and it came out crooked." Antonio loosed the soil with the shovel, then bent over and pulled out a blue fescue whole. It came out easily and without spraying too much dirt on the patio.

Eric reached for a trash bag and tossed the chopped-up grasses and flowers inside. "You always think you know better." Eric shook his head, still bothered after all these years about his father wanting to run his life.

"Give me one of those bags," Antonio said.

Eric noticed he was trying to keep up with him, but he was already winded and sweating heavily. He tossed his father a bag. "And my birdhouse didn't come out crooked."

Antonio laughed. "Yes it did." He hurriedly dropped the rejected plants into the trash bag and got back to pulling more.

"It was the tree I hung it on."

Antonio continued to laugh as he worked, and it only annoyed Eric more. He lifted his shovel and dug more intensely, carving up the soil, cutting into the roots of the plants. Now sweat poured off his forehead. He wiped it with his shirt, but a drop of sweat got into his eye and stung. "Damn it," he shouted, and threw the shovel up against the fence. "So what if it was crooked? So what?"

Antonio continued to work, ignoring him. "So if you had listened it could have come out better."

"It was *my* damned birdhouse."

Antonio paused, his face red. "But I was trying to teach you something. That's what fathers do."

"People learn by making mistakes. Why couldn't you just let me make mine?"

Antonio maintained eye contact for a moment. A flash of emotion crossed his face. Then he took his shovel and gently dug up the impatiens, pulling up the flowers with the roots. "Victoria might want to plant these somewhere else," he said. His voice had lost its warmth.

Eric cursed. Wasn't he going to answer him? Wasn't he going to tell him why *he* was the only one that could screw up and had to be forgiven, while Eric had to do things just right? "Just throw the flowers out. We're not going to use them."

"Why not? There's nothing wrong with them."

"We're not going to use them."

"That's crazy."

"We're not going to use them!" He stalked over, pulled the flowers out of Antonio's hands, and tossed them into the trash bag.

"You fool," Antonio shouted. "What did you do that for?"

"You don't listen!" Eric shouted back.

"*You* don't listen." Antonio reached for the trash bag. Eric pulled back, ripping the plastic and spilling the contents all over the concrete patio around the pool.

"Now look what you did," Antonio said.

"Ah, shit." Eric dropped the torn bag. "Now look—"

"No, you look. I came to help you and all you've done since I got here—"

"Help! You call this helping?"

They both continued to shout back and forth, neither hearing what the other said. Their voices got louder and louder.

"Hey!" Victoria interrupted. "Oh, my God. Look what you two have done."

Dirt and plants covered Eric's area. Antonio's was nice and neat except for the mess Eric had made when he ripped the trash bag. His father had smudges on his face, and his shirt was drenched. Eric imagined he looked the same.

Just like that, Victoria had yanked Eric out of this crazy place inside himself where his emotions had regressed fifteen years or more. Here he was with his father acting just like he had as a teen: feeling powerless and angry and fighting back irrationally. He drew a breath, looked down at the mess, and shook his head.

"Good morning, Victoria," Antonio said. "I brought a couple of trees. We're going to plant them."

Her horrified expression changed when she turned her focus from the massacred plants to Antonio, and she smiled. "They're beautiful. How thoughtful of you."

Eric got back to work. He picked up a rake and tried to collect the mess he'd made into a pile.

"I'm going to the grocery store," she said. "Can I bring you guys anything? Doughnuts? I made coffee. Or maybe something less stimulating and more calming."

"No, gracias querida," Antonio said.

"Eric?"

He hadn't meant to make a scene or to embarrass himself or her. He wiped his face and glanced at her. "I'm fine."

"You sure?"

His heart skipped a couple of beats as he looked at her. The look in her eyes told him two things. She was trying to help, and she was concerned about him. "Yeah, I'm sure."

"Okay, I'm leaving, then."

Eric nodded. Once she was gone, he turned to Antonio. "Look, I don't need you to teach me anything anymore," he said. His voice was still rough and cold, even though he was through fighting. "I know better than you that pine trees this close to a pool won't work." He pointed and gestured to the trees standing beautifully in their pots.

Antonio tossed his shovel down now and came almost nose to nose with Eric. "I stopped trying to teach you anything the day you walked out," he said in a low, menacingly calm voice.

"Right," he said. "At that point, you just stopped talking to me. Because I didn't do things your way."

"I was wrong to do that," he admitted, stepping back. Whatever anger Eric had sparked in him was fading. Victoria had helped them both take a breath and calm down. Antonio returned to pulling out grasses. "I wish I could turn back time, but I can't." He picked up the shovel. "All I can do is go on from today."

Eric felt drained. "And what would you do if you could turn back time?"

"Not what I did." That didn't say much, and yet it said a lot.

Eric took a new trash bag from the box on the ground, and refilled it with the contents he'd spilled.

"For years I thought I should have forced you to stay home and go to that damn law school." Antonio spoke quietly, contemplatively. "I should have had your tuition. I shouldn't have lost the little I did have."

"Yeah." Eric sat at the edge of the planter, his shoulders slumped. "But I didn't want to go to law school." He was tired of this old barrier between them.

"It was our plan," Antonio reminded him.

"It was *your* plan. I was so thankful that you couldn't afford to send me to school anymore. It set me free."

Antonio came to sit beside him. "You were spoiled and ungrateful, and you didn't appreciate what we were trying to do for you." He put an arm around Eric's shoulders and looked at him. "You think running out on your own made you a man?"

"Maybe I did." He *had* been a spoiled, hotheaded fool who thought he knew best. Still, he had to mature his own way. And he had.

"It didn't make you a man. It made you an idiot," Antonio said matter-of-factly. "It made you a menial worker just like me. You stupid boy." He gave Eric a hard slap on his shoulder.

"You think I would have been a better person if I'd become a lawyer, Papi?"

"No, no. Of course not. But you would have had an easier life, hijo."

Yeah right. He couldn't think of a more miserable existence than being cooped up in an office all day or having to wear a stuffy suit all the time.

"And it would have made me feel good about myself," Antonio continued. "So I could finally say, I did something good in my life." His voice was rough. "I helped my son become a professional. A man others look up to." He shrugged. "Stupid."

"Hell, that's not stupid, Dad. I get it."

"When you have a child, you want so much for him. You want everything to be perfect."

"Perfect." Eric chuckled. "You mean, your version of perfect."

"Probably."

Why was this so hard? Why had he always had to fight to carve his own path? Because he was the son of an immigrant, he decided. His father had something to prove. And the expectations for Eric had simply been higher. "I'm doing what I love, and I'm happy. It's not always easy and I sometimes think I should have listened to you, but... that life you wanted for me wasn't right. It wouldn't have fit."

Antonio nodded and slapped Eric's back one more time before standing. "I know." He stared at the half-cleared planter. "So should we take those trees back?"

Eric laughed. "That would be great."

"Let's do that first."

"No, let's finish with these plants before it gets any hotter."

Antonio opened his mouth like he was going to argue. "Bueno," he said, instead.

They finished clearing the planters. Eric shared stories of some of the places he'd been to, and Antonio shared his woes of the various jobs he'd held over the past seven years. And Eric decided his father *could* teach him something after all. He learned that working with his dad wasn't bad at all. In fact, it was good. They had a lot in common. And he loved the man.

"So have you seen Eric naked yet?" Carmen asked.

Victoria laughed into the phone. "Of course not," she answered Carmen.

"But you want to, right?"

"Did you call just to harass me?"

"No." Her voice took a more serious tone. "I need to tell you something."

"Okay."

"I'm coming home after this quarter and not finishing the bio degree."

Victoria knew this wasn't good. "Because?"

"I can't do anything with it unless I continue on to a master's and a PhD. The field is saturated, and I can't see myself continuing on for another four or five years."

"But you love science and you're good at it. And you were going to continue on to med school. I figured we'd have a doctor or vet in the family soon."

"I have another idea. I need to talk to Dad about it when I come home for Christmas."

"Carmen, Dad's going have a fit. You know that. Just finish what you're doing. You don't have to continue with a master's, but finish out this last year. It's just until next June."

"You dropped out before you finished."

"This is going to sound obvious, but you're not me." They both knew that their parents had different expectations for each of them. "Besides, I'm going back to school now." She told her about the Institute of Design.

"That's fantastic."

"But I should have finished out the business degree. It would have helped me out. Don't quit before you get your BS. Promise me."

"Vic, I don't know."

"Carmen, you've come this far. Don't do something you're going to regret."

The line was quiet. "Okay, I promise. I'll graduate, but then I'm coming home."

Having Carmen home thrilled Victoria more than she could let on over the phone. They had been right to apply for an away college for Carmen, but Victoria had missed her. "Good. I'll talk to you soon."

She clicked the phone off and went to the kitchen, which was now completed. She started screwing switch plates around the outlets. Eric walked in and took out a bottle of water from the refrigerator. He drank the whole bottle and tossed it in a trash can. Then he smiled. "Plants are in."

She'd noticed that the trees were gone and in their place Eric and Antonio had brought in gorgeous leafy plants. "How do they look?"

"Perfect." He angled his head. "How are you doing?"

"Good."

"Good?"

She smiled and nodded. "Good."

"All right. Sorry about the screaming match out there. My dad has a way of driving me crazy, and I lost it."

"No need to apologize. I understand, believe me."

He nodded. "I'm going to go shower."

He strolled away and she watched him, thinking of Carmen's question about seeing him naked. Ignoring the interest, she kept working. Seemed like the safest thing to do lately. With her father creating an empire, her mother returning to her youth, and Carmen probably wanting to come home because she was worried that her family was falling apart, contemplating anything where Eric was naked seemed too irresponsible. But it was there. In the back of her mind. And she wasn't sure how long she'd be able to keep the thoughts and building desires locked up. Didn't the obvious always find a way of expressing itself?

Chapter Fourteen

Saturday was the only day that neither Lucia nor Antonio had obligations, so when Antonio got back from helping Eric they sat on the couch together and watched television. Lucia rested her head on his comfortable shoulder. He caressed her upper arm absently as he watched a cop show. Waiting for the commercial, she thought about how to approach the idea of the cruise with Jaqueline. She decided to just come out with it and hope he understood.

"Antonio?" she said, the second the screen went from a murder investigation to a flashy new car.

"Hmm?" He kissed the top of her head.

"What do you think about Victor and Jaqueline's marital problems?"

"What marital problems? They had a fight."

"It's deeper than that."

"Oh. Okay, I think you shouldn't get involved."

She lifted her head and gazed into his eyes. "I'm not getting involved."

"Good."

"Well, I did have one small idea."

"I knew it." He drew a breath and focused on her. "What?"

"I told Jaqueline we could take a little vacation together."

"Go on vacation with those two? Are you crazy? They're not even talking to each other."

"Not the four of us. Just she and I."

His eyes narrowed. "Where would you go? And for how long?"

"We decided on a restorative cruise."

"Oh, you decided?" He eased back so their bodies were no longer in contact. "What if I don't want you to go?"

"Antonio, don't be a baby. Do you want our best friends to get divorced?"

"I don't care. That's their problem."

"Victor is your friend."

"I don't want to be his friend if it means I have to lose my wife."

She chuckled and kissed him. "You're not losing me, amor. I think it would be good for me to get away for a little while. Spend some girl time with a friend, relaxing."

He frowned. "We don't have the money for that."

"I knew you'd say that. Jaqui wants to pay for it all. She insisted."

"Great. And what about Eric? Now that he's home you want to leave?"

"Actually, I thought about that a lot. It will only be for a short time, and it will give you the opportunity to be with him alone. Do some male-bonding activities together."

"I'd rather bond with you."

She smiled. "Listen, I won't go if you really don't want me to, but I'd like to. Jaqueline is a little lost these days. And she was always there for me when people were talking about me being a bad mother at the club. Remember? She always stood by me."

Antonio gazed at her and she could see he was coming around. "I'm not going to tell you not to go if you really want to, but... we've never been on vacation without each other."

"I'm sorry, amor." She snuggled in close. "I don't like the idea of being apart from you, either. But some time off where I don't have to cook or clean or do anything, even worry about you, sounds...I don't know...nice? I know that probably sounds incredibly selfish."

"No," he said. "You never do anything for yourself. I would never think you're selfish." He ran his fingers though her hair. "You should go," he added reluctantly.

Lucia slipped her hands around him and squeezed tight. "I knew you'd understand. You're the best husband in the world."

He chuckled and kissed her. "You're a good manipulator, Lucia."

"I mean it," she said, full of love for the man she'd chosen so many years ago. "I couldn't have dreamed of a better husband than you."

"You could have done way better."

"No." She placed a finger on his lips. He was always too hard on himself. "I'm the luckiest woman alive, and if you say I'm not, I'm going to get angry."

He chuckled again. "Okay, okay." He kissed her, and reached for the remote. He turned the TV off. "What do you say we go back to bed?"

"I was thinking the same thing."

The board approved a Mexican fiesta and decided it would be next May in honor of Cinco de Mayo. Jaqueline was excited and called Hugo to give him the good news. He answered on the third ring. "Hugo, this is Jaqueline."

"Hey," he said. "Hold on." The line grew silent for a couple of seconds. "Sorry, I was inside an office, fixing a fax machine."

"Is that what you do when you're not entertaining audiences?"

"Yep. I work for the school district. Puts food on the table and lets me work pretty much the same hours as my kids."

Too bad the man wasn't younger, Jaqueline thought. He would make Victoria a good husband after all. "Did you buy your daughter that dress?"

He chuckled. "Yes, and she was beautiful. And I took pictures. Want to see them?"

"Oh, well, sure."

"Are you at the club? I'll stop by on my way home. I'll have the kids with me, though."

"No, I'm on my way home." Then impulsively, she added, "Bring them to my home. I'll make them dinner tonight. No McDonald's."

"Seriously?"

"Sure." She was tired of eating alone. And the idea of having children in the house again made her suddenly happy. "Take down my address."

He wrote it down. "We'll be there. About five? Is that too early?

"It's perfect. See you then."

Jaqueline disconnected the call and realized she hadn't even given him the good news about the Mexican fiesta. Oh well, she'd tell him over dinner.

She hurried home and went straight to the kitchen. She pulled out slices of veal from the freezer, defrosted the meat as she peeled potatoes. Let's see, she thought. Vegetables. What vegetables do children like? None, she decided, but she had to include some kind of vegetable, so she reached for carrots. She also took out the eggs to prepare a flan for dessert.

A couple of hours later, she had breaded veal parmesan, mashed potatoes, honeyed carrots, and beautiful flan chilling in the refrigerator.

Hugo arrived right at five with his two adorable kids standing on either side of him.

"This is Augustine. We call him August, and he's ten. And this"—he put his hand on his daughter's head—"is Daisy, and she's seven."

Jaqueline shook their hands. "Welcome. And thank you for coming to dinner." She showed them inside, and Hugo told them to go wash their hands.

He stood in the living room. "Nice," he said.

"Victoria decorated it all."

"Looks great. Is she joining us for dinner?"

"No," Jaqueline said. "I didn't invite her."

"I thought she lived with you."

"Not anymore. Come to the kitchen."

The kids joined them, and were well mannered as they took their seats.

"So tell me about your piano recital," Jaqueline said to Daisy.

The girl brightened. "I played Sonatina by Beethoven. And I didn't make any mistakes. My dad bought me a great dress that went almost to my ankles and had beads in the front. I wore shoes that had a little heel even."

"Really?" Jaqueline served the mashed potatoes. "I bet you looked beautiful."

She nodded. "My dad brought pictures."

"I can't wait to see them."

She put the veal and carrots in the center of the table. She served the children while Hugo served himself.

"I made lemonade. Do you like that?"

"Yes," the kids said in unison.

"And August, your father tells me you like soccer."

"Yeah," he said. End of conversation. She'd never had a boy, but she knew they were more concise.

"Do you enjoy it?"

"Sometimes."

"He doesn't enjoy getting kicked or losing," Hugo said.

"My team sort of sucks," he said.

Jaqueline smiled and finally joined them at the table.

Hugo asked his son to say grace. The boy quietly obeyed. Then the three of them dug into their food. Jaqueline watched them for a second. They all ate like this was the first dinner they'd been given all week. She enjoyed that children appreciated her cooking again.

Hugo smiled. "I don't make anything this fancy. Lots of Hamburger Helper and sandwiches. Thanks for inviting us."

"Not true," August said. "He makes great fajitas and carne asada. And grilled fish. You should try his fish."

"I don't have time to cook on a regular basis, though," he said.

"That's okay," she said. "I didn't always have the time when I was raising my girls, either. You do the best you can."

He smiled.

"I called you to tell you that the club has accepted your program."

His eyes lit up. "That's wonderful."

"In May. We're going to have a Mexican fiesta. So I'm going to invite a couple of other performers."

He wiped his mouth with a napkin. "Excellent idea. I can't wait. Your club is really going to enjoy it."

"I'm sure we will. Can I get you more?" she asked the children, who had finished eating and were sitting politely. They both shook their heads. "Well, I have some flan for a little later. If you would like to play in the backyard or watch TV." She glanced at Hugo. "Is that okay?"

"Sure." He told them to place their plates in the sink and they did. Then they hurried out to the backyard, following Jaqueline's directions to the back of the house.

"Wow," she said. "They're great kids."

"Thank you."

"You seem to be doing a terrific job raising them."

"I try." He chuckled. "But it's hard."

"Do you have any help?"

"My mother and sister help out. They see their mother a couple of weekends a month."

Jaqueline was surprised that their mother wasn't more involved. "Not much."

"No, not much, but enough. She's not good for them."

"Why not? If you don't mind me asking."

"I don't mind." He leaned back in the chair. "She's a performer, too. That's how I met her. Unfortunately that's how she meets most men, and the fact that she was married and had children didn't seem to sink into her head. She still felt free to drink and take her costume off for anyone who interested her."

"How awful," Jaqueline said.

He shrugged. "I wanted to kill her, but I decided divorce was more socially acceptable."

Jaqueline smiled, even though the situation was sad. Some women didn't appreciate good men when they found them.

"Daisy was two when I kicked her ass out the door—sorry."

"It's okay."

"So, I'm over it. I wish the kids didn't have to see her at all, but they're stuck paying for my bad judgment."

"You've got two great kids out of that bad judgment, so it wasn't all bad."

He grinned. "You're a nice lady, Jaqueline. Where's your husband, if you don't mind *me* asking?"

"Working late," she said, not willing to share her marital

problems as freely as he had. Not with another man, whom she hardly knew. Maybe that wasn't fair since she'd delved into his private business, but she wasn't divorced and she owed Victor her consideration. "Finished?"

He nodded.

She picked up his plate and cleared the table. Then she pulled out the flan and poured some coffee.

"This was beyond delicious. Thank you."

"Oh, I loved having you all. With my girls gone, and Victor busy with his business, I eat alone a lot. It was nice to have company."

He put a teaspoon of sugar in his cup and nodded, as if he understood.

"Call the kids in, will you? I'll cut them a piece of flan each."

Hugo took a drink of his coffee. "Mmm. In a minute. I want to enjoy the silence for just a few more seconds."

She laughed. "I'd forgotten how nice it is to have a few moments of peace."

"It never ends. After working all day, you have to go home to noise and more work. Then they wake up at night with bloody noses and bad dreams." He shook his head. "It's damned exhausting."

"It was." She remembered. Victor never helped with any of those things. She hadn't wanted to bother him, because he worked hard. But he never once thought that she'd also worked hard all day.

He laughed. "Hell, I'm whining like a chick."

"Sometimes you need a little girl talk."

"Yeah," he blushed. "My guy friends can't relate. And women . . . well, I don't want to . . . you know."

"Show any weakness?"

"Right. I want them to think I've got it together. But I don't."

"You can call me up and whine any time you want, dear. And in fact, drop the kids off every once in a while. I'll watch them if you need a break."

"I couldn't impose."

"It wouldn't be an imposition. I'd really like it."

He drew a breath, then released it. "Thanks. My mom is in her seventies and my sister is busy with her own kids. They're both great, but... thanks."

She patted his hand. "You're welcome."

He went to call his children who were out-of-their-minds thrilled with the flan. They ate two huge pieces. Then they moaned when they had to leave.

"I'll bring you back sometime," he promised. Then he hugged Jaqueline. "Thanks again."

"It was dinner and a little chat. Nothing to thank me for."

As she watched them leave, she was glad she'd invited them. And also glad, for some strange reason, that she was watching from a distance. Child rearing was the most exhausting, pleasurable endeavor a person could undertake.

She returned to her kitchen to clean up in the silence of the empty house. Only the sounds of the refrigerator, the clock ticking above the stove, and the water running into the sink filled the kitchen. Jaqueline smiled. This was nice. Quiet was nice. A reward, she thought. And she enjoyed every second of it.

Antonio parked his car in the driveway of Victor and Jaqueline's place Sunday after spending the afternoon at the Argentine Club. Jaqueline and Lucia went inside to purchase their cruise tickets online, excited like little girls. He smiled as he watched them, glad he hadn't been selfish and told her she couldn't go. She probably would have gone anyway—the woman was so damned independent, and then they would have been angry with each other. Who needed that?

"I'm going to check on Victor," he said, as they headed into the house. Victor hadn't been back to the club since he and Jaqueline had that fight.

He looked in the garage, where Victor had a nice setup with one recliner chair, a TV, and clothes hanging all around. "Che, loco," he said.

Victor looked over his shoulder. "What are you doing here?" He looked sort of pleased to see him.

"Just brought the women back from the club."

"Mmm," he grunted.

"I lost fifty bucks at poker today."

"So what else is new? You can't play."

"I can play," Antonio said defensively.

"Right. That's why you always lose."

Antonio sat on a box. "So how long do you plan to live out here?"

He shrugged. "I'm not home much these days, anyway. The restaurants are going up and I have to spend so much time away that I stay in hotels."

"Yeah, it's so far for you drive back and forth from Santa Monica, right?"

Victor shot a cold glance his way. "*And* Newport Beach."

"Look, I'm with you. I think our wives and our kids are a little nuts."

"Why are the kids nuts?"

"In my opinion, moving in together is a little nuts. I'm surprised you let Victoria do it, actually. Don't get me wrong, Eric's a good man, but... he's a man." He raised an eyebrow. "You know?"

Victor sat up straighter. "Victoria moved in with Eric?"

"Yeah. You didn't know?"

"No," he barked. "I didn't know. No one tells me a damn thing."

"Sorry."

"Shit, what's wrong with that girl lately?" He ran a hand up and down his stubbled face. "It's my own fault. I told her to move out, figuring she wouldn't. She called my bluff."

"Well . . . they're adults."

Victor snorted. "That makes me feel better. Thanks," he said sarcastically.

"Listen, Lucia can get back home by herself. Why don't we go out? Have a drink? Get out of this garage."

Victor stared into the empty space opposite the TV and slowly nodded. "Let's go."

Antonio stopped by the house and told Lucia he was going out with Victor and would meet her at home. He handed her the car keys. Distractedly, she kissed him good-bye and told him to have fun.

But Antonio and Victor drove around town, unsure what to do for fun. They hadn't been single since they were kids. Every event they attended was either at the Argentine Club or with their families. Work seemed to be their only solo activity.

"In Argentina, I used to go to the field to play soccer almost every day. And spend the evenings strolling el centro, looking at the chicas," Antonio said.

Victor smiled. "I can't remember what I did before I fell in love with Jaqueline. I think she was the only girl I've ever loved."

Antonio gazed at him. He wanted to ask how he could let his marriage fall apart, but it was none of his business.

"And I spent hours learning English," Victor said, as if he suddenly remembered what he used to do. Then he shrugged. "I knew I wanted to come to America and that I wanted to marry Jaqui. That's all I ever cared about."

"Ever think you're too focused?"

"Yeah," he said. And pulled off the freeway in Newport Beach. He followed the busy streets to the beach. "Want to see where the restaurant is going up?"

"See, too focused."

Victor shrugged again. But Antonio couldn't help being impressed with the location. This restaurant would have the most amazing view of the Pacific Ocean. And not only that, but it was located in an area that catered to affluent vacationers and wealthy residents in multi-million-dollar homes. Victor parked the car, and they got out to admire the shell of the new building.

"The entire west side will be windows, and these seats here will be reserved months in advance."

Antonio nodded, his hands in his pockets. The late August heat hung in the air, but here by the beach the breeze tempered the oppressive summer. Victor would easily get away with serving a heavy steak even at the peak of the summer heat. "You going to remember your buddies when you're a millionaire?"

Victor grinned and placed a hand on Antonio's back. "You know millions would be great, but right now, I just want it to work. I want Jaqui to see I was right to want this."

Antonio was certain it would. Some people managed to make magic happen whenever they tried. Others, like him, couldn't get a break. But to be fair, Victor had spent years preparing for this move. Working his one restaurant, day and night. Saving. Establishing himself. All the while, Antonio had been impatient, risking the little he had, hoping to make a fast buck. Taking frequent vacations with Lucia whenever they had a spare dollar. Victor and Jaqueline never went anywhere.

If Victor succeeded, it was because he deserved it. "I hope it all works out for you, loco."

"Me too," he said, with just a tinge of concern.

In some ways, Antonio was starting to realize that even with all his mistakes and his failures, maybe he was wealthy in ways Victor wasn't. Lucia never made him feel he had to prove anything. Although he wanted to give her more, he knew she loved him even if he didn't. "Let's go."

They found a noisy, touristy bar, where they ate some sandwiches and ordered beers. "I'm not very thrilled with Lucia and Jaqueline going on this cruise."

"What cruise?"

"You really don't know anything about what's going on with your family, do you?"

"She's going on a cruise?"

Antonio took a bite of his burger and nodded. "With Lucia."

"You were okay with that?"

"No, but... she wants to go help your wife deal with the fact that you're a bastard."

"Thanks."

Antonio sipped his beer and nodded, sending him a wordless *You're welcome.* "You know, Victor, I've decided I'm nothing like my father. Back in his day, women did what men said."

"And children, too," Victor said, drinking his second beer.

"You can say that again. Children respected their parents' wishes."

"Women didn't move in with men. They married them."

Antonio nodded. "So what did we do wrong?"

After a prolonged silence, Victor said, "We didn't listen to our own parents and moved to America."

"Yeah. I guess we weren't exactly perfect kids, either, were we?"

They finished their beers in silence. Finally, Victor said, "Let's switch to coffee. I have to drive back."

Antonio agreed. "Moving to America may not have been the

best idea in the world, but I love my American son and my independent wife."

Victor didn't say anything, but Antonio knew he also loved his wife and daughters. But right now, he didn't know how to show it. Antonio hoped he figured out how to open up to them before it was too late.

Chapter Fifteen

Eric put on a tie and looked at himself in the mirror. Damn, he looked good. He fingered his lapels. Expensive suit, crisp white shirt, fresh haircut, clean shave. He smiled a lady-killer smile. Yep, he was blessed. But he wanted female confirmation. In particular, he wanted to see the look of appreciation of one female. "Victoria," he called.

"Yeah?" she answered from her own room.

"I need your opinion." He didn't actually want to go to this high school reunion. He'd reconnected with the people he'd wanted to see again on the dinner cruise. But he was sort of excited about going out with Vicki. She'd moved in almost a month ago, and seeing her every day was nice. Who was he kidding—it was great. A beautiful woman to share breakfast with in the morning, read newspaper articles with on Sundays, laugh at silly things that happened during the remodel, and unwind with at the end of the day. The daily grind was growing more and more special each day. But he liked the idea of dressing up and going out, too. He felt like they'd skipped a few important steps. Not if they were going to remain just friends and business partners; in that case, things were as they should be, but that was not what he wanted at all. He wanted the dates, the romance, the—

She walked into his room looking like... wow, like a magazine model. No, better than a magazine model, dressed in a form-fitting, smoky-colored dress with a scoop neckline that displayed a respectable but enticing amount of cleavage. She'd lost a lot of weight since she started her diet. He didn't want to ask her how much, but if he had to guess, he'd say probably about twenty pounds. Not that it mattered to him. She looked beautiful regardless. And maybe it wasn't the weight loss at all that made her shine but her new confidence and endless excitement about everything.

"What?" she asked.

He couldn't take his eyes off her. "You look amazing."

"Thanks. So do you."

Turning to look at himself in the mirror, he remembered why he'd called her. "Do I?"

She walked farther into his room. "Very handsome."

He turned to face her, fingering his gray and blue tie. "I'm not sure this is the right tie."

She gazed into his closet and pulled out a more colorful satin bow tie. "This one."

"No," he said. "I'm not going to an awards show."

"Then no tie at all. This one makes you look like you're going to work on Wall Street."

He pulled off his tie and unbuttoned his top button. "Better?"

"Much."

He wanted to touch her. "Are you ready to go?"

"Not that I want to go, but yes."

"Why don't you want to go?"

"I don't know. I'm nervous." She angled her head. "Should we forget it and not go at all?"

He placed a hand on the small of her back. Hell no. "I'd be nervous if I were you, too. Guys are going to be jumping out of their skin to get their hands on you tonight. But don't worry—I'll protect you."

"Eric," she laughed. "You're crazy."

"And their wives are going to be pissed big-time. You're going to make some enemies." He guided her to the front door.

She wrapped an arm around his waist. "I'm so glad you're going with me."

"I'll be right beside you all night. Let's go."

He knew they weren't a couple. She hadn't shown much interest in anything romantic. And since that day at the club when Victor and Jaqueline had their fight—the day she reminded him that she wasn't just a girl he could fool around with and move on, he was reluctant to start anything he couldn't make permanent. But tonight he didn't give a damn. Victoria would have to make a verbal and maybe even a physical objection if she wanted him to keep his hands to himself.

On the drive, she chatted easily about this and that. Nothing in particular. A neighboring dog that kept jumping the fence into their backyard—that would be fixed as soon as they put up the new fence in a week or so. A TV show she watched in her bedroom the night before. A new recipe she wanted to try in the kitchen next week. Eric enjoyed listening. Most of the time he had nothing to listen to but his own thoughts or the radio. No wonder his father always looked so content when his mother was in the same room.

He rested his arm behind her seat. "I feel a little guilty that I haven't called my parents in a week. I'm surprised my mother hasn't called to tell me what a terrible son I am."

"She's busy planning a cruise vacation with my mom."

"A what?"

"They're going on a cruise together."

He kept his eyes on the road, but wished he could look at Victoria instead. "That's a shocker. My mom is going somewhere without my dad?"

"My mom said they're going to enjoy a relaxing ladies-only vacation."

"Why would they want to do that?"

"Because it's fun to hang out with your girlfriends."

This time he glanced at her quickly. "Sure, before you're married. After you're married, you go places with your husband."

Victoria laughed. "Oh, really?"

"Don't you think so?"

"I don't see anything wrong with spending time with your friends every once in a while."

"Hmm." He contemplated that as he drove. He bet his dad wasn't thrilled about his mother going away without him.

Once they got to the Marriott in Burbank, Eric valet-parked the car and took her arm. She hesitated for a second, and he thought she was going to ask him not to touch her as they walked in, but she didn't.

They were greeted at the door and offered name tags.

"Want a drink?" Eric asked, as soon as they walked in.

"No." She glanced around the room. "Oh, God, there's Susana. Let's avoid her if possible. She will definitely make me feel like I'm back in high school. I get my fill of her at the club."

Mrs. Apolonia's daughter had never been the nicest person in the world, but Eric sort of felt for her. How else could she have turned out, when her mother was such a busybody? "Fine by me. How about that drink? It'll help you relax."

"I'm relaxed."

"Liar." He ran a hand up and down her back.

"Okay, maybe I am still a little nervous about how I look."

He dipped his head closer to her neck and whispered, "You look hot in that dress."

She smiled and angled her head. "Really? Hot?"

"Totally?" Her lips were so close he wanted to swoop down and taste them.

"Thanks." She reached across and squeezed his hand. "I appreciate that."

He smiled.

"Hey," a voice interrupted. "Eric Ortelli?"

Reluctantly Eric turned away from Victoria and found himself facing an old friend he had lost touch with. They started chatting and catching up on their lives since high school. The next three hours were filled with more of the same. A friend. An acquaintance. The varsity football player everyone knew, who now worked at SportMart. Shaking hands with one person, then another. The evening was interesting, but mostly he wanted to go back home with Victoria. He wasn't sure how she felt, but she seemed to be in a great mood and not in a hurry to leave. She received lots of compliments on her looks and that made tonight worth it.

For a while he lost sight of her when he found a couple of friends he used to hang with, and they started discussing those carefree high school days when all they really cared about were girls.

"Things haven't changed all that much," his friend said.

"Not really," Eric agreed. "In fact, I better find Victoria." He held out his hand. "Good to see you again."

"Call me, Eric," he said, and handed Eric a card.

"I will." Eric strolled the hall, searching for Victoria, and found her standing with a couple.

"You remember Giselle," Victoria said. "She's now married and has two children."

He didn't remember her. "Hi," he said.

"Oh, yeah, I do remember you," Giselle said. "Are you two married?"

"No, we're—"

"Dating," Eric interrupted, because she'd been telling everyone all night that they were business partners, and that was getting on his nerves.

She turned her head and stared at him.

He put an arm around her. “Dating,” he repeated. “Living together, actually. And no, we don’t have any kids.” Since that always seemed to be the follow-up question.

Giselle smiled. “Wonderful.”

The music system in the background played an early 1990s ballad, “More Than Words,” about a woman in a guy’s life not needing words to show her love, just her body. Sounded good to him. Actually, he’d never liked sappy love songs, but tonight, all the Whitney Houston, Celine Dion, and Bryan Adams lyrics of passion and emotion were getting to him. He let his hand slip down and took Victoria’s fingers in his grip. “Let’s dance. Excuse us.”

He pulled her into his arms.

“I’m not even going to pretend to understand what that was about,” she said.

They danced to Mariah Carey’s “Always Be My Baby.” Eric held her close. “Sorry Victoria, but you’re full of shit and I couldn’t listen to it anymore.”

Her arms rested stiffly on his shoulders. “Why am I full of shit? You were the one who lied. You were implying something else with that ‘living together’ comment.”

“Are you seriously going to stand in my arms and look in my eyes and tell me I’m nothing to you but a business partner?”

“I didn’t mean it like that, Eric. You know we’re friends. But we’re all theoretically friends here. I think the fact that we’re working together is sort of cool and different.”

Maybe he was being overly sensitive, which wasn’t like him. He pulled her closer and lowered his lips to her ear. “I want you to admit that something is happening beyond friendship. We’re not kids anymore, Vicki.” He lifted his head. “I’m attracted to you. I love being with you. I think about you all the time, and I look forward to waking up because I know you’re going to be there. I... why are you looking at me like that?”

One of her hands crept up his neck and behind his head. "Because I really want to kiss you."

He angled his head and brushed his lips against hers, then eased back, letting their breaths mingle, before dropping down for a fuller, deeper kiss. He pressed his lips hard against hers, passionately taking possession of her mouth, enjoying the taste of her kiss.

When it ended, he took her hand. "Let's go home."

They said quick good-byes to a few friends and promised to keep in touch. Eric couldn't have cared less if he ever saw any of those people again. At least that was the way he felt at that moment.

He took Victoria home. The second they walked through the front door of their house, he took her hand and, before she could say a word, shamelessly flattened her against the freshly painted living room wall. He kissed up her soft, sweet-smelling neck as his hands moved along the curve of her waist. Sexy, curved waist in the Kate Winslet style that he loved.

She breathed heavily and moaned, "Eric."

He covered her berry-painted lips with his mouth and molded his body against hers. His body was on fire. Her hands traveled down his back, to his buttocks, maybe encouraging him, maybe just getting used the feel of his body close to hers.

Drunk with desire and frustrated with the voice in his head that cautioned him not to rush into something from which there was no going back, he slowed down. His hand moved up her body a little at a time until he reached her breasts. The feel of them, even covered by a bra and a dress, made him growl like an animal. "Victoria, I want to touch every inch of you."

Her lips found his again. "Touch me, then," she whispered hotly against his mouth.

Damn. Those three words nearly made his mind blow a fuse. One hand skimmed down her body, pulling on her dress, sliding it up her leg until his hand could slip under. Her skin was pure silk. His fingers played with the lace of her panties. The heat of her body penetrated the fabric. And he wanted to be consumed by it. Now. Immediately. "I want you so bad."

"Let's... go to one of the bedrooms."

He lifted his head.

Her voice was tight. Her eyes dark with passion.

Dropping a kiss on her neck and another on her shoulder, and sliding his hand back down her leg, he asked, "Is that what you want?"

"What do you think?"

"I mean, really what you want?"

Her face was flushed, and she looked confused. "Things have gone from zero to ninety in a matter of hours, haven't they?"

He took his time, letting her dress fall, kissing her breasts through the tight fabric of her dress, pressing his hips against hers. Slowly drawing in his need. Fighting to keep from doing what his sex-starved body craved. Finally, he cupped her face and dropped a gentle kiss on her swollen lips. "I think we should date."

She laughed deeply, way too sexy. "I love that idea."

"Me too. Love the idea. That's why I'm giving up what... damn it, I want right now."

He stepped back. She sighed.

"You deserve the romance, the magical dating phase," he said, more to convince himself that he was doing the right thing than to inform her.

Her fingers combed through his hair, and her eyes warmly studied him. "Are you trying to make me fall in love with you?"

Her question stopped his thoughts cold, stiffening his back. Was he?

"Because my heart is doing some pretty crazy flips right now."

He took her hand and kissed her fingers, then walked her to

her bedroom, ignoring the question he couldn't answer. "I had a great night. You wanna go out again tomorrow night?"

With a smile, she nodded. "You dropping me off at my door?"

"Yeah." He leaned a hand on the doorjamb. "See you tomorrow?"

She gave him a quick, soft kiss. "Maybe. Call me." Then she slipped into her room

Eric chuckled and went to sit outside for a while. He wouldn't be able to sleep for probably a couple of hours.

Chapter Sixteen

Victoria awoke early. Normally she would have slept in after a late night, especially one when she'd stayed up sexually frustrated and emotionally shaken, replaying the scene with Eric over and over in her mind. The man was beyond sweet, and he made her insides melt in so many ways. But life called for her to get up and take care of her responsibilities. She took a quick shower, trying not to let her heart take over her head. When she saw Eric this morning, she had to be cool. She dressed in a pair of jeans and a spaghetti strap top. Her mother would probably be going to the club today, and she would, too. She prepared a plate of fresh fruit. She placed it on the center of their small card table in case Eric wanted some as well when he woke up. Then grabbed a yogurt cup and her cell phone. As she enjoyed her breakfast, she speed-dialed her mother.

Jaqueline answered on the second ring.

"Good morning, Mom."

"Victoria, how was the reunion? You didn't stop by and let me see you all dressed up."

"No, we got back late. But it was fun. Are we going to the club today?"

"Yes," she said, not sounding very excited.

Eric walked into her field of vision, in a pair of shorts and a T-shirt. The sleepy, intimate look of him, actually brought warmth to her face. "I'll, ah, pick you up around one?"

"All right, querida. I'll be ready."

Victoria said good-bye and stared at Eric.

He took a seat across from her. Reached for a bunch of grapes and popped a few in his mouth. "Want one?"

"I have some." She pointed to the plate she'd loaded with grapes, blackberries, and a banana.

But he reached across and held a grape to her lips anyway. Victoria took it, even though she felt sort of silly.

He smiled, stood, and walked around the table. Bending down, he eased a spaghetti strap down her right shoulder and gently dropped kisses and little nibbles on her skin. As if every touch of his lips raised her body temperature five degrees, her skin grew hot. When he finished, he crouched by her knees and looked up at her. "What would you like to do today?"

She lifted an eyebrow and swallowed. "I'm *going* to spend the afternoon with my mom at the Argentine Club. I'd *like* to get started on those dates as soon as possible, but I guess that will have to wait."

He placed both hands on her knees and moved them seductively up her jean-clad legs.

"Can I go to the club, too? I promise to behave." His hands jumped from her thighs to her waist, where he rested them lightly.

She hooked her own hands behind his neck. "Do you really want to go?"

He nodded. "I actually do. I want to be where you're at."

She lowered her head and rested her forehead against his. "I'm really starting to like you," she said, overwhelmed with the whirling sensations of pleasure just his words stirred in her.

He kissed her lips and sat back on his heels. "That means I can go?"

"Of course, but you don't need my permission. It's your club, too, Eric."

"Part of our shared history."

"That's right. We've both been cursed with all the crazy Argentine traditions, and they're part of you, just like they're part of me." And maybe that was the biggest attraction between them. The bond they shared ran deep and would always be there.

"Maybe it's not a curse after all. I didn't want to be part of all that when I was younger. But lately I've realized I've become part of nothing, and it doesn't feel good. I need life to have a deeper meaning."

"Deeper than what?"

He grinned wryly. "I don't know. Deeper than traveling around, seeing places on my own, and making money. I can't remember why I wanted to do that anymore."

"Maybe you needed to figure out who you were apart from your parents and your culture."

"Maybe." He winked. "Is that what you feel?"

"Yes."

He entwined his fingers with hers. "Maybe we can help each other. I'll take a step back in and try to reconnect, and you take a step out and leave some of that behind. It'll be a new beginning for both of us."

She'd already taken many steps out. She was figuring out who she was and what she wanted. Now she needed to help him return home. And she wanted to, more than anything.

Jaqueline spent the morning reading. She was starting to understand that she wasn't insane, and that there was nothing wrong with the feelings she'd been having lately. Women who spent their entire lives dedicated to their children and husbands often felt at a loss when that family was all of a sudden gone.

She bought a journal and a planner to create a new plan for

her future. That was another thing she was coming to realize. The future wasn't something only for her husband and her children. Why couldn't she create a fulfilling new life different from the one she'd had as a mother?

Excited, she logged on to the online community she was coming to enjoy chatting with. She spent about an hour and a half sharing her ah-ha moments and her plans for the upcoming cruise. She looked at pictures of young men and women in military uniforms from other members who were not simply missing their children because they'd moved out, but had the added worry for their safety. At least she didn't have that fear.

Victoria arrived with Eric shortly after noon. Although she was surprised to see them together, she tried not to show it. She wondered how many things they did together now and if they were becoming an actual couple. Jaqueline didn't see how that was possible when Eric was here only temporarily. She hoped Victoria kept that in mind.

"Oh, my God, Mom, are all these boxes in the living room things you're going to get rid of?"

Jaqueline poured them both a glass of orange juice. "Yes. I'm going to have the Salvation Army pick it all up this week."

Victoria looked through some of the boxes. "All our board games?" she complained.

"If you want them, take them. I have no use for those anymore."

Victoria gave Eric a look as if to say, *Can you believe she's getting rid of this stuff?*

He stood beside her. "Tell me which ones you want to keep and I'll put them in your car," he said, placing a hand on her shoulder.

"This one." She picked up Monopoly. "And this one." Scrabble. "Oh, and these puzzles." She piled them into Eric's arms. "Am I taking too many?"

"Take what you like, but I'll have to make another trip if you add any more."

"My dad's chess game; he won't want to lose that. Okay, that's it."

Eric staggered to the car, and Victoria sat at the kitchen table and accepted the juice.

Jaqueline looked her over. "You're getting terribly thin. On your body type it doesn't look good to be too skinny."

"I feel great. I go for a run every morning and am up to three miles."

Jaqueline wanted her to feel great, of course, and to be healthy—but a little meat on a woman's bones was healthy. Why did these American kids all think they had to look like mannequins? "You're probably not eating much living with Eric. Are you cooking?"

"Yes, but not too much because we want the kitchen to stay in new condition. But I'm eating fine. In fact, I'm looking forward to an asado at the club today. Are you ready?"

Eric walked back inside. He went back to the boxes.

"I'm ready," Jaqueline said. "Let me get a sweater. The air-conditioning is always too high at that club. There's juice on the table," she said to Eric.

"Oh, thank you." He picked up her camera. "Nice. You aren't getting rid of this, are you?"

"I'm thinking about it," she said, still not certain she wanted to give up entirely on her passion for photography.

"I'll buy it off you, if you decide to get rid of it."

"You like to take pictures?"

He blushed. "I just want to take some pictures of Victoria. I have a digital I use for my houses, but I bet this one will take some really nice shots."

She gazed at the young man Eric had grown into. Did he love Victoria? Was that possible? And if he did, how long would it last before he found another woman to love and hurt Victoria, erasing the pure feelings she might have for him? "Take it," she said, as she turned away. But before she reached the hallway she turned back. "Borrow it. And bring it back when you're finished."

"Thank you, Mrs. Torres."

"I'll have to show you how to use it. That's a complicated camera. The lenses take some work."

"I'd appreciate that," he said, full of sincerity.

Jaqueline headed to her bedroom, knowing that if she didn't, she'd say things she shouldn't. The boy was too charming and handsome for his own good, and Victoria would fall for it all, just like she herself fell for Victor. She had to fight the urge to tell him to stay away from her daughter.

Of course Lucia was thrilled to see them all at the club. And Victoria was her new best friend. Lucia hugged her and pulled her aside. "Eric looks so happy when he's with you," she said. "I'm not implying anything. But you look great together, like you fit."

That wasn't implying anything? "Thank you, Mrs. Ortelli."

"You know since you two decided to work on that house together, he hasn't mentioned leaving even once."

"I guess you're hoping he sticks around a long while, huh?" She felt for Lucia, she really did. She'd been so heartbroken when Eric left. She remembered Jaqueline sitting on the couch, holding Lucia while she cried. She'd heard it all from her bedroom and had hated Eric back then.

"He belongs here with all of us. A man has to be surrounded by those who love him in order to reach his potential. Love makes him stronger and happier and healthier."

"Well, he can't even think of leaving until he sells the house, so don't worry. Okay?"

"But there could be other houses, right?"

"I really don't know his intentions."

Lucia patted her face. "You're right. Let's not worry about that now. The wonderful thing is that he's here and he's happy, and you're a big part of that reason."

Victoria blushed. "Mrs. Ortelli, I don't think that's true." If she was responsible for Eric's happiness and desire to stick around, when Eric left would Lucia also feel that she was responsible for him leaving? "I'd better get to the classroom to help out. Excuse me."

She hurried away, leaving Eric, who had found a table to sit at and fiddle with her mother's camera, in the main hall. If Lucia had any more questions, she could direct them at her son.

A couple of hours flew by. She loved working with the kids, even if they complained about having to do anything at all. Alyssa was one of her favorites, but she was a heavy complainer. Today she found issue with everything.

"But you get to do crafts and fun things," Victoria said to the precocious seven-year-old.

"This is boring." She waved the collage of fall images in front of Victoria's face.

"When I was little they actually had Spanish lessons here on Sunday." Victoria eased her hand down and cocked an eyebrow. "It was like school. You're lucky. I wouldn't complain—it could be worse."

"I could be home playing DS or playing with my friends."

Victoria sympathized with her—but hey, this was part of the burden all Argentine kids had to bear. Sundays at the club. When lunchtime arrived, everyone was happy, including her.

That was until Lucia cornered her again at the table. She set down a bowl of salad and gave Victoria a hug. "Would you and Eric like to come over for dinner next Friday night? I can't invite Eric without inviting you anymore. You've always been like family, but now that you and Eric are so close, you're even more like a daughter."

"Oh, thank you." But she didn't know what to say. It seemed strange to go to dinner to her mother's friend's house. And what if Eric didn't want to go? She couldn't decide for him. "I'm not sure what Eric wants to do on Friday."

"Why don't you two talk it over and let me know?"

"Mrs. Ortelli, did Eric say anything about...us being a couple?"

"No, no, no. I know you're not. Are you?"

She glanced at Eric and was happy to see him playing cards with Eduardo, off to the side. They were laughing and joking. Eric would win them all back one at a time. They'd all see the same amazing man she did. And for those who didn't, it was their loss. "We're just friends, Mrs. Ortelli. I need to have a friendly chat with him. Excuse me, I'm sorry."

Victoria hated to interrupt, but Lucia was driving her crazy.

"Hey guys. Having fun?"

"Hey Victoria," Eduardo said. "Killing time until lunch."

"Is it time to eat yet?" Eric asked. "We're starved."

"Ah, almost." She spoke to Eduardo. "Can I pull Eric away for just a second?"

Eduardo shrugged. "Sure."

She motioned for Eric to stand.

Moving off to the side with Victoria, Eric smiled. "Pulling me away for a kiss?"

"Shh, no I want to talk about your mom," Victoria whispered.

He angled his head closer to hers. "My mom?"

"Eric, you have to talk to her. She's fishing for information about our relationship. Inviting us over for dinner. Telling me I'm like her daughter..." She sent him a pleading look. "I don't know what to say."

Eric laughed. "Tell her the truth."

"You tell her, and tell her not to broadcast it to the entire club." Especially when there wasn't much to broadcast. They'd agreed to date. Nothing more. And if something more did develop then it should stay between the two of them.

"She likes you. She probably will want to shout it to the whole town."

"First of all, she'd like any woman she believed could keep you around for a while."

"True."

"And secondly, Eric, we decided to go on a few dates, not get married. Please, tell her it's no big deal."

He nodded. "She's going to make a big deal about it, but I'll try to keep her calm."

"Thank you. I need some wine. See you at our lunch table."

"I'll meet you there."

Eric returned to sit with Eduardo and sighed.

Eduardo picked up his cards again. "Game over? Or you want to keep playing?"

"Mmm," Eric murmured, thinking about Victoria and his mother and what to say. "I think we're done."

Eduardo stood. "You and Victoria... hooking up?"

Eric watched Eduardo for judgment, condemnation, acceptance. "I like her a lot. But I may just be passing through. I don't want to be a jerk, not with her."

Eduardo nodded. "Maybe you stick around." He looked around the club. "We're a strange group, but we're family. You know, Eric?"

"I know. But I gotta go where the work is."

"Right." He tapped Eric's shoulder with the back of his hand. "I saw you at the high school reunion with Victoria on the dance floor." He put his index finger under his eye in an Argentine gesture that meant *watch out.* "I'm sure Susana and a couple of others saw it, too."

"There aren't any secrets in this place. I'd forgotten." Maybe that was why his mother was giving Victoria the third degree. Gossip had probably already made the rounds and the stories had most likely been exaggerated or changed five times. He'd better talk to his mother and fill her in. He got up and went to find her.

With lunch over and done with, Jaqueline helped clean up, then went in search of Victoria and Eric to see when they wanted to go home. Lucia said she and Antonio could take her home, but she wanted to spend what few minutes she could with her daughter. After all, she could have driven herself. The whole point of leaving her car behind was to drive with Victoria.

She didn't see Victoria right away but found Eric off in the corner, playing with her camera. They had stopped on the way to the club and she helped him buy rolls of film. Curious, she sat with him.

"Figuring it out?"

He glanced at her and smiled. "Sort of. It's complicated, but I like the idea of controlling the process rather than having a camera decide everything for me."

"Let me see," she held out her hand, and he passed her the camera. "I started out with simple cameras and slowly learned the features that make a good one. I'm sure there are better ones today, but this was the top of the line when I bought it. Victor took me shopping and ordered me to choose the best."

"Great guy," Eric said. He leaned back, and crossed his ankles carelessly.

Jaqueline raised an eyebrow. Was Lucia's boy tossing in his

opinion on her separation from Victor? "My point is that I worked my way up to this camera. It might be too much for you to start with."

"I've had cameras before. But they're the point-and-shoot digitals that focus and do all the work for me."

"But you'd probably get better prints from those specifically because there are fewer variables to control."

"What variables do I need to control?"

She sighed, wondering why she was so reluctant to teach him the basics of using her camera properly. Maybe because she preferred to box it up and not think about it anymore. Holding the camera up for him to see, she said, "The shutter controls how long the film is exposed to light. This is important because what you're doing with a camera is recording the light patterns of real images on a layer of light-sensitive material—the film. So this is your first variable, controlling shutter speed."

Eric leaned closer, resting his forearms on the table, to see what she was doing.

"Basically, you want to balance film speed, aperture size, and shutter speed."

"Okay."

"With film speed, you want to choose the correct ISO rating. Like I explained at the store you want to choose lower ISO for places with more light, like outdoors. Higher ISO for dark places."

"Got it."

"Now the lens. That's the key to a perfect picture. And you'll have to play with it until you get the right focal length." She adjusted the lens. "What should we focus on?"

Eric grinned. "Her." He pointed to Victoria, who was listening to Nelly.

Jaqueline aimed the camera at Victoria. She changed the lenses and turned them until she found the angle and focus she wanted. The weight of the camera felt great in her hands. She remembered all the times she'd photographed the girls as babies and kids. She had sometimes followed them around for hours trying to get the right shot. "Getting the perfect picture is sometimes a matter of patience," she said. "Waiting. Watching."

Across the room, Victoria nodded and listened to Nelly. She looked bored. She crossed her arms, she shifted on her feet. Jaqueline noticed again how thin she'd gotten. She looked good, but she didn't look like *her* Victoria anymore. The sadness in her heart intensified. Then something changed in Victoria's expression and she lowered her arms and laughed at something Nelly said. Her chin lifted and her face lit up. Jaqueline immediately clicked and took the picture. "If you're lucky, you catch the image you've been waiting for."

Eric nodded. "I'll have to practice."

Jaqueline smiled at Eric and handed back the camera. He'd made her remember the joy of catching the perfect image. He was so young that he didn't see it yet, but life was nothing but a series of perfect moments, perfect images caught in memory for that instant and then they were gone. She had boxes of pictures. But all they were now were moments of the past that were gone, no matter how beautiful the shots or how many hours she worked to get them just right.

She gazed at the camera. Loving it, missing it, and at the same time knowing that she wasn't the same person who used to strive to capture the perfect image. She didn't believe in holding on to moments anymore. Because you just couldn't. It was all an illusion. Time moved on.

Eric stared at Victoria through the camera's viewfinder. Jaqueline wondered what he wanted to capture. What aspect of her daughter did he hope to pick up and hold on to? He lowered the camera but continued to stare at her with a serious, faraway expression.

"Keep practicing," Jaqueline said. "You'll know the perfect shot when you see it."

"Thanks," he said, almost sleepily smiling at Jaqueline. "I'll take good care of her."

Jaqueline couldn't help thinking that he was referring to more than the camera. Her heart skipped a beat. Young men were so full of promises. "I don't think cameras are females."

"They are in Spanish. *La camara*, right?"

"You're right." And though it pained her, she added, "And if you really promise to take good care of it—it's very precious to me—you can keep it."

"I promise," Eric said, and reached across to hold and gently squeeze her hand.

Chapter Seventeen

Monday morning, Victoria found a furniture rental company that worked with real-estate investors on a week-by-week basis. She walked through their gallery looking for just the right items. Since this wasn't going to be her home, she wouldn't decorate it the way she would her own personal space. But she didn't want it to lack the warm energy that would make a potential buyer fall in love with the house.

So she chose basic pieces to make the rooms look pulled together, and she planned to bring items from her home and borrow some from hers and Eric's parents to display. She chose just enough for the house to look lived in and appealing. Lucia gave her an adorable picture of Eric when he was five. She framed it and set it on the coffee table in the living room. Once she'd selected everything from furniture to kitchen dishes, she scheduled the items to be delivered. She made it out of there in time to attend her classes. The rest of the week was spent the same. Organizing the furniture that arrived on Wednesday and studying. Transforming the remodeled house into something that resembled a home. She barely had time to talk to her mother.

Eric reminded her Friday night that Jaqueline and Lucia were leaving the following morning for their cruise and they had agreed to drive them to Long Beach.

"Oh hell," Victoria said, as she arranged a small group of vases on a corner coffee table.

He reached for her arm and pulled her onto the couch. "This place looks amazing. I can't believe what you did in one week."

"I'm exhausted."

He pulled her closer so her body rested against his. And he dropped a kiss on the top of her head. "I'll make some dinner, then you can go to bed early."

Eric felt so warm and strong, and she wanted to close her eyes and fall asleep right there next to him. But she was hungry. "Okay," she said.

He slipped off the couch. "Don't move." He hurried to her room, and when he came back he had the book she'd been reading at night. "Here you go. Lay back, relax, and take your mind off everything for a while."

Victoria took the book, touched by his thoughtfulness. She held his fingers and pulled him forward. He bent down, filling her nostrils with his sexy masculine scent, and their lips met in a sweet kiss that made her want so much more of him. She wanted to spend hours getting to know more of the man he'd become. "You're a great kisser," she said.

He grinned. "This weekend I plan to take you out on our first date and show you just how good a kisser I can be."

"Mmm," she said. "I can't wait."

As he slowly stood, he watched her. "Stay there a sec." And he disappeared down the hall again. This time he came back with her mother's camera. She groaned internally. He'd been photographing her all week as she worked putting the house together. He changed the lens and focused on her, then snapped shot after shot of her sitting on the couch.

"That's enough," she said.

"No, wait. Stay there. Relax."

She laughed and reclined on the couch, resting her head on her hand. "What are you going to do with all these pictures?"

After he took about another dozen pictures, he lowered the camera. "Keep 'em."

"All of them?"

"The best. That way I can take you with me wherever I go."

Hearing him mention leaving sent her heart plunging down to her stomach.

"I want to remember this house, and our time together here."

"Oh." She pulled herself up and gazed down at her hands, then placed the book on the coffee table. "When will you be leaving?"

He placed the camera on the coffee table beside her book, and crouched down to look her in the eyes. "Victoria."

She lifted her gaze and met his.

He reached across and placed the palm of his hand on her face. His fingers caressed her skin, and wove into her hair. "What are you thinking?"

She shrugged. "Nothing." She eased away from his touch. "I'm hungry. I'll help you make dinner."

"No," he stood. "I'll do it." He looked like he wanted to say more, but he turned away and a few moments later she heard him working in the kitchen.

Victoria sighed. Damn it. She didn't want him to go.

Saturday morning Victoria dragged herself out of bed. If she hadn't promised to take Jaqueline and Lucia to Long Beach she probably would have stayed under her covers all morning. As she showered, she thought about her parents. Although she was happy that her mother had decided to take some time to explore herself, that she and Lucia had planned such a fun trip together, she worried about her parents' marriage.

Victor hadn't made an attempt to talk to her or Jaqueline.

Carmen told her that if she didn't call him once a week, he didn't call her. Was her father going to simply let his family go? Were these restaurants so important to him that it didn't matter if his entire family fell apart? She turned the water off, reached for a towel, and dried her body. She almost felt guilty for feeling so happy about her own life lately, when her mother and father's relationship was disintegrating.

She wrapped the towel around herself and left the bathroom.

"Hey," Eric said, coming out of his room.

So caught up in her own thoughts, Victoria startled and jumped.

"Whoa." He laughed. "Sorry." He pulled her into his arms in a bear hug from behind.

She held on tight to her towel, but rested her head back on his shoulder. "You scared me."

He bent his head and kissed her neck. "Mmm, Victoria. Drop the towel and come to bed with me."

She turned her head and looked at his profile, surprised by the direct invitation even if he was just flirting. "And when both our moms miss their cruise, what excuse will we give them?" she played along.

"My mom will completely understand." He chuckled and brought his lips to her ear. "She is so hoping we fall for each other."

"I bet. What did you tell her?"

"That I'd use all my charm to convince you I can be your knight in shining armor."

She smiled as he gently nibbled on her earlobe. She wondered about their conversation. She used all her willpower to lift her head and turn around in the circle made by his arms. "I'm not looking for a knight in shining armor."

"What *are* you looking for?"

"I don't know. But I'm not sure I believe in fairy tales. Especially ones where the prince rides into town and rescues the grateful princess, making all her dreams come true."

His arms were loosely wrapped around her, his hands rested on her lower back above her bottom. "That's too bad. I'd kind of like to be the hero of a girl's fairy tale." He smiled and kissed her chin. "Or maybe her fantasy would be better. Do you have any sexy fantasies I can fulfill?"

Victoria laughed. "Cut it out. You're making me blush."

"Good." He groaned. "Okay, okay. I'll let you go, because we do have to get on the road, and because it's kind of unfair that you're almost completely naked and I'm not. It gives me an unfair advantage, right?"

"Right."

"And it makes me a bad guy to get so excited about that fact. Doesn't it?" His hands slipped lower on her bottom.

"Eric," she warned.

He growled and lifted his hands in the air and stepped back. "Fine. Get dressed, damn it."

He wasn't the only one who was excited. Not by a long shot. But this wasn't the right time. She got ready to leave and met him back in the living room, a little disappointed that he seemed completely recovered from his moment of crazed passion.

Even in early October, the temperature was in the seventies. Eric wore a pair of shorts and a light button-up shirt. And an out-of-place baseball cap on backward. She handed him the keys to her Saturn. "Want to drive?"

He took the keys and her hand. "Yep," he said, as they hurried out of the house. They picked up Jaqueline first. Eric helped her with her bag while she got settled in the car. Then he rushed to Lucia's house and honked. Victoria frowned. "Have you exhausted all your gentlemanly manners?"

"I don't need to get out for her. My dad will help her."

"I'll go to the door." Victoria got out of the car, but before she could reach the door, Antonio and Lucia walked out. As Eric said, Antonio loaded her suitcase into the trunk. Then gave her a long hug and kiss. Victoria got back into the car.

"What did I tell you?" Eric said.

Victoria ignored his smug smile.

"I should drive you," Antonio said.

"Don't be ridiculous. The kids can do it." Lucia patted his back and walked around the car.

"No use in both of us going," Eric said, hanging his head out the window.

Antonio agreed and opened the door for his wife.

"Call you later," Eric told him, and got on the road before the good-bye could drag on any longer.

Lucia and Jaqueline chatted for the entire drive, barely letting Eric or Victoria get in a word. When they finally got to the dock, Victoria and Eric watched them walk up the gangplank to the ship. Victoria let out a sigh of relief. "I hope they have fun."

"I don't like her going off by herself."

Victoria turned to see the frown on his face. "Give me a break. She's a grown woman."

"My dad was a basket of nerves this morning. Didn't you notice?"

"He'll live."

"That's a shitty attitude to have."

She opened her mouth to say something but changed her mind. Instead she turned around and strolled along port, enjoying the warm day and the awesome view of Long Beach. "My mom needs this break to relax and think about what she wants."

Eric followed along, with his hands in his pockets. "I don't know. Marriages don't stay together by people avoiding their problems. Leaving to spend time by herself isn't going to fix your parents' problems," he said.

Victoria stopped walking. "Eric, give me a break. What do you know about staying around to work out problems? You're the expert on leaving and doing what makes you happy, without one thought about the people you leave behind."

His eyes narrowed and he frowned. "I didn't leave a wife. I left my parents. That's different. I went to create a life for myself."

"Well, that's exactly what my mother is doing. After all the years she spent being a mother and wife, she deserves to spend a few weeks on herself. And so does yours."

"You talk like being a wife and mother is a jail sentence."

"Maybe it is." She turned away and headed to the car. The last thing she wanted was to fight with Eric, but he pissed her off.

He opened the car and got behind the wheel. "Want to hang out in Long Beach for the day? Not a fancy date, but a date just the same."

"I don't care."

"I'm sorry we disagree." He sighed. "But let's not fight."

She didn't want to fight, either. "Fine." Maybe she was just tired.

"And I did think about the people I left behind."

Would he think about her when he left again? Of course he would. He'd have his damn pictures of her. Damn it—she couldn't get the irritation out of her system. She was definitely tired. "I want to go home," she said.

He reached across and touched her shoulder.

She pulled away.

"Okay," he said. "We'll go home."

Jaqueline and Lucia enjoyed a fabulous dinner and met three couples who were assigned to their dinner table. Jaqueline partly wished that she was on this cruise with Victor, but another part of her thought it was nice to be here with her best friend.

After dinner, they caught a lovely show with dancing and

music in the lounge. Lucia seemed to be enjoying every moment. As they made their way back to their cabin, she couldn't stop talking about the costumes.

Jaqueline nodded. "Gorgeous." And those women had *some* bodies. Even when she was young she didn't remember looking like that.

Lucia prepared her bed. "I feel a bit guilty. This is the first time all day I've thought of Antonio. I hope he had a good dinner."

"Call him."

"Good idea."

Jaqueline went to the bathroom to take off her makeup, wash her face, and brush her teeth. When she returned to the room, Lucia was still talking.

"I love you," she whispered, full of emotion, and disconnected. She sat on her bed with a gratified look. "Eric is such a wonderful son. He went to have dinner with his father."

"Good. See, you didn't have to worry about Antonio."

"He told me not worry and to have fun. He and Eric ate Subway sandwiches and watched sports." She giggled. "Men."

She wondered what Victoria had done that night. They were obviously a couple now, though Jaqueline didn't know the extent of their relationship.

"I'm so glad Eric is home. This is exactly what Antonio needs. Time alone with his son." She undressed and pulled a nightgown over her head. "Antonio said that Eric seemed upset about me leaving him alone. Isn't that adorable?"

"Victoria has always been like that with her father. She worries about him all the time. Until recently anyway. But it's not the same as having a boy. I sometimes wish Victor had a son."

"He has two wonderful girls. And he'd better open his eyes and see what he's got before it's gone," Lucia said. "I haven't said much, Jaqui, but after all you've done for him, he's acting like un hijo de puta."

"We've never been enough for Victor."

"Then I feel sorry for him."

They changed the subject and chatted about everything and nothing until about three in the morning, when they both finally fell asleep.

Victor spent the whole week in Newport Beach. The structure was really beginning to resemble a restaurant. He'd planned the new menus and, though the food would be pretty much what he currently had, he updated the look of the menu and adjusted the prices for the locale.

But as the weekend rolled around and he hung out at the original La Parrilla, still operating at full capacity and needing his attention, he found himself less focused than usual. He sat in his back office staring off into space. Victoria had stopped by early Saturday to pick up Jaqueline and take her to the cruise ship. His heart hammered in his chest as he peeked out of the garage and saw Jaqueline leaving. He worried for her safety and worried that she'd have too good a time without him. What if she decided she actually enjoyed the single life? What if even after working so hard to build his restaurant empire, Jaqueline didn't fall back in love with him?

He decided to go to the Argentine Club on Sunday. Maybe he'd run into Victoria. He missed working with her. He missed seeing her and knowing what she was up to.

But he spent all afternoon at the club and Victoria never showed. Instead he wasted hours playing cards and losing money. He watched other families laugh and enjoy being together while his family was scattered all over the place. As he got ready to go home, he felt like a loser in more ways than one.

"I finally got lucky," Antonio said, gathering his winnings.

Victor smiled. "Had to happen."

"Going back to your garage?"

"Quiet," Victor said, looking around to make sure no one heard Antonio's big mouth.

"They've only been gone one day and I want to charter a boat and go find them. Want to go with me?" Antonio asked.

Victor shrugged. "Enjoy it. She'll be back telling you what to do before you know it."

Antonio rested an arm on his back. "Yes, she will."

Victor grew uncomfortable. He headed to the door, waving good-bye to the others.

Antonio walked beside him. "Eric came over last night worried that I'd fall apart without his mother. I told him I'd be fine, and he said his mother never should have left me alone."

"He's right."

"No, he's not. And I told him so. He got into a fight with your daughter because he told her women had no business leaving their posts as mothers and wives." He laughed. "I guess little Vicki let him know what she thought of *that* idea."

Victor felt a hot flash of indignation at any man arguing with his daughter, even Eric. And he was proud she'd stood up for her mother and women in general. "Maybe we haven't set the best examples as fathers."

"I've always treated my wife well. I don't know where he gets these things. I told him to go home and apologize."

Victor scowled. He hadn't always treated *his* wife well. He'd taken her for granted more than he cared to admit. What had he inadvertently taught his daughters to expect from men? In a way, he was glad Victoria wasn't going to accept the same treatment from a man. "I might have some apologizing to do myself. To my girls. And to my wife."

Antonio nodded. "When Eric left home to work as what I considered a construction worker, I didn't talk to him for a whole year. And even after that, I kept him at a distance, to punish him, I guess. And because I was ashamed, because I'd failed him. But I lost a lot of years with him because of my stubbornness. If I had to do it again, I'd support any damn thing he decided to do, even if it killed my dream for him. No dream is worth losing your kid."

Victor stared at Antonio. He swallowed a lump in his throat. "You're right." He took a breath and stood. "Take care, Antonio." He went home. Correction—to a garage in the back of an empty house that used be a home. How the *hell* had his life come to this?

Chapter Eighteen

Victoria had her iPod firmly plugged into her ears as she poured over her books and design plans. And not because she was intent on ignoring Eric. Their argument had been long forgotten. He'd been a fool to tell a woman like Victoria, who was just now enjoying her independence, that women didn't deserve some time alone once married. He was lucky she hadn't packed her bags and left that night. But she hadn't. She'd apologized to him, as soon as he got home from having dinner with his father. Even before he could tell her *he* was sorry. So they'd spent the night enjoying a late swim in the pool and talking. If that counted as their first date, it was perfect, because he learned tons of little things about her, like that beer made her throw up. And big things, like how many kids she wanted. And huge things about himself, like maybe he'd like to see what she looked like with her belly swollen with a baby someday. Crazy. Insane. But the thought had definitely been there.

So thanks to his father's good advice, she wasn't angry with him. But she was annoyed. Eric hired two guys to put up crown molding, and the constant hammering was driving her crazy. It wasn't doing much for him, either.

He tapped her shoulder. She pulled out one of the earbuds.

"Want to go out to lunch? Get out of here for a while?" He motioned toward the door.

She sighed, turned her music completely off, and nodded. "Sure."

All the large projects in the house were complete, but the finishing touches needed to be done before the open house. Crown molding was one of those details that made a house stand out.

"They're awfully slow," Victoria said, as they drove away from the house. "They've been at if for four days."

"And when they're finished, I've hired guys to redo the lighting in the backyard."

"What? The lighting is fine. Why do that now?"

He pulled into the parking lot of a little family restaurant. "It'll look better."

"But the lighting is fine."

"Fine is not good enough." Besides, as soon as they were finished, the house would go on the market, and he honestly couldn't deal with the fact of moving out yet.

"Then why didn't you have the work done simultaneously? That's going to add another week to your building time."

He took her hand. "Next time I'm going to make you my project manager. You're good."

"Why aren't you worried? You wanted to be done by the end of September and it's close to the end of October."

He pulled her into his arms and backed her against the truck. "I guess I'm enjoying myself too much to be worried. Just think, next time we go swimming, the lights in the backyard will be awesome. But maybe we'll leave them off and swim naked. What do you say?"

She smiled. "I'm ready for you to see me naked, if that's what you're asking."

He lifted an eyebrow. He and Victoria were having such a good time, he didn't want it to end. Although he probably should have been worried about getting the house on the market—and he would be later—right now he couldn't have cared less. "Let's have lunch first. Then if you want to take your clothes off, I'll kick those guys out."

"No. Please. Let them finish." She laughed. "But I'll give you a rain check on that naked business."

He kissed her and then, with a wink, pulled her toward the restaurant. "I'll take it."

Eric spent a week looking for new properties to renovate, but he didn't come across anything promising. So he decided to put shutters in the extra bedrooms where Victoria had hung drapes. When she got home and saw what he was doing, she wasn't pleased.

"The drapes looked good and were inexpensive," she said, pointing out the absolute truth.

He seriously needed a new project. Instead he'd cooked dinner and convinced her to play board games with him. His mother and Jaqueline had been gone ten days. And when he looked around the house, he admitted that he could have gotten all those minor fixes done in a couple of days. And he shouldn't have put the shutters in. He'd wasted two weeks. Hell.

But as Victoria raced around the Monopoly board, he smiled. Their relationship had gotten better and better every day. And that was worth the extra house payment he'd have to make. "I'm going to hire a Realtor. I think we're ready."

"Sure you don't want to redo the fireplace? Marble might look good," she teased.

"No, smart-ass. I'm done."

"You also owe me two hundred dollars for passing Go."

He shoved the board aside. "How about two hundred kisses instead."

"Sorry, I've got work to do tonight. I spent all my free time playing this game."

He ignored her and crawled across the floor, climbing over her. "Victoria?"

She smiled. "What?"

"You've done a great job with this house. And with my room at my mom's house." He studied her pretty face. "Thanks."

She kissed his lips in a feather soft brush. "You're welcome, Eric."

Tonight was Halloween. Eric waited excitedly for her to get home from school so they could attend the Argentine Club Halloween dance. Unfortunately, the holiday fell on a Tuesday night and she had classes. He rented a knight suit to surprise her. The darn thing was hard to get into, too.

When he heard her car pull up, he positioned himself by the front door. Victoria walked inside, bags and backpacks hanging from her arms, and when she spotted him, she screamed. Then she started laughing and dropped all the bags on the floor by her feet. She reached forward and lifted his face mask. "Oh my God, I love it."

"Your knight in shining armor, ma'am."

"Mmm." She ran her hand up and down his chest, which was covered in soft spongy stuff that looked like metal. "You are one sexy knight."

"Careful, ma'am. This costume is tight and I can't risk having it stretch in the wrong places."

She gave him an evil look from the corner of her eye and her hand traveled down. But much to his disappointment she stopped at about his navel. "I'm going to go get dressed," she said. "Stay put."

"I can't move. Don't worry."

She laughed and disappeared down the hall and into her bedroom. When she came back, she was wearing a short white dress with an apron like the ones home store employees wear, with the words *The Home Wrecker* written across the chest. The front pockets held a variety of plastic tools. On her head she wore a matching scarf, and her legs were encased in knee-high boots.

"Wow," he said.

"You get it?"

The only thing he got was instantly aroused.

"I couldn't find anything that went with being an interior designer. But this was pretty funny." She pulled out a robe. "I'm going to wear this at the club, too, because the outfit is a little bit revealing."

Not revealing. Sexy. And short. "You are the best home wrecker I've ever had the pleasure of working with."

She laughed. "Well after seeing you, I sort of wish I'd chosen a princess costume."

"I could tear all this off, get in a pair of jeans and a baseball cap and spray sweat all over my chest, and go as a sweaty construction worker."

She narrowed her eyes. "There will be children at this event. I think we'd better save that look for my private enjoyment." She slipped the robe over her costume, adjusting the apron over the robe. "There we go. Better."

"I don't agree."

"Come on," she chuckled. "Let's go. I feel guilty that I didn't help set up this year. I usually spend all day before Halloween making sure things look great for the kids."

Eric couldn't remember enjoying anything more than he had this corny Halloween party at the Argentine Club. The women had the entire meeting hall decked out with spooky spiders and webs, and black and purple streamers. And on the tables were various games that the kids could participate in. They stationed him with a couple of other guys at a bowling table. He had a great time encouraging the kids. The little monsters, goblins, and princesses ran from booth to booth, picking up goblin tickets that Victoria said they would cash in for prizes at the end of the night.

During the dinner break, after all the games had been picked up, he sat beside Victoria at his parents' usual table. For tonight everyone brought simple salads or finger sandwiches and, of course, *empanadas* in a major potluck. No one cooked, and they used paper plates, which made it nice for everyone.

"That was a blast," Eric said, and discreetly kissed Victoria on the cheek.

"Victoria created all these activities years ago," Antonio said with obvious admiration. "The kids look forward to Halloween night all year."

"So what happens after dinner?"

"Costume contest onstage," Victoria said. "Adults included."

"The winner gets the witches' brew," Antonio explained.

When they'd arrived, every person donated five dollars to the witches' pot. There were a couple hundred people here tonight. Eric widened his eyes as he looked at his father. "So the winner gets about a thousand bucks?" he asked in amazement.

Antonio leaned across the table. "Yeah and last year little eight-year-old Mariela won. She was so excited. The women all made her mother promise that Mariela could use the money any way she wanted. Can you imagine being a kid and winning all that money?"

Eric grinned, sitting back and enjoying the night. The only thing that would have made it better would have been if his mother was here, too. She and Jaqueline would be back that weekend, and he knew his father was counting down the days.

He rested his arm behind Victoria's chair. "You should have dreamed this thing up when we were teens."

"No one would have listened to me back then. I was powerless. But now"—she raised one adorable eyebrow—"I'm the party queen."

Antonio nodded. "When it comes to parties, her word is law."

Eric slid his hand onto her shoulder. "I'm ready to let her make all the rules."

She laughed and stood. "You guys are nuts. I'm going to go get the costume contest ready."

Eric decided to go to the restroom before the contest began. While in the back, Mrs. Apolonia cornered him. "Eric, since your mother isn't here, I thought I should offer a few words of advice."

"About?"

"Your obvious relationship with Victoria."

"Okay," he said, bracing himself. He knew he wouldn't appreciate anyone's advice on the matter of his "relationship." But he knew that everyone in the club made it their business to butt into everyone else's life, so he resigned himself to listening.

"She's a very pretty girl and she's single, so I can understand why you didn't waste any time showing your interest in her."

He shifted in his uncomfortable suit, feeling his back muscles flex.

"And no one can really blame you for seeing the opportunity that she was vulnerable with all the nonsense going on in her family, to convince her to move in with you—"

"Mrs. Apolonia—"

"Not that she's blameless. After all she's a grown woman and could have said no. But when you both flaunt your sinful behavior here at the club, you make her look—"

"Sinful?" He stopped her before she went on and really pissed him off. "Not that it's any of your business, but there's nothing sinful going on. She and I work together, and though we live together, too, she has her bedroom and I have mine."

"I'm not naive, Eric. And Susana saw you together at your high school reunion."

"You didn't let me finish. I was going to say that even though our relationship has been platonic to this point, I'm not about to let how things look to others stop me from pursuing a woman I'm definitely interested in."

"I think that's extremely selfish of you."

"Hey." Victoria came up behind him. "We're about to start the contest." She smiled, her gaze bouncing back and forth between them. "What's going on?"

"Nothing," Eric said. He smiled at the older woman. "Nice chatting with you."

Mrs. Apolonia shook her head and walked away.

Victoria placed a hand on his arm. "What's up?"

He hooked an arm around her waist. "She was just...giving me some advice."

"Uh-oh."

"Yeah."

"Don't listen to her. I never do." She rested her arms on his shoulders and played with the hair touching his neck.

He smiled gently at the adorable woman who always made him feel better about everything. "What if she might be right?"

"Highly doubtful."

"She thinks I'm making you look bad. That I'm taking advantage of you."

She smiled. "Well, you haven't yet, but a girl can hope that you might soon."

He wanted to smile again but couldn't. He released her, stepping back and leaning his butt on a rectangular table. "Vicki, I know you probably have the same thoughts going through your head."

"What thoughts?"

He gripped the edge of the table with both hands. "That you shouldn't get involved with me. That I can't offer you anything permanent. That—"

"I haven't had those thoughts at all."

"Vicki, let me be honest. I wasn't planning on coming back home and falling in love with anyone. Not even you. But I think I am."

She stared at him, a pink flush appearing on her cheeks. Her expression told him she was surprised and maybe uncomfortable with his admission.

"And I'm having a hard time having to justify that to anyone. Even you."

"Justify?"

"Yeah. I love you. And I don't want to explain why or how it happened or defend it or make promises that I'm not sure I can keep."

She still looked stunned. "I'm not asking for any of that."

He released a breath from deep in his chest. Pushing off the table, uncomfortable in this ridiculous costume, he took a step toward her again. "I feel like everyone is waiting for me to make a grand statement about my intentions regarding you. My mom, your mom, our so-called friends, people at this club."

"Me?"

"Not so much you." He reached for her, placing the palm of his hand against the side of her face and caressing her cheekbone with his thumb. "Although I know the fact that I'll probably have to leave bothers you."

"Well, yes. To be honest, it does. But I like you and we're… involved, so of course I don't want you to go. That's natural, isn't it?"

Her words made him feel instantly better. Of course it was natural. And it showed she cared, which was amazingly wonderful. "Yes."

"And I promise, I'm not waiting for any declaration, even the one you just made."

"But the truth is, I do love you, Victoria."

She looked away, making his hand fall from her face.

"Neither one of us has to do anything about it," he added quickly. "Love is a feeling that doesn't really require any action. I'll love you whether I stay or go. Whether our relationship grows or doesn't." He tucked her hair behind her ear and brought her eyes back to connect with his. "I told you before that I think I loved you even when we were teens. I love you differently now. Deeper. More intensely. And I don't think that'll ever change."

She touched his chest, laying her hand flat over his heart. "You say these things, these amazing things. And you make grand, sweet gestures that make me want to close my eyes to reality and strip down to nothing in front of you."

He arched an eyebrow. "Don't let me stop you."

She smiled. "I mean strip down emotionally, and mentally, and yes, physically. Just give you everything. I've never felt like this before, Eric, and I don't know what to do about it."

His heart pounded and he was sure she could feel it. He pulled her into an embrace. "You don't have to do anything." She felt great in his arms.

"Neither do you," she said, looking up at him. "Don't let Mrs. Apolonia get to you. I really don't give a shit what she thinks about me."

Eric cared. He cared a lot, and it pissed him off that anyone would dare say anything negative about Victoria. But he had a feeling that Mrs. Apolonia would always find things to criticize others about. "You're right. Let's just enjoy what's happening between us and not try to define it."

"Agreed." She kissed him softly.

He hurried to the restroom, while she waited for him. Then they headed back to the main hall together and participated in the costume contest. Neither of them won, but he didn't care. He felt like a winner no matter what. And aside from that old woman trying to ruin his night, he had a blast.

Victoria made some coffee when they got home. Eric followed her into the kitchen. "Wait," he said, and took off her apron, making her drop her robe, then he reattached the apron. "Now the costume looks the way it's supposed to look." He sat at the breakfast table and watched her prepare the coffee.

Victoria enjoyed the way he looked at her. She'd never considered herself much to look at. Lots of women were overweight and still felt sexy, but she never had. Her weight had been a barrier between her and men. But Eric had made her feel beautiful from day one. She filled his coffee cup and placed it on the table. He reached across and ran his hands up the back sides of her thighs.

"Congratulations," he said. "You've reached your goal. You're officially hot."

As he continued to touch her, she knew she didn't want it to end here tonight. He'd actually told her that he loved her. She'd been speechless. How had life taken away a boy who was her friend and returned this man who left her breathless? A part of her knew that she loved him, too. She couldn't say that she always had. Of course she hadn't. What she loved about Eric was his passion for taking something ugly and broken down, and fixing it with his care and patience and loving attention until it slowly transformed into a thing of beauty. He saw the potential hidden within that others didn't. She loved that he could be strong and determined yet vulnerable. A fighter and defender of his dreams, while at the same time bowing his head with remorse for the pain he caused others. These were all part of the man he'd become—that hadn't existed the last time she'd known him. So this love she felt was new and fresh and something she couldn't voice, because she didn't know how to put all those feelings into words.

But she did know that she wanted him. At least for tonight. And she wanted him to know that. Finding the strength to be bold, she straddled him, her short dress riding up her thighs.

Eric groaned and his hands continued up the back of her legs to cup her bottom. Victoria leaned into him and pressed her lips to his. He pulled her intimately against his body. She wanted to get lost in all the sensations, in her emotions for him, in the relationship that had somehow blossomed into something beautiful and unexpected. "Eric," she whispered against his lips.

"You're gorgeous, Victoria."

"Let's take these costumes off," she said.

"But we're supposed to be dating before we—"

"I don't give a shit about those dates. We're way beyond that."

He pulled his hands from under her dress and untied her apron, leaving nothing but the flimsy white dress. Then, a fraction of an inch at a time, he lifted the white dress over her head, leaving her in her bra and panties. His breath grew harsher.

She began to help him out of his tight costume. The top part came off in one piece, and she stared at his gorgeous bare chest. Tan, hard, with a narrow line of hair that ran between his abs and below his belly button.

He caressed her back, and she his shoulders. His thumbs hooked onto the back of her bra and unsnapped it. She inhaled and closed her eyes. Softly his fingers slipped the straps down her shoulders. Even before the bra hit her lap, his hands were on her breasts. She leaned into his touch, lowered her head and kissed down his jaw to his neck. On the outside he was strong and rough, but inside he was gentle and loving. And he was hers. She was claiming him tonight.

“I can’t believe this is happening,” she breathed into his ear.

His right hand fisted in her hair and pulled her head back, taking her mouth passionately. His tongue delving hotly into hers, sparking dark, erotic thoughts of the pleasurable things they could do for each other without ever leaving the kitchen.

He broke away, kissing and nibbling down her neck until he reached her breasts. Arching her backward, he claimed her nipples, one then the other. The roughness of his stubble rubbed against the delicate skin, inflaming the liquid heat inside her.

“Oh, Eric,” she moaned. One hand clung to his shoulder, the other worked its way down their bodies, unsnapping the top button of his pants.

“Victoria,” he said against her breast, as he let one of her throbbing nipples slip from his mouth. “Man, Victoria. Oh, man, you’re beautiful.”

She reached for his face, framing it with her hands, bringing his lips up to hers. “I want to make love to you.”

“I want to make love to you, too,” he said.

She slipped off his lap and took his hand. He didn’t question her but followed her down the hall. When they got to her bedroom, she pulled him inside. She was glad they had decided not to label what they felt for each other or to question where things were going. It gave her the freedom to just enjoy him and what they had. As they spent the remainder of the night in each other’s arms, she didn’t have to debate with herself if she was doing the right thing or wonder how long this would last. Nothing mattered, except the natural expression of love between two people who wanted to be together. Life could sometimes be that simple.

Chapter Nineteen

Jaqueline didn't want the cruise to end. Tomorrow the ship would dock in Long Beach, and the peace and happiness she'd felt the last two weeks would vanish. She'd have to face her life again.

Lucia couldn't wait to get home and see Antonio, although she had had a blast. While Jaqueline spent many hours on the deck of the ship simply thinking, Lucia participated in as many ship activities as she could. She'd painted and sculpted, played bingo, gone to aerobics classes with women half her age. Every night they shared dinner and a show together, but during the days, they did their own thing.

Jaqueline finally finished reading all the books she bought. They helped her tremendously. And she realized something very important: No matter what, she couldn't turn back the clock. Of course, she knew that in the logical sense, but she had been considering picking up her childhood goals and continuing with them as if she hadn't lived a lifetime between then and now. How ridiculous that would be. She didn't want to be a photographer anymore. She had no dreams of seeing her photographs in magazines. What did that really matter? What she really wanted was to have what she had: a family that needed her. Sadly, she had to accept that they didn't need her in the same way anymore. She'd done her job and she'd done it well. And her reward had to be watching her girls tackle life on their own.

Lucia, who had been swimming laps, finished and sat beside Jaqueline. "Oh, that felt so good."

Jaqueline smiled. The day was beautiful. Warm and cloudless. The ship seemed to barely sway at all.

"You look sad," Lucia said.

"I was just thinking about... I don't know, the girls."

"Excited to see them? Well, Victoria at least?"

"I am, but I was thinking not of seeing them, but about a lifetime of raising them. I swear, Lucia, I can still remember how they smelled when they were tiny, pudgy babies."

Lucia smiled. "Nothing like the smell of a sweet baby."

"No, nothing. And holding them in my arms, especially late at night when it was just me and them, was magical. Looking into their eyes as I fed them from my body while swearing I'd protect them and love them forever."

"I sang to Eric and he giggled and reached for my nose. He was probably trying to get me to shut up."

Jaqueline inhaled a shaky breath. "I was their whole world back then. They didn't want to be separated from me for a second. When Victor picked them up, they screamed and cried. Both of them. And the second I took them into my arms again, they calmed down and the world was right."

"Eric was the same. Used to make Antonio so mad." She chuckled. "He felt that Eric was a boy and was supposed to want to follow him around instead of me. Antonio didn't understand that it takes time for little guys to turn into men and that they need their mamies during those few years."

"When do we start losing them?"

"Oh, Jaqueline," Lucia said, sounding so strong. So unlike the woman who cried every day when Eric first left. She'd gotten stronger.

"No, really. When does it happen? When we send them to

school? I cried more than they did when I had to leave them the first time. Especially with Victoria. She held on to my hand so tightly and she begged me not to leave her." Jaqueline's eyes filled with tears all over again. "It was the most painful experience of my life at that point."

Lucia reached across and took her hand. "It happens a little at a time, I guess. Little by little we become less important in their lives. But it's a good thing. I remember the first time Eric didn't want me to kiss him good-bye in school. My heart shriveled up inside me and I thought I would die. I went home and cried on Antonio's shoulder." She laughed. "My little baby was becoming a boy, and I didn't know how to deal with it."

"And what about when they become teenagers and don't even want to be seen with you?" Jaqueline added.

"You want to slap them silly and remind them that you were the one who changed their dirty diapers."

Jaqueline somehow found it inside herself to laugh. "God, it all happened so fast."

"Too fast," Lucia agreed.

They were silent for a few moments.

"The first time I kissed Eric and felt bristles on his face, I was heartbroken. He was turning into a man. He was no longer a baby or even a boy. I tried to hold on to that boy and I think I drove him away."

"No," Jaqueline said.

"Yes, I did, Jaqui. I wasn't the sole reason he left, but I was part of it. He needed to become his own man away from me and Antonio, and our demands. I see that now."

"It's not easy to let go."

"It's impossible."

Jaqueline agreed. "And yet we have to. I can't live with my heart lodged in my throat anymore. I'm not the mother of little girls. I'm going to be the mother of a doctor and of an interior designer. Two competent, beautiful women who will want to get married and have children of their own."

"We've done good, huh?"

Tears fell from Jaqueline's eyes, off her lashes and onto her lap. This was almost as painful as the first day of school. "We have."

Victor intended to call Victoria two weeks ago, but he'd gotten so busy he hadn't had the chance. He hadn't even been able to attend the Halloween event at the club. Not that he cared to go to that silly thing. Halloween had nothing to do with Argentina, so he didn't know why they bothered with all the craziness. But he'd wanted to drop by the club to talk to Victoria.

He sat in his office in La Parilla, reached for the phone, and dialed her cell.

She picked up immediately after the first ring. "Dad?"

"Ah, yeah."

"Is anything wrong?"

"No, nothing," he said. "I wanted to..." Apologizing wasn't easy for him. He didn't know what to say. "Do you want to come have lunch here at the restaurant today? To talk."

"Oh, well, that sounds nice, but I'm actually on the way out the door. Mom and Lucia are coming home today, and I'm going to go pick them up. Well, pick Mom up. Antonio will be there for Lucia."

Jaqueline was coming home. His heart picked up speed. He wished he were the one that was going to be waiting on the dock to collect his wife. Like Antonio. What if he did? What if he were standing there waiting for her? What would she say? Would she be happy or refuse to get in the car with him?

"Dad?"

"I see. Well, that's good news. I mean, that your mother is coming home. I... bet you missed her."

"Yes, I have," she said in a whisper-soft voice.

She was so grown up. She made him feel so old. Like after all these years she could see right through him the way he used to be able to see though her. "Well, we can have lunch another day. During the week I'm sort of swamped with work."

"Me, too," she said. "Next Saturday?"

"Sure, next Saturday is good."

"Okay, Dad. Thanks. It's good to hear from you."

"Yeah."

"I... I'll see you soon."

Was she going to say she loved him? She used to all the time. He hung the phone up and leaned back in his chair. Maybe he should have been the one to tell her *he* loved *her*.

Victoria cried in Eric's arms.

He patted her back and chuckled. "I don't understand why you're crying. He called. That's a good thing, isn't it?"

"But he sounds so sad, so alone. So distant."

"Victoria, I'll go pick up your mother if you want to go have lunch with him. To hell with the real-estate walk-through. I'll call our Realtor and tell her to do that on Monday."

"No." She shook her head and wiped her eyes, pulling out of his arms. "I want to go pick up my mom. And you need to do the walk-through and get the house on the market."

He placed his hand on her cheek. "I don't need to do anything. Except make you happy."

Eric filled a void in her heart that she had never known was there. With her, he was sweet and considerate and always said the right thing. "You do make me happy. Too happy."

"Too happy?" He laughed. "How is that possible?"

"It all seems too perfect, doesn't it?"

His hands slipped behind her neck. "Love is supposed to be perfect."

What did either of them know about love? "Is it?"

He eased her back and crawled over her. "Yes. And just for the record, you make me happy, too."

She hooked her arms around his neck. "Make love to me before I have to go."

Her request made him smile. "We don't have much time."

"We won't need much time."

They made love passionately, taking off enough clothes to satisfy each other. Victoria's worries melted away. Life really was perfect with Eric, and she didn't want it to ever end.

Victoria picked up Jaqueline. Antonio was there to pull his wife into his arms and kiss her in a way Victoria had never seen her parents kiss. The moment was so touching and personal that she and Jaqueline left them alone and headed to the car. Other than driving her home and listening to all the exciting things she'd done, they didn't spend a long time together. Victoria could tell her mother was tired.

They walked into her childhood home. The house felt cool, and a lack of air gave the house an oppressive feel. "You need to open the windows." Victoria stood in the living room looking around, not feeling the comfortable sensations that used to greet her when she came home. Instead everything seemed strangely foreign.

"I'll do that later. Right now I want a shower and to get some sleep."

Victoria couldn't stand it. She opened the living room window. "There. I guess I'll leave you alone to rest. Call you during the week?"

"Sure." Jaqueline came forward and wrapped her arms around her daughter. "It's so good to see you."

Victoria closed her eyes. "Good to see you, too." She held on to her mother tightly.

Jaqueline drew back. "Is everything okay?"

"Fine."

"You seem a little different."

Was she kidding? Everything was different lately. She was simultaneously deliriously happy and nursing a sense of loss where her family was concerned.

"Maybe it's just me," Jaqueline said. "You know my mother used to say that it's easy to see when you open your eyes—sounds better in Spanish." She gripped Victoria's shoulders and placed a soft kiss on her cheek. "I'm seeing a grown woman for the first time when I look at you, though I know she's been there all along."

Tears sprung to cloud Victoria's vision. Her mother didn't know what those words meant to her. She'd wanted her mother to see her as a mature adult for so long. "I guess I'm finally acting like a grown woman," she said.

"I'm proud of you, mi vida. I'm proud that you're following your heart. That you're strong and independent. Just let me baby you every once in a while, okay?"

Victoria nodded. "You got it."

She drove home, savoring the bittersweet shift in her world.

Victoria turned in a project, incorporating all the design details into a presentation board. Her instructor asked her to wait after class.

"Your project looks fantastic, Victoria." He said. "You obviously spent a lot of time working on it."

"I guess so. I never notice the time passing by." She wished she could say she struggled to get it done just right so it would sound more like she worked hard, but the truth was she didn't consider it work at all.

"You can be proud of the natural talent you have, Victoria," the instructor said.

"Thanks, but it was a blast. I loved it."

"I just wanted to congratulate you and tell you to stick with this. You're going to be very successful if you do."

She thanked him and, on cloud nine, hurried off to work. The few hours she spent at the design firm seemed to be paying off. It certainly was another thing she was loving. She didn't get paid much, but the work experience was worth more than money right now.

Still, when Eric sold the house and paid her for her work, she'd welcome the money. She'd been dipping a bit into her savings, and she didn't want to do that. Once she had to start paying rent, she'd need that money.

But for now, she decided not to worry about any of that and enjoy her life, which got greater every day.

Victor made sure a perfect lunch was prepared for him and Victoria Saturday morning. By the time she arrived at noon, everything was ready and waiting for her. He filled her glass with wine and sat across from her. She looked amazing. Happy. Healthy. Alive in a way she'd never looked when she worked at La Parrilla. "Raining outside?" he asked.

"Drizzly. Not bad for the middle of November." She took off her coat.

He nodded. "I had them prepare a full parrillada. I hope you're hungry."

The waiter brought a plate of empanadas for them to start with.

"Starving," she said, taking one of the meat pies. "How are the new restaurants shaping up?"

"Great. You've got to come see them. My favorite is the one in Newport Beach."

She smiled a wide, bright smile. "I'd love to see them." She took a bite out of her empanada.

"It's been much harder than I thought, though. The expenses. And dealing with contractors and banks and, hell, everyone. And keeping up here."

She swirled the wine in her glass, then took a sip, washing down the food. "I'm sorry I left when I did, Dad. It was bad timing."

He shrugged. "Don't apologize." He was the one who was supposed to be apologizing. "You look happy and that's what's important."

"I'm done working on Eric's property. It's just a matter of getting the house sold now. I might have some time to come help you out."

Of course he'd love that. To see her more often. To get her involved again. The right way this time. He wanted to jump all over her offer. "Thanks, Victoria. I'll think about it, and give you a call if I need you."

"Oh," she said. "Okay."

He didn't want her to think he was rejecting her, but he wanted her to follow her own path now that she'd started. Hell, being a parent was hard, even now that she was grown. What was the right thing to do? "I never realized that you had desires to explore your love of decoration. With Carmen, I knew. She loved school, she got amazing grades. I knew what she wanted. But with you . . . you didn't seem to want anything in particular."

She nodded, but he felt it wasn't really an agreement.

"I wanted you to be free to do nothing."

"Most daughters would be happy to play the role of pampered princess," Victoria said. "But I felt useless."

Victor could understand that. He was only sorry he hadn't seen it. "So now you're enjoying whatever you're doing?"

"I'm loving it. I'm taking classes at a design institute. I'm working for a design company and learning a lot. And staging Eric's real-estate investment was the most fun I've ever had."

Fun. What was it with young people always having to think of work as fun? Work was work. Challenging, satisfying, lucrative. But fun? He didn't understand that. "What are you going to do when he sells the house?"

She lowered her gaze and shrugged. "If he decides to flip another house, I guess he'll use me again."

Victor pinned a look on her and he couldn't help himself—he'd never been able to keep his mouth shut when it came to the men she dated, and this was no exception. "Interesting choice of words. What are you doing living with a man, Victoria?"

"It's not like that." She looked him in the eye. "Well, it wasn't like that when it started."

Victor cursed.

"I... love him."

"He's going to leave you once he sells his house and has had his fill of you." That was harsh, but she needed to hear the truth.

"I'll still love him. Besides, I've always known he wasn't going to be here forever."

"Then I'm surprised at what you're doing."

"Dad, please."

The waiter placed the steaming parrilla, a grill, in the center of the table. Victor stabbed a slab of short ribs and a chorizo. If he got his hands on Eric, he planned to bruise a few of his ribs. "Look, Victoria, I wasn't always the best husband, but—"

"Especially lately."

He held her gaze, not liking the look of condemnation in her eyes. He thought of Jaqueline and how he never felt he was good enough for her. Always wanting to prove to her that she made the right choice in marrying him. "It's torture to be married to someone you never feel you're going to measure up to, and with your mother, I always knew she deserved more than me."

Victoria frowned as she cut into her beef.

"So I've spent my whole life trying to become the man I'd promised her I'd be, and almost no time being a husband she could love."

"There's still time," Victoria said.

Was there? Or was it too late. "I think our marriage may be beyond repair, Victoria."

"Dad, Mom loves you. But she needs to know you love her back."

"I do."

"Then tell her. Show her."

"She doesn't even want to talk to me."

"Try it."

He nodded.

"And Dad, she needs a life of her own."

"I realize that too. She's spent years raising you girls and supporting my dreams. And none on her own." He reached across and gripped her forearm. "I don't want you to make the same mistake, Victoria. You only get one life, so be sure you do what you most want while you can. Don't throw your life away being a man's...anything, including wife—I'm not saying get married."

"I'm not planning to," she said. "Don't worry."

"I *am* worried. I love you, damn it. I don't want you to get hurt."

She lowered her fork and her eyes misted. "Eric won't hurt me. But thank you for caring."

"Of course I care. You're my daughter. I know I've been busy.

I've been preoccupied. But, Victoria, that's just me. You know me. I'm not... very sensitive... to other people's feelings, I suppose." He paused, unsure how to continue.

"I know." She locked her eyes with his. "I do know. And I love you, Papi. Just the way you are."

Victor smiled. He actually felt like smiling. He'd gotten through to her. He didn't know how. Except that Victoria had always known him best. And he hadn't realized how dead he'd felt lately without the closeness they'd always shared. He nodded.

"Well, let's eat," he said.

"Let's," she said with a big smile, digging into her food.

Monday morning when Victoria got home from work, a real-estate sign flapped in the wind of the front yard, announcing to the world that the house was for sale. She paused to look at the sign, and instead of feeling a sense of completion, she felt as if another chapter of her life was coming to an end before she was ready.

She dropped her things in her bedroom and went in search of Eric. He sat on the back porch, bouncing a handball against the new wooden fencing. He appeared in deep thought.

"Hey," she said. "What are you doing?"

He looked over his shoulder for a second, then threw the ball again. "Nothing."

"The sign is finally up. Exciting, huh?"

"Just the next step in the process." He caught the ball and threw it again.

Victoria leaned on the patio post. The sun had almost gone down and only a slight orange glow remained on the horizon. The breezed chilled her. "Think it'll sell fast?"

"We're going into Thanksgiving week, and usually December

isn't a good month for real-estate sales." He held on to the ball this time. Squeezing it in his hand.

She moved forward and placed a hand on his shoulder. "Are you worried?"

"No."

But he seemed worried, even though it wasn't like him to stress. His easygoing, carefree personality could be considered one of his few faults. Not by her—she loved his personality—but by those who didn't understand what a hard worker he truly was. "Good," she said. "Because we've done a great job. Someone's going to snatch this place up before we're even ready for it. You'll see."

He stood abruptly, facing her, but not particularly looking at her. "Listen, I'm going to go for a drive."

A bit stunned, she stepped back. "Where?"

"I just need some air."

Air? He was sitting outside. "Are you okay?"

"Fine." He leaned forward, dropped a quick kiss on her lips, and left.

Victoria wasn't sure what to think about his strange behavior. Was it just that it was time to move on and he didn't know how to let her down easy? Once the house sold he would leave, and maybe he felt guilty about that. Or was he just worried? Victoria stood outside long after he left, playing different scenarios in her mind, until she finally snapped out of it, deciding that it wasn't doing her any good trying to guess what was going on in his mind. Instead she went inside and made some dinner. Then she went to bed—his bed. Alone.

Tonight was one of those nights Eric wanted to be alone. He drove to Hollywood Boulevard and stopped at a touristy burger joint with flashing pink and baby blue neon signs, loud music inside, and way too many people crammed into one place. He had a greasy bacon cheeseburger, fries, and a vanilla shake. He people-watched through the glass window as he ate, not really seeing anything but a blur of humanity.

When a house went up for sale, he always started to question everything. Had he spent too much? Had he taken too long on the project? Had he made the right choices? Always caused a little edginess inside him until the house finally sold.

But it was more than that this time. As soon as the sign went up outside, he started to feel sick to his stomach. Something was wrong. But what? He knew he had taken too long on this remodel. Truth was, he didn't want to finish. He was having too great a time with Victoria and being back in Burbank. The house should have been sold by October, but he'd dragged his feet and now he might be stuck with it until the new year.

Still, that wasn't such a big deal. An extra house payment or two wouldn't kill him. The real problem was that it was almost over. He and Victoria would need to start looking for a new place to live soon.

The plan had originally been that he'd go back to his mother's house, and if he didn't find a new property to buy he'd leave town and return to Austin, where real estate wasn't as overinflated. Victoria would get her own place. They'd shake hands one final time and agree to get together next time he was in town. But that was before. Shit. Way before.

He took out his wallet and laid a few dollars on the table and left, then walked down the street toward his truck. Who was he kidding? He'd expected—well, *expected* was too strong, maybe *hoped*—he'd hoped that when she moved into the house, they'd get sexually involved. Why the hell not? He was single, she was single. And he was attracted to her.

But he and Victoria had started something special that went beyond a sexy little romp he could walk away from. Now they were supposed to go their separate ways because it was time to sell the house? That was crazy. He had to talk to her, but he wasn't sure what to say. Maybe after Thanksgiving, they could have a chat about their future. He didn't want to ruin the holiday by bringing all that up now. As he reached his truck he saw a little shop with scarfs and wallets and all sorts of fancy bags. He went inside and asked the woman to help him choose a nice purse. He'd rather buy her some lingerie, but this would do. And some flowers, he decided. He'd apologize for being a moody ass, tell her he needed some time to think about his business. He wouldn't admit that it was because his life was one big question mark right now and he was fucking miserable.

When he got home, she was in his bed. He woke her up with a kiss.

"Hey," she said in her cute sleepy voice.

"I went shopping," he said, and gave her the flowers and store bag.

She sat up in bed and frowned, the blankets and comforter dropping to her waist. "Shopping?" She rubbed her eyes.

"I didn't want you to be mad at me. It's a bribe."

"But I'm not mad at you." She peeked inside the shopping bag and pulled out the Louis Vuitton purse, wallet, and key chain. Her eyes grew to the size of golf balls. "Eric...oh, my God. What did you do? Cheat on me? This must have cost you a fortune."

Yeah, he'd almost fainted when the girl gave him the total. He hoped she would keep this for the rest of her life. He smiled. "I'm just sorry for walking out tonight, like I did. I wanted to be alone. Wanted to think."

She turned concerned eyes on him, her gifts completely forgotten. "What's wrong? Whatever it is, you can talk to me."

"I will, but not tonight."

"Is it me? Are you—?"

"You're perfect. It's just...business. The house. I'm a little stressed."

"Stressed," she said, as if she knew there was more to it than that.

"Yeah."

She sat there, just looking at him. Waiting. Finally she nodded. "I can relieve your stress," she said, lowering her eyelids, a sexy invitation that had him immediately aroused.

He pushed the items he'd purchased to the floor and moved the blankets aside. He climbed into bed with her. "Yeah?"

"Yeah. If you had said that to begin with, we could have taken care of it hours ago, and saved you a lot of money." She wrapped her arms around him. "Though I do love the bribes. Great taste."

"Thanks." He reached between them and pulled her nightgown off. "I'll remember that next time."

His hands covered her breasts. She placed her hands over his. "Hey. I'm serious, though. I'm happy to give you alone time, or to listen, or to hold you if that's what you need. Just tell me, okay?"

God, he loved her. "I need *you.*"

"You can have me."

Gratefully, he lost himself in her. In her kisses, in her caresses, in her body. And he didn't care if he never got out of this bed or moved out of this house. He just didn't care anymore.

Chapter Twenty

Lucia prepared Thanksgiving dinner, going all out this year. With Eric home, Victoria at his side, and Jaqueline joining them, her house was full of the people she loved most. Eric and Antonio watched football while Victoria and Jaqueline helped out with the last-minute preparations.

During dinner, they bragged about the wonderful cruise.

"I hope you enjoyed it, because you're never going anywhere without me again," Antonio teased her. Though she was sure he wasn't really teasing.

"We wanted to take more trips together. Once a year to renew our spirits."

"Your spirit is going to clash seriously with mine if you decide to do that," he said.

Jaqueline changed the subject, describing the feeling of being surrounded by water. "I think I should have chosen to live closer to the ocean in my life. I would have felt more at peace."

"It's never too late," Eric said.

"Oh, honey," Jaqueline said. "It's too late for me."

"Why? Tell me your dream house on the beach and I'll find it for you."

Jaqueline laughed, but then played along. "Okay, well, it's on the beach."

"Okay," he said, and laughed.

"I mean *on* the beach. It's small, but comfortable, but sort of rustic. Has a fireplace made of river rock. A nice kitchen with a breakfast nook. A couple of bedrooms. And only one story," she said. "Oh, and it has a small yard for a little flower garden."

Eric listened and ate as she spoke. "Easy enough."

"Then every morning I can go for a walk on the beach. I could even get a little dog to walk with me."

Lucia enjoyed Jaqueline's daydream. "Don't forget that you can always invite your good friend over on the weekends to walk with you."

Everyone laughed.

Jaqueline enjoyed spending Thanksgiving with Lucia and Antonio, but it wasn't the same as cooking for her family. Carmen called her earlier that day promising that she'd be home for Christmas. She had a cold and would be spending Thanksgiving alone in bed. Jaqueline wanted to fly out to Pennsylvania and make sure she ate and took care of herself. She even mentioned it to her, but Carmen told her she was being silly. That it was just a cold and that she'd be fine in a few days.

As she and Lucia cleaned up, Victoria and Eric snuggled on the couch. He continually whispered in her ear and made her laugh. He never let her out of his sight for long, and always seemed to make an effort to touch her.

"What do you think about Eric and Victoria?" Jaqueline asked Lucia.

"You know I think it's wonderful."

"Do you think they're in love?"

"Or do I think they're just playing house?" Lucia asked. She wiped the dishes dry and put them away.

"Exactly."

"Doesn't make any difference." She placed the towel on the rack. "As long as they're happy."

"I don't agree. Happiness comes and goes. Love and commitment makes you stay together during the times when things aren't so happy."

"Does it really?" Lucia asked, lifting an eyebrow that reminded her that even love and commitment ran its course in time.

"Yes," she said stubbornly.

"I knew I loved Antonio from the first day I met him. How about you and Victor?"

"I didn't love him right away. I'm not sure I even liked him." She smiled when she remembered how cocky and annoying he was.

"I think the kids have loved each other since they were... well, kids. Not like now, of course, but they've always been so perfect together."

Jaqueline looked past the door into the living room. She watched them sit side by side on the couch and wondered at how perfect things could be in a world where a generation of young people thought pretending to be in love was the same as the real thing.

She left soon afterward, leaving the two couples to enjoy coffee and dessert. She parked in the driveway and glanced at the garage. Victor stood at the side door of the garage.

"Happy Thanksgiving," he called.

Through a lump in her throat, she thanked him and wished him the same. "Did you eat?" she asked.

"Oh yeah," he said. "I bought a turkey dinner from the grocery store. It had everything, and it was good."

Jaqueline's heart ached, knowing he'd spent Thanksgiving alone.

"Not as good as yours, of course," he added.

"Do you want to... come inside for coffee?"

"Sure," he said.

She unlocked the house and they walked in. She went into the kitchen and he followed. He sat at the kitchen table. The sight of him at the table looked so familiar she almost started crying right there and then.

"I heard you went on a nice cruise."

She turned away and started making the coffee. "Yes."

"Did you like it?"

"Beautiful."

"Good." He tapped his fingers on the table. "I talked to Carmen this morning. She's sick."

"I know. I told her to get some rest."

"She promised to come home for Christmas," Victor said.

"It'll be wonderful to see her." Jaqueline sat at the table and waited for the coffee to drip into the carafe. "Have you spoken to Victoria?"

"Yes."

"I'm glad to hear that. She needs you in her life, Victor."

"I'm sorry I told her to move out. I never thought she'd move in with that man."

"They put that house up for sale. Maybe she'll get her own place now."

Victor scowled. "I doubt it."

"Why?"

"She told me she loves him."

Jaqueline stared wide-eyed at Victor. Victoria hadn't told *her* that. "Love? She used that word?"

"Yes."

"Oh, boy."

Victor smiled, then stood and started pouring the coffee.

"Oh, I'll do that."

"No, stay there. I'll do it." He poured both their cups and placed them on the table.

Neither of them spoke as they added sugar and cream.

Then he stared at her with his smoky gray eyes, searching and warm. Jaqueline stared back. He looked away first.

"The restaurants are almost finished. Except for the interior."

"Great."

"I'd love it if you came to see them on opening day."

"Of course I'll go. I'd love to."

"Are you still planning a trip to Argentina?"

"I don't know. I'd like to go and see what our country looks like after so many years. Walk the streets that I did as a child. See our flag flying proudly in the capital. But I don't need to go to figure things out anymore."

He drank his coffee. "No?"

"No, my life isn't there anymore. It's here." She wanted to say *with you,* but she wasn't sure it was with him anymore.

"I feel like I should apologize about that."

"About bringing me here? No. I've had a good life here with you and the girls."

"But not what you thought it would be. Away from your family and friends."

"I made new friends."

He nodded and gazed at her for a long time again.

"Besides," she said, her voice cracking, "nothing ever turns out the way you think it will. That doesn't make it bad. Just different."

He cradled his coffee cup, not meeting her eyes anymore. Then he stood. "I'd better go. Thanks for the coffee."

"You're welcome. Victor, I..."

"Yeah?"

"Are you okay out there? Do you need anything?"

He shook his head sadly. "No, I don't need anything."

"Okay," she said, wishing that for once, he'd tell her he needed *her.*

"What about you?"

What about her? She missed him and was lonely. She needed what she always needed: his arms around her, wanting her. But she hugged her arms around herself. "I'm fine, too."

"Okay. Good night, Jaqui."

"Good night."

He walked out and closed the door. She locked it and shook her head. Why couldn't she stop loving him once and for all?

Victoria stopped by La Parrilla to see if she could lend a hand, see how things were going. She found the manager that her father hired to be very efficient. The cooks and waiters worked as well as, if not better than, when Victor ran the restaurant. With Victor, they had wiggle room. They were family to him, and though he worked everyone hard, he also didn't mind if they took care of personal matters or just rested during the lulls. The new manager wasn't their friend. He was their boss, and they knew it.

Victoria spent Saturday and Sunday with him, and when she told him she was there to help, he gave her specific tasks in the office, nothing in the restaurant itself. Here, too, he had reorganized the office. On the desk, Victoria found bids from various interior designers for the new restaurants. She studied each. When Victor stopped by on Sunday night, Victoria asked him about them.

"I haven't had time to look at those very closely. But I have to," he said, running a hand through his hair. "What to you think of 'em?"

"I don't think any of them are capturing the essence of La Parrilla, the Argentine tone that will distinguish it from other steak houses."

Victor put his feet up on the desk and leaned back in the

chair. He drank a bottle of cold water. "Those were exactly my thoughts when I scanned them."

She picked up one of the proposals. "This looks too much like any other chain restaurant. There's no warmth to it."

"I told those people I wanted an outdoorsy look, but not too outdoorsy. Leather. Cows. As if the customers were spending the day at an estancia."

She nodded. "Right. This isn't it."

"No."

"Neither are the other two."

He studied her. "What would *you* do?"

"Well." She shrugged and picked up a pencil. She sketched on a piece of drawing paper as she spoke. "An estancia. Let's see."

"You don't even know what an estancia is, do you?"

"A farm, Dad."

"No. More than a farm. It was the gaucho's life. His spirit was part of the land."

Victoria frowned. "But I thought gauchos were sort of wanderers and the rich Europeans owned the land."

"Don't argue with me. Americanos think of Argentina and they think of gauchos. Beef. Tangos. That's what we have to have."

"Okay." She thought. "Gauchos, outdoors, beef, tangos. Outdoors," she repeated, and started drawing.

Victor watched her sketch. "What's that in the center there?"

"It's a grill."

"What the hell is the grill doing in the middle of the restaurant. The kitchen's back there." He pointed to the back on her drawing.

"Well," she said. "I was thinking that if you wanted to make it like a weekend at an estancia, you should have a big fire pit. Right here in the center of the restaurant. People could choose their cut of beef, barbecue it, and take it back to their table."

"Cook their own meat! Are you crazy? What if they don't do it right?"

"Wait a minute," she said. "Hear me out. You'll have a cook stationed at the grill, of course. Giving advice and marinating the beef." She glanced at Victor to see if he was following. A frown wrinkled his forehead. "People love being in control. This way, they'd participate in the making of the meal. And it would be all they could eat. It would give the restaurant a modern feel, and it would look really cool with an open grill in the center of the restaurant."

Victor seemed to be considering it as he studied the sketch. "Maybe you have a point. The grill could be sort of an attraction bringing everyone together."

"Right, people could chat and laugh as they're standing around the huge grill, like they would in their backyard."

He stared at the drawing. "So would the circle be sort of doughnut shaped? The cook in the middle?"

"Exactly."

"But what if they don't want to cook their own food?"

"You'd still have a menu for them to choose from, and cooks in the kitchen."

He arched an eyebrow. "I think it's... brilliant," he said simply. "It will make La Parilla stand out. But I'm going to have to run this by the architects. And probably by the marketing team I hired. See if they think this idea would appeal to customers."

"Sure."

"But I like it." He smiled. "A lot."

"Thanks. And the name will make more sense since La Parrilla means 'the grill.'"

"So is this something you know how to draw up to give to an architect and design crew?"

"I can do this for you, sure," she said enthusiastically. This was something she could help him with that she'd actually enjoy.

"Then you're hired. Give me a real bid to present to the bankers."

"I wasn't going to charge you for this, Dad."

"Of course you're going to charge me. This is your new career, no?"

"I haven't opened up my business officially, but yes."

"Then this will go in your portfolio."

Victoria was so happy, she dropped to his side, and wrapped her arms around him. "Thanks, Papi."

He patted her back. "Don't thank me. Just do it right. I'm counting on you."

And she wouldn't let him down. This was the kind of collaboration she'd always dreamed about having with her father. Having him really listen to her opinions. Taking her suggestions seriously rather than giving orders. Even if she had to go without sleep, she'd make sure she executed every detail of this design flawlessly.

Eric couldn't believe that a week after Thanksgiving he got an offer on the house. Excited and nervous at the same time, he stopped by the real-estate office to meet with the agent. But when he saw the offer, his good spirits sank. The number was much lower than he expected. He sent a questioning look to the agent.

"Sorry," she said. "But prices keep dropping. And buyers are few these days."

Eric stared at the number and nodded. "I'll get back to you," he said.

When he got home, Victoria was home for a change. He didn't mention the offer. She sat in the living room, poring over design books. He sat beside her. She leaned over and offered him a kiss.

After the sweet kiss, he winked. "What do you say we spend the weekend in the mountains. No snow yet, but we can rent a cabin, make love in front of a fireplace, sleep on a bear skin."

Victoria wrinkled her nose. "Bear skin? Yuck."

He chuckled and wrapped an arm around her waist, caressing her soft skin where her jeans and her top met. "Okay, we'll skip that part."

"I'm going to help my father out at La Parrilla this weekend. I'm sorry."

Help her father out? That shocked the hell of him. "When did you start working there again?"

"I didn't start working there again. He offered me the interior design job for the three restaurants," she said, barely able to contain her excitement. "I've got to meet with the architects and go over preliminary sketches, and—why are you looking at me like that?"

He dropped his arm. How was he looking at her? "I guess I'm surprised. Actually, I'm fired up for you. That's a huge step for your dad. A major compliment."

"I know." She placed a hand on her chest. "I wanted to cry, I was so happy."

He smiled. *Way to go, Mr. Torres,* he thought.

She angled her head. "What's wrong?"

"Wrong? Nothing. Like I said, I think it's awesome."

"You just don't seem . . . that happy."

"Well." He sighed. "I wasn't going to tell you yet, but we got an offer on the house."

"That's great," she said, looking a bit confused at his own lack of enthusiasm.

"Not great. The offer is low."

"Oh. How low?"

"It'll cut my profit by a third. And with the extra expenses . . . well, it wasn't what I expected."

She placed a hand on his knee. "I'm sorry."

He shrugged. "At least it's an offer. We can finally be done with this."

She nodded. He sort of hoped to see a look of disappointment in her eyes. He certainly wasn't thrilled about having to move out. But her feelings didn't show.

He leaned back into the couch, thinking maybe it was time they had the talk. "Remember that night that I went out to think, and you wanted to know what was bothering me?"

"Yeah. The night I got the best purse and wallet and key chain I've ever had in my life?"

He smiled. "Yes, that night. Well, that night I was kind of wondering... what we were going to do when the house sold."

"I don't understand? Celebrate?"

"I mean *we*, Victoria. You and I."

Her face grew serious. "What did you have in mind?"

"I had always planned to go back to Austin. And after seeing what this house is going to sell for, that might not be a bad idea still. California real-estate needs to plateau before an investor can work it well."

"But you don't want to leave," she said. "You've been so happy being back. You're enjoying being with your parents and even hanging out at the club."

And being with her. She forgot that part. But yes, he'd miss the other things, too. It was damn depressing. Lately, he'd been considering asking her to go with him to Austin. But after her announcement that she planned to be the interior designer for La Parrilla, that wasn't going to happen. He wasn't even going to mention it. The job for her father was a great opportunity for her. Much better than helping him stage another property. "I gotta go where I can make money, Vicki. It's my job," he said.

She stood. "Your mom isn't going to take this well."

He reached for her hand. Then stood and hooked an arm

around her waist and pulled her against him. "You're taking it well."

She rested her arms on his shoulders. "Not really. I'm trying not to be a needy girlfriend that smothers you like your well-meaning mother did. So, I'll support whatever you feel you have to do, Eric."

"You're something special," he said. "Aren't you going to miss me?"

"*So* much that I don't want to think about it." She kissed his chin. "I'm still hoping you find another property out here. You'll keep looking?"

"Of course."

Her fingers played with his hair. "Good, because you do belong here, you know."

With her? Why wasn't she saying it? "I don't want to go. That's the truth."

She responded only by moving her lips over his.

"Victoria," he said between her kisses.

Her hand traveled to his belt buckle. "I don't want to talk about any of this anymore. You're here now. Let me enjoy you." She unzipped his pants.

He looked down. "Ah, okay."

Her hand slipped into his shorts and he inhaled sharply as she touched him.

"Shit," he said. And he lifted her into his arms and carried her to his bed. Fine, they wouldn't talk about it anymore. The plan was to find another house to flip and hope he didn't lose his ass on the next one like he would on this one. They made love, but something was lacking. The passion they always shared. The feeling he felt that their souls had come together. And almost immediately afterward, she slipped out of bed.

"Where are you going?" he whispered.

"I've gotta finish what I was doing. I'll come back later."

He rested his back on the headboard and watched her walk out. She was pulling away from him. And damn it, there wasn't anything he could do about it, no promises he could make. At some point, he fell asleep waiting for her to come back. But when he awoke in the morning, he knew she never had.

Chapter Twenty-one

Victor was still congratulating himself Monday morning as he drove to Santa Monica over the interaction with Victoria. He'd listened to her, given her the benefit of the doubt, hadn't criticized, and had been rewarded immediately by the look of satisfaction on her face and gratitude in her eyes. He'd felt the wall between them crumble. And a new connection between them emerge, different from the one they'd shared when she was a child. Because she wasn't a child, he reminded himself. She might always be his baby, but she was a grown woman. Good and bad, in his opinion. All the complexities of a woman that made it hard to relate to her sometimes, but wonderful in the sense that she saw things he missed.

Mostly he was happy that he'd have her close by again. Not working for him, but working with him. He was damned proud.

When his cell phone rang, he answered using his Bluetooth.

"Hi, Dad."

Carmen. "Hola, mi amor."

"Are you busy?" she asked.

"Driving to the Santa Monica site. What's up?" Mostly she called to check on him lately. She didn't like that he was alone. Since she never worried about him in the past, he had thought that endearing. Carmen was growing up, too. Instead of leaving everything to Victoria, she was finally showing some interest in her family.

"I wanted to talk to you about something before we see each other for Christmas."

"Okay, I'm listening."

"I was going to wait until we were face-to-face, but I don't want to ruin the holidays."

Only for an instant did he fear she'd confess she was pregnant or getting married or some other awful thing parents dreaded to hear. But then he caught himself. Carmen wouldn't be that stupid. He and Jaqui had raised her well. "Qué pasa, nena?"

She drew a breath. "I can't continue to lie to you and Mom anymore."

"Lie about what?" Now she had him worried.

"I haven't been doing as well in school as I've let on."

Was that all? A wave of relief made him actually sag in his seat and the cars in front of him ceased to be a blur. "Carmen, you don't have to lie about that."

"When I started the bio degree, I was so excited and I loved it. But I've come to realize that I'm not as good as some of the other students in my classes. And the competition for jobs in this field is tough. I'm never going to be able to compete with my grades."

"So take a lighter load and concentrate more on your studies." He pulled off the freeway and waited in a long line of cars for a streetlight to change from red to green.

"I don't see the point in continuing with my bachelor of science degree."

He wasn't going to have a second daughter drop out of college. "Carmen, the point is that you don't give up when things get a little tough. You work harder."

"I've *been* working hard."

He tried to control his words even though it was on the tip of his tongue to say, *you're going to finish because I said you're going to finish, end of discussion.* "You're less than a year from graduating. Don't you think it's a little late to realize you don't like what you're doing?"

"I'm sorry."

"Sorry?" Traffic moved again. "Are you kidding?" His grip on the steering wheel made his knuckles ache. "Do you think I'm going to tell you I'm okay with you dropping out now?"

"I'm not suggesting dropping out, just changing my major."

"No."

"Dad, I'm not asking your permission."

"What?" he shouted. "Someone in this family better damn well ask my permission. I'm sick and tired of you women doing one stupid thing after another against my wishes." He pulled off the side of the road, before he got in an accident.

"Dad—"

"Your mother decides she's going to start acting like a single woman, Victoria is living with a man—living with, not dating—and you think you're going to throw away three years of college just because you don't like what you're doing? No way. Do you hear me, Carmen?"

The line was quiet, though he thought he heard sniffling. "Carmen," he repeated forcefully.

"How can I not hear you? You're shouting," she said in a weak voice. She was definitely crying.

"I'm sorry, but you just can't do this."

"I understand that you're upset with Mom and Victoria, and that this is bad timing on my part, but listen to me, please."

He didn't want to listen anymore. But Victoria flashed through his mind. All the years he'd refused to see what was right in front of his eyes. Dreams she'd buried to please him.

The real self she'd hidden. He didn't want to do the same thing to Carmen. He had to at least hear her out. "Go on."

"I'm not dropping out of college. I'll finish, I promise. But it doesn't make sense for me to get a degree in something I know I won't use. It's better if I change course now than later. I know this is disappointing to you, but—"

"Yes, it is."

"I know. I'm sorry." She paused and sniffled. "I wish I'd done better. I did try."

His heart ached. He wished he could wrap an arm around her. "I'm sure you did."

"I know you always wanted Victoria to be the one in business. The one to help you with the restaurant. But Papi... I'd love it if you let *me* work with you."

"Doing what?" He'd never considered including Carmen in his plans. She was too bright to get stuck slaving away at a restaurant. She could do so much more.

"I want to change my degree to business. I've taken quite a few classes in management and marketing, and I was so excited to hear about your expansion... I'd really love to... help out."

Victor was stunned. He got out of his car and stood on the sidewalk of some residential neighborhood in Santa Monica. He looked up at the sky, wondering if God liked to mess with his mind. "You want to help run the restaurants?"

"I think the idea of building a chain of restaurants is fabulous, and then opening them up to franchises... When Victoria told me your plans, I knew I wanted to be a part of it, and I felt sort of guilty that I was happy she wasn't going to be involved."

He blinked at the brightness of the day, almost blinding him. Not Carmen. This wasn't the life he'd envisioned for her. "So... you're thinking of getting... a degree in business."

"Something in the business field. I'll have to look into it. But mostly I want to work with you." Her voice grew softer. "I know your dream was for Victoria to be by your side. She was the first-born, and you've always been closer to her, but—"

"No. Carmen. No, it wasn't like that." He sighed and leaned on the car, his strength weakening. "You were so smart. Your teachers all told us how effortless learning came to you. You were in the gifted program and took advance placement classes, and I didn't want you to waste a second of your life at La Parrilla. The whole world was yours if you wanted it. And I wanted you to have it. Your sister was different. She didn't care to study much and never focused on anything long enough to excel. I figured I'd keep her close, show her what I knew, and maybe one day she'd have the restaurant to run. At least, she'd have that if nothing else. Maybe get married and have her husband provide for her. But I was wrong about Victoria."

"Yes, you were."

"She's smart in her own way. And she's talented."

"She's amazing," Carmen agreed.

His eyes filled with tears, not because of the glare of the sun, but because all his life he thought he knew his family, and he didn't know any of them. He hadn't paid attention. They were strangers. "Carmen," he said. "I'm speechless. I'm proud that you want to work with me, but I wanted something—"

"More. I know. But you said yourself, this is going to be an empire. And I believe you. I see it as if it already happened."

She saw it. His heart sang a strong beat, and energy started to flow though his body again. "When you come home for Christmas, we'll talk some more."

"You're not mad?"

"I can't be mad at you for knowing what you want, Carmen."

"I love you, Papi. So much."

"I . . . I love you, too."

* * *

Today Victoria actually understood the feeling behind the phrase *being on top of the world.* She rushed home to start the design of the future La Parrillas. The architects had looked at and approved her preliminary designs. Now she had to create the actual plans. Her bedroom had turned into her design studio. She slept in Eric's bed most of the time, so she didn't use her own. Before they got an offer on the house, she kept it looking like a bedroom, because they had needed it that way for staging purposes. But now that Eric had a buyer, she'd moved the bed up against a wall so she had more room to work.

She went to the kitchen for a cup of coffee, and the doorbell rang. She answered it, finding the real-estate agent on the other side of the door.

"Hi, Victoria."

"Hi," she said. "Come in."

"Is Eric around?"

"No, I'm not sure where he is."

"I paged him, but didn't get a call back."

"Want some coffee? I was just getting a cup for myself."

"Sure."

They sat at the breakfast nook with their coffee cups.

"I'm afraid I have some bad news."

Victoria braced herself. "About the house?"

"Yes. The buyers fell out of escrow. I'm sorry."

"So we have to start all over from scratch."

"We do."

Eric walked in. "Hey," he said, with a smile, carrying a bag of groceries. He placed it on the counter. "What's going on?"

The real-estate agent gave him the bad news, and Victoria saw his smile fade.

"I think you might want to lower the price of the house another five thousand, Eric."

He frowned.

"We want to stay competitive and a lower price will help you sell faster," the Realtor added.

Eric shoved his hands into his pockets and leaned on the counter. "Every month I'm here, it costs me another four grand."

"I'm sorry."

"Take it down another ten," he said.

"Will do." She made a note, then stood. "You both have a good week. I'll show myself out."

Eric walked her to the door anyway. Then he stood at the entryway by himself. Victoria perched herself on the arm of a couch. "Eric, I've been thinking. I can start paying half of the mortgage."

"Don't be ridiculous." He walked past her, back to the kitchen. He pulled the grocery items out of the bag and started putting them away.

"I'm serious. I'm living here."

"You worked for me. So far for free. You're not paying rent." He ripped open a bag of pasta and dumped it into a canister.

"But once we sell it, I'll get paid. In the meantime—"

"In the meantime," he said, his eyes flashing, "I've got it covered."

"Why should you carry the brunt of the expenses when—?"

He slammed a can of corn on the counter. "I said no!"

She gazed at the can he'd used to hit the brand-new granite counter, and wanted to take the can out of his hands and smack *him* with it. And how dare he raise his voice at her? "I'm just trying to help."

"It's not a big deal, okay?" He turned away, tossing things into the fridge. "Sorry. But I've got things under control. I found one buyer, I'll find another."

"And until you do, this is our place. We should both contribute."

"It's not *our* place. It's *my* place. I'll take care of it."

Feeling as if she'd been put in her place, Victoria swallowed the humiliation with as much composure as possible. But she had no control over the heat that rose to her face, nor the stab she felt in her heart. And he must have seen it—the change in her expression, the hurt look in her eyes, because all of a sudden he stopped his angry, jerky movements, and the color drained from his face.

"Victoria—"

"I'll start looking for a place of my own."

"Whoa, whoa," he said, holding up a hand and coming out of the kitchen.

"It's okay," she said. "Don't apologize."

"I didn't mean that the way it sounded. I only meant the responsibility is mine."

"You're right about one thing. You hired me to do a job. My job's done." She picked up her coffee cup. "There's no need for me to stay here anymore."

"No, no, don't do this." He stepped in front of her and took the cup from her hand. "You know there's a reason for you to stay. Come on, Victoria. I love you, you *know* that."

She looked around at the house they'd fixed up together. Everything looked new and shiny and beautiful. But all of it was fake. Nothing inside belonged to them. Even their relationship was on loan. They were on a time clock. And that was what bothered her the most. "What I know is that none of this is real. It's time for both of us to leave."

He cursed. "I know, damn it." He put the coffee cup back on the table and took her hands. "I shouldn't have yelled at you. I shouldn't have taken my frustrations out on you. But as I see this damned market getting worse and worse every day I get more and more...worried. Not because of the money, Vicki, but because I want things to work out with my business so I can stay close to you."

Tears blurred her vision. "My heart tears in half when I hear you talk about California real estate sucking and how you're going to move on. I can't pretend it doesn't bother me anymore, Eric. If it's going to be over between us, then—"

"No. Remember when we decided not to define our relationship and just let things happen? Well, we have, and what's happened is incredible, and Victoria, I don't want to lose it."

She fell into his arms. "Neither do I."

He pulled her back and kissed her. "Then let's not."

She gazed at him with a deep sadness in her heart. "How can we hold on to it if you might not be around?"

"I'm going to be around."

"Are you telling me you aren't leaving town after you sell the house?"

"I'm telling you I'm not leaving *you.* I love you and I need you, and I want to hold you in bed tonight. And the next night. And the next."

"I love you, too," she said, not knowing how long this was going to last, but she was going to hold on as long as she could.

Eric stopped by the Torres house, hoping Victor was around. He noticed the door to the garage open and headed there first. He knocked on the outside wall. Victor was studying some papers he had laid out on a box.

"Sorry to bother you."

Victor glanced up. "What do you want?"

"Just to talk."

Victor stood and took a few steps forward. "I don't want to talk to you; I want to punch a few teeth loose from your mouth."

Eric blinked and raised his chin. If the man wanted to hit him, he'd take it.

"I have no respect for a man who lives with a woman instead of marrying her."

"I understand. And I'd love to marry Victoria. That's what I wanted to talk to you about."

Victor frowned, but the harshness faded from his eyes. "Oh," he said. "In that case, come in."

Eric walked into the garage that Victor had made his house. He felt for the man. To come to his stage in life and be in this position. He'd never let this happen. "Sir, I love your daughter."

"That's supposed to make it okay for her to be living with you?" Victor's words were sharp and told Eric that he'd protect his daughter from any harm. But Eric wanted to be the one to do that from now on.

"I understand that I haven't been very... clear about my intentions." No matter how old-fashioned this seemed to him, if he wanted Victoria's very Argentine parents to approve of him, he had to actually ask Victor's permission. And he realized he was acting a little late as far as Victor was concerned.

"Clear? You mean, you had no intentions that I would approve of when you asked her to move in with you."

"I'm... sorry."

Victor frowned. "So now you've decided you love her."

"Yes, sir."

"Wonderful."

Eric sighed. "Not so wonderful. I've got a lot of money. Not millions, but a lot. Still, it won't last forever. And all I know how to do is buy and sell properties. If I ask Victoria to marry me, I'm just not sure that I'm going to be able to support her here in California. And I don't want to ask her to move. I know you all wouldn't want that."

"No."

"So, do I string her along for months or years while I wait to see if I'm going to be able to make it or not?"

Victor returned to his chair and told him to sit in a second chair across from him. Eric wondered who visited him in the garage.

"You really love her?"

"Yes. I want to marry her. I want to have kids. We're completely right for each other, I know that. But I saw my parents struggle. My dad couldn't always make ends meet. And my mom suffered. She never complained or anything, but I knew. How can I do that to Victoria?"

Victor rubbed a hand on his chin. His eyebrows drew together in almost a straight line. "You know, when Antonio and I were young, it was a different time. The man was supposed to support his wife. Especially in our culture."

Eric nodded.

"You young men have it easier. Not only are you not expected to do it all, but women don't want you to, either. Victoria is very excited about building her career. Quite frankly, I don't think she's going to need your money."

Eric smiled. "I know that. Still—"

"Quiet. Listen. You do what you love to do. What you're good at doing. And let her do what she's doing. If you love each other, then you should be together. The right way. Not what you've been doing."

"I don't think I can stay in California."

"Bullshit. You can make money anywhere if you try hard enough. Truth is, you're scared. And you're using the market as an excuse. If she doesn't see a future with you eventually, she'll leave. No woman is going to stay with a man she can't build a future with."

Eric understood that.

Victor frowned pensively. "I know, you're thinking who the hell am I to give you advice when I'm living in a garage?"

Eric laughed. "No, sir."

"Well, you'd be right to think that. I've been a shitty husband, and if you marry my daughter and ever make her miserable I'll dig a hole in my backyard and put you in it."

"I won't make her miserable. That's what I'm trying to avoid."

"I'm going to fix things with Jaqueline." He patted Eric on the shoulder. "Go make things right with Victoria."

Eric nodded and stood and offered his hand to Victor. "Thank you."

Victor shook his hand and nodded.

Eric drove home to put his plan into action.

Chapter Twenty-two

Victoria had lunch with Douglas to catch up on what was going on at the boutique. She missed working with him as well as the slow pace of the small store.

"I hired a nice college kid to work part-time," he said. "She's smart, and the customers like her."

"I'm glad." She sipped a cup of tea, washing down the great Chinese food they'd shared. She checked her watch.

"Almost time to get back to the office, or do you have a class?"

"The office. They're so wonderful, letting me take off whenever I need to go to class, that I don't want to take too long for lunch."

"I'm proud of you, kiddo," he said. "You're heading down the right path."

She rested her elbows on the table and clasped her hands, and gazed at him.

"What? I know that look. What's wrong?"

"Nothing. Well, not really."

He chuckled. "That means something. Don't tell me you're not enjoying the interior design program."

"I'm loving it. It's perfect."

"You're worried you ate too much, and will put back on some dreaded weight?"

She laughed. "I ran five miles this morning and had a light breakfast. I'm good."

"Let's see, you're happy with work, not obsessing about your looks, then it must be a man."

"Why must it be a man?"

"Wild guess." He shrugged. "And you're twenty-eight. Besides, I had two sisters and a wife. I remember."

She sighed. "My personal life is a little sticky, yes." She laughed. "I can't believe I can say that. I actually have a personal life."

"Good." Douglas gave her a warm, caressing appraisal. "Eric?"

"Yep. He's wonderful. And we love each other. It's just that..."

"He snores?"

Victoria laughed. "No." She shrugged. "It's nothing. Forget it." She checked her watch again. "I've got to go."

"Victoria. Follow your heart. If you love each other, don't let anything come between you."

She stood. Nothing was coming between them. But her feelings for him overwhelmed her sometimes. She felt like they'd skipped quite a few steps in the relationship process by moving in together. The slow buildup, the wondering if they *should* move in together, the conversations of taking things to the next level. Hell, they were having those now, after the fact. "Okay, Douglas." She hugged him. "Thank you. I'll see you soon."

She hurried to work. As soon as she got there, she got involved in a project for a gymnasium. The work was challenging and different from designing the interior of a residential property. As she was basically an assistant covering for actual designers, her jobs were minor. And anything she did was double-checked by whomever ran the project. But the two designers she worked with had started relying on her more and more as soon as they realized she could do the work.

Before she knew it, it was six o'clock and time to go home. The company VP paused at her cubicle. "Victoria, you're still here."

"I got busy and lost track of time," she said, standing.

He glanced at her desk and inspected her blueprints. "Very good. How much of this have you done on your own?"

"Only part of it. Dana told me pretty much what she wanted done."

"Dana and Angie both have told me they're very impressed with you."

"Good," Victoria said, gathering her purse. "I appreciate everything I'm learning."

"How would you feel about continuing on in the new year?"

Victoria put on a coat and pulled her hair loose of the collar. "I thought the work-study program only lasted for one quarter."

"I mean permanently. I can give you your own projects. Not too many until you finish your degree, but you'll be a full-time employee."

"Well." She didn't know what to say. Sounded like a great offer. Even though she wanted to start her own business and do more residential designs rather than the big corporate things they did here. "I promised my father I'd complete a design for his restaurants. He owns La Parrilla downtown; I don't know if you've heard of it. And he's expanding."

"Yes, I've eaten there a time or two. In downtown Burbank?"

"Yes. And he's opening up a few more. He asked me to work with his architect on the design."

He nodded. "Interesting. Well, I can give you one project. I've just signed a contract with an office complex in Washington State. Can you wrap up your father's project this month and be ready to take this one in Washington?"

A million thoughts were flying through Victoria's mind.

This was an amazing opportunity. She'd get to travel. Be a real designer. "I can wrap up my father's project soon, yes."

"Then I'll team you up with Karrie, who's experienced in these large office projects, and the two of you can work on it together. I'll have Human Resources contact you and get you hired on." He nodded. "Welcome aboard, Victoria."

Victoria was stunned. Had she said yes? Well, why would she say no? This was awesome. She grabbed her purse and headed home.

Eric waited for Victoria to decorate the Christmas tree. When she got home at close to seven that night, he made her close her eyes and led her to the living room. "Okay, open them."

She did, saw the tree, and tears touched her eyes. "You got a tree. I didn't even think of it."

"You've been busy."

She walked up to it and closed her eyes as she drew in a breath of the evergreen scent. Damn, she was gorgeous.

"Smells wintery and amazing. Now it's starting to feel like Christmas."

"If you're not too tired, I thought we'd go shopping for ornaments," he said.

She gazed at him, and walked forward, still wearing her coat. She narrowed her eyes and angled her head. "I *really* love you," she said. She could get used to coming home to him every day.

He smiled and mentally patted himself on his back. He'd done the right thing. "Love you too, Vicki."

They hurried out to the mall and bought tons of ornaments. Then stayed up until close to midnight decorating the tree. They fell asleep in the living room, sitting on the couch together, staring at the tree.

* * *

Victor never participated in any of the Argentine Club preparations. He didn't have any interest in that or in any skill whatsoever in that department. But when Jaqueline told him she was going to go prepare the club for the Christmas celebration, he'd impulsively told her he was going to go help, too.

She'd looked surprised.

"I can drive us, if you want."

"All right," she said.

He felt like a teenager, like he had when they were in Argentina and he was trying to convince her to date him.

"When am I going to get to see the new restaurants?" she asked on the drive.

"Well, I decided that I want to wait until the grand opening to take you. I want you to see them when they're finished. Victoria is going to meet with the architects this week to present her final plans. They're amazing. I can't tell you how impressed I am with that girl."

"She's so happy, Victor."

"Yeah."

"I'm sorry she never got very excited about running the restaurants. I know you're disappointed about that."

"No. Not anymore." Especially not since talking to Carmen.

When they got to the club, she got involved in hanging decorations. Victor and some of the younger men went to purchase trees. They bought two huge noble firs for either side of the stage. The ladies, pleased with their selection, immediately began decorating them.

Nelly congratulated him on helping. "It's not the same without your daughter this year," she said. "You know, ever since she got involved with Lucia's boy, she's practically dropped out of everything."

Not true. Victoria still attended club dinners almost every Sunday. She didn't have much time to donate to things like this—and Victor couldn't be happier. He'd always thought these club events were things for old ladies to occupy their time with, not young girls. "Eric has inspired her to live her life." He winked. "It always takes a man to jolt you women into action."

Nelly gasped. "Really, Victor. Do you actually approve of what Victoria is doing?"

"What is she doing?" he asked.

"The way she's living with Eric, giving away what she should save for a husband."

Victor had felt the same way. And he'd been glad that Eric had come to him with the promise of rectifying his mistake. But hearing Nelly voice such stupidity made him realize that they'd all carried away from Argentina very antiquated and stupid ideas. He was a modern man. And he honestly didn't give a shit if his daughters decided to experiment with a dozen men until they found the right one. Well, okay, a dozen might be a bit much, and he hoped they'd be safe. But the truth was, they were smart girls and he planned to support all their choices from now on. "Nelly," he said. "I'm not sure what she's giving Eric or what he's giving her in return, but I do know they've always got smiles on their faces, so they must be having a damn good time."

She raised an eyebrow.

"Oh, and I'd appreciate it if you kept your opinions to yourself from now on when it comes to my daughter. She'd always been too nice to tell you to mind your own business, but I'm not that nice."

"Of course," she said stiffly, obviously offended, which gratified him immensely.

Victor's mood stayed high after that until they were about to leave, and Jaqueline decided to have a little talk with him before they got home.

"What do you mean you want a divorce? Are you crazy?" Victor shouted as they stood outside by the car.

"We can't live like this forever," Jaqueline said. "Apart, alone, and yet still married."

"I agree. We need to stop all this nonsense."

"It's not nonsense. We've outgrown each other."

He scowled. "Stop all this crazy talk. I love you, Jaqueline. I always have. You can't tell me you don't love me."

"I don't know you anymore."

"Yes, you do." He took her hand possessively. "You've always known who I was and what I wanted."

She looked down at the ground and nodded. "I know what you've wanted. The American dream. I guess I hoped you'd give up all those fantasies."

"They're not fantasies. But they *are* dreams. And dreams sometimes come true." Victor gazed in Jaqueline's eyes as the sun began to set and the cool air blew her hair. "They come true if you believe hard enough."

She swallowed and nodded. "I hope so, Victor. I know how much you need to have success. Money..." She smiled. "I hope these restaurants bring you everything you've always wanted. I really do."

"It's not about the restaurants. You don't understand. I saw the opportunity to finally accomplish my goals and decided to take it. I thought if I could make this happen it would mean I was finally a success." He squeezed her hands and urged her to grasp the importance of what he was saying.

"I know. But the problem is that without that success you refused to be happy."

He shook his head. "No. Well...yes. But that's because I've been stupid and blind. I didn't appreciate that I've always had what I wanted and needed to be happy. It's you, Jaqueline. I swear it."

"I was only part of the little packaged dream you made up when you were a young boy in Argentina."

"You were the most important part. Jaqueline, nothing is worth it without you. I've always wanted to make you proud. To be a man you could look up to. I know you could have married someone better than me. Someone more educated. Someone who wouldn't have dragged you away from your family and friends. I know I was a wild card. And I want this wild card to pay off for you."

She looked stunned. "Victor, you've always been more than enough. I never wanted anyone else. And I've always been proud of you."

He closed his eyes and shook his head. "I haven't been proud of myself. I promised you so much and . . . gave you so little."

She touched the side of his face. "You gave me a lot. A good life, two wonderful daughters, a nice home in a safe neighborhood. A lot."

He opened his eyes. "But not enough. Not the attention you deserved."

"That's true. But maybe I shouldn't have expected you to be everything. I drove you away. To . . . women who weren't so needy."

"No." He tightened his lips to keep from cursing the bastard he had been. "I was an insecure boy. When I didn't see the appreciation I needed in your eyes I went to find it elsewhere. I hurt you and me and our marriage, and I'll never forgive myself for that."

The hurt in her eyes was just as fresh as it had been years ago.

"I've needed to prove to you, to myself, to everyone that I was something special." He shrugged. "I'm sorry." He was so busy being self-absorbed he didn't have anything left to devote to her.

She brushed decoration ribbon off her sweater. "Your ambition is what I loved most about you. But after so many years . . . I just can't compete with it anymore. I want peace."

Swallowing the lump in his throat, he nodded. The last thing he was going to have in the next couple of years was peace. Not with all the restaurants opening. "Jaqueline, I don't know what to say. We've been married for so long. I've loved you since I was a boy. I don't know how to let you go."

"You're going to have a huge business to run and all this money to spend." She paused. "I know you, Victor. You'll be so busy, you won't think of me often."

Oh, God. He was going to be sick. He was actually light-headed. "Jaqueline. *Please.* Give me one more chance. Give me some time to show you I can be different. That I can do both—be a businessman *and* a husband. I'll take lots of time off to relax from the pressures of the business world. We can get to know each other again. Then if there's truly nothing left, I'll concede."

A smile crept to her lips. "Don't you ever give up on anything?"

"Yes, but not on you. I adore you, mi vida, and I'm so close to giving you everything I promised."

"Victor, I don't want—"

"I'm not talking about things. I'm talking about what I promised in our wedding vows. Love, fidelity, cherishment, my heart. Let me try again."

She didn't exactly agree, but she didn't disagree. And she didn't bring up the terrible word *divorce* again. This gave him hope. And he'd take what he could get.

Jaqueline hurried home from the club because she'd promised to watch Hugo's children while he did some last-minute Christmas shopping. He had been dropping them off every once in a while, and she enjoyed it. The kids brought life back to the house. She made them special treats and spoiled them, and pretended for just a little while that they were her own grandkids.

"Watch this," Daisy said, showing off one of her ballerina moves.

August reclined in a chair, playing an electronic game.

"Very good, Daisy. I'm glad your father enrolled you in ballet class."

"Me, too."

Hugo was a good father. She wished Victor had taken this kind of notice of her girls. But he hadn't had to. She had done it all. And it had worked out. At least now that they were women, Victor paid more attention to them. She was sensing a change. A thrilling change. Victor wasn't just doing what he was supposed to do. He seemed to really want to spend time with his daughters. He was so excited about working with Victoria again, and about Carmen coming home for Christmas in a few days.

"Miss Jaqueline, are you watching?" Daisy said as she spun.

"I'm watching," she said, and applauded. She looked at the boy again and stood. "Okay, let's go to the kitchen. We're going to make dinner together."

Daisy jumped up and down, but August continued to play his game as if he hadn't heard. Probably hadn't. She ruffled his hair. "You, too."

"What? Oh, sorry," he said, sitting up straighter. "Did you want me to do something?"

"Yes, help me make dinner."

"But I don't know how to make anything."

"I'll teach you. You're a big young man. You're father needs help around the house, and it would be great if you, too, could help him by making dinner every once in a while. What do you say?"

"Yes, ma'am," he said, not sounding every excited.

Jaqueline put the kids to work. "Okay, August, take out some potatoes from that drawer there, and bring them to the sink to peel. Daisy, get the carrots out of the refrigerator."

By the time Hugo came to pick them up, they had a warm shepherd's pie, steamed vegetables, and a fruit salad ready for him. He ate happily and thanked her repeatedly. When he was ready to leave, he stood in the living room with tears in his eyes. "Merry Christmas, Jaqueline." He presented her with a small gift. "Just a small thank you for all you've done for us this year."

"Oh, Hugo, that wasn't necessary." She pulled out a lovely scarf and a little angel pin from the gift bag.

"You're our angel," he said, and leaned forward to kiss her cheek.

She blushed. Just like a young girl. "Wait here," she said, and brought back the gifts she'd gotten for the kids. "Take them. Put them under the tree and open them on Christmas morning."

The kids hugged her and left happily with their father.

Jaqueline went back to the kitchen and prepared a plate of food for Victor. They'd come straight home from the club and she knew he hadn't eaten. She still wasn't sure she wanted to put her trust and hope in Victor again. She'd convinced herself that divorce was the best option for the both of them. And that hadn't been an easy choice. But she'd made it, and to backpedal now... Well, she just didn't know. She put on a sweater and walked back to the garage. She knocked on the door, and he opened it.

"Thought you might be hungry," she said.

"I am." He took the plate. "All I bought was a bag of chips at the store yesterday. Want to come in?"

"No, thanks." It struck her as crazy to be invited into her own garage.

"Did you enjoy babysitting?" he asked. "I saw the kids leave."

"Yes, but they've worn me out. I'm not as young as I used to be."

Victor smiled. "Hugo seems like a nice man," he said.

"Yes. It makes me wish we'd had a son, Victor."

He shrugged. "I like my girls."

"Me, too, but a boy... might have been nice."

"Should we try again? We're not *that* old."

That made her laugh out loud. "Trust me, I'm too old for that." They gazed at each other with a smile on their faces. "Good night," she said.

"Good night." He held his plate up. "And thanks for this."

"You're welcome." The problem with divorce was that she still loved him after all these years.

No one celebrated Christmas at the Argentine Club. Christmas was reserved for family gatherings. However, on December 23, the club had its own celebration. Eric went out and bought a new suit with a red bow tie. He got a fresh haircut and even had his rough hands manicured. Not just because of the holiday celebration, but because he planned his own celebration for tonight.

They arrived around nine that night. The dinner would be formal. Instead of the customary Argentine dinner, turkeys and hams were served by hired waiters. Everything smelled delicious. Christmas lights twinkled from the various decorations. "Silver Bells" played softly from the speakers. Everything was perfect.

The joy he felt inside, he almost couldn't process. This club held everything he loved. His parents, Victoria, bits of history that made him who he was, and a community that had always considered him one of their own—a lost son, but their son.

He found himself smiling every time he looked at Victoria, who was dressed in a beautiful dark blue gown with gold lacy trim molded to her body and flowing to her ankles. The missing parts of his life could only have been put together by this woman.

During dinner, his parents and hers sat together, because they knew Eric and Victoria would not be separated. The evening flowed with synchronized perfection.

So later that night when Eric pulled Victoria out to the dance floor, he knew it was the perfect time to break his surprise.

She rested her head on his shoulder.

"Victoria?"

"Hmm."

"Are you happy?"

She lifted her head, a soft smile on her lips. "Very happy."

"How happy is that?"

"On a scale of one to ten, I'd say a nine point three."

"Not bad. But I want it to be a perfect ten." He pulled a gift from his coat pocket. A small box he didn't bother to wrap. A squashed red bow sat on top. He held it in the palm of his hand. "For you."

She sort of smiled in a confused way. Glanced at the box and at him with a question.

"Take it. Open it."

She quickly scanned the dance floor, appearing hesitant to take the box from his hand. But she reached for it and held it between them. Her fingertips caressed the soft velvet; her eyes studied the outside as if it would give her a clue to what was inside.

"Open it," he urged again, whispering in her ear, hoping that she liked what he picked out. Wondering if maybe he should have let her choose.

With shaky fingers she flipped open the hinged lid. The two-karat diamond winked at them both as the lights from above caught each cut and angle. They had stopped moving on the dance floor, and some eyes were on them. Victoria stared at the ring without speaking. Time seemed to stand still the longer she was silent. Then she snapped the box closed rapidly, and walked off the dance floor without a word.

Victoria couldn't breathe. Oh God, what had Eric done? She pushed past other dancers. Felt like the crowd was closing in on her. Needed some space. A quiet spot to look at this ring. To look into Eric's eyes and try to understand what he was thinking.

As she finally burst through the heat of bodies, and ignored a few people who called out to her, she reached the back room where school was usually held. She drew in a deep breath and told herself to calm down. Eric was *not* going to ask her to marry him. And if he was, then this would become the most wonderful day of her life. But it would not be with everyone from the club watching her reaction. She heard footsteps behind her and turned around.

Eric frowned as he stared at the most gorgeous woman he'd ever seen in his life. She had a hand to her heart and didn't look like she was breathing too easily. "What's wrong?" he asked.

"Nothing. It's a nice ring. Thanks."

"Nice ring? It's an engagement ring."

"I know."

He smiled, trying to ignore the knot that had begun to grow in his stomach the second she walked away from him. "Well, you didn't wait around for the question that goes with that ring."

"Eric..." She shook her head. "It's Christmas."

Christmas music still played out in the main hall—only the faint melody of "Everybody's Home Tonight" floated into the back rooms.

"Victoria, I know. Listen, I decided I don't want to sell our house. I want to live in it with you and buy our own furniture and decorate it, and live together in it for as long as we want, as a married couple."

Her eyes were wide as she stared at him, seeming unable to take in what he was saying. He'd shocked her, but not in the joyous way he'd expected. Why not?

"And so you went out and bought a ring, and decided to propose? Here? Tonight?"

"Sure, it's a special night. And a special place. What's wrong?"

She closed her eyes and shook her head. Her hands gripped the small blue velvet box tightly in front of her, putting strain on her knuckles. "Eric, I've wanted to tell you something for a couple of weeks and kept putting it off, because I figured it wasn't a big deal. But... I sort of got a promotion at work."

"You mean at the design firm? I thought you were finished with them as of this week."

"They offered me a permanent position."

He smiled. "Great."

"Yes," she said, but didn't smile back, and he wondered, again, why not.

"And?" he urged.

"And my first project is going to take me to Washington State for a few weeks. I was going to move all my things out in case you sold the house while I was gone. I knew you'd be looking for a new place to flip, and... but, you've been thinking... wow, marriage."

His stomach tightened more painfully. "Don't you want to get married?" She didn't seem thrilled with the idea.

"I, ah, think... it might not be the best time to get married, Eric."

"Well, I wasn't suggesting we run out and do it tonight."

"I know. But I'm starting this new job, and finishing my degree. And you're going to try to establish your business here, and—"

"Whoa, wait a minute, Victoria."

She looked miserable. Uncomfortable.

"I thought you'd be happy about this." His voice came out cold and held a question he couldn't put into words.

"I'm incredibly touched. I mean, Eric, I *am* happy." She closed the few feet that separated them, and placed a hand on his arm. "But I'm going to want a long engagement."

"How long?" He knew he shouldn't be getting pissed, but he was. Women were supposed to jump up and down when a man proposed. Not negotiate a deal on when she'd give in and accept the inconvenient proposal.

Victoria could see him getting angry. Feeling hurt. And damn it, she wasn't sure what to say or how to say it so that he would understand. The back rooms were hot, and all of a sudden the dress flowing around her felt more like a straitjacket. She ran her hand up his upper arm. "I expected us to date longer. We've only been together for a little over five months."

"Five great months, I thought."

"Yes, but five great months mostly as friends."

"What does time have to do with—"

"I'm still getting used to the idea that you're actually going to stay in town," she interrupted. "And that we're going to be able to deepen this relationship."

"I though we might deepen it with a commitment."

A commitment, yes. A permanent bond that would last a lifetime... was she wrong to think it was too soon? That they needed more time to contemplate such a huge step? But she did love him. And spending the rest of her life in love with Eric couldn't feel more right.

"Forget it," he said, shaking his head.

"Eric. Wait. Don't get angry."

"Look, I rushed into this. I'm sorry."

"No," she said. "Don't be sorry. I love you for thinking of this. For this beautiful presentation of the ring. And..." She paused for just a moment, to see if she could put into words the conflicting feelings inside her. "But I have to be honest. Can I be honest?"

Her heart had begun to beat so hard that the thudding pulsed in her ears. But something inside told her that if he really loved her, that if they were going to have a chance together, she should be able to voice her honest concerns and he should be able to listen. She didn't want to end up like her parents twenty or thirty years from now. Not talking. Not communicating. Not knowing the deepest needs of the other person.

He stared at her and waited for more, with a closed expression that wasn't encouraging, but she spoke anyway.

"I've felt so confined living with my parents all my life," she started. "This is the first time I've had any freedom. That I've been able to do my own thing without worrying about what they thought." She paused and gazed at him.

"Yes. I know. But what does that have to do with me? With us?"

She forced herself to express her thoughts with strength and continued. "The thought of getting married makes me feel confined all over again."

"*I* make you feel confined?"

"No, it's not *you*." She shook her head. "I simply want us to spend more time dating. I need to be *me* awhile longer before we become an *us*."

Eric's jaw was so tight he though it was going to snap. The night that had started out so wonderful had now taken on a dark shadow, making it difficult for him to focus. On one level, he understood what she was saying, but on another level—the one taking over his emotions right now—he understood that she obviously needed her independence more than she needed him. And she could have it. He was bending over backward trying to fit her into his life, to make her happy, because he thought it was what she wanted. Why the hell had he bothered?

"Yeah, okay." He turned away and headed for the door.

"Eric," she called after him. "Stop."

He paused and looked over his shoulder. "You said when I needed time to be alone, you'd give it to me. I need time now."

She rushed to his side and took one of his hands. "This isn't you needing time alone. This is you running away from me. Don't do it. I love you, Eric."

Gazing into her eyes, her soft face, the sexy lips he loved to kiss almost convinced him to stay. He angled his head and kissed her cheek. "I love you, too. But damn it, Victoria, if you can think of marriage to me as a trap of some sort, then..." He was going to say *it's over,* but he couldn't say it. "Then, we both need some time to think about what we want."

Her grip intensified on his hand. "I didn't say no." Tears touched her eyes, glistening, threatening to fall and break his heart.

"Vicki, you didn't say yes." He pried her fingers loose, and waited for just a second to see if she'd say it. If she'd say, *Yes, I'll marry you.* The second came and went in silence, and he turned away and left.

He went home. Packed a bag, got in his truck, and started driving. He headed east on the 10 Freeway. The one that led him out of California. The one he'd taken the last time he'd left, when he was full of anger and resentment at his father. This time his feelings were deeper and more complex. This time he really didn't want to leave.

Chapter Twenty-three

Victor and Jaqueline drove Victoria home. Antonio and Lucia followed in their own car. When they all got there less than an hour later, Eric was gone. Victoria rushed to their bedroom and noticed he'd taken his things. Not all of them, but enough to fit in a large suitcase.

"Oh, Eric," she said. She sat on the bed and dug in her purse for her cell and called him. Voice mail—big surprise. "Hey," she said. "Where did you go, Eric?" she sighed. "I'm sorry. But you know I love you, and that I want you." She was about to click the phone off, but her thoughts wouldn't stop. "You made me believe in myself again, Eric." She sniffled and realized tears were running down her face. She wiped her tears. "You're my best friend and the crazy thing is I know you understand exactly how I'm feeling. If you weren't my boyfriend you'd be telling me, 'Don't marry this guy yet, Victoria. Go to Washington, build your career.' You know you would. But right now you're acting like a guy, and that's okay. You're entitled. I love you anyway." The phone beeped. Her time was up.

She went back to the living room, where her parents and his stood talking among themselves. Victoria, too rattled to think logically, just paced back and forth. She wanted everyone gone.

Lucia stopped her with her hands on her shoulders. "Tell me what happened."

Victoria groaned inwardly. God, the woman was going to kill

her. "Maybe he went back to your place," she said, avoiding the question.

Lucia looked over her shoulder at Antonio. "Maybe."

Victoria held her forehead. "I'm sorry, Lucia. I was just shocked and I thought he'd understand."

"Understand what?" Victor asked.

She turned her attention to her father. "He wants to get married, and I told him I wasn't ready for that just yet."

The older adults all glanced at each other. Victor moved first, stepping forward and kissing her on the forehead. "No man takes it well when the woman he wants rejects him, but he'll—"

"I didn't reject him. I *love* him—and he knows that."

"Still hard to swallow. Give him a few days to cool off." He turned around. "Let's go," he said to everyone else.

"Can you call me if he's at your place?" she asked Lucia. "Just so I know he's okay."

Lucia was clearly upset, but she nodded.

They all left her alone. She sat on the couch in her beautiful gown and waited. She didn't sleep. She couldn't. Lucia called to tell her he hadn't gone to her house. Somehow, Victoria knew he hadn't.

"I'm sorry, Lucia."

"Get some sleep. We'll talk tomorrow," she advised.

But she didn't sleep. Thoughts kept her up all night. And at some point she stopped being upset or even angry. Eric needed time to sort this relationship out. She did, too.

The next morning, Victoria dressed in a pair of jeans and a sweater and drove to Lucia's house. It was Christmas Eve, and if Eric didn't come back home no one would be celebrating.

They sat at her kitchen table to share a cup of coffee.

"I came to drop off a set of keys to the house. I'll move my things out and notify the Realtor to contact you if she wants to show it."

Lucia held on to the keys, stared at them as if they held answers about her son that Victoria hadn't shared. "I don't think you should move your things out yet, querida."

"I'm leaving for Washington on January second." She told Lucia about her new job.

"But you'll be back," she said.

"Yes."

"Then stay in the house. I'm certainly not going to show it or sell it. It's Eric's responsibility."

Which was why she thought it best to take her things out of the house. But maybe Lucia was correct. If Eric came back and saw all her things gone, he'd think it was all over between them. And Victoria didn't want him to believe that. Just because she wasn't ready for marriage just yet didn't mean she didn't want him. "Okay. I'll stay," she said.

Carmen made it home for Christmas, arriving on December 24. Victor picked her up at the bustling Burbank Airport, which was full of holiday vacationers leaving and arriving. She had a couple of carry-on bags, and two full and heavy suitcases.

Victor loaded it all onto a cart. "All this for one week?"

"You never know what I might need."

"Sure you do. A couple of shirts, a couple of pants, underwear, and socks."

"A week consists of seven days. A couple of anything isn't enough."

"Hmm." He loaded her bags into the trunk of the car. Then they got in.

"I'm starving. That nasty food they allow you to buy on flights these days is barely edible. I can't wait to eat some of Mom's good food, and to eat at La Parrilla, and to eat good

Mexican food." She laughed. "I'm going to do nothing but eat for an entire week."

"Good." She looked too thin. Probably didn't eat much. He wove out of the airport terminal and onto the freeway.

"I do need to go shopping this evening. I'm going to drag Victoria out and have her take me to the mall."

"Might do her good. She had a fight with Eric, and she isn't in the best mood."

"About what? And when did this happen? She didn't tell me about it."

"Happened last night." He shrugged. "Talk to her."

"Ugh, men. I've dated five different guys this year. Each worse than the next. I swear I don't get guys. Most of them have the attention span of a two-year-old and the memory of... what has a terrible memory? Anyway, late to dates or they forget all together. Unless it concerns sex or sports they can't focus."

Victor shot her a stern glance as he drove. She dated *five* men? A little much.

"Sorry, I know you're a man."

"Thanks for noticing." He took the off ramp he needed and headed for home.

"But trust me. Guys these days, they're not like you, Papi. They have no character. No substance."

He needed her to change the subject. Not that it would be difficult to do. Carmen could talk nonstop about anything.

"So tell me about your idea to work for La Parrilla."

"Well, when I originally thought about it, I thought I'd help you run the restaurant. Take care of payroll, hiring, and most of the back-office business stuff. Give you a chance to retire soon."

"Retire? Who said anything about retiring?"

"Eventually. Aren't you the man who has always talked about retiring to Argentina?"

"Well, that's not going to happen for a long time."

"Whatever. That's what I was thinking. But now that you're opening the other two restaurants, well, the stakes are even higher."

"I've thought of this a lot since we spoke on the phone. If you're determined to go through with this, you should change your major to business management. I'll train you to run the restaurant. Victoria can help you as well."

"She doesn't want to be involved."

"She won't mind training you. Although it won't be for a while. She's—"

"Leaving for Washington. That I know."

He wondered if he would ever get to finish his thoughts with all the interruptions. He turned onto their street. "If I think you can do it, I'll move my current manager from Burbank to Newport Beach and leave you the original to run. It'll be the easiest since it's established. But, Carmen, if I think it's too much for you or that you're not serious about this, I won't hesitate to remove you." He pulled into their driveway and cut the engine. Then he turned to look at her. "Clear?"

She looked serious for a change. "Absolutely. I can do this. And I want to."

"You wanted to follow a career in science, too."

"No, I was good at science. It was fun. You and Mom decided I should make it my life. But, Dad, I want to make money. I want to be rich someday."

"Doctors make good money."

"And they're stuck inside a clinic with sick people all the time. Not for me. I want to be around people who are happy, having a good time, eating a good meal. You've got the best job in the world."

He'd never thought of it that way. "All right. You make the

degree change and when you're finished with college, we'll start your training."

She threw herself across the seats and wrapped her arms around him.

"Your mother is definitely going to divorce me now."

"I won't let her." She pulled back and opened her car door. "Let's go."

Jaqueline welcomed her baby home, tears in her eyes as she hugged her for a good, long minute. Victor stood at the door, watching.

"Come in," Jaqueline said to him, grabbing his arm.

He walked inside and closed the door. The three of them sat on the couch while Carmen talked about everything on her mind, jumping from one topic to another. Then she grew serious. "I need to tell you something, and you can't freak out."

"Okay," Jaqueline said cautiously.

"This was my idea. My decision. And I begged Dad to consider it."

She glanced at Victor who looked scared. That didn't make her feel any better. Carmen went on, explaining how she planned to change her major and eventually move back home to help Victor in the restaurant business. That was the crux of what she was saying, but she danced around the idea for nearly fifteen minutes and took another ten minutes to explain how it would work.

When she was finished, she stared at Jaqueline. "What are you thinking?"

They both looked at her expectantly. Carmen was coming home. She couldn't think of a better Christmas present. She pulled her forward for an embrace. "Whatever makes you happy, amorcito."

* * *

In a suburb of Austin, Texas, Eric cruised the neighborhood, a list of repos in his hand. Pulling over, he killed the engine. He slid out from behind the wheel of the truck and crossed the yard, like he'd done millions of times in the past. The house was nice, didn't seem to need much work. Someone probably overpaid for it and found they couldn't handle the expense. He glanced at the sheet of paper listing the specs of the house. Three bedrooms, two baths, one story. Typical. The kind of house most families liked.

In the backyard, the previous owners had left a playground. He checked it out. It was in good condition. He sat on the swings, bummed, not finding a thrill in much of anything these days. He'd missed Christmas with his family, and he'd thought that it might be the first he'd actually spend with them in seven years. Now tomorrow would be New Year's Day, and the only resolution he'd made was to wake up the next day.

He'd called the Realtor in California and told her to take the house off the market. He'd called his mother and apologized for leaving so abruptly. She hadn't been very understanding this time around. She'd told him he was immature and unreasonable, and he owed Victoria an apology. He probably did. At first he'd been angry and just needed to get away. His ego had been bruised and he wanted to drift in his self-righteous anger. But once he reached Austin he crashed in a motel room, sleeping for almost two days, and he stopped being angry. And when he checked his voice-mail message, he almost turned right around and went back to her. But as he thought of how he would apologize and beg her to reconsider his marriage proposal, how he would do everything in his power to convince her that they'd be happy forever, he realized he couldn't do that to her.

This was her moment. She was absolutely right. He was the

one who'd encouraged her to do exactly what she was doing. Explore herself and all her possibilities. Leave the comforting security of the known for the unknown. He was proud of everything she'd accomplished in the last few months. He'd watched her grow and blossom, and his heart swelled with something much stronger than love. Respect. Real affection—he liked her and enjoyed her and wanted the best for her. He was completely devoted to her. And for that reason, he decided not to return home. Not to make her reconsider her decision. Not to appeal to her emotions.

He couldn't explain any of this to his mother, of course. He told her he didn't owe Victoria anything, and that he'd be back to wrap everything up once she was gone. She assumed he didn't want to see her because he was hurt. But he didn't want to see her because he knew himself, knew he would have a difficult time doing what was best for *her* when his heart was crying out to do what was best for *him*.

He swayed gently on the swing. The outside air held a crisp chill and he shivered. He reached for his cell, turned it on. Most of the time he had it off now, because Victoria called three or four times a day. This time, he didn't have any messages. He dialed his favorite contractor in Austin.

"Hey," he said, when the guy answered. "Happy New Year to you, too. I think I might have a small job for you." He glanced at the house. "Yeah, let's meet in a couple of days." He clicked the phone off and headed back to his truck.

Victoria flew to Seattle with a heavy heart. She hadn't been able to reach Eric, and she couldn't believe he'd been so unreasonable. She hadn't declined his marriage proposal, after all, she'd just told him it wasn't the right time. His anger was way overblown, and she just didn't get it.

But now she had to put her personal problems on the back burner. At least for the next few weeks.

Her company put her and her project partner, Karrie, up in a condo close to downtown. They met with the client the second week of January to clarify her vision of the new building they would be moving into at the end of the month. From there, she and Karrie worked from sunup to sundown locating the perfect art pieces for the walls, the right furniture for each office and lobby, and creating the ideal look in general.

Victoria had created the design for the washrooms almost on her own, so she put them together while Karrie worked on the larger offices. The men's room had black walls, which she contrasted with shallow white porcelain bowl sinks that rested on a slatted blond wood stand. The faucet tabs set into the mirrors were simple. She was happy with the dramatic masculine effect of the room. For the women's washroom she allowed herself a few more frills. Even though this was an office building, women appreciated a few luxuries. Limestone counters, wicker baskets to hold the paper towels, a couple of pots of dried leaf plants, candles, colors. Everything subdued but still pleasurable to the eye.

As the end of the month approached and the project took shape, both she and Karrie were pleased with the result. Their clients also seemed happy on their final walk-through. Victoria had loved working as a designer. Even with the constant Seattle rain and the pangs of loneliness she felt at times when she wished she could spend Sunday at the Argentine Club or having dinner at her parents' place, she knew that at least careerwise, she'd found a home.

Eric put his contractor in charge as project manager of the Austin house he purchased. He hoped he could get it turned around in less than a month. Having worked with this crew before, he felt comfortable leaving it in their hands. He drove back to Burbank and settled in to the home he and Victoria had invested so much time in. She had left it in perfect condition, but it lacked life. The Christmas tree was gone. He spent his first day home dusting, vacuuming, polishing. Then he went to see his mom. Although Lucia was obviously still disappointed in him, she was happy to see him back home.

"So what are your plans now, Eric?"

He'd thought long and hard about what he wanted to do. "I'm moving back for good."

His answer seemed to surprise her.

"This is home. With or without Victoria. She helped me see that." He smiled. "Which is sort of ironic. But this is where I fit in. This is where my family is.

"I may have to travel every once in a while for certain projects, but I'm going to keep the house I have here. Pay it off. Pay my subs. And wait for Victoria to come home."

She ran a hand through his hair. "I hope she decides to do what you'd like her to do, but there are other women, Eric."

"Not for me."

She kissed his forehead. "She was devastated when you left. She really was."

"I needed time to get my head clear. And she needed time away from me."

"I'm not sure I agree. But everything will work out."

"I'm not worried," he said. "And I'm not in a hurry. She's doing the right thing, Mom."

Lucia nodded. "Yes, she is. And I'm proud of you for seeing that. You're a good man, hijo."

He chuckled. "Thanks."

"And I have to show you something." She pulled out a bank statement. "The money you sent us month after month. It's all here in this account, and it's yours."

Eric looked at the amount and widened his eyes in shock. "But this was for you and Dad. So you wouldn't have to work so hard."

"The first monies you sent, Antonio used to pay off some debt he didn't want to talk about, but once that was paid, you kept sending money."

"I know. I wanted you to have it."

She shook her head. "No, my love, Antonio and I both agreed we didn't want it. So, here. Use it for your wedding. For your first child?"

He raised an eyebrow. "Don't get ahead of yourself."

She leaned across the table and kissed him. "Aside from your father, you have been my greatest love. Do you know that?"

Tears touched his eyes despite the fact he tried not to let her get him all emotional. "Oh, hell," he said, swallowing a lump in his throat. "Well, to be honest, Victoria isn't the only reason I wanted to live close to home again."

She smiled, and stepped back away from him. "Oh, yes, she is. But I don't mind. I love her, too."

He stood, gave her one last hug and kiss. "And I love you. But I gotta go."

There would come a time, in the next few years, when they would need him more. As they got older. As they were less able to be the strength always supporting him. He hoped those days were far into the future. But as he walked out of his childhood home, he was ready for the tables to turn when they had to. They were all the family he'd ever had, and he finally understood how precious that made them.

Later that week, he searched for a new property he could restore. Homes weren't difficult to find. Seemed like a quarter of all California real estate was up for sale. An exaggeration, but he certainly had many options. Still, great deals were always hard to find. He got one lead on a beach house. This interested him. He went to check it out.

The wind blew off the Pacific. Dark clouds didn't let much sunshine reach the beaches. The only people enjoying the sand and the waves were a few runners and a handful of die-hard surfers. Eric, wearing a black raincoat, walked along the beach. He could have parked in front of the beach house he was interested in, but he'd decided to spend a little time outside. The cool salt air, the cries of seagulls, and the crashing waves relaxed him. His thoughts seemed to flow more freely when he was outdoors.

And what he was thinking of doing was investing in a few quality homes in nice family neighborhoods, fixing them up, and renting them. This would bring him some income while the market steadied itself. People continued to need places to live. If they couldn't afford to buy, they'd have to rent. He was also playing with the idea of restoring commercial property. This appeared to be more profitable right now. No matter what he decided to do, it would involve restoration of real estate. He loved his job, and he'd always found ways of making money in the past. That didn't have to change now.

He came upon the house on his list. The beach house was small and dwarfed by the neighboring homes. It had a nice wraparound porch, but it was practically caving in on itself. Inside he found worn maple floors that could be restored, a small kitchen in need of renovation, but stunning windows. He could rent this place by the week and make a killing. With the famous Santa Monica pier and Venice Boardwalk close by, and the tons of shopping and restaurants available on the Third Street Promenade, this was a vacationer's heaven. He stood on the crumbling patio and listened to the far-off calls of seals on Santa Monica Bay, and he imagined sitting out here in the mornings with a cup of coffee. That was enough to help him decide he was going to own it.

As he looked out at the horizon, he saw an older couple holding hands, walking along the surf. A look of contentment on their faces. For some reason, Jaqueline and Victor came to mind. He frowned. Turned around and looked inside the house again. Hadn't she... mentioned a beach house? Had she been serious?

Getting a spark of inspiration, Eric rushed out of the house and jogged back to his truck. He called Victor on his cell and asked him to meet him at the beach house, and he drove to Burbank to pick up Jaqueline. She questioned him for the sudden need to pull her away from her photo organization project but went with him, laughing at his enthusiasm.

Her eyes sought his when she saw Victor waiting in front of the beach house. "Eric—"

"Come on, you'll see." He got out of the truck and hurried around the passenger side to open the door for her.

"Hey Victor," he said, and opened the door with the key he'd been given by the Realtor. "I wanted to show you both this place."

"Why?" Victor said, frowning as he took in the dirty walls, cracked ceilings, broken lights, and trash on the floor.

Jaqueline seemed equally perplexed until she walked to the large living room window and stared at the view. "Wow."

Eric stood beside her. "I thought you'd like that. Great for early-morning walks."

"How did you find this?"

"Luck. Not many cheap houses right on the beach. Not that this is cheap. You're paying for the land the house sits on. But I can fix this up and have it looking like new."

Victor joined them at the picture window. "Am I missing something?"

"Mrs. Torres told me her dream was to own a beach house somewhat like this one."

"I didn't say it was my dream," she corrected. "I said it would be nice."

Victor let his eyes take in the house with a more open expression on his face. "Nice floors," he said.

"They can be," Eric said.

"You want this place, Jaqui?" he asked, disbelief in his voice.

"Oh, I can't afford this."

"The price *is* steep," Eric agreed.

Victor drew a breath and slipped his hands into his pockets. "Ah, thank you, Eric. Can we talk a little in private? I'll lock up."

"Oh," he said, stepping back. "Sure." He handed Victor the key. "I'll get it from you tonight?"

"Sure. I'll drop it off at your place."

Eric slipped out the front door. Victor heard his truck start and drive off. Jaqueline walked gingerly around the small house.

"I never knew you wanted to live on the beach."

She laughed. "I told him how much I enjoyed waking up every morning on that cruise and seeing the ocean. It felt so freeing and wonderful. I never had any illusions of living on the beach."

Victor shrugged. "Why not?"

She looked embarrassed. "I was kidding. Dreaming. The way people say it would be nice to win the lottery. I'm sorry Eric dragged you out here."

Victor gazed at his amazing wife. Never asking for much, never wanting anything from him but his love. "I wasn't far. In fact, the Santa Monica restaurant is down the street." He pointed in the general direction.

"Really? Great location."

"I'll drive by it when I take you home. We don't have to wait for the grand opening."

She nodded. Then she turned and peeked into the bedroom. This house was a disaster, but Jaqueline didn't seem horrified by the look of it.

"What do you think?" he asked.

"About the house?"

"Can you see yourself living here?"

She smiled wistfully. "These days I can see myself doing lots of things I wouldn't have considered in the past. You and the girls are making me think I need to take more chances. Live while I still can. Enjoy life a little more without expecting any of you to meet all my needs." She faced him. "You know what I love?"

He arched an eyebrow. Him? "What?"

"That both Victoria and Carmen are doing the opposite of what we expected them to do."

"You love that?" He was okay with it all now, but love it? No.

"I love their strength, their determination. It's inspiring and refreshing to see them grow up and take control of their lives. In a way, we did that when we moved to America. But then we forgot to nurture that spirit of adventure. At least I did. And I'm sorry I stifled yours."

She was apologizing to him? "No," he said. "I'm the one who's sorry for making such a momentous business decision without talking to you first. The least I could have done was tell you my plans. I was afraid you'd point out the very real possibility that I could fail."

"I probably would have pointed out all the possible reasons why it was a bad idea. I'm sorry, Victor."

"It's been good to have a balance between security and risk. We made a good pair."

Her eyes skittered away and she stood in front of the window.

"Maybe moving out here is just the change we need," Victor said.

"We?"

"New house. New start. Just for you and me. No kids."

"Oh, Victor. You can't afford an expense like this, either."

He stood beside her and placed a hand on the side of her cheek. His thumb caressed her beautiful face that had grown wiser and more lovely each year. "I can. And if you'd like to live here with me—or without me, if that's what you decide—I'd love to buy it for you."

"To answer your earlier question, I *can* see myself living here. But I don't know that I want to move. We've lived in Burbank all our lives. Raised the girls there. The club is close by. We have a home."

She looked at the crashing waves. A man walked his dog as the water touched their feet. Victor thought he might like to have a dog. Retire on the beach? Not quite Argentina, but as much as it hurt to admit, his life was here now. He was never going back to live.

"Maybe we're too old to start over," she continued.

He took a chance and let his hand slide down her back. He eased her closer to him. "I'm still in love with you, Jaqui. We're not too old to move to the beach and go for quiet walks in our bare feet on the sand. Or to read the paper on that patio once it's fixed. Or even to have a passionate, romantic affair together." He smiled. "We're not too old to fall in love all over again."

She smiled, too. "You don't think so?"

"No, I don't." He angled his head and touched his lips softly against hers. They shared what he hoped was the first kiss of many.

She hugged him and drew a shuddering breath.

"I'm sorry for how much I've hurt you, Jaqueline. I promise

you that I'll do things right this time, if you'll trust me one more time."

She nodded against his chest.

Victor closed his eyes and thanked God for his good fortune. If this house got him his wife back, he'd do what he had to buy it. "I love you," he said.

"I love you, too," she echoed.

Chapter Twenty-four

A week later, Eric helped Victor make an offer on the house and worked out an amazing deal that would get Victor the house way below market value. Because of Victor's already tapped resources and debt from the restaurant, Eric actually bought the house like he did every other flip. He would fix it up and sell it to Victor in a private deal. He didn't intend to make any money on this project. He was happy to help out Victoria's parents.

"Pibe," Victor said, when they left the Realtor's office. "I owe you."

Eric smiled. "You don't owe me anything." He pulled out his truck keys. Not only had he purchased the beach house, but he was headed to the post office to mail in a check to pay off the Burbank remodel, which would now be his house.

"You can't imagine how excited my wife is."

"I'll meet with her later this week. She can tell me how she wants to fix it up, and I'll get the contractors working."

Victor slapped his shoulders. "Gracias."

"You're welcome," Eric said.

"And Eric, maybe I didn't give you such good advice with Victoria. I'm sorry. I shouldn't have rushed you into proposing before you were ready—"

"It was fine advice." He nodded. "I proposed because I wanted to, not because you told me to. Remember, I came to you."

"I know, I just feel... horrible."

"Don't." He got in his truck and waved as he pulled away. He headed to the dealership where his father worked.

Antonio looked surprised when Eric walked into the showroom. Eric thought Dad looked good in his spiffy little suit.

"Selling any cars today?"

"Not many. What are you doing here?" he asked with a wide smile.

"I need a car, of course."

Antonio laughed. "You have a car."

"I have a work truck." He leaned close to his father's ear. "Not exactly a sex machine, if you know what I mean."

Antonio crossed his arms. "I'm not selling you that kind of car," he said.

"Show me a nice family car, then," he said.

"Come on," Antonio clapped a hand on his shoulder and strolled with him through the lot. "Your mom tells me you're going to roll the dice and stay around here."

"Yep. Paid off my house today."

Antonio whistled. "Do you know I've got five more years on mine?"

"Want me to pay it off?"

"No," he said. "I'm going to be able to do that myself soon."

"Yeah?"

"Yeah, remember those tax lien certificates you told me not to get involved in?"

Eric narrowed his gaze. "I remember."

"Well, I didn't listen to you. I would have if you had let me invest in your flip. But when you didn't want to partner up with me, I used the money to buy a couple of those."

Great, Eric thought.

"One person got current on their property taxes, and so I got my money back with heavy interest. The other abandoned the property, and so now I have a house in Arizona to sell. I'm going to sell it and pay off our place. If I have enough left over, I'm going to take your mother on another cruise. She had too much damn fun without me, so I figure I'd better take her on another one and show her an even better time."

Eric stared at his father with his jaw slack. "You bought some certificates, and you . . . you made money? I mean—"

"It's taken me a lifetime, but I'm learning. Yeah, I made money."

Eric chuckled. "Hell, Dad, that's great."

"I'm not sure what condition this home in Arizona is in, but maybe we can go take a look and you can fix up whatever needs to be done."

Damn, his viejo had his first investment property. "All right," Eric said, nodding. "You've got yourself a deal."

"You really should look at these tax lien things, Eric. With the downturn in the market, there are thousands of properties with back taxes due. Great opportunities."

"Yeah, but I sort of like fixing houses up." And a part of him didn't like the idea of making money off of someone else's misfortune. It was business, and a way for the state to get their money. He knew that. Business was business. And the world was cold and hard, and the Donald Trumps of this world got rich because of it, but that wasn't for him. He smiled at his father. "Mom will really like another cruise. You better tell her about that before you tell her you're sending me to Arizona."

He frowned and rubbed his chin. "Yeah, she's not going to like that part much. But it'll be temporary."

"Yes, that's true."

"And when I sell the place, I'll surprise her with the cruise."

He chuckled. Antonio was a good man. Eric wanted to be like his father, which was a hell of a thing for him to want, because for so many years he wanted to be nothing like him. "So about my car. What do you recommend?"

"Save your money. Get married. Have a kid. Then let Victoria pick out the car."

"Victoria, huh? She turned me down."

"Not what I heard."

Eric nodded and shoved his hands in his pockets. "It was exactly what I heard. Wish I'd have listened better, because that's not what she said. I'm an idiot."

"Happens to the best of us." Antonio headed back to the showroom. "Well, when she comes back, apologize, beg for forgiveness, and if all that fails, come back for the love machine." He laughed.

Eric grinned and detoured to his truck. "See you on Sunday."

"Ciao."

When he got home, he prepared the rented furniture for the afternoon pickup. Everything was going back. By tonight the house would be empty. And that made him happy.

The truck arrived at about three in the afternoon. Victoria arrived unexpectedly at around four. His heart began a frantic beat. She got out of the car and frowned as the men loaded the truck with the items from the house. Eric forced his legs to move and he met her in the front yard.

"Welcome home," he said. Damn, she looked good.

She held a suitcase in her hand. "Thanks, but what's going on?" she asked.

He looked over his shoulder as the guys loaded the truck. "Can't keep the rented things forever. We were only supposed to have it during the staging period."

"Right. It must be costing a fortune."

"Story of my life these days. Let me help you with this suitcase. I assume you're staying here still."

"Your mom said I shouldn't move my things out. And I tried to call you, but—"

"Many times, I know." He took her suitcase from her hands.

"You took the house off the market? I don't see the sign anymore."

"I paid it off. It's mine free and clear now."

She stepped forward. "Wow."

They walked inside the house. He put her suitcase in the living room. "I've been back for about three weeks."

"I know. My mom told me. She called me as soon as you came back."

"Of course."

She sat on the arm of the chair. "I missed you," she said.

The guys walked back into the house. One picked up the coffee table. "Sorry," he said as he stepped between them. The other picked up a large vase.

Eric moved out of the way. When they walked back out, he looked at Victoria. "I missed you, too. How did it go?"

"Great. I learned so much. The experience was fabulous."

"Good. Then I'm glad you went."

"Eric," she began, but the furniture people returned.

"Excuse us. Is that chair going?" He pointed to where she sat and checked his inventory list. "Yep, I'm supposed to take it back."

"Oh, yes." She stood so they could take the chair from under her.

Eric placed a hand on her elbow. "Let's, ah, go outside."

"Sure," she said. "Don't take anything on that table," she told the furniture guy. "It belongs to a friend of mine." She pointed to trinkets on an end table that she'd gotten from the boutique where she used to work.

"Just what's on the list," the guy agreed.

She let Eric lead her outside to the back patio. "Should I make us some mate or something?"

She looked as distracted as he felt. "Ah. No. Thanks."

"I didn't mean to get so bent out of shape at that Christmas party." He plopped down on the patio chair, suddenly exhausted. At least this was not rented. It belonged to his mother. For tonight, he could keep it. "I guess I thought marriage proposals were supposed to be like they are in the movies." He laughed. "You know, all romantic and happy."

"They are." She sat beside him. "I didn't mean to ruin it."

"My timing was all off." He shook his head. "And I didn't know you had this great opportunity with your company. If I'd known, maybe I would have waited."

"I should have told you as soon as I found out."

Noise from inside the house flowed out of the French doors. Men maneuvering furniture. Grunting, swearing.

"They better not bump our walls," she said. Then her eyes flickered to him. "I mean your walls."

He didn't mind the slip at all, and in fact he hoped it was indicative of what she planned to do. "Have you spoken with your mom?"

"Not this week. I knew I was coming home and figured I'd see her. I came here first to see you."

He told her the story of the beach house.

"Eric," she said, full of awe and gratitude in her voice. "That's the sweetest thing I've ever heard. I can't believe you did that for my parents."

"It was fate. Finding that house was a stroke of luck." He leaned back and rested his woven fingers on his stomach.

"So it's a done deal?"

"Done. I'll be spending the next two or three months getting it ready for them to move in."

"Thank you," she whispered.

He was going to say it was not a big deal. But it was, and he knew it. "You're welcome."

"Hey, we're done, dude," one of the movers called from inside the house. "Need a signature."

Eric stood. "Be right back." He went inside to sign.

Victoria drew a breath. The outside air was cold, and she shivered. She stood and followed Eric inside. The house was completely empty, and her footsteps sounded loud on the wooden floors. The movers left and closed the front door behind them.

Eric buried his hands in his pockets and looked around. "Damn. Want to stage my house again? With permanent items this time?"

She laughed. Her eyes met his contemplative gaze, and her heart beat hard against her chest. "Maybe. I need to see where we stand. I'm still not sure why you came home this time. Not sure if you're still angry with me. Or if you're going to leave each time things don't go your way. If I should take my things and go, or if... the marriage proposal is still on the table."

"Fair enough. I came home because this is where I want to settle down and live my life. I'm *not* still angry with you. I'm *not* going to leave each time things don't go my way. You shouldn't pack your bags and leave, and the marriage proposal is most *definitely* still on the table."

"Hmm." She walked the empty living room, stopped at the front door and leaned her back against it. Watching him as he took up the entire room all by himself. Gorgeous.

"But you're angry with *me*," he said.

"Yes."

"Why?"

"You just *left*."

"I didn't want to get in your way. I wanted you to go do this job in Washington." He moved forward, his hands still in his pockets. "I want you to be successful and be free to do whatever makes you happy. I want to be your biggest supporter, not the weight around your ankles. I thought if I came home before you left, my pitiful crying might make you want to stay."

"Your crying?"

"Oh yeah, it would have been an ugly scene." He continued to approach. "I would have bawled my eyes out. You would have felt guilty and stayed." He gave a playful shudder. "Ugly."

"So let me get this straight. You stayed gone because you weren't strong enough to watch me leave?"

"You got it." He stepped closer, standing only a few inches from her now.

She fisted her hand at her sides to keep from touching him. "So instead you disappeared, refused to take my calls, and made me cry *myself* to sleep each night."

He pulled his hands out of his pockets and placed them on the door by her shoulders. "Let me make it up to you."

"Don't you dare touch me." Although her breath was already coming in thicker.

He stepped closer and dropped his forehead on her shoulder, his hands still on the door. "I'm sorry," he whispered. "I didn't know how to stay out of your way while still being by your side." He angled his head so his lips touched the side of her neck. "Tell me I didn't blow this with you, *please,* Victoria."

Tears clouded her vision. She closed her eyes and brought her hands up, placing them on his chest. Then she turned her head and found his lips.

He responded immediately. Growling in response, kissing her hungrily. His hands sliding down the door, but still not touching her body. But every other inch of his body came in contact with hers. He pressed her hard against the door. Bit her bottom lip, kissed down her neck, along her breastbone, to her breasts. Her knees grew weak, and she began sliding down. He finally let go of the door, wrapped his arms around her, and helped her to the floor.

She should have stopped this. The wood floor was cold and hard. They still had much more to talk about. And sex wouldn't mend the wounds they'd inflicted on each other out of sheer stupidity. But none of that mattered in those minutes where the clothes came off and their bodies came together hard and feverishly. The explosion of passion came quickly, and left them both breathless and drained.

Once she caught her breath, she put herself together as best she could and sat up, her back against the wall. He lay sprawled on the floor. "Vicki?"

"What?"

"The older I get, the more I realize I'm not perfect."

She laughed because that sounded so funny. "You mean you thought you were?"

He pushed himself up on an elbow. "Yes."

"Well, welcome to reality."

"So, you knew I wasn't perfect?"

"Honey, you're pretty darn close."

He smiled. "Does that mean I'm forgiven for wanting to claim you for myself and never let you go?"

She stared at him. Although she'd been angry and hurt that he cut off communication the way he had, she was as much at fault. In her mind, she was already planning a fabulous career, finally traveling away from this town. Finally free. And a marriage proposal from a man who wanted nothing more than to return home and settle comfortably into it sent her into a panicky, emotional dive. But looking at him now, she understood that he wasn't going to tie her down. With him she'd been able to soar. Look how far she'd gotten. And he came back to continue to support her. "Okay," she said, as they waged a staring war across the room. "You're forgiven."

"I was starting to sweat waiting for your answer."

"If we still have a bathtub, I'll help you get nice and clean."

He pushed himself up. "Shit, this floor is hard." He stood and took her hand. "I like that idea, but I'm not done getting dirty yet." He led her to his bedroom, where at least he had a mattress on the floor. They took all their clothes off and got under the blankets. It was still early evening, but she didn't care. She didn't want to be anywhere else. They snuggled together, their legs wrapped around each other.

"Will you have to travel a lot with your design company?" he asked.

"Not really. I think most of their contracts are around here. But occasionally they get work in other states. It won't affect me regardless."

"Why not?"

"I'm going to go ahead and open my own design studio right here in Burbank. That way I can finish my classes, get my own clients, and stay close to those I love. What about you?"

He drew a breath. "I'm going to need to travel back and forth between Austin where I just bought a place, somewhere in Arizona where my dad just bought a place, and here where your parents just bought the beach house."

She raised an eyebrow. "I hope you're going to need a traveling interior designer for all these places, or I'm going to be upset again."

"I absolutely need an interior designer." He kissed her forehead. "But don't worry, the guy I left in charge in Austin is really good. I'll go back three or four times to get it completed, then I'll try to stay local."

"Promise?"

He held out a hand. "Promise."

She placed her hand in his to shake, but instead brought it to her chest. "Then, when all that's done, I'd like to officially announce our engagement."

"Why wait?"

"I don't trust you," she said, but with a smile. "You might decide to take off again. Your track record sucks."

"It does. You're right." His hand slid up her chest and curved around the back of her neck. "And every time, I come back and decide to stay because of you. Must mean I'm crazy in love with you."

"And every time I welcome you back. What does that say about me?"

"That you're crazy in love with me?"

"Or just plain crazy."

He laughed and kissed her. "Just marry me before we have our first child, okay?"

"Deal," she said, with a prickly feeling in the base of her spine as she thought about how that reunion by the front door a few minutes ago had been condomless, and she couldn't remember the last time she'd taken a birth control pill.

Oh, what the hell. She'd deal with whatever life brought her. Although this time... "Get the box of condoms," she muttered.

He chuckled as he kissed his way down her body.

Chapter Twenty-five

Six months later, sitting on the newly constructed and stained wraparound porch at her mother's beach house, Victoria was happily *not* pregnant. In fact, she was weighed down by very little these days.

In the last few busy months, Eric finished the Austin house and flipped it for a decent profit. Then they both spent a month and a half in Arizona, fixing up Antonio's house. Eric turned it over to a real-estate firm to sell.

They returned home and Victoria spent most of her time studying and taking classes. In May, the Argentine Club had its first-ever non-Argentine event, celebrating Cinco de Mayo with some fabulous performers and delicious, spicy Mexican dishes. The day was a huge hit, and Jaqueline received all the praise she deserved for organizing it.

And then there was this beach house. After weeks of reconstruction and designing the inside just right, Victoria spent the weekend helping her mother move in, and now they were taking some time off to relax.

"Eric did an amazing job on this house," she said under her floppy summer hat.

"You've got to convince him to take your father's check. We never expected him to work for free."

"Dad paid for all the materials. All Eric did was donate a little time."

"You *both* donated a lot of time," Jaqueline corrected. "And Victor now wants you both to get our old house ready to sell."

"No, he doesn't." Victoria lifted her head to gaze at her mother. "Carmen is going to live there for a while when she comes home next month."

"I thought she'd stay here, with us."

Victoria smiled. "Dad told me you were thinking that, and he said no way in hell was he going to share his time alone with you." She raised an eyebrow. "I'd let Carmen use the old house if I were you."

Jaqueline blushed.

"Where is Dad anyway?"

"I think he's at the Santa Monica restaurant today. Do you know that that place alone has practically paid for the construction loans? It's done better than the Newport Beach restaurant."

"Well, the land alone cost him a pretty penny in Newport."

"The investors are very pleased," Jaqueline said. "I don't think he's going to have any problem when it comes time to build the other restaurants."

Victoria opened the bottle of suntan lotion and spread some on her legs. "He told me. How *do* you feel about him planning to open even more restaurants?"

"I asked him to wait a year. We just got these open a few months ago, and I want to make sure, you know, things continue to go well."

Victoria knew her father probably wasn't thrilled about that. "Hmm."

"He told me that was a great idea. That he was happy to sit here on the beach for a year and enjoy all his good fortune. And we're going to take a month off to visit Argentina." Jaqueline sighed—a content, happy sigh that said everything was finally right.

Victoria smiled and stared out at the vast sea spread before her. Her parents hadn't crossed an ocean to build their life in America. No weeks on a ship, experiencing seasickness and disease. Their struggles had started once they got here. Would they make it? Would they be accepted into this new society? Would their dreams really come true, or would it become a nightmare? And like all immigrants, they'd suffered and almost lost the spirit that had brought them to this land to begin with. But they had also survived and had helped build a better America. She, as their daughter and as a proud American, benefited from their hard work and sacrifices, and was grateful. So very grateful.

Dear Reader,

The Argentine Club that sets the stage for much of this book became a catalyst, a sort of time machine for me to take a trip back to my own childhood. I have vague memories of my family attending "the Argentine club." We didn't go often, because my mother didn't like going. She shared with me recently that the women sat around gossiping most of the time, or trying to one-up each other. My mother didn't find a sisterhood, but rather, as she says, a bunch of silly women she'd rather avoid.

My father, however, must have felt a different type of connection. He enjoyed being around other Argentines. He wanted to be reminded of his birth country, which he missed as if he'd left behind part of his soul. I remember many Friday evenings when he would go to the club to play cards, then return Saturday morning while my mother was cleaning the house and my brother and I were watching morning cartoons. If he won money (because they played for money), he'd walk in and toss twenty-dollar bills into the air and watch them rain down on us. My brother and I would excitedly pick up the bills as if they were candy that had spilled from a piñata. We were usually allowed to keep one each. If he lost, he walked in quietly, sat at the kitchen table, and talked to my mother about his night.

I wanted to share with you that "the club" was a part of my life; however, it wasn't the central part, as it is for my characters. The club in the story comes from my imagination. Bits and pieces that I remember combined with, perhaps, wishful thinking. For instance, children didn't learn Spanish or have a school at the club—I wish we had. We ran wild around and between the tables set up in the main and only hall.

I don't know the exact history of the club, but I do know that it disbanded eventually. Today there exists an Argentine Association of LA in Burbank, which holds weekly dinner shows. I took my mother to a dinner event when I was doing research for this book. I thought she'd enjoy it. Good food, tangos, and jokes that went way over my head but she found funny because she connected with Argentine humor. We had a nice night out together, and she indulged me as I drove around Burbank taking pictures. Since I grew up in the San Fernando Valley of California, and I know there actually are large concentrations of Argentines in that area, I knew I wanted this to be the setting for my story. But I do want to make it clear that my fictional club is not intended to resemble what exists today.

As a child, like Eric in my story I didn't see the point in getting together with a bunch of strangers only because they happened to have been born in the same country as my parents. I didn't "get" my father. I'm happy to say that today I do. I don't belong to an Argentine club, but I *am* a member of a number of Latina organizations. And I'm passionate about writing stories with Latino characters.

I think the beautiful multicultural fabric of our country makes us such an amazingly wonderful and strong nation. I'm glad that we have groups that keep bits of foreign cultures alive. I love Cinco de Mayo fiestas, and St. Patrick's Day parades, and churches that hold services in various languages.

I love my memories of the real Argentine club that helped make me aware of my roots in a minor way, and I hope that you enjoy being a part of my fictional club.

Reading Group Guide

1. The Argentine Club was the glue that kept all these people together. What do you feel groups such as these do for a community? Does it keep immigrants from becoming Americanized? Or help make the transition easier?
2. Every character in the story was seeking, in some way, to fulfill the American dream. Is the dream still a possibility in this country? If no, what has changed? If yes, is it still the same dream that early immigrants came to this country to achieve?
3. How do you think Victoria's relationship with her father affected her blossoming relationship with Eric?
4. In Latin America it is not unusual for a child to live with his or her family until marriage, which could be in their thirties. Do you see a problem with children staying to live with their parents longer?
5. As mothers, our jobs are to help our children mature and prepare them to live life on their own. Did Jaqueline perform this job well? Did Lucia?
6. What do you think caused Victoria's weight issues? Was it simply a lifetime of unhealthy habits, or was there another, more emotional cause? How do you feel that her decision to follow her dreams helped her shed the extra pounds she carried?

7. Did Victoria hold traditional Latino values? How did they affect the way she lived her life? What are traditional Latino values? Is there such a thing?
8. Independence is one of the themes of the book. Are we ever truly independent or is that a myth?

Guía del Grupo de la Lectura

1. El club de Argentina era el cemento que guardaba a toda esta gente junta. ¿Qué hacen grupos como éstos para la comunidad? ¿Impiden a los inmigrantes a integrarse? ¿O hacen la transición más fácil?
2. Cada carácter en la historia intentaba, de cierta manera, satisfacer el sueño americano. ¿Es el sueño americano todavía una posibilidad en este país? ¿Si no, qué ha cambiado? ¿Si sí, es el mismo sueño que los inmigrantes de antes soñaban?
3. ¿Cree usted que la relación de Victoria con su padre afectó la relación de ella con Eric? ¿Cómo?
4. En la América latina no es insólito que un niño viva con su familia hasta su matrimonio, que podría ser a sus treinta años. ¿Ve usted un problema con los niños viviendo con sus padres por mucho más tiempo?
5. Como madres, nuestros trabajos son ayudar a nuestros niños madurar y prepararlos para vivir sus vidas propias. ¿Realizaron bien este trabajo Jacqueline y Lucia?
6. ¿Qué causó la preocupación acerca del peso de Victoria? ¿Era simplemente un curso de la vida de hábitos malsanos, o había otra causa más emocional? ¿Cómo le ayudó a perder sus libras adicionales esta decisión de seguir sus sueños?
7. ¿Tiene Victoria valores tradicionales latinos? Si sí, ¿cómo

afectaron la manera en que ella vivió su vida? ¿Cuáles son algunos valores tradicionales latinos? ¿Hay todavía tal cosas?

8. La independencia es uno de los temas del libro. ¿Es posible ser realmente independiente, o es un mito?

About the Author

JULIA AMANTE had the misfortune of growing up away from the extended family that is so valued in the Latin culture, but she missed out on very little of what it means to be Argentine. Asados were sacred meals shared together on weekends. Cheering for the Argentine soccer team was a must, as were the pilgrimages to the Argentine Club in Los Angeles, where the young Americanized kids hid under the tables and watched the adults dance tango until the wee hours of the morning. Julia giggled right along with the rest of the kids at how geeky the parents looked, but secretly she was intrigued by the romantic culture and passionate music.

Julia lives in California with her husband, son, daughter, and two pampered pound puppies. She is hard at work on her next novel.